THE THREATENING SKY

E.R. Mason

Editors

Frank MacDonald
Contact: SciFiProofreadingDoneRight@gmail.com
Web Site:
https://sites.google.com/site/scifiproofreading

Tom Macomber
contact info:
proofing@wowrec.com

Sam Thornton, PE PhD
https://www.facebook.com/SamThorntonPE
SamThorntonPE@outlook.com

ISBN: 978-1-7328697-0-7

Chapter 1

Cassiopia Cassell stood with her hands on her hips, eyeing the gray sliding doors with mischievous intent. The locked doors were the latest challenge proffered by her professor father, Theopolis Cassell. He so loved to keep his current projects secret. But it was a game to him, a taunt to his meddlesome genius daughter. Ironically, Cassiopia's relentless tenacity, inherited from the Professor himself inevitably resulted in the yielding of his project's secrets.

It was a gunmetal entrance with a seam down the middle with no knobs, no locks and no keypads.

She turned to survey the room while thinking out loud. "I see no infrared eyes or miniature microphones anywhere which means access must be by radio frequency, maybe Bluetooth or more likely some simple pulse code modulation transmission, or perhaps hidden wires in the wall linked to his computer terminal. He's been working in there for months. It's time I know what it is he's up to."

Scott Markman sat in a chair tilted back against the wall, his feet crossed atop a lab workbench. The beauty of Cassiopia was so compelling it was difficult not to stare. So many expressions, each like a reflection of a completely different woman yet all of them mesmerizing. Her blue eyes seemed almost too bright and there was a shadow about them that pulled him in. Her small mouth was always slightly rose colored even without makeup. A tiny button nose that seemed like it belonged on a child and not an adult. Markman stiffened as she noticed his lustful gaze. He tried to sound condescending, "Boy, you are so nosy, you know that? You have two PhDs but snooping on your father is still your favorite pastime."

Cassiopia pulled her long ivory hair behind her head. "Am not nosy. I'm only concerned. It's not safe for him to be doing this again. What if he got into trouble in there? How would we know? How would we get in there to help him? We'd have to use a torch to cut through the doors!"

"Admit it, you just always want to know what he's working on," insisted Markman. "He's got a cell phone if he needs help."

"Cell phone access! I'll bet you that's it. I'll bet the door opens to a program he's set up in his cell phone."

"Personally, I really think he's got you stumped this time," mused Markman.

Cassiopia narrowed her stare in defiance. "I still have one trick up my sleeve."

Markman linked his hands behind his head and smiled. "The robot? You think Tel is going to help you? That would have been the first block your father put in place."

"Tel can never refuse me. Let's go see," said Cassiopia.

Markman swung his athletic shoes off the counter, stood and adjusted his jeans. His reflection in the side panel of a stainless-steel lab oven made him pause for just a moment. Were his gray-blue eyes as appealing to her? His dark blond hair was slightly too long near the shoulder. Was that an age line forming by the left eye or just road wear on his well-tanned face? He straightened the collar of his tan cargo shirt and gestured toward the exit. "Elevator or tower stairs?" he asked.

"You like this place a lot, don't you?" mused Cassiopia.

"A castle home located in the mountains? I've got a lawn chair on the tower roof. It's the best view of the stars I've had since Tibet. Who wouldn't like this place? I know your father does, that's for sure. Six separate laboratory rooms for his experiments down here in a private dungeon. This is Shangri-La as far as he's concerned. Don't you like this place?"

Cassiopia strolled close by him toward the elevator and seemed hesitant to answer. As she passed Markman couldn't help but eye the formfitting blue and white tie-dye

Maxi dress chosen for this morning's wear. Her sleek figure shaped the dress so nicely it was difficult not to stare.

"Not going to answer me?" he asked.

Cassiopia pressed the elevator button. The doors opened. She turned to him. "I'm afraid to let myself like it here. I'm not sure I feel okay about the arrangement." She stepped into the lift and waited for him to enter.

As the doors closed Markman pressed the issue. "The Celestial Order? You're worried about working for the Celestial Order?"

"We're not supposed to mention that name out loud, Scott. You know that."

"Geez, it's just you and me," replied Markman as the elevator started up.

"There could be listening devices or something. You know the rules," said Cassiopia.

"Or you might be paranoid. For someone who has doubts about the secret organization she now works for you sure are a stickler for the rules. Don't you trust our beloved leader, John Paul?"

"I believe I do but he's just one person. Just because he recruited us and is our main contact doesn't mean the entire organization is legitimate, especially considering the things we've seen them capable of."

The elevator doors opened. Cassiopia stepped out. Markman followed.

"Well, all I know is I have a Corvette downstairs that can change colors automatically or come to me all by itself if I'm in trouble and that's really cool."

"The way to a man's heart is through his car," said Cassiopia and she turned and headed down the ornate hallway in search of the robot.

Markman followed close behind. "Well okay, you're the high IQ and I'm the spiritualist. What makes you think the organization shouldn't be trusted?"

"You're the spiritualist who spends hours a day practicing fighting forms and weapons technique."

"Oh boy, how many times are we going through this? A sage once said, *'When confronted by only bad choices a wise man who is prepared will choose correctly.'*"

"Okay, Sensei."

"That's Japanese. I keep telling you I'm Tao Chane, a branch of Chinese Kung Fu."

Cassiopia stopped and looked around. "Where is Tel anyway?"

"The last time I saw him he was in his room in his docking station."

Cassiopia resumed her walk down the red-carpeted hallway, past the heavily carved doors and paintings that lined it. She came to an open door that gave access to a small utility-styled room. Among the shelves of electronic equipment, special tools and stacks of books stood a shiny, chrome-finished TEL model 100D robot. It was in a wall mounted recharging station alive with colored lights, display screens and push buttons. The robot's visul began sweeping gold light in response to Cassiopia's entry. As always, she stood admiring the handsome machine for a few moments. Somehow the robot seemed at attention in her presence.

"Good morning, Tel," said Cassiopia.

"Greetings, Cassiopia. May I be of service?" replied Tel.

"How was last night's surveillance, Tel?" asked Cassiopia.

"No unauthorized activity was detected, Cassiopia."

Cassiopia took a moment to look around the room. "Tel, where is Speedy?"

"Speedy is presently outside performing olfactory inspections in the courtyard."

"He's smelling around the courtyard? I take it his new tracking collar is working well?"

"It is frequently providing invaluable data that would otherwise require extensive use of corporeal scanning, Cassiopia."

Markman asked with annoyance, "What?"

Cassiopia laughed and turned to him. "He likes the dog's new tracking collar. He was spending too much time looking for him before." Cassiopia looked back at the robot. "Tel, I have a few questions for you."

For some unexplained reason the robot suddenly looked uncomfortable.

Cassiopia continued, "How do I open the Professor's project room door downstairs?"

Markman leaned back against the wall and folded his arms. "Here we go."

The robot seemed pressed to answer.

"Tel?" persisted Cassiopia.

"I am inhibited from responding to that query, Cassiopia," replied Tel.

"Okay, then we'll do it a different way. Please show me the last file Professor Cassell accessed," ordered Cassiopia.

To her dismay the robot suddenly began playing waiting-style music from the game show Jeopardy.

Cassiopia stepped back. "Tel, what are you doing? Stop that!"

"I'm sorry Cassiopia, I am mandated to provide this rendition for a period of not less than 120 seconds each time you query a file attributed to Professor Cassell."

The music continued.

Markman turned away, squinting to contain his laughter.

Cassiopia wrinkled her brow and tapped one finger against her mouth.

"I do believe he's got you this time," joked Markman.

"I'd have to plug in a maintenance terminal to get around this," she replied thoughtfully. "I'd have to get in through the firmware."

"You're gonna get in tra-aa-ble," warned Markman comically. "Is it really worth it?"

"He's been receiving crates from machine shops and companies that deal in custom molds. It's driving me crazy."

"Still, seems like getting through that door is a dead end if you ask me."

"I already know it has to be wireless remote control or computer terminal entry and now I know Tel knows."

"Why don't you just ask your father?"

"Oh, he'd love that. He'd gloat for a week and he still wouldn't tell me. Whatever he's building is pretty big. If I can figure out what reference material he's using...."

The robot spoke, "Cassiopia, there is a vehicle at the main gate. The occupants have the gate code and are entering."

Cassiopia quickly decided to concede her dilemma for the moment. She took Markman by the arm and tugged him back out to the hall. "To the rotunda, Sir Scott."

"Where?" replied Markman.

"The front door, silly."

"You really do like this place, don't you? Admit it."

"We must see to whom it is that so honors us with their presence, Sir Markman."

Markman followed along the red carpet, reaching for the elevator button as it came into range.

"The stairs, my good man, the stairs. It be but a single floor beneath us, My Lord."

"See? That's the trouble living in a mansion. It's too easy to get used to being rich. One day you're living a life of luxury then the market crashes and you're back out on the street remembering what the good life was like."

"Fear not, good Scott. The Cassell coat of arms will remain on high, a noble and well-respected line." Cassiopia turned the corner to a large cloak room and led Markman down a wide, winding corridor of stairs.

"Noble and respected family? You have a crazy scientist father who conjures up magic doorways to other worlds and a robot who owns a beagle named Speedy. Does that sound like well-respected nobility to you?"

"Quiet yourself, oh loyal knave. We must be gracious in greeting our guests."

"Did you just call me loyal knave?"

The pair emerged from the side stairwell into the grand receiving hall, a two-story chamber with pillars and ascending stairways on either side. Decorative stone balcony circumvented three-quarters of the second level. The floor was large polished stone tile with smaller tiles dividing. At the opposite end of the chamber carved double doors stood open offering access to a social meeting, entertainment area.

"You know, I think I've only been in this part of the place twice," mused Markman as they crossed the huge foyer.

Cassiopia gave a condescending stare and stepped up the short row of steps leading to the front doors. She pulled one of them open and peered outside.

A long black limousine was parked in the drive. A familiar figure strolled up the walk tapping a golden-brown cane as he went. His dress was Victorian in style, a single-breasted brown morning jacket with a striped light brown vest beneath, topped by an outdated bow tie. Light brown plaid trousers and deep brown leather boots completed the ensemble. A pocket watch chain led from one button to a vest pocket. He wore a dark derby hat and carried a worn brown briefcase in his free hand. Upon seeing Cassiopia in the doorway, he paused and smiled then hurried his approach.

"John Paul!" exclaimed Cassiopia and dashed out the door to meet and hug him.

Markman waited to hold the door.

"John Paul, I always feel better about things when I see you," declared Cassiopia and took her mentor by the arm.

"And it is always my great pleasure to see you as well," replied John Paul.

They strolled through the doorway past Markman. John Paul nodded and smiled in passing. As Markman closed the doors Cassiopia finally released her grip and stood back to look at John Paul. The age lines in his weathered face never seemed to deepen. He smiled back at his favorite protégé.

"Have you settled into your new home?" asked John Paul.

Markman stepped down to join them. "The truth is I haven't been able to find where it ends yet," he said.

"And you, Cassiopia? Is it to your liking?"

Cassiopia stuttered, "It's a great deal to take in and get used to John Paul but it is so beautiful."

Markman added, "A janitorial team showed up yesterday. We didn't call for them but they said you'd authorized the service so we let them in."

John Paul nodded. "They are a specialized service, Scott. They not only do the maintenance they also secure the entire estate from eavesdropping devices or anything else which does not belong. You should feel quite at ease after they've visited."

"Wow!" replied Markman.

"Is the Professor here?" inquired John Paul.

"He's asleep in his room. He's been spending his nights in the lab downstairs. That allows his daughter to snoop around his work during the day." Markman smirked.

Cassiopia snarled at Markman then smiled at John Paul. "John Paul, do you know what he's working on down there? The door to the project room is always locked."

"I'm sorry, my dear Cassiopia. We have found that the best, most surprising results come from eccentric scientists who are left to their privacy. I'm sure whatever it is he's doing we'll all be amazed when he finally lets us in on it."

"John Paul, please forgive our manners. Are you hungry? Or would you like something to drink? Can I take your briefcase?" asked Cassiopia.

"Perhaps later, thank you. Actually, I am here to give the two of you your first official assignment. I know it's a bit soon for that. It's something urgent that just popped up and happens to be well suited for the two of you."

"Assignment?" said Cassiopia as she tried to hide a flush of doubt.

"Don't worry. You are free to decline if you so desire. As I've said, I know this is a bit soon, especially since you're not quite at home here yet."

"What's it about?" asked Markman with more interest than John Paul had expected.

"We should discuss it in the briefing room. We'd be much more comfortable there."

"We have a briefing room?" asked Markman.

"Why yes. It's on the third floor but is only accessible from the east elevator."

"We have more than one elevator?" asked Markman.

John Paul laughed under his breath. "It is the last door on the second-floor hallway. It looks like a bedroom door and is locked to anyone but you two and the Professor. Why don't I show you? There is an exceptional espresso machine up there. We can have coffee."

John Paul took a step toward the main elevator but paused and looked back, waiting for the other two to dismiss their surprise.

In the elevator, John Paul continued, "So I'm of the impression you have not requested household staff yet?"

"Household staff?" asked Markman.

"Do we really need those, John Paul?" replied Cassiopia.

"It is provided for in your residential services manual, my dear. Though you may think it somewhat decadent, you will find after a time the walk from the dining rooms to the kitchen is too lengthy to allow you to enjoy your meal. You will also find some mundane tasks such as answering the door or gate intercom take up far too much of your time and energy, especially if you are working on the third floor or in the subterranean labs. Beyond that you will be traveling on business from time to time during which I have no doubt the Professor will need to be looked after by more than just the TEL robot."

Cassiopia wrinkled her brow in thought. The elevator doors opened.

They followed John Paul down the second-floor hall to the last of the adjoining doors. There he twisted the decorative knob and opened the door to a shiny metallic elevator. The group stepped in and as the door shut itself a cage barrier also closed them in. A brief ride up and the grated door opened to a moderately sized office densely packed with electronics. Lighting came on automatically. There were large display screens on three of the walls along with computer stations beneath them. A sizeable panel on the right appeared to be filled with various types of radio equipment. In room's center, a dark oak table had a dozen heavily cushioned dark leather chairs around it. The brown carpet was unusually plush.

John Paul emerged from the elevator, plunked his briefcase down on the table and headed for the stainless coffee maker built into the wall near the head of the room.

"I'll mix you my blend and if you don't find it deliriously wonderful you can come mix your own," he said as he worked the machine.

Cassiopia and Markman stood at the center table, marveling at yet another elaborate room they'd been unaware of.

"You have another of these delightful espresso machines in your main kitchen. You should master it as soon as possible. It is its own reward," said John Paul.

"How much more is there we don't know about?" asked Markman.

"A great deal you would not expect," replied John Paul. For example, there are numerous cave entrances in the woods farther up the mountainside. Most have steel grating over them to prevent anyone from falling in. I'm told the caves go on for miles."

John Paul brought the first two large china cups over to the table then made a second trip to retrieve his own. "Shall we sit, my friends? I believe you'll find my proposal more than interesting."

Markman plopped down onto a seat and tilted back. Cassiopia sat beside him.

Markman asked, "Is this room specially shielded or something so that we can say anything we want?"

John Paul sat across from them and nodded. "Yes, in fact it is. There are white noise generators along with every other kind of sound abatement technology in the walls, floors, and ceiling. There are not many bubbles of space more secure than this room."

"So we could even talk about the Celestial Order here then?" asked Markman.

"You should never mention that name out loud anywhere ever, Scott, unless it's a matter of life and death and there are no other alternatives. The first rule of our organization is invisibility. If an organization's name is never spoken, for all intents and purposes there is no evidence of its existence."

"Okay, sorry," answered Markman.

"In fact, you will find the premise of invisibility to be a key element in the objective we are about to discuss. It is a rule you should live by in all the work you do from this point forward."

"John Paul, do you have surveillance equipment installed here that is watching us?"

"No, Cassiopia. By not installing those types of devices it makes it much easier for the cleaning crew to spot any equipment planted by adversaries. But I should remind you that each of you has the implants we installed when you agreed to work for us. We can track your location and hear everything you say though we never do except in an emergency. Your implants continue to be monitored by a computer system programmed to respond to key words you can use to call for help. It will also transfer commands to your car when you call for it. Other than that we are notified only if you appear to be in an unexpectedly hazardous location or situation. As always, you are free to have those implants removed anytime you wish. A simple command from us dissolves them."

Cassiopia nodded. "John Paul, does my father know about this room?" asked Cassiopia.

John Paul shook his head. "Not yet. A true eccentric genius, that man. Although he arrived here three months ahead of you he paid little attention to these wonderful surroundings. His only concern was setting up his labs and resuming work on whatever it is the man has in that locked lab downstairs. Our coordinators found it to be quite humorous. They would visit periodically to restock the refrigerators with food and do maintenance as necessary but the Professor took no notice of their visits other than to eat the food without even questioning from where it was coming. Nor did he question how the household chores such as laundry and trash where being done. Our only concern has been that perhaps the man is spending too much time locked away in the labs. Has he always cut his own hair when it starts getting in his way?"

Cassiopia looked annoyed. "You are describing my father to a tee, John Paul. That's the way he has always been. When he was still teaching at the university I had an endless battle keeping his appearance marginally acceptable. I'm glad to hear he is at least eating."

"It is reassuring you're here so we have a better understanding of what is normal for Professor Cassell. I must say it puts my mind a bit more at ease. Whatever he has behind that door, considering the new working environment and tools available to him, I have no doubt it will be something extraordinary."

"You have no idea at all what it is?" asked Cassiopia.

"None whatsoever. He has been like a man guarding a treasure. We would need to violate our own protocols to find out what is in that project room and that could interfere with his obsession, and obsessions of his kind often lead to spectacular discoveries."

As Markman sipped his coffee, his eyes suddenly lit up. He pointed at his cup. "John Paul, this is the most fantastic coffee I have ever had. How do you do it?"

"I shall text you the formula, sir. But perhaps we should turn to the business at hand. Your first mission, should you decide to accept it, if you don't mind me quoting an old television show I'm rather fond of...."

Cassiopia interrupted, "John Paul are you sure we're ready? I mean I'm not even perfectly sure of what we've gotten ourselves into here."

"What better way to understand than to go to work, my dear?"

Markman leaned forward and rested his chin in his hand. "I, for one, am ready. Lay it on us."

John Paul pulled his briefcase in front of him and unsnapped the latches but left it closed. "You are both already aware races more advanced than our own exist on and off the Earth. I know it takes some time to accept such a thing but in our previous dealings you've been exposed to some of that. You now know not all UFO sightings are swamp gas and not all ancient artifacts were made by primitive man. However, this knowledge is not for everyone. You would be surprised how many people would be harmed if they learned there are races far in advance of their own. Religion would be irreparably damaged whether it was contradicted or not. We go to great lengths to discount Bible stories which describe visitors descending in towers of fire or sightings of firmaments in the heavens. It is important for now to preserve the façade we are the only people in the universe so that this system we all participate in while we're here on Earth can continue as it is."

John Paul paused to sip his coffee. He eyed his two counterparts carefully for disapproval then continued. "Occasionally evidence of the more advanced races accidentally gets into the wrong hands and sometimes such evidence can give someone power or notoriety they are not mature enough to possess. In those cases it is our job to recover said evidence before any significant damage is done to society."

John Paul sipped again and waited for questions. Cassiopia and Markman stared with great interest.

John Paul continued, "Recently, a small group of nonhuman intruders entered Earth's restricted space without authorization. More simply put, an alien species that does not have rights or permissions to be here landed either to collect something or meet someone. We do not know which or why. We detected their arrival and landing in a densely wooded area outside of New Providence, New Jersey. An intercept team was dispatched to deal with them. The invaders did not have time to get far from their vehicle before they were met by our operatives. There was a brief military action. The invaders retreated to their ship and made their escape, but they had to leave one member behind. There was a foot pursuit which went on for quite some time. The intruder was finally cut off and captured. He remains in custody but has been uncooperative."

John Paul paused to sip again, taking time to evaluate how such unearthly information was affecting his friends. They continued to stare silently back at him. Cassiopia's eyes had widened somewhat.

John Paul continued, "What we did not know at the time was that the captured intruder had been carrying a handheld disruptor weapon which he lost in the woods during his escape attempt. This all took place in the Great Swamp National Wildlife Refuge near New Providence. To our dismay, before we could recover it two children illegally racing around the refuge on dirt bikes found the disruptor. Fortunately, that weapon is made to fire only for its owner and no one else. But to complicate matters further, one of the kids took the thing home and gave it to his father who happened to work for Bell Labs. He thought it was an expensive Star Wars toy and took it to work for a joke.

"The research group played around with it and eventually realized they couldn't figure out how to take it apart. Suddenly urgent calls were made to higher company officials and meetings quickly scheduled. The story gets hazy after that. Normally we have connections with Bell Labs and would secretly have been brought in on this but at some point the disruptor simply vanished. That's not surprising, however, nor was locating it a problem. Only a limited number of individuals had access to the disruptor weapon at any given time. Once a list was compiled our team began twenty-four hour scans of all the people involved. Since the disruptor contained materials not available on Earth, we eventually detected those kinds of signatures at one particular location. Bell Laboratories executive Robert Duran also owns Advanced Aviation Systems Incorporated. Mr. Duran was found to be the culprit who had made off with the disruptor. Obviously, he knows it is an item not of this Earth and has stored it in his company vault on the fifth floor of Advanced Aviation Systems in New Providence. Your mission is to recover that disruptor and replace it with this."

John Paul opened his briefcase and withdrew a dark black case about the size one would expect for a target pistol. He placed several other odd-looking items alongside it. He unsnapped the case and from the tight black padded foam drew out a strange looking gun. The grip was dirty brown and well worn. The gun looked like an undersized hand drill except the body was made up of dull silver cooling rings that led to a short fat chrome barrel with more silver rings at the end of it. From the way John Paul handled it the thing seemed to be very lightweight. He placed it on the table and slid it over to Markman who quickly snatched it up for closer inspection.

John Paul said, "As I've mentioned, the real disruptor has materials and technology unknown to Earth. This replica is identical in every way except it uses only common Earth elements and does not function at all. We even placed patent IDs from various Earth companies inside to complete the suggestion it's simply a sci-fi toy. When scanned, however, this unit will reflect exactly the same way the real one does so there will be no way anyone will know a substitution has been made. Your mission is to get into Advanced Aviation Systems, recover the real weapon and put this one in its place. You will then insert the real weapon into this same case and return it to me. This case cannot be detected by any scanner. If you get into trouble you may dispose of this case anywhere you need to and we will be able to quickly find it, whether it is at the bottom of a lake or buried deep in a landfill dump site. The trick is, no one is to know you were ever at Advanced Aviation Systems. Complete invisibility during this exchange is essential. That is the tenet of invisibility I talked about earlier. So, having completed this rather lengthy dissertation I am ready now for your questions."

Markman looked up from the weapon. "John Paul, I'll probably seem stupid asking this but don't you guys have equipment that you could just beam the thing out and beam this one back in?" Markman glanced at Cassiopia to see if she was laughing. She was not.

"Actually, it's a fair question, Scott. And since you now officially work for us I am at liberty to answer it. Yes, we do have such equipment. It's referred to as a Teleportation System. We do not customarily use such equipment on humans as it tends to disrupt the electrical signals in the brain. Often several minutes is required for a person to reorganize their thoughts after transit. Special in-depth training is required before a lifeform can safely use that system. And as for inanimate objects, unfortunately teleportation cannot be used on certain classes of objects including this one. This weapon contains a power cell of a very high order. Power cells of this type are encased in a containment vessel. If that type of containment vessel is dematerialized in any way the energy within it is released all at once, resulting in a high order detonation and contamination of the surrounding area to a degree proportional to the size and capacity of the power cell. So, in more common Earth terms, we cannot beam this type of disruptor up."

"Wow!" said Markman as he handed the duplicate disruptor to Cassiopia.

Cassiopia inspected the item with both interest and disdain. "I take it this company has an elaborate security system and a vault which must be very modern."

"You are correct, Cassiopia," replied John Paul. "I see that idyllic mind of yours has already gone to work on this. I am not surprised."

"So how do we get in the building?" she asked.

"I have no idea, Cassiopia. Although we will provide you with some very useful tools."

"And the safe? How can we get in a modern high security safe?"

"Again, I have no idea, my dear. I only know you will do it and leave without anyone knowing you were ever there," replied John Paul.

Cassiopia stopped her inspection and looked up. "You mean you're not going to help us at all?"

"Oh no, you will have all of our resources at your disposal. We will provide you with exact drawings and schematics of the building, alarm system and safe along with any special tools you require. If there's anything else we'll be at your service twenty-four hours a day."

Cassiopia furrowed her brow. "You're saying we have to figure out how to get in, exchange the gun and get out of the place without anyone knowing we were there?"

John Paul sat back. "Yes."

"But we're not safecrackers!"

Markman burst out a laugh, then thought better of it.

John Paul smiled calmly. "Yes, Cassiopia. You are."

Markman's penchant for humor took over. "I don't know, John Paul. She can't even break into her father's project room!"

Cassiopia stiffened. "Of course I can. I've only just started! Just wait!"

John Paul smiled once more. "I rest my case."

Markman laughed out loud.

John Paul folded his hands in his lap and spoke reassuringly, "Cassiopia, you underestimate yourself. Sitting before me is a master of the martial arts who grew up in the Tibetan mountains, a man who can move as silently as a cat in the night and disarm an assailant before he knows it's happened. And then there's you, the cute girl who graduated college when she was only fourteen, the same girl who once started a fire in the snow using jet fuel and a landing gear piston from a crashed airplane. And who then figured out how to carry a 180-pound man twenty-one miles down an icy cliff. Do I need to go on?"

Cassiopia narrowed her stare at John Paul. "When's all this got to be done?"

Chapter 2

Cassiopia sat in the sunlight from the mansion's second floor windowed alcove, there especially for tea times. She was wrapped in her rose terrycloth robe nibbling at toast, still half asleep, a tablet with the morning news in one hand. The rising sun brightened her view of the distant Culpeper City beyond the mountainside forest that seemed to be waking along with her. She soaked in the wonderful view, enjoying the sentiments of a new day's nature for it was far too early to think about things.

"I see you've found your morning spot," said a voice behind her. Markman stepped into view and tugged at his jeans. He fastened a button on his plain blue collared shirt and took a seat.

"John Paul was right. It's a very long walk to the kitchen."

"At least *you* can find it."

"Not really. I took a wrong turn and ended up in the servant's quarter's kitchen."

"How could you tell?"

"There was no food there. I saw my father also."

"The Professor? You've seen him too? The ghost of Cassell Castle?"

"Very funny. He was grumpy. His project must not be going well. He was on his way to bed."

"Did you sleep okay?"

"You're always gone when I wake up."

"Sunrise is very special," replied Markman.

"Can't you do your morning meditation later?"

Markman took the empty china cup which had been placed there in anticipation of his arrival. He poured from the matching teapot and tested the brew with a cautious sip. "There is nothing as good as sunrise," he replied. "There's a secret during the time between each night and new day. It's a time when, using meditation, you can learn to see and even visit the next higher plane very easily. You can actually do that kind of meditation without ever even getting out of bed but it's too easy to fall back asleep. If you use some version of the lotus posture it helps keep you conscious so you can study the lower portion of the astral plane."

"Maybe I'll try it sometime," said Cassiopia as she sipped.

"You need to practice a bit first. It's very important you know yourself and who you are before attempting a higher plane."

"I'm not sure I understand."

"The astral plane is a very emotional place. It's very easy for influences there to affect you. You must know your own space and not let anything from outside invade it. It's like here on the physical plane when someone stands too close to you; they are in your space so to speak. They can influence your feelings doing that. You must be self-assured and in control to prevent them from bothering you. That's what it's like on the astral. You need to think of yourself in an egg-shaped bubble. Everything inside is your space. No influences from without are allowed in."

"Did you say the lower portion of the astral plane? The lower portion?"

"Yes I did...Grasshopper. The lower portion of the astral is where most people go when they sleep. Dreams often come alive there. It is a very emotional place. But the higher you go the more pleasant it becomes."

"We're getting too heavy for so early," replied Cassiopia.

"Sorry."

"I just wish you were there when I wake up. It would be nice to wrap up in you in the morning."

"Sounds like I don't know what I've been missing. From now on I will meditate and then come back to bed. Boy, men are stupid."

Cassiopia laughed and smiled. "Did you look at that stuff John Paul left us on the flash drives?"

"I had trouble getting the new computer to work. Do you believe the 3D those screens put out? And you can reach in and touch the pictures and move them. It's mind-blowing."

"Well I, on the other hand, took a good look at everything. The building we're supposed to sneak into has every form of security there is but I think there is a way."

"Okay...."

"My plan is based on an old saying they use a lot at the Kennedy Space Center: Keep it simple stupid."

"Sounds like my kind of plan. Wait... that didn't come out quite right."

Cassiopia laughed once more. "You'll need your best stealthing clothes. Will you wear those baggy black robe things the Ninjas use?"

"Actually, I would use a type of free climber's boots and a skin-tight body suit and hood. Those loose black Shinobi Shozoku uniforms brush up against stuff and can get caught on things. But apparently none of that matters. In my John Paul notes it says he's going to send me a chameleon suit. I have no idea what that is, but he said I'll like it and should keep it on hand for other missions. In this plan of yours, will you be joining me inside the place?"

"Only part way. It will be up to you to get me to the security room."

"Do we crawl through the air conditioning ducts or something?"

Cassiopia rolled her eyes, "That's only in the movies, Scott. Very few buildings have ducts big enough to crawl around in and even if you could the sheet metal screws would tear you to pieces. We won't be opening deadbolts with a credit card either."

"Boy, this little talk of ours really has gotten just as heavy for so early in the morning, hasn't it?"

Cassiopia nodded and sipped her tea. Markman smiled and did likewise.

Cassiopia said, "I was trying to take my mind off this sickening morning news. I wish I hadn't read it."

Markman raised an eyebrow and held out his hand for the tablet. She handed it over. The front page title was indeed repulsive:

KESTRY WOMAN MURDERED

The first few paragraphs carefully detailed a grisly murder scene discovered by police at the home of Maria Landers after they'd been sent there by concerned coworkers. The victim had missed work for two days and was not answering their calls.

Cassiopia sipped. "Why does the news media have to be so gruesome? Isn't it shocking enough that the poor lady was a victim of terrible violence? Wouldn't it be a much better world if they used their literary talents to dispense the information without creating images of horror in people's minds?"

Markman continued to read as he spoke, "Cass, maybe I shouldn't say this but from my experience doing police work I'm guessing the crime was probably uglier than the press or the police are letting on. Where is Kestry, anyway?"

"That's the scary part," replied Cassiopia. "It's not far from here. It's a new community about thirty miles southeast of Culpeper. Such a wonderful area to have this sort of thing happen. It's like you can't get away from it anymore."

Markman became distracted by a secondary news article:

FREDERICKSBURG BOY HIT BY DUI DRIVER MAY LOSE LEG

The victim was just seven years old. He was trying out a new bike, a birthday present from his aunt. The driver did not stop but police had a good description of the vehicle resulting in the man being arrested a short time later.

A pang of fear along with a faint touch of nausea surged through Markman. The article made it clear the boy, Mark Delan, would lose his right leg above the knee. There was no doubt about that. The child was in the Gifford Orthopedic Surgery Center in the intensive care unit waiting to be stabilized enough so the surgery could be performed.

Markman's private ethical dilemma had abruptly surfaced once more. It was a closely guarded secret known to only one other person on Earth. Growing up at a secret military base outside of Lhasa, Markman had spent many hours with Tibetan monks learning the philosophy of Tao Chane, a martial art based on the movements of animals. Tao Chane was intended to be used only to protect people, animals and nature in general. On numerous occasions he had watched in amazement as the old masters fiercely rubbed their hands together and then used them to heal an injured student, but that amazing power had always been possessed only by the old ones. It was said a lifetime of Tao Chane knowledge was needed to acquire it.

For Markman there was now no escaping the truth. Through a strange set of exotic circumstances he had unexpectedly acquired that healing power prematurely and at a much greater level than his old masters. Not only could he heal others, he could levitate small objects simply by concentrating on them. He had never sought such abilities through meditation so discovering them had come as something of a shock. The old masters had borne their talents casually as though they were a natural part of life. They did not appear to be conflicted in any way. But for Markman the new talents were an endless source of confusion and concern. Each healing he'd secretly performed had drained him of energy, sometimes to a dangerous level. So how was this gift to be apportioned? How many per day should he try to attempt? At what point was he guilty of not doing enough?

The only other person who knew the secret was a doctor he'd once saved. The man had promised to keep quiet. He'd also tried to help with Markman's dilemma. He'd explained anyone on Earth could spend every waking hour trying to help others but at some point that would be harmful to the person doing it. In the end his answer had been to do as much as Markman could without harming or losing himself in the effort. Markman continued to struggle to apply that philosophy.

Cassiopia's voice brought him back to reality. "... and so I thought it would be good... are you listening to me, Scott?"

"What? Yes... of course. Go on."

"I'll spend most of today going through the materials John Paul left us then you and I can go over how I think it should be done. Does that sound good to you?"

"Yes... great."

"What were you planning on doing today?"

"I thought I'd go for a drive just to clear my head. This has all been a bit much for me if you know what I mean."

"Good, you can bring me back some potato chips. It's the one thing we don't have."

"Sure. What kind?"

"Regular, but no salt if you can get those."

"I will make it my quest, fair maiden."

Markman finished his tea and tried to look casual. He stood, stretched, and yawned. Immediately Cassiopia began to look suspicious.

"Regular potato chips, no salt. I'm on it."

"Take your time. There's no rush."

"As you wish."

Cassiopia chuckled and watched as he casually strolled away down the corridor.

As soon as he was out of sight Markman broke into a run. He paused momentarily and tapped at his left collarbone where the Celestial Order implant was located. It was an unnecessary gesture but to speak to the car without a switch or turn-on of some sort was difficult to get used to.

"Core, pick me up at the east entrance."

Markman thought to bolt straight down to the car but again stopped. Hospitals were no longer easy places to sneak into these days. A plan was needed. He hurried down the corridor and turned left toward the master bedroom. Once there he pulled out his only dark suit and found his seldom used briefcase tucked away in the closet corner. In it he grabbed the old FBI badge and ID he'd once been issued while on temporary duty for the Bureau. There was a pair of dark-rimmed reading glasses and a black leather notebook as well. With suit bundled up and the other items tucked away he carefully checked to be sure the hall was clear, skipped the elevator and slid down the stairway banister toward the east entrance. At the bottom of the stairs he darted around the necessary corridors and dashed out the double metal doors to find the shiny black Vette waiting with the driver's door open. He slid down and in, dumped his possessions on the passenger seat and spun off toward the main gate.

Through the barely opened wrought iron entrance he spun onto Mountain Road and sped along the tree-lined roadway, wondering about the wisdom of what he was about to do. Route 3 would take him directly into Fredericksburg. Core would locate and take him to the Gifford Orthopedic Surgery Center. From there he would need to get in and out as quickly as possible without attracting attention.

Fredericksburg was only 30 or 40 miles away, probably an hour's drive by the speed limit. Markman decided a quicker trip was needed.

"Core, is your radar on?"

"Radar is currently active," replied Core in its raspy masculine voice.

"Core, please keep speed safe up to 90 miles per hour. If you see traffic or people ahead go back to the speed limit. Go ahead and take over steering control."

Core beeped understanding and the steering wheel and gas pedal began to move on their own. Gradually Markman leaned back and loosened his grip on the wheel. The car accelerated and held 90 on the straights and ever so smoothly slowed for curves.

The self-driving mode made for a quick trip to the outskirts of Fredericksburg. Markman took back control and asked for the location of the hospital. The dash display appeared showing the best path. It was fast and easy, north up Route 1 and a right onto East Hospital Drive.

The hospital complex was big. Markman drove around to side parking. A green security van pulled out as he turned in and a police car was parked in one of the first lots. The emergency entrance was on the left. Markman backed into an empty space and sat in thought.

"Core, is there a floor plan online for the Gifford Orthopedic Surgery Center?"

A PDF file opened on the car's display screen with the layout for each of the floors at Gifford Orthopedic. Markman moved them around with his index finger and did his best to commit them to memory. For a moment he wished Cassiopia was assisting him for she, with only a single look, would have memorized the entire place down to the smallest closet.

But she could not be included in this. Absolutely no one, including Cassiopia, must ever learn of his powers. It could be too life-changing a revelation. Cassiopia might look at him differently. She might consider him some sort of deviant. It could affect their relationship, and nothing was worth taking a chance on that. As for John Paul and the Celestial Order, they might want to do testing on him. He could become a lab rat with no real life of his own. No, there could be no chance of anyone finding out. It was too much of a risk.

For these reasons, getting in and out of Gifford Orthopedic without being noticed was essential. If the healing worked they'd be left only to wonder. It would be a miracle associated with no one but God. That was the way it had to be.

ICU was on the far east side of the second-floor. There were utility and mechanical rooms near a side entrance on the ground floor, good places to hide if things went badly.

This would be perhaps the trickiest job Markman had attempted but it had to be done now before the kid's surgery was started. There would be surveillance cameras everywhere. The FBI ID would provide the best chance to get in. Markman climbed out of the car and stood within the open door, struggling to change into his dark suit and tie without attracting attention. He tucked his ID into an inside breast pocket, put on the big dark-rimmed glasses, grabbed the thin black leather notebook and shut the door. His brownish-blonde hair was a bit long for the part, but it would have to do. With a deep breath for courage he headed for the main entrance.

The large sliding doors gave way to a grand receiving area. Gray tiled floor led to a wide circular receptionist desk. Above, a high, domed white ceiling opened to the second-floor. Plants and oil paintings filled the surroundings.

A very attractive blond lady in a beige suit top straightened her headset and looked up to greet Markman.

"Yes?"

Markman awkwardly adjusted his dark-rimmed glasses and pulled his ID from his jacket. "Special Agent Wayman. I'm here to sign off on your patient Mark Delan." Markman held up his ID being careful to conceal the name.

The receptionist's expression darkened. "Oh.... Yes, he's in ICU on the third floor. I'll print you a badge." She turned and busied herself and a moment later handed Markman an adhesive badge he stuck to his lapel. The receptionist promptly returned to her computer screen.

"Too easy," thought Markman as he rode an elevator up. "Bet it gets tricky now."

The elevator door opened to cool air. It smelled of disinfectant. Worn green carpet lead to the left and right. Far to the right two large windowed doors with aluminum push guards bore an ominous gray sign that read *ICU*. There was no one in sight in either direction. Markman took another breath for courage and headed that way.

Door handles with no latches meant the speaker and red access button by the door were mandatory. Markman pressed the button and waited.

A terse voice answered, "Yes?"

"Special Agent Wayman."

A buzzer sounded. Markman pulled the open. Inside, a circular station took up the center of the ICU. Glass enclosures along the walls separated patient areas. There were faint pump sounds and the clicking of machines. A stern looking nurse in dark blue scrubs behind the counter eyed Markman as an interruption. Her brown hair was very straight and she wore little makeup. Her expression suggested impatience.

Markman held up his ID before she could ask. "Special Agent Wayman. I need to do a quick check on your patient Mark Delan."

"What is this about?"

"I'm not at liberty to discuss the case, Ma'am, but it's just a sign-off so we can close out our paperwork. We contributed some lab work on this. I just need to verify Mark Delan is a real person."

The nurse slowly began to nod. "I think I understand. He's in the third cubicle over there. You just missed his mother. She's been keeping a vigil. The boy is due for surgery in two hours. You must not disturb him in any way. He's heavily sedated."

Markman tried to sound sympathetic. "It'll only take a moment to note his condition. I'll be very quiet." Markman tucked in his fake ID and turned to head for the boy's room. At the same moment a second nurse entered the ICU with two steaming Styrofoam cups of espresso. There was muted jubilation as one was delivered to the person on duty. An excited conversation in low tones broke out. As Markman crossed over to the boy's area he was able to make out some of it.

"I just saw Dr. Morrison, the medical examiner. They brought the body of that Landers woman in, the one that was murdered. I don't know what happened to her but it was bad. Morrison won't talk about it and he looks really grim."

"The woman from the Kestry community?"

"Yes. Whatever was done to her they won't talk about it."

"Oh my God!"

As Markman paused to open the glass door he glanced back to see the two opening their coffees and giving each other looks of dread. He gently opened the glass door, concerned there was not enough concealment for the little time he would have. The two nurses sipped their espressos and one gave a momentary glance his way.

The boy was asleep. There were IV tubes coming from each arm. A heartbeat monitor was also alongside the bed, turned on but not attached to the patient. An automatic blood pressure reader was hissing depressurization. The boy was in a white hospital gown with the blankets pulled up to his waist. He looked peaceful, sedated from the horror of a smashed leg. Markman stood where he could still see the nurse's station. There were too many quick glances coming his way.

One of the nurses put her coffee down on the counter to fetch something from her pocket. Markman opened his black folder and held it up as though he was studying it. Ever so carefully he raised his free hand to his chest and pointed the first finger toward the nurses steaming coffee cup. With the first concentrated movement of his finger the coffee cup obediently began to slide ever so slightly. Neither nurse noticed and as one of them reached up to hand the other something, Markman made a full jerk with his hand.

The coffee cup tipped over and spilled the nearly full cup onto the counter of folders and documents.

There were muted cries of alarm and despair and a rush to save whatever possible from the espresso tsunami.

Markman snapped his folder shut and stepped over to the boy. With a quick breath for inner strength he placed one hand on the boy's chest. There was the familiar snap and jolt of electricity between his hand and the patient, then the magnetic locking between the two. A rush of power began to flow into the boy. In his mind Markman could see the life-force charge immediately, targeting the injured leg. At the same time the life-energy within Markman began to drain dramatically. Markman had to fight to stand his ground and not pull away in self-preservation.

But the leg was being reconstructed, almost like turning back time. Markman could feel it. His knees weakened. He dropped his notebook to the floor and braced himself against the bed rails. As he did, something new and unexpected began to happen. Part of the life stream of healing power diverted and flowed upward toward the boy's head. Somehow Markman knew there was damage to the boy's brain that had not been detected. It was a critical bleeding of some sort, more a threat to his life than the leg had been. Markman struggled and strained not to pass out as two rivers of life force raced to the boy's injuries.

Then the merciful snap of completion jolted Markman. His hand slid away from the boy. He fell to one knee, holding to the bed rail to keep himself up. There was no way to tell how long the treatment had taken. Certainly the nurses would be looking in at any moment. Markman's energy level was so depleted he could not muster enough strength to take a breath but the fear of being seen by the nurse drove him on. He managed to grab his fallen notebook and pull himself up by the rail. A wave of dizziness pulled him backward. He backed into the wall and fought with weak knees. A glance outward showed the spilled coffee crisis was nearly under control. Another attempt to breathe resulted in a choked off half a breath. A second attempt filled the lungs. In desperation, Markman opened his notebook and pretended to be checking it. A nurse with a coffee cup stuffed full of wet napkins looked up to check on him. He managed a quick nod. She turned away and looked down at her friend, out of sight, mopping the wet floor.

Markman straightened up and tried for the door. There was not enough strength to open it. Not all of his attempts to breathe were successful. He focused and pulled the door open enough to squeeze past it. Heading for the exit, there were staggers which went unnoticed by the preoccupied nurse. A lean against the exit door allowed a quick look back and an abbreviated wave to her.

The hallway was deserted. A pause to lean against the wall brought more choked off breath attempts. Someone passed by the hallway in the distance but took no notice. Using the wall, he managed to reach the elevator. Mercifully the elevator doors opened quickly. There was no one within.

A deep breath allowed marginal speech. "Core, meet me at the west entrance."

The *Emergency* signs were the only things that allowed Markman to find his way out. In the emergency waiting area a dozen people were too preoccupied with their own discomfort to notice the drunken man leaving.

Pressure doors swooshed open. Outside a black Corvette with heavily tinted windows waited with the driver's door open. No one had paid any attention.

Markman fell into the driver's seat and had an urge to shed a tear or two in self-pity. When enough strength had been garnered to pull his legs in, he spoke. "Core, close."

The driver's door shut.

"Core, return to home base. Autonomous mode."

The obedient Corvette dropped into drive and slowly pulled away from the entrance. Markman fell into a semiconscious state. He could feel the Corvette stopping at intersections and making turns but there was not enough strength to actually see what was happening. There was the sensation of G-force as the car accelerated on the main road home. Breathing slowly became closer to normal. Vision began to focus. Apparently escape had been successful. Now all that was left was the self-doubt. It seemed like a stupid, impulsive thing he had just done. He was still wearing the dark-rimmed glasses but they were hanging on the left side of his face. He pushed them away.

All was not assured. The implant in his neck would have tracked him all the way. Would it notify the monitoring computer that he was at a hospital and possibly in distress? The adrenaline had been pumping. Could it interpret that as physical illness? The hospital cameras would have recorded the FBI agent in glasses and dark suit. A good video processor might be able to electronically remove those for a better ID. When they unwrapped the boy's leg for surgery there would be many questions. Had an incorrect diagnosis been made? Was someone at fault? There was no denying that he was not necessarily in the clear.

But he had known all of these things and had gone ahead anyway. Markman rubbed his chest with one hand. There was a big mental hole there. Vegetarian or not, power food needed to be taken and it had to be meat of some kind, something packed with protein.

"Core, take me to the nearest drive-through restaurant."

The map display on the dashboard changed to show a McDonald's along the way. Core pulled into the drive-through ten minutes later. There was difficulty speaking to the clown-faced speaker and awkward fumbling of the wallet and credit card. Markman ravaged the two fish sandwiches before Core even had time to pull away from the parking lot. The attendant inside had eyed him curiously.

Fish sandwiches jammed in the mouth gave way to deeper breathing. A soulful strength flowed through Markman. His head began to clear. Cassiopia's potato chips managed to find a place there.

"Core, take me to the nearest Publix."

The Corvette's display screen changed once again.

Forty-five minutes later the castle gates swung open, welcoming the Master home.

Chapter 3

Markman sat in the lotus position atop the castle tower, seeking the life-stream flow within, meditating for its rejuvenation. He opened his eyes briefly to find Cassiopia sitting across from him, her own lotus attempt looking incomplete and painful. She noticed his wince at the sight of her awkwardly crossed legs and threw her head back in playful laughter.

"You are like spaghetti, Markman. I am normal."

"Don't be discouraged, Grasshopper. The yoga positions were made for Asian people, sometimes called a state of Jing. Their bodies match the yoga disciplines perfectly. We Americans usually don't fit those exercises very well. So yes, you are normal. Growing up over there I had a lot of time to practice."

"I was surprised to find you here at this time of day."

"I was meditating on the tough choices life sometimes forces on us."

"Tell me about it. Why are we here? Should we be here? Why isn't life easier to understand?"

Markman smiled. "There's a little fable they tell in India about that. One day God decided he needed to shrink reality down to something very small so we could better understand him so he created the universe."

Cassiopia thought for a moment and laughed. She loosened the fold in her legs and breathed a sigh of relief. She leaned back on her hands and smiled. "Thanks for the potato chips, by the way. They were sooo good. Where'd you go?"

"They were from Publix."

Cassiopia rolled her eyes. "I know that! Where else d'you go?"

"Oh, just for a ride in the country. It was nice."

"You didn't stop anywhere else?"

"I got a couple fish sandwiches at a drive-thru."

"You? Fish sandwiches?"

Markman opened his mouth to reply but was interrupted by a distant droning. He searched the sky to the northeast, pointed and said, "Look! What is that?"

The two stood and stared at a strange dark object approaching. As it neared they realized it was a black, four-propeller drone carrying a satchel. Rather than pass by it slowed and descended directly toward them. As they stood in silent awe, the aircraft lowered just above their heads and dropped the package on the tower floor. It rotated and sped off much faster than it had arrived.

Markman looked at Cassiopia. "Airmail?" he joked.

Cassiopia kneeled and unzipped the bag. "It's from John Paul! It's the stuff we asked for. Your suit is in here! Wow! It almost feels like liquid!"

Markman leaned over to look down. "When are we supposed to pull off this heist anyway?"

"It's not a heist, Scott. Don't call it that. You make us sound like bank robbers."

"Well, it is someone's private property, isn't it? I mean we're just gonna take it from them."

"No, we're going to give them a different one in its place so no one can be harmed by the real one."

"So that's not stealing then?"

Cassiopia stood with two small black items in her hands. "Wow, look at these electronic lock decoders. This one decodes combo locks and this one actually picks a key lock and turns it open!"

"Right, not stealing at all," replied Markman.

Cassiopia straightened up with an annoyed look. "We can decline this mission. Is that what you want?"

"I didn't say that. Is that a spool gun in there?"

"Yes! I asked John Paul for one. So, you do believe someone needs to recover that alien weapon to protect society, right?"

Markman tried to look innocent. He fumbled around trying to put his hands in his pockets, forgetting his dark Wushu-styled robe had no pockets. "Man, that drone just made it here. Look at the black sky over there. It really looks threatening. What'd you want to have for dinner?"

"I shall take such evasiveness as meaning you concur," said Cassiopia. "Soup and salad."

Once the new burglar items had been put away they went to the main kitchen and Markman sat as Cassiopia ladled soup into their bowls.

"Scott, sometimes you eat enough for a horse. Why don't you ever gain weight?"

"It's the forms, Cass. Like you said, I still do the forms. That's another thing I love about this place. Out in the courtyard I can work the Bo and the shurikens in the garden and still be around nature."

"How come I never see you use those numchuckie things?"

"Because I've hit myself in the head too many times. I still use the butterfly sword Isn't that good enough?"

"Oh yeah, maybe you could carve the turkey this Thanksgiving."

"Very funny. When do we do the caper anyway?"

"Tomorrow night."

"That soon?"

"In John Paul's text messages he is concerned the weapon might be moved."

"Are you ready already?"

"Yes."

"Do we get to practice?"

"We'll use the displays in the meeting room along with some visual aids but it will be mostly mental practice only. You will get to do some laser net practice, though. There's no time for anything more than that."

"Laser net?"

"Just wait and see."

"When will we do all this?"

"Tonight."

As the two paused to enjoy their soup the sound of rain replaced the silence.

"Wow! Sounds like a typhoon has started out there," said Cassiopia.

"Wonderful, isn't it?" replied Markman.

"Not if you can't find your raincoat."

"Huh?"

"My father stuck his head out of his lab for a few minutes today."

"Really? Did he see his shadow?"

"Very funny. Actually, it was what he didn't see. I guess he noticed the weather report and went looking for his hat and raincoat. Blamed me for taking them, as if I'd wear a Dick Tracy long coat and hat. He's had them for decades."

"The absent-minded professor."

"He can't find his boots, either. I told him the whole outfit is so old it probably became self-aware and walked off."

"We're going upstairs and beginning training then?"

"As soon as we take care of these dishes. You washing or drying?"

When cleanup duties were complete Cassiopia led the way to the hidden elevator. On the way up Markman's humor again kicked in. "Did you ask your father how to get into his project lab yet?"

Cassiopia responded, "Tsk." She pointed her nose up and looked away. "You know I won't do that. Don't need to."

"It must be killing you," mused Markman.

"Let's focus on the business at hand, shall we?"

The elevator doors rattled open. Lights came on. Markman stepped out and plopped down in the nearest seat at the conference room's center table. He locked his hands behind his head and pushed side to side in the seat.

Cassiopia went to the head of the table and tapped at a few keys built into the table's surface. Monitors around the room came alive with diagrams and data. Most surprising for Markman was the 3D image of a building layout which hovered and slowly rotated just above table's center. Transparent green rooms, stairwells, duct work, alarm sensors, along with an array of other information all projected there.

Cassiopia went right to work. She moved over to the floor plan image and leaned against the table. "This is the Advanced Aviation Systems building where the weapon is locked away. Seven floors, the vault is on the fifth floor, the main security room is on the first. Your initial task is to get me into that main security room. There are cameras in various places on every floor. You cannot approach this building from ground level on any side; all are covered by surveillance cameras and motion detection alarms in case the guard isn't paying attention."

"Are you saying there's a guard on duty in the security room 24/7?"

"Yes. You have to get in there and put the guard to sleep without hurting him or letting him know you were ever there. Once you've done that you can open the front door and let me in. My entry will cause the ground cameras and front door to set off alarms in the security room but there will be no one to hear them. Once I'm in there I'll cancel the alarms and go to work on the camera and alarm software. I'll replace all the video using previous recordings from the same time of day. I'll change the dates on the videos and delete all the alarm entries."

"How did I get in the security room without setting alarms off or being seen?"

"That's the trick. There is one place they did not install cameras, the roof. There is a high rise next door to Advanced Aviation Systems. The ninth floor is vacant. There's no security. The exterior plate glass windows can be opened for cleaning. That's what the spool gun is for. You will need to shoot a line across and use it for a zip line. Ever done that?"

"Sure, but not ninety feet up in the dark."

"Can you do it?"

"Yes."

"Once you're on the AAS roof I will reel in the cable and your harness, seal up the room and hurry down to get into position to enter the main security room when you signal the coast is clear."

"So I'm on the roof."

"Yes, now the tricky part."

"Tricky part? I thought the Flying Wallenda across buildings was the tricky part."

"The rooftop elevator motor room will be locked but easy for you to open with the unlocking device John Paul provided."

"You want me to ride an elevator down to the first floor?"

"No. You can't do that. At night the guards on patrol are the only ones to use them. Someone using an elevator would probably get their attention."

Cassiopia paused to study the building's image. She used a pencil to point to a section near the elevator shaft. "See right here? There's a small cable drop adjoining the elevator shaft. It's just big enough for a man. It goes straight down to the first floor. There's ladder rungs going the length of it for servicing cables. That's your way down. You'll need to remove a panel to get access to it. Whatever you do don't drop the panel."

"Right." Markman rolled his eyes. "The tricky part is getting into and down the Jefferies tube."

"The what?"

"Star Trek! Jefferies tube! Haven't you ever heard of a Jefferies tube?"

"That's not the tricky part."

"You're kidding."

"On the first floor you can't crawl out into the lobby. The cameras would spot you and the security monitor would be notified."

"Okay...."

"The entire first floor is built on a raised floor so cables can run underneath. It's a twenty-four inch space. You'll need to work yourself under the raised floor then worm yourself around and make your way underneath the security room. You'll use a headlamp and a cable map I've made for you."

"There aren't any rats under there, are there?"

"There's no food products under that floor, Scott. And don't get claustrophobia because you can push up on any floor panel and climb out if you need to but of course you'll set off alarms. Once you're beneath the security room the guard will be sitting just above you. Your goal will be to push up slightly on a floor panel and release an odorless gas into that room. The guard will go to sleep without realizing anything is happening. You'll be wearing a gas mask. Then you climb up into the main security room, check on the other roving guard and come open the front door to let me in. We will go back into the security room where I will attend to the sleeping guard and you will change into your Spiderman suit."

"I have to admit, I don't really see any problems so far," said Markman.

"It's a perfect plan but it's not as easy as it might sound. Access the building and take control of the main security room and as far as anyone knows no one is there."

"John Paul's invisibility law."

"Yes, for all intents and purposes no one will have entered the building. You will be a dirty mess when you finally climb out from under that floor but you'll be wearing special black coveralls and change into your chameleon suit right there in the security room. From that point there's only one danger. We need to get everything done and be out of there without any of the sleeping guard's associates stopping by to visit him. There's no way we can guarantee that so we have to be quick so the odds are in our favor. I can busy out his phone and cell but if any of them stop by I would have to give the guard the wake-up nasal spray and hide while he wakes up. We'd probably need a John Paul type of rescue then and that would be undesirable."

"Couldn't you use the sleep gas through the building? Ta-da! Take our time, a walk in the park."

"No. Some of the guards would wake up on the floor and who knows what else might happen. They'd know something was done to them. The object is for none of them to notice anything. I can get away with the security room guard because I'll set him up leaning against the counter with his chin in his hand if I can. When he wakes up he'll think he just nodded off for a few minutes. His panels will all be green, his videos normal."

"Will I be able to breathe under the floor?"

"You'll have that filter gas mask."

"So I'm in the security room in my Spidey suit. What then?"

"I will begin by erasing the video and panel alarms from when I entered the building. From there I'll replace all the video feed with a previous day's identical video. I'll go into the system software and change the dates and sensor logs. I'll alter enough video and system time for you to get to the vault and exchange the weapon."

"And while you're doing that I'm on my way to the fifth floor then?"

"Yes, by way of the stairwell. Remember, no elevators. The fifth-floor door will have a special keypad. It will want a four-digit number and a palm print. John Paul's keypad decoder device will give you the number and there will be special plastic gloves in your backpack. They have Robert Duran's palm and fingerprints."

"Cool."

"Once you've entered the fifth floor it gets tricky."

"No, really?"

"Very funny. There is a guard stationed at a desk which you must get past to reach the main vault. The second roving guard periodically walks that floor also, sometimes two of them do."

"Man, talk about paranoia."

"That part's not so bad. From the security room I will be able to track them and when they are in range of a surveillance camera I'll be able to see them. Basically, I'll talk you through to the vault. Then comes the really tricky part."

Markman folded his arms and raised his eyebrows.

"There's another keypad-palm print needed to get into the room with the main vault door. Inside there is an invisible vertical laser net. Break any laser beam and alarms go off I can't stop."

"Are you saying I have to play laser tag? The Big Bang Theory?"

"Exactly. There will be three columns of laser net. You must work your way through them one at a time. You'll have a fog spray to help you see them."

"What if there's no way through? Can't you shut the thing down from the control room?"

"It's an independent system which also keeps a record of who turned it on and off. I can't get to it and you can't shut it off or it will be recorded. But never fear. I know there's a way through it. I have the schematics and layout for the laser emitters and the mirrors. I know the exact pattern of each net. John Paul sent along the stuff and I've set up an exact duplicate here in this room. When we're done here you can put on your chameleon suit and start practicing. I was able to get through it myself. Fifty-seven seconds. Beat that or lose your man card."

"Gee! I might actually like this part!"

"Your chameleon suit is amazing. The pullover hood has little lenses for the eyes that change color and imagery with the suit. The material almost feels like a second skin. The suit reflects the space behind you perfectly. It's the best optical illusion I've ever seen."

"Does It have pockets?"

"Not a one. You'll wear a flatpack on your back underneath the suit. The suit has a slit in the back just above the waist that lets you reach underneath it to access the stuff in the flatpack. The weapon and decoders will be stored there."

"I make it into the vault and through the laser net. What then?"

"All that will be left is the main wall safe. It will take a combo from your hand-held decoder. Once you have it open there's another single layer laser net. You will have six seconds to find the opti-panel just inside the door somewhere. It needs the print from Robert Duran's right forefinger so be ready with the plastic glove. There's no recording done with that laser net, but you must remember to turn it back on before sealing the safe."

"And that's all?"

"I guide you back to the security room. We set the security room guard to wake up a minute or so after we're gone. Then we simply walk out the front door. Sixty seconds later undoctored video and alarm system data will kick back in. There will be no sign anyone was ever there or that anything unusual ever happened."

"You are a devious woman."

"Look who's talking."

"We take the Corvette to New Providence tomorrow, get a room somewhere and visit Advanced Aviation Systems after dark?"

"Yes. If anyone asks we are in New Providence to look at some property on the Passaic River."

"Sounds like you have all the answers."

"I do."

"What could possibly go wrong…?"

"You'd better get going playing laser tag."

"So I'm Leonard?"

Chapter 4

Markman leaned out the open service window on the ninth floor of the Verotech building and stared down into the darkness. The air was cool. He could make out some of the windows on the eight and seventh floors, but ground level was veiled in black. Not far away, a single dull street lamp illuminated a narrow street that ran between the Verotech building and Advanced Aviation Systems. It was a right-of-way not used by city traffic and no cars were in sight.

Markman tugged on the gray cable running out the window across to the other rooftop. It had taken two attempts to catch the steel ladder bolted to the elevator room atop Advanced Aviation Systems, but the grappling hook seemed to have latched securely.

Cassiopia pushed in alongside him and stared down. "Maybe this wasn't such a great idea." she said, half under her breath.

Markman looked over and shook his head reassuringly. "No, no it's fine. I don't see a problem."

He backed away and turned to check the near end of the cable. The abandoned ninth floor was virtually wide open and only support columns here and there interrupted the floor plan. The support columns were perfect places to anchor a cable and safety line. As Markman studied the newspaper-strewn surroundings Cassiopia tugged at his body harness. She clipped a nylon rope to it and finished zipping up his black stretch coveralls.

"Do I really need the rope?" he asked.

"I'll be unreeling safety line as you go. If the cable fails for any reason, you'll swing back down against this building. You'll need to break your impact with your feet. Okay?"

"That would be interesting. I'm ready."

"Not without your ear buds you're not." She reached in her coverall pockets and pulled out two small ear pieces. Markman accepted them with a smile and fixed one into each ear.

"I don't get it. No boom mic?"

"These earpieces are so sensitive they pick up the vibrations from your throat. They are their own microphones."

Cassiopia pushed a switch on a small black box on her belt. "Can you hear me?"

Markman nodded. "Great. Clear as a bell."

"And I hear you just fine. So, don't forget the brake lever on the pulley. You'll need it to stop over there. And, once you're safely on the roof release the safety line and the cable so I can reel them back in. Then I'll gather everything up and hurry down to Core. He'll drop me off with my pack at a spot where I can watch the front doors without setting off any detectors. As soon as you put the guard to sleep make sure the lobby is clear and come to the front doors and let me in. Got it?"

"I think I've got it."

"Don't count on anything."

Cassiopia reached up and adjusted the headlamp on Markman's forehead. "Don't forget to switch your headlamp to red light when you go under that raised floor. You can't take a chance on a guard seeing light leaking through the floor panels."

"Yes, dear. Um, why aren't we using infrared goggles again?"

"Because their vision is too narrow for such a cramped area. You'll need to be looking everywhere to find your way."

"Okay, so can I go now, Mother?"

Cassiopia cast a sarcastic look and gestured to the open window.

Markman stepped one foot outside and balanced himself on the narrow ledge. He hooked onto the cable pulley and tested it. Cassiopia stepped back. Her expression had changed to one of hesitancy and concern.

With a last smile back at her, Markman pushed out into dark empty air.

There was an abrupt gut-wrenching sag in the cable. The momentary fall jerked into a downhill race, the slide pulley whirring from the acceleration. Markman held to the pulley clamp and focused on the AAS building's approaching rooftop. He kicked with his feet to keep straight. Cool night air rushed by his face and forced him to squint.

Halfway across the abyss, Markman began to worry at how much speed had been gained. It seemed the landing on the roof might need to be a controlled crash. And, as the roof edge approached, he realized the cable sag was taking him too low. An impact with the building's wall would be ugly.

Now traveling with too much speed, Markman struggled to maintain control, but as the roof edge lurched forward at him he yanked his feet upward, swinging high and barely across. Dragging his feet on the gravel rooftop turned him around backward, but the slide gradually eased so that no crash into the elevator room was needed. Stopping a few feet from it he stood, unhooked his harness and looked back at Cassiopia still staring wide-eyed at him in alarm. He waved and did a short celebratory dance move. He unclipped the harness and line and gestured with open arms for approval. Cassiopia was shaking her head as she began pulling the lines in.

The door to the elevator room was a heavy-duty knob lock. Markman drew out the key lock device from inside his coveralls and snapped out the key insert. Carefully he slid it into the doorknob key slot and waited. There was a slight pulsing and vibration as the lock decoder searched for the right tumbler combo. A few seconds later he felt the key insert turn and the door jumped open.

It was a darkened chamber with large gray motors and cable sheaves straddled by fat steel cables. Dirty steel girders were positioned everywhere. Markman was able to balance on one and look down into the elevator shaft. A cable array led down into the darkness of the pit.

Somewhere far below an elevator car hung at the end of them.

The electrical cable shaft Markman needed did not reach this level. It would require a climb down to find the desired access panel. Markman switched on his headlamp.

Cassiopia's voice interrupted. "What do you see?"

Markman replied in a low tone, "Elevator's way down there. Stand by."

Markman kneeled and lowered himself onto another I-beam cross member. He hung over the side and searched the shaft below. On the south wall, just where it was supposed to be, a rust-colored four-foot by four-foot hatch cover allowed a few power and data cables to flow past a cutout in its base. The cover was held in place by Phillips head screws. There was an I-beam cross member below the cover. Markman swung down and positioned one foot on it. With slow caution, he managed a position which allowed him to draw the mini electric screwdriver from his leg pocket and begin removing screws.

Cassiopia's voice sounded impatient. "How's it going?"

"Almost there. Hold on."

The last of the screws released the rusty panel from its place. Markman moved it to the side and carefully leaned it against the wall on the I-beam. The newly opened black hole looked menacing. Markman leaned in and searched with his headlamp. The cable drop looked like a closet-sized hole descending into the earth with cable flows surrounding it. The small rusty welded ladder rungs were opposite him. With a shake of his head he wormed his way in and jockeyed around to pull the cover inside with him. The cover would have to be re-installed on the wrong side but it was doubtful anyone would ever notice. Markman maneuvered the panel so that one corner screw could be set, then let the cover drop into place to do the rest.

"I'm in the cable tunnel. It's a tight fit."

"Can you do it?" asked Cassiopia in nearly a whisper.

"I think so."

Markman started down, one rung at a time. In some areas the passage was so narrow he had to raise his arms to squeeze down in.

"It's like exploring a cave," he whispered.

"How far down are you?"

"Two floors. I can see where the cables exit at each floor and there are more hatch covers to the elevator shaft."

Three more floors made the passage even more cramped. The number of data and power lines were multiplying. The air was becoming musty. Markman paused and brought out his breathing mask. He fit it in place and continued.

Another twenty minutes of squeezing through tight spaces and maneuvering to find footholds brought Markman to a point where added cables were making his passage nearly impossible. He paused and twisted around to point his headlamp down in search of the bottom.

It was there, another fifteen feet or so. In fact, the cable drop opened to an eight-foot by eight-foot cement chamber that appeared to be below the ground floor, almost like a small basement. One last tight squeeze and he was able to slip down and drop onto the floor and search the hidden room. There was a ten-foot opening at eye level. A forest of raised floor stanchions supporting floor plates came into view. To his right, power and data cables entered through a portal in the cement. The path underneath the raised floor did not look as foreboding as he had expected. The rows of stanchions disappeared into distant shadow. There was room between cable runs to crawl through.

"I've reached the bottom," he whispered.

It took a moment for Cassiopia to reply. "Oh, that's so good. That was the part which worried me the most. But can you make it under the floor?"

"Doesn't look too bad."

"I'm parked in the next parking lot over. I'm ready to make a run for the entrance as soon as you've secured the security room."

"Standby."

Markman mentally charted his course through the floor stanchions then switched his headlamp to red light.

"Don't forget to switch to red light," whispered Cassiopia.

"Yes, Dear."

Markman checked his canister and hose for the sleeping gas and pulled himself up into the raised floor area. Grabbing onto the floor stanchions made progress easier. As he paused to get his bearings he suddenly remembered his fear of rats. A quick search around did not reveal any or any other signs of life, just dust and dirt everywhere. He pulled himself ahead, counting stanchions along the way. Headway was fairly easy until nearing the halfway point. Suddenly sounds from above made him stop and fumble to shut off his headlamp.

Footsteps. Someone was walking on the floor above. They were the heavy steps that had to be those of a guard patrolling the building's entrance. Markman held his breath and listened. There was the sound of a door being tested. A closet was opened and shut. There was silence for a moment. The guard was still there. Suddenly nearby stanchions squeaked and a sprinkle of dirt showered down on Markman's shoulder as the footfalls passed directly over him. The footsteps faded into the distance. With red light back on, Markman tried to hurry his way along. Ahead were cement support columns marking the security room perimeter. Squeezing between them was easy enough.

New sounds caused him to take pause once more. A chair was being pushed around the room above. It was the security room guard at work. He was rolling in his chair from console to console. Not far away Markman could see a floor panel missing where cabling passed up into the room. Silently, he inched his way there.

Looking up revealed the underside of a countertop. He was inside and beneath a security console. Craning his neck to see above, there were cooling grills in a panel facing outward into the room. It was the perfect place for gas flow into the security area. He wrestled to pull the small hose from his suit and blindly ran it up and over the tile to the vent. The guard continued to roll around in his chair. Markman checked his mask to be sure the gas would not affect him then twisted and squeezed at the gas release valve. The gas bottle against his chest became cold from the flow.

It was only a minute or so until the guard ceased rolling his chair. Markman waited another lingering few minutes. There was no sound. He worked his way back then found a floor panel easy to push up. The first crack let in bright fluorescent light. There were no sounds of alarm. He pushed the panel all the way up and over. With great determination he pulled and pushed his way up into the main security room. Video monitors were running everywhere. Colored system lights were spread out around the room. Gently he slid the floor panel back in place.

The uniformed guard was tilted back in his chair, head hanging forward, body slumped to one side. Markman adjusted his gas mask and turned the chair for a better look. The man was out cold. Markman searched the rest of the room. There was a wraparound counter with keyboards and displays. Monitors for the building's different floors were located overhead. There was a small bathroom next to the entrance. He took a moment to study the overhead monitors. Each had a number and letter in the bottom right-hand corner marking the camera location. On the centermost monitor, the second-floor east, a guard was checking doors. A monitor to the left showed another guard on the fourth floor south strolling down a hallway. On the right, the fifth-floor guard was at the security counter leaning back in his chair.

That accounted for all of them. Markman spoke in a low voice, "Main security room secured."

Cassiopia sounded breathless, "I'm ready. As soon as the monitors show no guards nearby tell me and I'll meet you at the front doors."

"It's clear now. Hurry."

Markman searched the countertop in front of the sleeping guard. There was a log-in notebook nearby. He grabbed it, checked the monitors once more, then hurried to the door. With a slow turn of the doorknob, he gently pushed it open and searched the lobby. It was clear. He stepped out and jammed the notebook in the door so it wouldn't close. As he headed for the front glass doors, he spotted Cassiopia already wearing her filter mask, briefcase and carryall in hand, running across the parking lot. He pushed open the door to let her run through. They rushed to the security room entrance and slipped inside, letting the door snap shut behind them.

Cassiopia stopped and gasped for breath from her mask. She looked around the room, stopped abruptly and gasped again at the sight of the sleeping guard.

"What's wrong?" asked Markman in a near whisper.

Cassiopia caught herself and shook her head. "Nothing. The reality of what we're doing is setting in. I've never drugged anyone before. I'm suddenly feeling pretty guilty about it."

"You don't have time to feel guilty," replied Markman. "Let's get going."

Cassiopia went to the counter next to the guard and placed her bag and briefcase on it. She reached into her coverall leg pocket and drew out a small nasal device. She stretched its elastic band over the guard's head and positioned it under his nose.

"This will keep him asleep until we're ready."

She drew out a small scanning device from her opposite pocket and took a reading in the room.

"The gas is almost dissipated. We'll be able to remove our masks in a few moments. Your chameleon suit is in the bag. Get into it."

With the greatest of care, Cassiopia pushed the guard to one side and pulled an empty seat into position. She sat at the main keyboard and began typing commands, looking up at the floor monitors in between typing.

Markman stripped off his coveralls and waited for Cassiopia to stand and stick the flatpack to his bare back. He could feel the shape of the fake alien gun inside it. Checking behind, he tested to be sure all the lower pockets could be easily reached and opened. As she returned to her station he slipped into the strange black material of the chameleon suit legs, pulled the torso section up and maneuvered his arms into the sleeves and gloves, then wrestled the suit and hood over his head. A bit of squirming fit the suit in place. The zippers just above hip level on each side smoothly closed behind almost as if they were motorized. He checked for the slit at the small of his back that allowed access to the flatpack and pulled the hood back and let it hang behind. Everything was in place and felt good. A moment later the suit came alive of its own accord. The entire front side of Markman projected the room behind him no matter how he turned or moved.

"How do I look?"

Cassiopia gave a glance but was too nervous and occupied to reply. She studied her scanner for a moment then peeled the mask off her face. Markman followed her example. Cassiopia swiveled in her chair, gave the sleeping guard a check and looked up at Markman. "The stairwell should be clear. Once you gain access to the fifth floor I'll talk you along depending on where the guards are. I have a floor puller in my bag. If anyone so much as knocks on the security room door I'll have to give the guard his wake-up spray and get under the floor. At that point John Paul will be forced to beam us both out of here and the mission will be blown. I sure pray that doesn't happen."

"I know all that. Let's do it."

Cassiopia gave a worried look and scanned the floor monitors. "Okay, the lobby is clear. Go ahead and get yourself to the stairwell. There's no cameras there so keep me informed of where you are."

"I know all that too." Markman rolled his eyes and headed for the door.

"Wow! Your suit is working nicely."

Markman looked down at himself. His suit had taken the soft blue of the surrounding walls. He gestured approval, gave Cassiopia a last glance and slipped outside the security room.

The stairwell door was close by. Beyond it, seldom used grated metal steps led upward. Markman bounded up. There was a keypad at the door for each floor. At the fifth floor he faced the keyboard, reached behind and drew out the decoder then attached it to the keypad. There was a moment of whirring and clicking and the door abruptly snapped open.

"Fifth-floor. Door unlocked," he said in a low tone.

"That first hallway is clear. Enter and the fourth door on your left is a bathroom door set back from the wall. You can use it for concealment until the next corridor is clear."

Markman did not reply. As silently as possible he slipped through the door and stealthily moved to the restroom cubbyhole.

"I see you now," said Cassiopia. "Okay, to your left is a four-way intersection. Turning right at that intersection takes you directly to the fifth-floor guard station. You will be visible from that guard station as soon as you enter the intersection so you must wait until I tell you it's clear. I know you know all that but for once at least I get the last word."

Cassiopia savored the moment until the realization of what they were doing crept back in. "The fifth-floor guard is at his station. He's milling around behind the counter sorting papers. You'll have to hold until he starts his patrol."

Markman looked down at himself. Half his suit matched the light brown wood grain door to the restroom. The other half was the dull green of the adjacent walls. With a start he realized he had not pulled his hood up over his head. Keeping tight against the door he carefully pulled the hood down over his face. The eye lenses quickly changed to the color of the door, but his view of the world was as clear as it had been.

"Okay, he's leaving. If he heads your way you'll have to take cover in the restroom. Get ready."

Markman wondered exactly what he was supposed to do to get ready.

"He's left the counter and is headed down the main hallway in your direction. He's taking his time, twirling his nightstick. Get ready in case he turns left in your direction."

Markman glanced behind him at the handle for the restroom door.

"It's okay! He turned right. He's heading away from you!"

Markman leaned out and quickly spotted the guard strolling along in the opposite direction. Without waiting for Cassiopia's okay he stepped into the hallway and moved silently along to the corridor intersection. Keeping an eye on the guard's back, he turned right. Ahead he could see the unmanned guard station. He moved carefully along one wall toward it.

"I didn't say go! What if there's another guard up ahead!"

Markman whispered, "At the guard station I take a left and then a quick right. That will lead to the main vault. Right?"

"Correct. And the way is clear. But at some point that guard will circle around toward the hallway to the vault room so you've got to be inside before he arrives."

Keeping low and moving quickly, Markman made his way to the deserted guard station and swerved around it.

At the end of the next hall a heavy metal door with a handprint scanner on the wall blocked the way. Markman straightened up to it, reached behind and drew out the plastic glove Cassiopia had provided. Looking back carefully, he put on the glove and held his hand in the lock's palm print. The result was immediate. Clicking marked the release of the weighted door. He pulled it open and slipped inside.

The new room had an air of entrapment. Gold carpet, tan walls decorated by expensive art and along the walls, oak tables with collectibles that would tempt any thief. At the opposite end of the room was a gray, rectangular vault door like one that might be seen at a branch bank.

But the first ten feet of this treasure chamber were deceptively bare, an invitation to thieves to walk right in and take what they wished. Markman drew out the small cold-spray canister provided him. He made one quick spray from left to right and there before him were the fluorescent green beams of the laser net.

His luck was holding. The patterns of laser beams appeared to be the same ones he had practiced on.

"I see that," said Cassiopia. "Is it the correct pattern?"

"Roger that," replied Markman.

"Thank God."

Markman went to the barrier of green light and stepped through the first layer. Standing stiffly, he skirted to the right, crunched up and eased on through the second.

"The guard is approaching the door to that room but he doesn't suspect anything. You'd better hurry."

Markman rolled his eyes and sidestepped left. He squeezed himself sideways onto the floor and snaked his upper body through the last V-shaped opening. A few seconds later he stood, safely beyond the barrier.

"The guard is outside your door. He's on his cell phone. He may be going to check that room. Don't use any more smoke. Oh! I see you're through it. Get ready to take cover."

There was no cover. Markman smoothed out his chameleon suit and adjusted the hood to be certain it was tight. He went to a portion of tan wall next to the vault door and stood stiffly with his back against it. He glanced down to check the suit. The bottom half of his boots matched the gold carpet. The rest of him was a perfect blend with the tan walls. He straightened up and stood stiffly.

"Oh God, he's got his hand on the lock pad. He's opening the door!"

To Markman, it felt like he was standing in plain sight.

The guard pulled the vault room door open and stared inside. He did not enter. He scanned left and right but to him Markman was a portion of tan wall and nothing more. He allowed the door to swing shut and went on about his business.

"Oh my God!" said Cassiopia.

Markman choked trying not to laugh out loud.

"I heard that! It's not funny!"

"Shouldn't you be changing the security program?" asked Markman softly.

"I am. I'm even ahead of schedule but the guard sitting here asleep gives me the creeps. I keep thinking he's staring at me. So hurry up."

Markman gestured in frustration and turned to the vault door. The dial lock and large spoke handle looked intimidating. Markman fumbled around to bring out his lock decoder. He snapped it in place beside the lock dial and the readout screen appeared. The device hummed for a moment. R 15 suddenly appeared on the display. Markman paused for another glance behind then twisted the dial to the right to the number 15. The decoder began humming once more. L2 25. Markman cursed under his breath that he had not practiced before this. He turned past the number 25 and stopped at it the second time around. The decoder hummed approval and displayed R 45.

"How are you doing?" asked Cassiopia. "He's turned around and is headed the other way. There's still no danger."

Markman spun the dial right to 45. There was a clunking noise loud enough to worry him. He waited, expecting Cassiopia to yell that the guard had been alerted but there was nothing. With a deep breath for hope, Markman turned the big spoke wheel. It moved cooperatively. There was the hiss of escaping air and the heavy door cracked open. He pulled it open just enough to slip behind it but stopped before closing it.

"Cass, are you sure I can reopen this thing from inside?"

"Yes, Dear. It's a Kerg Standard. It has emergency release handles on each bolt. Please continue and hurry before someone knocks on my door."

Ignoring the 'Yes dear,' gibe, Markman turned and inspected the vault. It was a ten-foot by ten-foot room filled with safe deposit boxes and other wall enclosures, some with clear Plexiglas compartments. There was a gray metallic table in the center with chairs. In the middle of the right-hand wall was the safe Markman was interested in, a larger gray panel with a spin dial and handle. Before Markman could take a step toward it, Cassiopia's voice interrupted.

"Oh no!"

"For Pete's sake Cass, oh no what?"

"There's someone coming in the front door with a keycard!"

Markman shook his head and went to the wall safe. He pulled back his suit hood, planted his decoder next to the dial and waited. The little machine hummed obediently.

"Oh thank God! It's okay. He's not coming to the security room. Thank God!"

A pregnant pause followed as Markman began dialing in the first number.

"Oh no!"

"Cass, you're killing me here."

"It's Robert Duran! He just stopped and waved to the security camera. He's carrying a silver metal briefcase. He must be going to his office. I sure hope he's going to his office. It's on the seventh floor."

Markman dialed in the last two numbers. The handle on the wall safe clunked open. Within the open safe sat the alien disruptor. Markman drew the fog dispenser from inside his suit and sprayed a tiny amount. The white cloud illuminated the green beams of the safe's laser net alarm. Searching the sides of the wall safe he spotted a small square of black glass.

"Oh my God! He's gotten off the elevator on the fifth floor. He may be coming to you, Scott!"

Markman slipped his gloved hand back into the rubber glove and pressed his first finger against the small mirror screen. The fading cloud of green laser net disappeared.

"He's stopped at the guard station and he's talking to the guard. He must be coming to the vault. It can't be anything else."

Markman hurriedly opened the back slit in his chameleon suit and withdrew the fake disruptor gun. He reached in and took the real weapon and quickly replaced it with the fake. With the real disruptor stowed back in his backpack, he reset the laser net alarm and shut the safe.

"They're both heading for the outer vault room, Scott! Have we set off a secret alarm John Paul didn't know about? You're boxed in! You don't have time to get back through the laser net and you can't get by them anyway! You've got to hide somewhere!"

Markman quickly double checked the safe door and turned to survey the vault room. There was not so much as a cubbyhole for concealment.

"He's opened the outer door! The guard is waiting outside. He's shutting down the laser net. He'll be at the main vault in a moment! We can't have John Paul beam you out now! You have the real disruptor with you! There's no time anyway!"

Markman considered the dilemma and chose his best chance. He went to the back corner farthest from the wall safe and stood with his back pressed into the corner, remembering to pull down his chameleon suit hood. Half the suit now reflected deposit boxes, the other half empty wall space. A quick pat down to be sure the suit was fit smoothly and the wait began.

"He's opening the vault door!" Cassiopia's voice had become a breathless whisper. "They can't suspect someone is in there because the guard is still out in the hall smoking a cigarette. Oh God! Here goes! He's opening the big door!"

Once again Markman felt like he was standing in plain sight. He dared a momentary glance down at his suit. The suit's projection of safe deposit boxes fit in with those on the wall perfectly. Markman straightened up, tightened his stance, and held his breath.

The heavy vault door swung open. Robert Duran stepped in, looking down at his fat silver briefcase. His gray suit coat hung open, white silk shirt, no tie. His wavy brown hair was uncombed. He was more concerned with the wall safe than anything else. At the table, he placed the case down and fussed with combination locks to open it. He was no more than six or seven feet away from Markman but he never looked up. He stared down at his wristwatch then turned to look at the main wall safe. He stepped over to it, brushed his fingertips on his jacket and began to dial.

Markman held stiffly at attention, certain that if Duran looked directly at him it would mean discovery.

Duran spun the dial and pulled the safe open. A careful touch to clear the laser net and the fake disruptor was quickly in his hand. He paused for a long few moments to study it with a gaze of greed and satisfaction. Still staring at his prize, he turned and carefully stored the treasure in the silver metal case. The wall safe was hurriedly reset and sealed. With a grunt of satisfaction he quickly turned and left the vault. The big door clunked shut as steel bolts thumped into the locked position. Markman exhaled.

Cassiopia whispered, "There's an HD camera in the vault but even I can't see you! The suit is amazing! He's turned the outer room's laser net back on and is closing the outer door. The guard is leaving with him. God please don't let him come down here to the security room!"

Relieved, Markman stepped away from the wall. On the inner workings of the big vault door he located each bolt release and within minutes had the heavy door unsealed and open.

"Oh God! He's in the elevator coming down. The guard went back to the guard station and is reading a paper."

With a wince for luck, Markman slipped out of the vault, quietly closed the big safe room door and spun the big spoke wheel. The locking pins clanked into the lock position. He knew if the guard had heard it Cassiopia would be at wit's end over the intercom. There was no exclamation.

The trip through the laser net was slower this time, probably from fatigue. At the outer door Cassiopia came on. "You'll have to wait. The guard is still at the guard station with his feet up. You can't get by without him seeing."

Markman quietly opened the final outer door, eased out and shut it as carefully as possible.

"What are you doing? He didn't hear you but if he gets up and comes that way he'll see you, well... maybe."

With a quick check for suit fit, Markman stood with his back against the hallway wall. He sidestepped along until almost at the intersection of the guard station. The left-hand corridor he needed to take was just a few feet away but the guard station was there.

"Oh no. The elevator is here on the first floor with Duran in it. Here he comes! He's waving at the camera! He's going to the front door! He's leaving! Thank God!"

Patience had never been a strong attribute for Markman. He worked his way against the wall to a point where he could see the guard's feet folded up on the guard station counter. A daring glance around the corner revealed the man was reading a newspaper and drinking coffee from a white Styrofoam cup. Spilling coffee had worked once, perhaps it could work again. If the guard were distracted for just a few seconds, he could certainly dash around the intersection and take cover at the men's room door.

Watching for the Styrofoam cup to be put down on the countertop, Markman raised one finger and concentrated. As soon as the cup was placed there he wiggled his finger and it skidded to the edge and tipped over.

Loud cursing and rustling of newspaper broke out.

Cassiopia's excited voice broke in. "He spilled his coffee!"

The big man knelt to recover his cup and Markman made his move. Keeping low in his best ninja sprint, he sped silently around the corner and backed up against the men's room door within the small alcove. A quick glance showed the guard standing and brushing coffee off himself.

Cassiopia's scolding voice came on. "Scott, what have you done? He spilled his coffee so you ran by and hid at the men's room door! Don't you realize the first place he'll go is to the men's room for paper towels?"

Markman wrinkled his brow and considered the error of his ways. With great care he slowly opened the restroom door just enough to slip in.

There were three stalls, two small ones, one larger handicapped. If he hid in one of the small ones and the guard chose that particular stall there would be no chance of concealment. But the larger, handicap stall probably had enough wall space to blend in with. Markman hurried over and entered there. He took a position in one corner alongside the toilet and stood stiffly against a dirty blue wall. His suit immediately became dirty blue, even matching stains on the wall and the dirt on the floor.

Cassiopia's prediction had been accurate as usual. The restroom door banged open, the guard still cursing to himself. Markman stiffened and wondered if the paper towel dispensers by the line of sinks were too much to hope for.

They were. Additional cursing erupted at the empty dispensers. Markman held his breath as the door to one of the smaller stalls opened and slammed shut to a chorus of even more cursing. The door to Markman's stall burst open as the big man partially entered. He was so upset with the stain on his uniform he wiped at it continuously with his hand then reached over the sink, pulling paper towels from the dispenser. Wet towels were dabbed furiously at the violated area of shirt.

Standing directly behind the offended guard, a spike of fear shot through Markman as he held his breath. What if the guard did not notice him and decided to use the toilet? His hiding place was just behind and to the right of the toilet seat! The man had to be two hundred and sixty pounds. Even if he somehow wasn't discovered Markman wondered if he could stand the explosions which would follow, much less the toxic fumes in the fallout area.

Markman prayed.

The answer came almost immediately. The guard turned and stormed out of the booth without ever looking up, still wiping at his coffee stains. Markman nearly collapsed with relief.

"What happened? I can't see. He didn't see you, right?" asked Cassiopia.

"All clear," whispered Markman.

"Well, stay put, okay? He's still cleaning up his desk. If you step out into the hall he'll see you."

"Yes, Dear."

Cassiopia scoffed. "Get by the door and when I say go, go fast and don't look back."

"Right."

At the main door, Markman stood and waited.

"Okay, he's finished cleaning up. He refilled his coffee cup and sat down. He's putting his newspaper back together. Get ready. His feet are back up on the counter. He's reading his paper. Okay! Go!"

Markman slipped out and dared a defiant glance at the guard. The open newspaper blocked any view. He tiptoed the rest of the way down the hall and disappeared off to the left.

"Thank God," said Cassiopia. "You should be in the clear the rest of the way down the stairwell. I'll be waiting here in security."

"You're ready to go, right?"

"Are you kidding? The whole thing's screwed up. Duran showing up messed everything. I've got to go back and implant the video from Duran's little visit now and preserve all the alarms he bypassed. Our guard will have to think he slept through Duran's entire visit. So just get down here. I'll get this done as fast as I can."

Back in the stairwell, Markman took the stairs in small leaps. At the bottom he tried to look through the narrow window in the door.

"I'm on the first floor. Is the lobby clear?"

"Yes. It's clear. Come on. I'll hold the door."

A moment later Markman was back in the security room. He eyed the sleeping guard with distrust and watched as Cassiopia returned to a keyboard and began furiously typing code.

"I'm just about done. Put on your street clothes. When I say go, we'll have sixty seconds to get clear of the building before the real security system kicks back in and Fred wakes up."

Markman looked again at the sleeping form. A small badge on his uniform shirt pocket read: *Fred*.

Markman slipped his street clothes over his chameleon suit barely fast enough. He slung the carryall over his shoulder as Cassiopia stood from her console and closed her briefcase.

"That's it. Help me get Fred set up. He needs to be in front of this monitor right where he was with his head down on his chest. When I hit the enter key, we'll have sixty seconds to be nowhere near here. Double check the lobby."

Markman went to the door and opened it just enough to scan outside. "It's clear."

Cassiopia finished setting up Fred and looked back at Markman. "Here goes…." She tapped the key and hurried over. Together they crossed the lobby and out the front doors. A sprint carried them across the parking area, beyond some lawn to the nearest sidewalk.

"Let's head around to the next side street and call for Core," said Cassiopia breathlessly.

As they walked, Markman's sense of humor returned. "I don't think we're your typical secret agents."

"What was your first clue?" Cassiopia looked around nervously.

"It was the, '*Oh my Gods'* that kept coming over my headset."

"Really? I thought it might have been sharing a bathroom with a very big security guard."

"Right. You know he came in the stall where I was hiding?"

"What bothers me the most is what we did to the first-floor guard."

"Gave him a nap? That bothers you?"

"Let's turn down this side street a few yards and call for Core. We drugged that man."

"Yeah, we did so that crook Duran wouldn't have a dangerous alien weapon to screw around with."

"When the guard finds out he slept through Duran's visit he may have a heart attack."

"Will he be awake yet?"

"He's been awake since we reached the sidewalk."

"Well, I don't hear any alarms going off."

"Aren't you the one who believes in bad karma?"

"Good and bad karma."

"Shouldn't there be bad karma from doing that to an innocent person?"

"Did we do any harm?"

Cassiopia stopped and whispered, "Uh-oh."

Markman stopped beside her and searched the area. Farther down the side street two figures in dark clothing were approaching. They did not look friendly.

Markman smiled. "Okay, you know the drill. If this starts to look like it's going badly, you stay directly behind me but you give me plenty of room to move. Got it?"

Cassiopia stared ominously in the direction of the nightwalkers. "I've got it. Core, this is Cassiopia. Please come to us immediately."

The approaching opportunists spotted the potential prey and picked up their pace. In the shadowy streetlight their faces were unshaven. They were both smiling bad teeth smiles. They wore red scarves under their dark windbreaker jackets. Their jeans were greasy and stringy. While they were still more than ten feet away the first called out, "Got any spare change, man?"

As they closed in they separated a few feet. The taller of the two, the one that had spoken, tipped his head as if to say, "Didn't you hear me?"

His partner began toying with something made of shiny silver.

Markman's voice sounded calm and unimpressed. "Yeah, I think I got some spare change. In fact, I'll give each of you a twenty to bug off. How's that sound?"

The tall man stepped slightly closer. "How much money you got, man?"

Markman's patience had already run out. "Gentlemen, there's only two of you. If we do this you're gonna leave here with pain and no cash. Wouldn't you rather just walk away with a twenty in your pocket?"

The tall man's partner coughed up a laugh and began flipping a butterfly knife open and closed.

This time Markman sounded threatening, "Guys listen, I've been in an awful lot of fights. That little toy's not gonna help you."

And that was it. The man with the knife lunged forward at Markman and flipped the knife open. He stood leaning forward as though ready to stab.

Markman shook his head in dismay. The man's weight was all on his forward bent knee. Markman sidestepped and drove a quick side kick directly into the kneecap. There was a crunching, cracking and the man went down screaming and holding his knee.

The tall one was at first alarmed, then surprised, then angry. What insolence was this that an average looking civilian would dare kick his friend? The guy hadn't even dropped his pack! Howling, he charged Markman and brought his right fist back, targeting Markman's face. Markman's right foot came up in a second sidekick and drove deeply into the man's rib cage underneath the raised arm. The man's own lunge drove him farther into the kick. There was a snapping followed by a gush of air escaping the man's choked off howl. Had he been able to breathe he would have cried out again. Instead, he went down holding his side, rolling from side to side, unable to speak.

"We should walk a ways back up the street to meet the car, don't you think?" said Markman.

Cassiopia's face was still flushed. She backed away, still staring in angst at the assailants writhing on the ground.

"Come on, we really should go. Let's just go." Markman took her by the arm and led her back the way they had come.

At the first intersection car lights in the distance were approaching. Cassiopia kept looking back in the direction of the two men struggling to recover. Only their silhouettes were visible now. One had partially regained his feet but was hunched over. The man with the damaged knee was still rocking back and forth on the ground.

Headlights closed in from the left. A moment later Core pulled up, its windows darkly tinted. Both doors popped open. Markman guided Cassiopia in and closed her door then ran around to the driver's side. On the road an atmosphere of relief ensued.

"I think you broke that guy's knee," said Cassiopia when she had finally gathered herself.

"He shouldn't have put it where it didn't belong," replied Markman.

"You've done this kind of thing quite a few times, haven't you?"

Markman choked back an indignant laugh. "You remind me of an old Schwarzenegger movie where his wife asks him if he's ever killed any people and under truth serum he says, '*Yes, but they were all bad.*'"

"See what I mean about bad karma?"

"Yeah, those guys really deserved some," replied Markman.

"That's not what I meant," said Cassiopia.

"You do know what they would have done to us if they could have, right?"

"Yes, but maybe we ended up in that situation because we assaulted an innocent guard."

"Putting someone asleep is not assault."

"It's a violation of sorts."

"It was your idea. Was there any other way to exchange that weapon without being detected?"

Cassiopia took pause. "No, not that I know of."

"Was anyone hurt tonight? Besides those two goons, I mean."

"Maybe emotionally a little bit when the guard thinks he was asleep on duty."

"Either he won't care or he'll try to be more alert, right?"

"Perhaps."

"Then have we driven this subject into the ground?"

"I guess."

"That Waffle House drive-thru is still open. Want to get an egg sandwich?"

"Uh-huh."

Chapter 5

Markman found Cassiopia in her breakfast cove having noonday brunch. She glanced up from her tablet just enough to acknowledge a good morning. Markman pulled out his chair and appraised the breakfast delicacies on the table as he sat. Still staring down at her tablet, Cassiopia pushed an empty cup across the table to him. He poured coffee and chose a raisin bagel.

"Is that the news? Any break-ins reported anywhere last night?"

Cassiopia bit down on a bagel and chewed, her eyes still narrow from sleep. "No. Apparently we got away with it despite ourselves."

"Not even any mention of the two trolls we ran into?"

Cassiopia's voice became musically sarcastic. "They were still people, Scott."

"Barely. Any other news of interest?"

"You want the good news or the bad news?"

"The good, please."

"Okay, but it's weird. That little boy who was hit by the car on his bike. He might not lose his leg after all. They've postponed the surgery and are doing more tests."

Markman almost choked but hid it well. "He must have taken a turn for the better."

"The doctors are calling it a miracle. His mother insists it was angels."

Markman coughed, causing Cassiopia to look up in concern. "You okay there, big boy?"

"So what's the bad news? Dare I ask?"

"Makes me sick. There was another murder. It was nearby again, too. Just east of Fredericksburg. Police won't release any details. The news media has already dubbed the guy *The Ripper.*"

"Really? As in Jack the Ripper?"

"That's how I read it. It's so scary."

"Hey! Maybe we should…."

"Stop right there, Scott. It's a job for the police. We are not man hunters."

"I just thought…."

"Subject closed."

Markman chewed and smiled. "As you wish."

After a moment of discord Markman asked, "Have you heard from John Paul?"

"He's on his way."

Almost in response to Markman question, the TEL robot appeared in the hall and coasted over to the pair.

"Cassiopia, a black limousine has just come through the gate. It is the vehicle most commonly associated with John Paul."

"The man is anxious to get his new gun," mused Markman.

"Thank you, Tel. And Tel, how do I get into my Father's project room?"

There was a pregnant pause. The robot began playing Jeopardy theme music, turned and coasted away.

Markman let out a laugh and watched the Tel drive away. "I'd swear that thing has a sense of humor."

Cassiopia scoffed. "I've tried to explain that's impossible."

"The thing has laughed at me more than once. You've heard it."

"Just a programming glitch. Nothing more."

"Right."

"It's my Father taunting me."

"Huh?"

"Don't you get it? The Jeopardy theme? He's making access to his lab a Jeopardy kind of question. He's waiting for me to answer it."

"You may be right."

"Would you go get the gun and I'll meet John Paul at the door?"

"Okay."

Cassiopia danced down the grand staircase and pulled open the huge double doors of the main entrance. There stood John Paul, a big smile greeting. He opened his arms and was rewarded by Cassiopia's bear hug. Markman trotted up from behind with the briefcase of alien treasure.

"Come on, John Paul. We're just having coffee," pleaded Cassiopia.

"Regrettably, I need to take the item to its final resting place right away," replied John Paul and he nodded toward the briefcase.

Markman handed over the case.

John Paul did not bother to open it for inspection. He smiled at his two charges and asked, "The operation was not without difficulty. Wouldn't you agree?"

Markman muted a laugh.

John Paul nodded, "We monitored you by special satellite. We know it was Duran himself who came into the vault while you were there, Scott."

Markman winced. "Lucky he was so obsessed with his gun toy."

"A few minutes sooner and he would have had the real one," added Cassiopia.

"And was there a near incident in the men's room, Scott?"

"I don't want to talk about it," replied Markman.

John Paul returned a pinched smile. "You two did an excellent job. I salute you both," said John Paul.

"Cassiopia's hung up on putting the guard to sleep, John Paul."

Cassiopia cast a contentious stare at Markman.

"The man has not called in sick today nor did he report any problems with last night's shift. It appears he intends to report to work tonight as usual. It may not be the first time he's napped for a few minutes on the job. Those are long dull shifts," said John Paul. "It seems your visit was executed perfectly. I'm feeling quite glib about it myself. I knew the two of you could do it."

Cassiopia smiled. "There was also some trouble after we left the building."

John Paul nodded. "Yes, we were watching. Once again I pride myself in anticipating Scott's abilities. We would have sent in help had the situation not been taken care of so expeditiously."

Markman tried to look indifferent. "John Paul, did you notice there's been two murders around here recently?"

"Yes, and they are particularly malicious acts of violence, especially for this area."

"Maybe we should look into those?" asked Markman.

"Your law enforcement background sneaking up on you is it, Scott?" asked John Paul.

"I've told him we don't do that kind of thing, John Paul," said Cassiopia.

"She's correct, Scott. The police must think of you two as reclusive, average, well-to-do citizens. Remember our invisibility mandate. You are just average millionaires living here to escape the multitudes. You must never forget that. But I will send you the police reports on those crimes since it's so nearby. If you see anything suspicious I'll call it in to the locals anonymously for you."

"I'll see he keeps busy," said Cassiopia.

"The two of you should take some time to celebrate an excellent mission. It may not be too long before the next one comes up. Oh, and by the way, we're stealing your father for a few weeks, Cassiopia. For the past few months I've had a group working on a reverse engineering project. Your father has been texting them advice from time to time. Now they want him to come in and prove the math. It may turn out to be quite an embarrassment to the group leader. Some of the group are new. I was hoping not to dispirit them. The group leader is a new recruit much like you two. If your father is able to complete the formula it will go a long way to earning their respect. But I suspect one or two of the group are hoping he can't take it all the way through. Personally, I have no doubt whatsoever he will tie it all up in a neat little package. I'll need to keep a close presence to make sure no one's feelings get too singed."

"Oh, I'd love to hear about this project," replied Cassiopia.

"Classified, my dear. Very classified," answered John Paul. "But, I will introduce you to Perseus Haiden, the young group leader. As I mentioned he's a recent inductee just like you and Scott, a brilliant scientist too far ahead of his time to be allowed to run free among mere mortals. You might like him."

With a brief salute, John Paul smiled and turned away, headed for the open door of his limousine.

After an early afternoon session of mediation which did not seem to work, Markman returned to the second-floor nook in search of Cassiopia. She was not there but had left her tablet on the table. With a quick scan to be sure no one was watching, Markman sat and turned on the tablet in search of the morning's news report. There he found the article about the injured boy's miraculous recovery. He read through it with concern but found nothing referring to a strange visitor. In fact, the doctors responsible for the original diagnosis had no comment. The hospital administration followed in suit by promising a statement at some later date. Those not afraid to speak mentioned the boy's remarkable recuperative abilities and were thankful for the wonderful progress being made. Markman gently placed the tablet back on the table and breathed a sigh of relief. His secret seemed secure. He rubbed his mouth with one hand and wondered why he had dared to be so impulsive. At the same time a beam of unavoidable joy arose within him.

He found Cassiopia standing in front of her father's project room door again, tapping at keys on her mini notebook computer. She glanced up after each group of commands, hoping the door would show some sign of movement. It had not.

"Aren't you afraid of being caught?" Markman mused as he entered the lab and stood with his arms folded, smirking.

"He's asleep in his bed. I checked."

"How do you know there isn't a Tasmanian Devil behind that door?"

Cassiopia laughed without looking up or slowing her attempts to open the secret room. "The only little devil around here is on this side of the door."

"You must mean you."

"No, I must not."

"Me!? Last night you broke into a research facility. Today you're breaking into this lab? Sounds pathological to me."

"Really, Mr. Markman. You must still be meditating in an alternate reality."

"Nope. Couldn't get there today."

"Did you want something other than to tease me?"

"Gonna hike up the side of our mountain. See how far up I can get. Want to come along?"

"It's tempting but John Paul's sending the limo back to pick up my father. I'm going to pack him a lunch and clothes and see him off."

"Then, back to breaking into his private domain?"

Cassiopia looked up with a warning glance. "Want to make a bet? You'll lose."

Markman stepped up and kissed her lightly on her neck. "I know. But I love losing to you."

Fifteen minutes later Markman was in hiking boots, jeans and a brown cargo shirt pushing up the hillside behind the castle home, winding his way through trees and brush and occasionally slipping on loose leaves. It was a steep climb. There were rotten smelling fallen tree trunks to climb over. Patches of fern hid the ground in places. A few dead trees were leaning among the healthy ones in a slow repose to the ground. There were patches of warm, dead air. Except for insects the forest was quiet as the local wildlife watched and wondered about the new intruder. Fifteen minutes into the ascent a small plateau with a clearing came into view. It looked as though brush had been cut away long ago. A pile of dead leaves looked out of place.

Markman went to the overgrown pile and began pushing leaves away with the toe of one boot. There was something hidden there, something iron. He knelt and wiped away the remaining leaves. An iron grate began to be visible. It was large, six feet by four feet, and beneath it there was a wide, ragged hole, a drop-off that descended steeply at a fifty-degree angle into the mountain. Markman tried to see into the depths but total blackness hid the secrets within.

Markman straightened up. A powerful beam light was needed. How far down did this thing go? Was it an ancient lava tube or had millions of years of water flow formed it?

With a juvenile smirk on his face Markman raced and slid back down the hill. Thirty minutes later he was back with a pack and a large flashlight clipped to his belt. He knelt and wiped away the shroud of leaves to fully reveal the rusting bars of the grate. It was bolted to rock, but with fasteners easy to remove with the adjustable wrench in his bag. Ten minutes of counterclockwise turning and he was able to drag the grill away from the ominous hole and peer down with the big beam light.

The entrance was a slide of small, loose rock. The tunnel appeared to level off forty or fifty feet below. Obscure markings on the walls meant others had already been there. Markman tied off his one hundred foot rope to the nearest tree, tossed the line into the hole and wished he'd had a longer rope available. With a last look around to get his bearings and a quick adjustment of the headlamp he'd brought he backed into the black hole.

The descent was a continuous slip in loose gravel, leaves and sticks.

He held to the rope all the way down, turning to one side to take the abrasive ground more easily. The bottom captured him sooner than expected. There was a small mound of loose stone at the ramp's base. Markman switched on his headlamp and flashed the big handheld beam around. Apparently Ray loved Amanda and he'd taken the time to scratch that into the wall here to prove his love. There was enough room to stand crouched over. He pushed himself up, began to study farther in and suddenly wondered if a bear from a different entrance might be using this cave as a den. A future newspaper headline flashed across Markman's mind:

Amateur spelunker mauled to death by local bear. Shouldn't have entered cave alone.

Silly thought. The tunnel formed a ragged path leading deeper into the mountain. The hard floor was uneven and V-shaped in places, requiring balance to climb past. Markman held firmly to his rope line. The cave quickly became damp. Wet rock walls sparkled in his flashlight beam. Finally, the passageway began to widen. He was nearing the end of the rope when suddenly his beam could no longer illuminate the entire tunnel. It had opened to a larger chamber the size of a gymnasium with a low ceiling. Stanchions of jagged rock were scattered around the place. Stalactites hung down from the ceiling. The place looked golden in color. A large opening to the right led further up the mountain. To the left a similar tunnel offered passage downward.

Markman was at the end of his line. It would be dangerous to proceed without it but something in the downward passageway caught in his light. It glinted from the shadows. He would need to drop the rope to investigate and from the looks of this place it would be easy to become disoriented and lost.

But, there was a trick Cassiopia had once taught him. To escape any maze place one hand on the left or right wall and never let go of it. That trick would lead out of any maze, not by the shortest route but out nonetheless.

The downward wall nearest Markman was available. He carefully placed the end of the rope where it could most easily be seen, leaned against the passageway wall and climbed and stepped his way toward the downhill opening. His headlamp bobbed and flashed from the effort. At the opening to the passageway the shiny object came into view. It was a woman's glitter purse. It was open on the floor of the cave, its contents scattered around. As Markman came up to it his detective instincts kicked in. He clipped his big light back onto his belt and drew his cell phone from its belt holder. In camera mode he began clicking pictures of the scene. Not far from the purse there were several spots where imprints with a boot pattern had been left in fine gravel. They were odd; they appeared to be partial prints. They were consistently lighter on one side. Markman went to the nearest one and made a print to compare. The strange print was much deeper as though the individual was heavy.

Markman returned to the purse and began gathering up the spilled items. There were a few handwritten receipts with no ID of any kind. Numerous cosmetics littered the immediate area. No wallet or credit cards. Obviously, the thief had taken those. Disappointed at the lack of identification he stuffed everything back in and stood.

The cavern suddenly looked very different. Which wall was the one he had planned to keep track of? There was a momentary pang of fear quickly replaced by the realization the downward tunnel had been in front of him. He turned with it to his back, tucked in the cell phone and brought the big beam light to bear. The wall on his right had to be the one. He followed it along and soon spotted his rope draped over a rock shelf. The word *idiot* briefly appeared in his thought train, causing a laugh which echoed off the hardened walls.

Purse under his arm, Markman climbed from the cavern. He thought to leave the grate off for a future visit but decided against it. Grate bolted back in place, he headed down.

Cassiopia was outside on the front steps waving to her father as he pulled away in a dark van sent by John Paul. Markman came up alongside her in time for a quick wave.

"Carrying a purse now, are we?" Cassiopia asked with a smirk.

"Found it."

"Where?"

"Would you believe deep underground?"

"There's never a simple answer with you, is there? Underground? Really? Where underground?"

"About a third of the way up the mountain there's an entrance to a very cool cave. I wish I'd had a longer rope."

"Scott, are you saying you found a cave and went exploring in it without letting me or anyone else know where you were?"

Markman again suddenly realized the error of his ways. "How long will your Dad be gone for?"

"Didn't it occur to you if something happened to you no one would know where you were?"

"I had a hundred-foot rope so I couldn't get lost."

"But what if you fell and were hurt or the place caved in? What would you have done then?"

"I would have realized I was in almost as much trouble as I am now?"

"Whose purse is it?"

"I don't know. It was dumped out and scattered around. There was no ID in the stuff."

"And you had a rope to find your way back with so you never let go of it, right?"

"I thought of you."

"Tell me, how did you pick up the contents of the purse if you never let go of your safety line?"

"You are devious, you know that? Maybe I tied the rope to my belt."

"But you didn't or you wouldn't have avoided the question that way. How far in did you go without the rope?"

"Damn it. I used the Cassiopia maze escape trick. Besides, we have the implants. John Paul could have found me if I screwed up."

"Only if the rock layer chemistry didn't block the signal. It's just a tiny transmitter you know."

"Can we talk about something else?"

Cassiopia took Markman's arm and began a slow walk toward the house. "You understand why I'm giving you a hard time, don't you?"

"Yes, Dear."

"You know you can't report that purse to the police, right? We're not to draw any attention to ourselves."

"Yes, but we could explore the cave together to see if there's any other evidence. You want to?"

"Yes, that would be fun with the right gear and backup."

"Okay, when you want to go?"

"I could go tomorrow morning after breakfast."

"Okay, I'll hold you to that."

Chapter 6

Cassiopia awoke from a sound, dreamless sleep. Had there just been a sound in the darkness? Markman was still asleep, leaning against her. She carefully worked herself away from his warmth and out from under the blankets. She pushed on her slippers and pulled on the cool blue cotton robe, not bothering to tie it. It took a moment for her eyes to adjust to the night light. Still sleepy and in the very dim light she felt her way to the door and listened but heard nothing. The door creaked slightly as she opened it. A strange faint chemical smell came from the hall. She stepped halfway out and searched the darkened hallway in both directions. To her left there seemed to be something. It took a moment to focus on the silhouette. It was a faceless figure at the far end of the hall wearing a long cloak and high boots. No other details were visible. It was impossible to be sure there was actually someone there. Was it just abstract imagery in the shadows? Cassiopia rubbed her eyes but when she looked again there was nothing. A wisp of chilled air flowed passed her. She checked in both directions once more but there were only spooky reflections everywhere. She withdrew back into the bedroom, shut the door and climbed back into bed. This house was designed to be safe from predators. It was all her imagination.

On the tower roof a bright clear morning greeted Cassiopia. An occasional warm breeze brought the fragrance of jasmine. Before her was a panoramic view of green hills and distant civilization. Markman sat in the lotus posture among potted green plants, hands clasped, head tilted slightly up, eyes closed. She approached quietly and sat in front of him. He opened his eyes and smiled.

"Earth calling Scott."

Markman smiled once more. "Good morning, Princess."

"Am I really?"

"More than you know."

"Where did you astral travel to this morning?"

"I was exploring."

"Exploring where?"

"Okay, you asked. All the matter here in this physical world also contains astral matter, so in the lowest regions of the astral plane the same Earth you see around you exists there also, although everything always looks a lot more like it's been decorated for Christmas. All the trees and buildings you see are still there but there are no laws. You can explore any building or house. You can talk to other people if they're able to. I was exploring a very big, old church. It had maybe six floors and lots of hidden rooms. It was very cool."

"You're making fun of me."

"No, I'm not. When you explore like that sometimes it really does get spooky, usually because you have some history with the place, like you've been there before, maybe in a past life or something."

"Can I go there?"

"With practice I could probably take you. But you have to be careful. You have to really know yourself."

"I'm pretty sure I know myself."

"Really? Here in this world if a bad guy comes up to you and grabs you, because of your physical body you know where you end and the bad guy's hand begins. But in the astral, you're in your astral body. You can pass through walls if you want to. So when someone presses up against you, it's not quite so clear where you end and the other person's spiritual body begins."

"Okay, yeah that *is* creepy."

"Not only that, if an unpleasant spirit tries to intimidate you or scare you, you must be able to recognize you are separate from it so the unpleasantness cannot get into you."

"I thought everything is just wonderful in the higher dimensions you always talk about."

"The astral plane is a place made up mostly by the emotions of the people there. And where the astral plane meets the physical, that's where the heavier astral inhabitants reside. So, there are dangers there if you are not perfectly secure about who you are. That's partly why we sometimes have bad dreams at night. If we're not feeling good or are bothered by something during sleep we are pulled down to those lower regions."

"Speaking of that, did anything wake you up last night?"

"No, not a thing. Why?"

"I woke up because I thought I heard something. I looked out in the hall and at first I thought I saw someone, but then there was nothing there. Did your spider sense warn you about anything last night?"

Markman laughed. "You must have been in the half-dream state. We sometimes see into other dimensions when that happens. Maybe that's it."

"Well, in any case, I'm brain drained. Want to go have breakfast with me?"

"I will always want to do everything with you."

Cassiopia smiled, leaned forward and kissed him on the side of the mouth.

Markman returned a sly grin. "You still want to go to the underworld with me?"

"I, sir, will always want to do everything with you."

Breakfast was bagels, cheese, and tea. The pair ate silently, stealing occasional glances in each other's direction, occasionally giggling to themselves. After breakfast there was an equally silent gathering of spelunking equipment. To avoid a long trip to the store Cassiopia gave in and approved the use of fishing reels, each with a thousand yards of 200-pound test line. Cargo wear made for passable expedition clothing.

A quick trip up the mountain, punctuated by undignified slips and laughter, brought the explorers to the cave entrance. Cassiopia gave Markman a look of displeasure after seeing the bolted down grill cover. "Didn't it occur to you this barrier meant there was danger down there?"

Markman stopped and gave an annoyed stare, "Cass, there's cave heart drawings on the walls down there left by kids."

"Oh."

Markman went to the nearest tree and tied his rope off. Back at the entrance he threw the remaining line in then stepped into the cave and let himself down to shoulder level. "You ready?"

Cassiopia nodded and watched him disappear down. She pulled open a leg pocket and drew out a headlamp. Once in place she switched it on and followed Markman.

Each step downward into the darkness brought more dampness and cool air. Cassiopia strained to see below but Markman's form blocked her view. Only the jagged rock walls were visible. It was more of a slide down in gravel than a climb. The safety line was becoming damp also but still provided a feeling of security. Now and then she could hear the faint howling of wind passing through a tunnel somewhere. It was like a creepy voice calling to her from the spirit world.

At the bottom Markman stood in a crouched position and took her hand. Stooping, they followed their headlamps to where the passage widened enough to stand. Markman's headlamp blinded her each time he looked back. They carried the rope together, dragging along it despite climbing over and around obstacles.

When the tunnel finally opened to a small intersection they stopped to explore with the large flashlights. Cassiopia made sounds of awe at the collage of formations surrounding them. Markman searched with his light in the direction of the downward passage where the purse had been found.

Cassiopia's voice echoed through the chamber. "Where did you find your purse?"

"To the left. The tunnel that heads down."

"Is it far?"

"No. I only had so much rope, remember?"

"Set up the reel and monofilament. I think we can go on safely."

"There's a small third entrance straight ahead between those two stalactite groups. I didn't see that before."

"Yes, I don't think we'd want to be in here during a long downpour. I bet this place becomes rushing water."

A distant, dull howl accented Cassiopia's warning. She looked at Markman. He smirked.

With the fishing reel set up they headed left and downward. There was more climbing. The passage became less defined, more of a winding path around columns and stalactite formations. Though mono-colored, the cave had enough shades of damp darkness to add beauty to its architecture. Cassiopia stopped continuously to study it.

"It's right over here. This is where I found it."

"We're quite a ways in. Why would a thief come all this way to search through his stolen purse? He would have had to bring a flashlight and have had to know his way out by heart."

"Some local kid ripping off his neighbors. Probably someone who grew up around here and knows the place well. Who knows what we'll find farther in? There's got to be another entrance. The crook didn't unbolt that grate. I was the first one to mess with those bolts in a long time. Wouldn't it be cool to find another entrance?"

"You're a spelunker at heart, Scott. You know that?"

"This place is pretty cool."

"Yes, I'll make maps of how far we went when we get back. Maybe we can chart this place for a hobby in our spare time."

"Count me in. Oh yeah, right over here are those strange imprints in the loose dirt. Any guess what they are?"

Cassiopia knelt to study the markings. "It's just boots or something heavy. I don't know, really."

"Gotta be another entrance probably ahead at some point."

"Okay. Let's go on. Maybe we'll find it."

Markman led the way down. The cave widened in places and became a series of room-sized chambers connected in series. There were dead-end alcoves on either side along the way and sometimes openings too small to enter. Finally, they climbed into a larger cavern heavy with stalactites and pools of water. Beyond it the tunnel became a steep drop-off. They both searched with their lights trying to see the bottom.

"It's too much of a drop to risk it without line," said Cassiopia.

"I can see something down there. Do you see it?" replied Markman.

"It's timbers scattered around. There really was some kind of mining operation in here."

"Boy, I sure would like to keep going and see."

"Not without real climbing gear, Scott. We've pushed our luck far enough already."

"Okay, let's hit a good sporting goods store, get some stuff and come back. Are you game?"

"I have to finish my written report to John Paul about the weapon recovery. You can go pick up what we need and I'll do that. Next time I'll bring a tablet and start mapping this place."

"Yeah, I'd like to see where this cave goes in the other direction, too. So tomorrow, then?"

"If I finish my report."

Markman turned to let his headlamp shine back the way they had come. "So back up we go then?" He gestured with one hand. "Lady spelunkers before gentlemen."

It was a much slower climb on the way out. At the ramp up to the entrance they went hand over hand using the rope. Cassiopia waited as Markman secured the iron grill over the opening then together they slid and hiked down the mountainside.

By late afternoon Markman was on the road. It was always a pleasure to drive Core. For some reason known only to it the car had chosen a dark golden color for itself on this occasion. Markman thought to ask it but then decided against doing so. He leaned back and enjoyed powering the unearthly vehicle down the back roads under his guidance. Somehow the car seemed content with the arrangement.

There was a very good sporting goods store in Culpeper and it had been some time since he had visited the wonderful calligraphy of the place. That alone was reward enough for the drive.

A slow idle down main street allowed him to spot his destination quickly. Core assisted with the parallel park. Inside Markman realized this was not necessarily the best place for him to shop on his own. The store had a full complement of weapons, including bows and other items of serious manly interest. Markman walked the store and debated with himself whether or not he really wanted at least one of everything. There was good quality here and they were well-stocked with line, climbing equipment and apparel. Pushing a shopping cart somehow seemed contradictory to these purchases.

At the checkout a young girl with heavy makeup and her hair tied back in a bun with a pencil sticking out of it smiled invitingly at Markman but something outside the shop window caught his eye instead. The Vette was visible across the street and had attracted three individuals of questionable character. They were dressed in typical black Goth, but they were not the peaceful, self-expressing followers of most Goth advocates. These three had dark auras, the signature of those with a disreputable past. Markman paid the clerk, avoiding the small talk she offered. He took his bags and stood by the front window where he could not be seen.

They had tried both doors. There was a lot of touching and leaning over to look inside. The tallest one, probably the leader, wore a long black jacket and high lace-up combat boots. His associates were less embellished in simple black jeans and black turtlenecks. The leader was nearly bald. His friends wore spiked hair, dyed black.

The appraisal became more aggressive. Markman smirked as he looked on. They had no idea of the machine they were messing with. Then one of them crossed the boundaries of good taste. He took out a small folding knife and opened it. Starting at the left front fender, he dragged the point of it along the full length of the car. The watchers bent over in muted laughter. The knife was refolded and tucked away. The three of them looked around to see if anyone had seen. The doer of the bad deed walked along the car to inspect his damage.

Suddenly he stopped with a look of puzzlement on his face. He bent over and studied the driver's door closely. He walked along, still bent over, looking for some sign of his mark. Apparently, there was none. The three searched in earnest for some sign of reward to mark their visit but found no scratch at all. They regrouped and looked at each other. The second subordinate held up a hand and drew a much larger knife from his boot. All three looked around again for witnesses. The coast appeared to be clear.

The leader and one associate stepped back and folded their arms to watch in admiration as the deed was done. This time the evil-doer began at the back of the Vette. With a last look around, he placed the tip of his knife on the fender and smiled back at his friends. This would be an especially cruel cut.

But the three had reached the limit of patience built into Core. At the first touch of the blade point, the knife-wielding gang member suddenly and quite unexpectedly shuddered, straightened up and fell into a heap on the ground, unconscious.

His associates stepped back further in surprise, expressions of alarm on their faces. They scanned the area looking for some cause that might explain. They went to their offended associate and knelt, trying to wake him. They again looked around worriedly hoping questions from local law enforcement would not need to be answered. They dragged their sleeping comrade to a nearby alley and set him in a sitting position against a red brick wall, slaps to his face medicinally applied to help awaken him.

Markman could not find any sympathy within himself. He clasped one hand over his mouth to muffle his laughter. He turned to see if anyone was watching only to find the store clerk standing shoulder to shoulder also looking on with great interest. Markman quickly collected himself and tried to look unconcerned.

"They were trying to key your car, Mister," she said angrily.

"Yes, I saw that."

"You going to call the police?"

"No, they didn't do any damage I can see. The police would have trouble pinning anything on them."

"Well. I'm glad you're not reporting it. I couldn't be a witness for you. If I was they'd come back and get me somehow for sure. They're a bunch of degenerates. That's such a nice car. I hope you're right. I hope they didn't hurt it too bad."

"It has a special coating. It's very hard to scratch."

"The tall one in the long black coat has been picked up by the cops a couple times. They think those guys have been breaking into homes but they haven't been able to charge them."

Markman nodded. "Probably just a matter of time."

"Yeah, *probly*."

"Well, I guess the coast is clear. Thanks for the gear."

"You're welcome. Please come again." The inviting smile returned. Markman nodded and left.

At home, Cassiopia was in the kitchen sautéing shrimp. They sat at a small serving table there and ate their seafood dinner with such savor that no pauses were available for conversation. Finally, Markman slowed enough to ask, "I got some great stuff for the caves."

"Where'd you go?" asked Cassiopia.

"They have a cool store in Culpeper. I got everything."

"Culpeper? I wish I could have gone now. Maybe I'm due for some shopping."

"We could explore in the caves tomorrow. You want to?"

"Oh yeah, about that."

"Uh-oh. Doesn't sound good."

"You want the partly good news or the not so good news?"

"What a choice."

"The partly good news is John Paul liked my report on the weapon recovery but wants a lot more detail, so I have to work on it some more tomorrow."

"*That's* the partly good news? What's the not so good news?"

"He wants the same kind of report from you. He wants the story as told by both of us."

Markman clanked his fork against his plate. "Please tell me you're joking."

"Nope." Cassiopia ate another shrimp and smiled at him.

"How about I dictate it to you and you type it for me?"

"Can't do it. He said I'm not allowed to help you because I might interpret what you say and he wants both viewpoints. He needs them tomorrow."

"Arrggh."

Chapter 7

Markman stood looking out the arched window at the end of the hallway on the third floor. The steady rain looked so beautiful. The green leaves on the trees bowed to each drop, capturing each precious offering, a watering direct from God. Light rays glistened from every direction. The faint drum sound on the rooftop perfectly choreographed the real-life artwork.

He turned to go back in the conference room but spotted the white light from his laptop screen and scowled and went back to the window. Unfortunately, the Celestial Order demanded intense detail about recovery missions. According to John Paul they wanted every step documented. There could be no chance something had happened they did not know about. Writing was not one of Markman's favorite things.

"It won't write itself, you know!"

He turned to find Cassiopia standing behind him smiling.

"It might be worth a try."

"I wish I could help you but I can't. It's a beautiful rain, isn't it? We couldn't have gone a-spelunking anyway." Cassiopia draped an arm over his shoulder and joined in the weather watch. She rubbed his back for a moment and said, "Come on with me. We'll sit in the breakfast nook and watch the rain together and I'll pump coffee into you until your motor is running enough that you have to do something, which will be work on your report."

Together they took the elevator down and sat at the tiny round table. Cassiopia poured the coffee and mixed it to Markman's liking. They sipped and stared at each other silently until both could not help but smile.

"You want some more good news or some more bad news?" said Cassiopia.

"Uh-oh, the last time you asked me that I ended up doing that damn report."

"The bad news has nothing to do with you."

"Okay, in that case what's the bad news?"

Cassiopia turned her tablet to face him. "Another terrible murder. This time near Stafford."

"Whoa! A third murder? In what, six days?"

"Yes, and I have the feeling it was another grisly one because the police aren't releasing any information. They're worried there will be a panic and they're right."

Markman's mind immediately switched to the news story. He scanned the tablet quickly and fumbled trying to advance the page. Cassiopia giggled, reached over and set it for him.

It was a male victim this time. Apparently, the Ripper was not biased by gender. Like the others it had occurred during the early morning hours. The victim had awakened during the night and left his bed to investigate. He had met with tragedy at the top of the stairs. There were no details of violation to the body but the story seemed to deliberately leave that possibility open.

Markman looked at Cassiopia with a grim stare. "What's the good news?"

"John Paul emailed you the police reports on the other murders."

Markman began fumbling furiously with Cassiopia's tablet, trying to open his email. She grabbed it from him and held it out of his reach.

"You can't have my tablet, silly! Take your coffee up to the conference room. You need to work on that...."

Markman was halfway down the hall before she could finish. She yelled, "Well at least I got you going... right?"

In the conference room he hurriedly brought his laptop to life, swiped away the weapons recovery report and tapped at his email icon. His inbox showed a single email from John Paul. There were two enclosures. The first was the Kestry murder report.

THIS ATTACHMENT CONTAINS CLASSIFIED MATERIAL AND IS ENCRYPTED. DO YOU WISH TO DECRYPT AT THIS TIME?

The translation was almost immediate:

Incident Report for Case #219-23850
Incident Type
Murder/Homicide
Deceased
Landers, Maria
Address
8240 West Park Street
Suspect(s)
No suspects identified at this time
Leads
During the evening hours before the incident, a neighbor reported seeing someone dressed in a long coat and high boots in the street in front of the victim's home. Suspect was possibly 6'2" or taller. No other details were available.
Victim(s)
Maria Landers, age 42.
Pronounced dead at the scene.
Details
The victim's coworkers became concerned when the victim did not show up for work and did not answer repeated calls to her home. One coworker, Jamie Stroff, 2994 Darling Street, Kestry, went to the victim's home to check and found the front door forced open. Upon entering the home she found the victim's body in the hallway outside a bedroom door and immediately called 911 from the victim's living room phone.

Based on forensic analysis it was determined the front door of the home had been forced open by the intruder. No evidence of a pry bar or battering ram was found. Both the doorknob lock and bolt lock were still in the locked position. Wood from the door frame had been torn out suggesting the suspect must have been someone of a large enough stature to have been able to impart that much body force on a double locked entrance.

No fingerprints other than those of the victim or her associates were found at the scene. No footprints were found inside or outside the home. No trace blood evidence was found anywhere other than on and around the victim.

Forensic analysis determined the victim was killed by a single blow to the head in the area above and to the right of the victim's forehead. A deep laceration indicated the single impact caused damage to the area of the frontal lobe resulting in death. Examination also revealed postmortem dismemberment of both hands which have not been recovered. Death is estimated to have occurred approximately 7 to 8 hours prior to the discovery of the body.

Reconstruction of the crime suggests the victim was awakened at or around 3:00 a.m. and left her room to investigate. She met the intruder outside her bedroom and was struck and killed by the single blow to the head. No items were known to be missing from the home. The victim's wallet was found in a nightstand drawer and still contained cash and ID.

Investigation is ongoing. For additional details contact Sgt. B. Raker.

John Paul updates (7/22):

Landers worked at InterTrans International Shipping, a very large conglomerate with huge warehouses around the world, one of which was located nearby in Alexandria. Landers was secretary to a Mark Furman, director of time-sensitive and controlled-substance materials management for that particular facility. II's warehouse is 1.2 million square feet. We have arranged for the FDA to do an informal audit of the place but obviously it will take a week or more and may not reveal anything suspicious. The *company may not have any involvement with Lander's murder, innocent or otherwise.*

Landers' movements and actions were routine over the past few weeks. She did not have any enemies. No judicial cases were open against her. She had not so much as a parking ticket over the past ten years. Random killing remains a prime possibility at this time.

Markman sat back and considered the gruesome details. Someone had seen a dark figure in a long coat before the crime. One of the punks outside the sporting goods shop wore a long coat. The police had recovered the woman's wallet but there was no mention of a purse. The purse now in his position could not belong to the victim, it would be too much of a coincidence. And why so little evidence? No prints. The assailant must have worn gloves. Those punks had worn black leather gloves. Still, connecting them was a long shot. And, there was nothing known to be missing from the home? The killer had left with nothing! Was the crime itself his reward? Was he that sadistic? Was the only thing taken souvenirs from the body?

Markman went to the second report.

HOMICIDE INVESTIGATION PROGRESS REPORT
DR   69-022   593
DECEASED: *MANNING, Robert, CC No. 69-8722*
LOCATION OF OCCURRENCE:
883 Borgden Drive
DIVISION OF OCCURRENCE:
DeAtlane Division
TO: *Lt. R. J. Hart, Supervisor of Investigations, Robbery-Homicide*
Div.
RESUME OF THE CRIME
According to associates at ConCom Holdings Inc., Mr. Manning had worked late in his office until approximately 11:30 p.m. to 11:45 p.m. He had indicated he was going directly home and would return early the next morning. Mr.

Manning's wife was away visiting relatives and expected to return by the end of the week. It is theorized that at some point Mr. Manning fell asleep on the living room couch. His body was found lying supine on the couch, still dressed. A laceration from a blow to the crown of the head was indicated as cause of death. There also appeared to be significant physical damage around the victim's eyes and mouth. The victims clothing was in disarray although there was no indication a struggle took place. It has been hypothesized Mr. Manning was killed while he slept. No prints other than those of family or friends were recovered. Entry to the home appeared to be from a foyer on the northeast first floor side of the home where French double doors were found to have been forced open. No other exterior evidence was recovered.

Later forensic examination by Trulane laboratories confirmed death to have been caused by a single blow to the frontal lobe area and also revealed postmortem extraction of both the victim's eyes. This enucleation appeared to have been accomplished by someone with some knowledge of medical procedure although minimum care had been exercised to preserve the optic nerves. Contact Dr. Maureen Steers at Trulane Labs for an amplified report of this examination.

Interviews with neighbors did not result in any additional leads or information. The victim's coworkers and family were not aware of any threats to Mr. Manning. There did not appear to be any items missing from the home even though a number of very valuable assets were available to the intruder. Nothing in the home was disturbed with the exception of the home's refrigerator which was found open and running. Several cabinet doors were also found ajar.

This case remains open and due to the postmortem mutilation of the body has been referenced to a recent murder in Kestry. Contact Sgt. B. Baker Kestry Homicide Division, case #219-23850, for additional information on that investigation.

Contact Lt. Brad Easly, DeAtlane Division, for additional details on this ongoing investigation.

Markman leaned back and tapped one finger against his lips in thought. He twisted in his seat to look over at the found purse sitting on a counter by the wall. It was still a very unlikely connection to the murders but there would be fingerprints on some of those cosmetic cases. The purse's owner could be identified. It could be returned to her. John Paul's orders were to avoid contact with the police. Okay then, turning the purse over to John Paul would make it his responsibility.

The murders played on Markman's mind. The lack of motive suggested a sadistic, deranged individual. A witness saw someone in a long dark coat before the first crime but that could have been totally unrelated. The third murder made this a very ugly little affair. If all three crimes really were related it meant there would be more. Markman set one elbow on the table and rested his chin in his hand. Maybe a skillfully worded email to John Paul might loosen the man up a little. Markman clicked *Reply* on the open email.

John Paul,

Found a woman's purse while exploring cavern on the hill. Sure it's evidence of some crime. I'll send to you for a look. Will have report to you shortly.

Markman

Markman scowled at the thought he had corralled himself back into John Paul's report. With a long sigh, he went back to work.

Thirty minutes later his email bleeped new mail.

Scott,

You must exercise great care when entering those caverns. The mountain is laced with them. Tunnels that are open one day are often closed off by rock falls the next. There is a high concentration of metals in some areas that can interfere with tracking signals. At the least, you should drop me a line when you're planning to venture in there and post a time estimate of when you expect to return. Sorry to sound like a doting parent.

I'll be glad to take the purse off your hands. If there is pertinent information from it we'll see that local law enforcement receives it in the proper way. If you notice anything related to the case files I sent you please notify me and no one else.

Glad to hear your report is nearly ready.

JP

Markman tapped his fingers on the tabletop and felt partially satisfied. After an hour of struggling with written reporting he managed to find his way to an end, then proudly transmitted it to John Paul. The rain was still pounding down even more than before. He stood, stretched and went in search of Cassiopia.

She was no longer at her windowed seat in the second-floor alcove. That meant the next likely place would be the basement lab area, probably there trying to get past her father's project room door again. Markman took the elevator down.

To his surprise, she was nowhere in sight. The lab area lights were set low. The place was stone silent. Deserted and shadowy, the chamber was suddenly eerie as though there were ghosts there. Markman walked around with his hands in his pockets to help avoid temptation. There were wires with electronics attached on one work table; empty lab trays, tubing and bottles of liquid on another. All of the doors to adjoining rooms were open except for the one that so tasked Cassiopia. He stood in front of it thinking what a coup it would be if he could figure it out, then smirked to himself and shook his head knowing that was not going to happen.

Off to his right, at the very end of the lab area, he suddenly noticed something not seen before. It was an old wooden door completely out of place compared to the other more modern architecture. He went to it. There was a wrought iron latch instead of a knob. He lifted it and pulled the creaky wooden door open to peer inside.

The place was so dark it took a moment for his eyes to adjust. There was a stale, dusty smell. Through the darkness he finally began to make out old furniture and boxes stacked almost to the ceiling. A narrow passage wound through them. Footprints in the dust meant the Professor had been in there. The room was deep enough that he could not see through the stacks to the other end. It looked like the perfect place for man-eating spiders to achieve science fiction level growth. Markman shut the door and latched it.

Cassiopia was found in a living area just off the main entrance foyer. Her feet were up on an expensive-looking, heavily engraved oak coffee table. The rest of her stretched out on a fluffy beige couch which looked like it might swallow her. Beside her, Speedy was curled up in a nap while the TEL robot stood silently beside the couch as though watching over the pair. Cassiopia was eating cashews from a bowl in her left hand. The TV was on with the volume so low it could barely be heard. She looked up and gave Markman a playful stare as he entered.

"Wow, Cassiopia Cassell not working!" said Markman.

"It's rain and rain and rain," she replied, turning back to the TV.

Markman sat beside her, opposite Speedy. "What are you watching?"

"Cartoons. Wile E. Coyote is about to fall off that cliff I'm pretty sure."

"Can I have a handful of those?"

"Did you finish your report, Mr. Markman? Or were you a bad boy as usual?"

Markman scooped out some cashews. "And what if I didn't?"

"You might have to be punished."

"Well, that doesn't sound all bad...."

Cassiopia smirked.

"For your information, yes I finished my report. I got an A."

"Well, in that case you should be rewarded."

"Wow! You are in a royal mood, my dear."

"I was planning on working in the garden. Guess that's not going to happen."

"Do I need to console you then?"

Cassiopia smirked once more. "What did you have in mind?"

"Let's see, it would have to be an indoor sport."

Cassiopia wormed the remote control out from under Speedy. "I couldn't have worked in the garden anyway. I need fertilizer." She turned to the robot. "Tel, did my father record any phosphorus or sulfur being put away anywhere?"

To her surprise, the robot seemed to stiffen and after a brief pregnant pause it began to play the theme from Jeopardy.

Cassiopia straightened up so abruptly she spilled some cashews. Her eyes became wide with excitement. "Tel, has my father opened any files for calcium?"

The robot seemed nervous. The theme from Jeopardy became slightly louder.

Markman began picking spilled nuts up from the couch. "What's going on?"

"How about iodine, Tel? Any recent files with iodine used in them?"

The robot continued its performance of Jeopardy.

Cassiopia broke out into laughter. Markman stared in confusion.

"Come on. What's this about?"

With great jubilance she turned to him, grabbed his head and gave a long passionate kiss. "I've got him now! I've got him!"

"What? Who?"

Cassiopia regained her composure but the wide smile on her face remained. "What do calcium, sulfur, iodine, and phosphorus all have in common, Scott?"

Markman stuttered, "They're chemicals?"

"Yep. They're all elements on the periodic table. How much do you know about the periodic table?"

"Nothing?"

"Well, CA is the periodic table symbol for calcium, and S is the symbol for sulfur, and I is the symbol for iodine. You put those all together and what do they spell, sir?"

"CA-S-I? Casi, as in Cassiopia?"

"I've got him now. I've got him!"

"Still not with you, ma'am."

"I'm sorry. It's easy. It's an old game my father and I used to play. You pick a number and the only clues you give your opponent are abbreviations from elements on the periodic table. Your opponent has to juggle the atomic numbers for those elements around to come up with the secret number. Tel has been programmed not to talk about the elements whose symbols spell my name. All I have to do is come up with a number sequence from the atomic weights of those elements and I'll have the passcode for my father's project room. Get it?"

"Yes?"

Cassiopia jumped up, waking Speedy. "Tel you remain here. Do you understand?"

The Jeopardy music from the robot stopped. A long moment of silence followed. "Yes, Cassiopia," answered the robot.

Markman barely made it to the elevator in time to join her. Cassiopia hammered on the *down* button even as the doors were closing. In the basement lab area she fumbled around on one of the work tables. "I need a piece of paper and something to write with!"

Finally finding those things, she began to plan out loud. "Okay, calcium is 20, sulfur is 16, that is used twice, iodine is 53...." Biting one lip she wrote down all the numbers involved. "And the last one has to be arsenic, AS. So it spells Cassiopias. Cassiopias is the password."

"What happens next?" asked Markman.

"You have your cell phone?"

Markman reached into his back pocket and gave it to her.

Cassiopia began nodding her head. "You see this list of local networks? Ours has five bars, the other three have just one bar of signal strength because they're our neighbors and are too far away."

"Yeah?"

"I say one of these weak networks is right here and has been deliberately disguised and set to be weak to make it look like someone else's home network. The atomic weights of the elements in my name add up to a total of 214. I'm betting if I keep trying 214 as a passcode one of these other networks will let me open that lab door."

"Geezz...."

Cassiopia clicked on the first network and tried her new passcode. A flag appeared, rejecting her attempt. She went to the second network with the same result. Holding her breath, she entered 214 into the third network's password screen. There was a brief moment where she did not receive the rejection flag. Then a loud swishing sound made them both look up at the Professor's project door. It opened wide.

Cassiopia gasped in delight. She pushed past Markman and entered the forbidden room. Markman followed closely.

There were stacks of fiber optic strands on a table to the left. Parts from disassembled miniature motors, along with some strange looking fibrous strands sat on the work table on the left. Test equipment was everywhere. Spots of tan-colored fluid marked the floor in various places. Several tower computers were located around the room, their screens dark.

Cassiopia turned slowly in a circle, taking it all in. Finally, she looked at Markman and grunted displeasure.

"What?" asked Markman.

Raising her hands in frustration, she complained, "It's not here! He's either hidden it or taken it with him so I wouldn't find it! That little sneak!"

"Well, it is his personal business. Maybe it's for John Paul and he's been ordered to keep it secret."

"No, no. I asked John Paul. He didn't know anything about it. My father is just playing his games. He knew I'd waste my time figuring out the door so he used it as a distraction. What a wily old fox."

"Well, like father like daughter."

"What?"

"So what's next? You going to start searching the castle even though you don't know what you're looking for?"

"Chocolate and ice cream," replied Cassiopia and she headed for the elevator.

Chapter 8

Cassiopia awoke from another restless sleep. Markman was hanging off his side of the bed, snoring faintly. She listened intently for the sound which had awakened her but heard nothing. Once again, she climbed out from under the warmth of the blankets, wrapped a robe around and in the dim light went to the door. Through the partially opened door the hallway was shadowy and spooky. She stepped out and listened.

There it was again. An ever so slight moan coming from somewhere to her left. She tied the terrycloth belt and walked barefoot in that direction. The air was cool and carried the new home smell. At the hallway's end the curtains were drawn. She wondered who had done that. The stairs to her left looked even darker and more ominous. She listened again but did not hear the mournful groan. Had she really heard anything at all? She waited and shivered slightly at the emptiness. With a quickened pace she returned to embrace of blankets and bed. Markman's arm was over her spot as though he'd been looking for her.

As she slid in under the blankets he spoke without opening his eyes, his voice a barely translatable grumble, a loving complaint, "Where'd jah go?"

"I think this house is haunted." Cassiopia pulled the blankets up to her neck.

"Uh-huh," replied the cracked voice an ogre. Heavy sleep-breathing returned.

In the breakfast nook, morning rays beamed through the colored window. Cassiopia nibbled at her toast and looked out at the freshly bathed world. In the garden below flowers had opened to the sun, their leaves still glistening from the past day's watering.

"Did you get up last night?" asked Markman as he took his seat.

"I think this house is haunted."

"Did you tell me that last night?"

"I heard a moan. I'm sure of it."

"The wind, blowing through cracks and corners."

"I don't think so."

"Did you get up? The bed was like cold for a little while."

"What am I, your bed warmer?"

Markman poured himself coffee, mixed in sugar and cream and smiled. "You are heavenly."

"Are you patronizing me? Don't stop."

"It's the spirit of your father, guarding his project while he's away. I feel it when I go down to the lab alone. It's like his ghost is down there standing guard."

Cassiopia looked up from her tablet. "Maybe there's a secret passage in this place that leads to a secret room somewhere where he's hiding his really good stuff."

Markman narrowed his stare and sipped. "You mean like Dr. Frankenstein's dungeon?"

Cassiopia tapped her tablet. "There's some interesting news again today."

"Oh please, not another murder. After reading John Paul's police reports I'm not sure I could stand another one."

"No, it's not another one but John Paul did send you the police report on the third murder."

Markman sipped again.

"Well, aren't you going to charge off upstairs again?"

"I'd rather sit here and look at you."

"You want something?"

"I was shorted some bedtime last night. I feel cheated."

"Oh... well...."

That afternoon Markman finally visited the conference room and called up the latest police report sent by John Paul.

STAFFORD LAW ENFORCEMENT
STAFFORD, VA
Incident Report Update #9003218 (7/21)
Case Title:

Incident Type/Offense:
1)Homicide

Reporting Officer:
Duley, Franklin (880)

Location:
9547 Pardenten Street

Approving Officer:
Jones, Wilson (348)

Victim:
Randolf, William, **Age:** *46,* **Phone:** *cell phone not located,*
Address: *9547 Pardenten St.,* **Next of Kin:** *not available*

Employment: Processing Supervisor, Advanced Materials Processing, 24 Vanhoy St. Stafford

Offender(s): No suspects at this time.

Cause of Death: Pending

Narrative:

The victim was found at 08:30 by a neighbor who noticed the front door ajar and broken. There were limited signs of a struggle in the home determined to be caused by the victim attempting to escape from an intruder. The decapitated body was located near the home's rear entrance, prone on the floor. Time of death has been estimated to be approximately 03:30 to 04:00. The victim's wallet and ID were found in an upstairs bedroom. No cash was taken; no other valuables have been determined to be missing.

Interviews of the victim's neighbors yielded no additional information. Victim was a senior supervisor in charge of volatile materials integration for Advanced Materials Processing Inc. According to relatives his employment was in good standing and he was in line for promotion.

Access to the home had been made by forcing the front door open with a crowbar or other tool. The door and its framework were fractured.

Partial footprints left in the blood evidence on the floor near the body revealed shoe patterns commonly known as piecewise lines, triangular in nature, a pattern commonly associated with combat boots or hiking boots. These partials were found not to be related to the victim. No prints or other forensic evidence was found at the scene. The missing body part has not been located.

For further incident profiling, contact Dr. Emily Resturn, Stafford Psychiatric Center, Stafford Va.

End of Update

Markman leaned back and winced. A momentary pang of fear touched him. The police were not formally connecting this murder in their reports, but there was no doubt they were operating under the assumption that one person or set of persons were involved in all of these recent homicides. Failing to reference all three murders was one way of trying to quell headlines declaring Jack the Ripper had returned.

Once again, little evidence was left behind. Forced front doors. Early morning hours. Mutilation of the victims.

In this last murder at least partial shoe patterns had been left behind. Triangular shoe prints. Markman narrowed his stare. The print pattern he had seen in the cave could have been described as triangular. Then something else flashed into his mind. The creeps who had messed with Core had worn lace-up combat boots. Wouldn't it be nice to see what kind of mark they made? The chance of those three being involved was remote but the idea wouldn't go away.

Markman opened an email to John Paul.

John Paul,

Can I drop that stolen purse off this afternoon?

Scott

An answer came almost immediately.

Scott,

I'll be in meetings all day but you're welcome to take the elevator down and leave it with my assistant, Shandra. But there is also a USPS Parcel Box in front of our building. If you place it in there and dial *123 on your cell it will drop down to us. Your choice,

J.P.

Markman pushed up and went in search of Cassiopia.

On the second-floor hallway the door to a large storage room was open. The sounds of a mischievous someone moving things around came through the open door. Markman smiled to himself and peered carefully in.

Cassiopia was searching. She stood biting her lip in thought. The expression on her face was one of disappointed determination.

"You're under arrest," declared Markman.

Cassiopia jumped, looked guilty and then annoyed. "Who says?"

"An officer from the Too-Nosey department."

Cassiopia came to him and pressed up against him. "Can't you overlook this just once, officer? Isn't there anything I can do to convince you?"

Markman tried to sound authoritative but his voice was shaky. "Well, miss...."

"I'll make it worth your while, officer." She pinched at his shirt.

Markman stuttered, "What was I saying?"

One hour later Markman was on the road to Culpeper, the stolen purse on the seat beside him. He had left Cassiopia to her relentless search, having been sworn to secrecy about her misbegotten quest to find her father's hidden project material.

John Paul's home office was located in a large, secret installation below the Taslam Building on Griffith Drive northeast of Culpeper. It was only a five-mile drive through the center of Culpeper. Taslam Industries was an extremely detailed cover for the Celestial Order's main base. Markman was tempted to take the purse down just to visit the unearthly installation but there was something else on his mind. The USPS package drop would have to do this time. He pulled up in front of the three-story glass building, smirked at the tower sign that read, 'Taslam Industries' and spotted the drop box. After inserting the purse, he keyed in *123 on his John Paul-issued cell phone and then could not resist looking back in the box.

The purse and all its contents were gone.

Markman laughed to himself and climbed back in the car. He headed back toward Culpeper and slowly cruised South Main Street, then turned around and headed for James Madison Highway where the sporting goods store was located.

It was late afternoon becoming early evening. Shadows were expanding to lead evening's quiet subversion. Color was fading. Markman scanned everywhere on the outside chance of spotting his Goth gang. There was no sign of them. As the downtown began to turn into country he looped around and headed back to the Walmart midway on James Madison. He pulled into the huge parking lot, found a good vantage point and parked. He leaned back and waited and watched.

As darkness set in the high lights around the parking area illuminated, flickered and slowly intensified so that one was shining into Core's windshield.

"Core, increase window tinting."

Immediately the light in the car's cabin dimmed, though Markman's view of the outside remained just as clear.

People came and went. Cars passed in front of Markman. There was no sign of the suspects. Markman started his engine and headed north on Brandy Road. He pulled into the Colonnade parking lot and parked again. Another thirty minutes quickly seemed wasted.

Once again, he started up and headed south and this time chose the parking area across the street from Walmart. It was a large shopping area with good lighting. He sat near a Big Lots where he could see all the way to the other end of the plaza.

Another thirty minutes and Markman began to scold himself for being so naive. He twisted the ignition, searched for the easiest way back on the road to home and began to pull out.

Halfway out of the parking space something stopped him. He jammed on the brakes and strained to focus.

Farther down the row of stores and shops an elderly woman was being harassed by someone. The exchange suddenly turned into a mugging for her purse. Markman stomped on the gas and watched as a thief dressed in dark clothes yanked the woman's purse strap off her shoulder, throwing her to the pavement. The man charged away between buildings.

As Markman closed in onlookers began to gather around the victim, attempting to help her to her feet. Markman slowly crept by the melee, straining to see down the alleyway between buildings. Once clear of the crime scene he jammed the gas pedal back down, scanning between the passing buildings for any sign of the thief. At the end of the shopping center Overlook Street gave exit. Markman slowed to a crawl and searched intently to his right, watching for the purse snatcher or possibly a suspect vehicle to emerge from behind the plaza. Markman cursed to himself. There was a fifty-fifty chance the robber had gone the other way. He rolled down the passenger window for a better view. He thought of cutting across the grass along the border of the shopping center to get on the road behind the plaza but before a decision could be made, his gamble paid off.

A rocking, speeding gray van came racing out from behind the last store. It had no windows, was unwashed and in rough shape. It ignored the stop sign at the end of Delivery Road and turned left in front of Markman. Markman paused at the plaza stop sign just long enough to put some distance between Core and the suspect. With the passenger window back up he followed the speeding van at a distance.

"Core, lock on and track the gray van in front of us."

Immediately, crosshairs on the windshield appeared. Core's machine voice spoke, "Please target desired vehicle using shift lever control pad. Depress pad to lock target."

Markman glanced at the shifter to find new controls had suddenly appeared. He passed a car which had moved in front of him, then moved one finger across the new shifter control pad. The windshield crosshairs moved obediently. The van was gaining ground. With the crosshairs lined up on the taillights he pressed the shifter pad and the windshield crosshairs disappeared.

Core spoke once more, "Target vehicle will require GPS tracking. Screen on."

A video screen appeared on the dash. Red nightlight illuminated it. A map display appeared. A red, flashing circular icon marked the suspect's vehicle. A steady green icon showed Core following.

"Core, make your body color black and increase window tinting to heavy."

The suspect vehicle turned right onto James Madison Highway heading southwest. It slowed, trying to blend in with traffic, keeping to the right lane. Two other cars pulled in front of Markman but with the tracking screen locked on that was not a problem. James Madison Highway became North Main Street. Markman had a chance to sit back and consider the situation.

John Paul's orders were to avoid contact with local law enforcement and always remain invisible. He could not call this in even though he knew he was following a robbery suspect the police would now be looking for.

A patrol car with lights flashing passed by in the other direction on its way to the crime scene.

Markman realized he could not even confront the criminal. That might mean he could be identified later. Even so he was not going to let them disappear into the night. As he continued to consider his options the van made a right turn onto West Piedmont Street. Markman dared not turn in to follow them down a side street. He pulled over and watched the tracking display.

A quick left-hand turn put the van on North West Street, then another quick left gave them West Edmonson Street. A moment later they turned right back onto North Main Street.

Markman pulled out onto the road and used the left lane to spot them. They were half a dozen cars ahead. The diversion off Main Street must have been to see if they were being followed. Now convinced of his successful escape the thief or thieves had settled back into the normal flow of traffic.

Nothing to do now but follow and maybe see where their hideout was. The van continued on to South Main Street and then took a left onto Fredericksburg Road. Markman's interest piqued further, knowing the suspects would probably pass right by Mountain Road, the entrance to his home. Suddenly this driver was passing by the area where the other purse had been found.

As the van passed by Highway 15 and onto Germana Highway, traffic began to fade. And, as the Mountain Road turnoff neared, Markman began to wonder if it would turn off there. The road had become dark from the discontinuation of street lights. There was now a chance the bad guys could pick up on Markman's headlights.

To his relief the van sped by Mountain Road without slowing. But now the roadway was a dark, empty path through the night. There was not another car in sight. The tracking screen was completely trustworthy but it was important to keep the vehicle in sight in case something changed.

"Core, shut off all outside lights and switch to infrared."

Immediately Core's headlights went out and the windshield became an infrared viewing screen. The world was suddenly shades of gray but the visibility was excellent. Markman dared to close in a little more but not so much that oncoming headlights would give him away.

Another few minutes put them past Lignum and a short distance beyond the van finally began to slow. It made a left turn onto Route 620 and as Markman turned to follow he could see the van slowly swerving from side to side as though something was going on inside. A moment later it slowed further, and something was thrown out the passenger window. Keeping his distance Markman waited patiently and pulled over at the drop sight. In the ditch along the road, the woman's leather purse was torn open with contents spilled out. Markman hurried out and gathered everything up then jumped back in and continued on.

A moment later he spotted the van pulling into a driveway. This was not a good time for a drive by. He pulled over, climbed out and stalked along the wood line along the road until in a position to see the van and residence. The van door creaked open and several people emerged. Three people. Though they were only darkened silhouettes, Markman could tell it was the same three he had encountered outside the Culpeper sporting goods store. The tall one was still dressed in his long coat and boots. His cohorts were in dark jeans and dark T-shirts. In the faint light from the home there was a glimpse of snake emblems on their shirts. Their conversation was casual. One of the cohorts had a paper bag which seemed to command the center of attention. They looked into it as they entered the house, like trick-or-treaters just home from Halloween.

Markman noted the address on the mailbox then crept back to the car. He climbed in, shut the door quietly and made a U-turn. The ride home became a time for soul-searching.

Maybe he could return when the gang was away to see if he could spot any matching shoe prints around the house. Perhaps he could gain entry somewhere and take a look inside. These guys were definitely guilty of theft but was there a connection to greater crimes?

At home Markman went to the conference room and made a map of the murder sites. He marked the gang's hideout. Their location was suspiciously central to the murders. The stolen purse sat on the table in front of him. Another item for the USPS package drop in front of John Paul's.

As he considered his options, Cassiopia arrived. She came up behind him and wrapped her arms around his neck.

"You were gone a long time. Where'd you go? Still on the case of the lost purse?" she asked but then she noticed yet another purse on the table. "What? Another one? Did you go back in that cave alone?"

Markman twisted his head around and gave her a peck on the cheek. "Nope."

"Well, what then?"

"I witnessed a purse snatching purely by accident."

"You're kidding! Trouble always seems to find you, you know that, Markman?"

"Well, you found me."

"Very funny. You saw a purse snatching and you got the woman's purse back? You know you're not supposed to get involved in that stuff."

"I didn't. I followed them back to their hideout. They threw it out the car window and I picked it up."

"Did they see you?"

"Of course not."

Cassiopia opened the purse and casually searched through it. "No wallet. No jewelry. Just papers and junk. So they got away with it."

"For now."

"You don't have something in mind, do you?"

"No... no. It will catch up with them sooner or later. It's one of your laws, isn't it?"

"My laws?"

"For every action there's an equal and opposite reaction."

"Karma? You're trying to equate Newton's third law to karma?"

"What is it you're always talking about? Perfect symmetry?"

"You're mixing up your science, Markman. Perfect symmetry has to do with string theory or M-theory, not Newton's laws."

"Yeah, but isn't that supposed to tie everything together or something?"

"Well I'm just shocked! You have been listening to me after all! But Scott, are you trying to bridge spiritualism with science? That's a big bridge to cross."

"About the size of the universe, maybe?"

"Okay, now you're starting to give me a headache."

"It's about time to sack out. You telling me you have a headache?"

"Oh, you're not going to get off that easily."

Chapter 9

The new day was bright and clear. Cassiopia sipped her tea and stared in serene thought at the glorious landscape beyond the breakfast nook windows. Markman appeared and sat across from her, smiling. "I want to drop off purse number two at John Paul's. Why don't you come along for the ride?"

"Is there an ulterior motive in your request, sir?"

"Well, I do want to take a slight detour on the way back. I want...."

Cassiopia interrupted, "You want to drive by the purse snatcher's place and check it out."

"You're scaring me, Cass. Am I that easy to read?"

"You're hoping that having me in the car will make you less conspicuous if you're seen."

"For Pete's sake."

"I'll do it."

"You will?"

"Yes, even though you only want me there as a diversion."

Markman leaned back, smiled and folded his hands in his lap. "Oh, I've got you on that one. I always want you with me. You know that."

Cassiopia smirked. "Okay, but on the condition you take me to the bookstore in Culpeper."

"No problem."

A comical moment of silence passed between the two as they sipped their tea. Markman's usual humor crept in. "Did you take this place apart yesterday trying to find your father's hidden project? And, did you find it?"

Cassiopia scowled. "No, I did not and don't you say anything about that."

"Say anything about what?"

"He must've taken his darn project with him."

"Did you check the old storeroom down past your father's workrooms?"

"Are you kidding? Did you see the cobwebs? There's spiders in there the size of small dogs. Did you look in there?"

"Uh, no. I didn't have the time."

"Oh, right. You, the man who runs away from small snakes."

"I do not run away. I advance in a different direction."

"By the way, during my exploration of this place I did discover something amazing."

"You found the real dungeon?"

"Almost! On the other side of the house there's a whole different section of basement. It has a big workout area with equipment and best of all, it even has a racquetball court. It's a good one too. You can play off the ceiling."

"Oh brother."

"Don't worry. I'll let you win sometimes. I practiced a little bit while you were gone."

"Let's go take that purse to John Paul's."

Thirty minutes later, Markman pulled up alongside the USPS drop box in front of the Taslam Industries. He climbed out with his newly acquired purse, went around the car and tapped on Cassiopia's window.

"What?" she asked.

"Watch this. It's cool."

Markman deposited the purse in the drop box and motioned to it like a performing magician. He closed the cover.

"Type * 1 2 3 on your cell phone."

Cassiopia drew out her phone and did so.

With a broad smile, Markman opened the drop box cover. The purse was gone.

He came to Cassiopia's window. "Somehow that's gone down to John Paul's office."

"Is it a drop tube or some kind of Star Trek transporter?"

"How should I know?"

"I'd like to know."

"Well, you can ask him the next time you see him. Hey, would you drive? I didn't email him about this thing. I'll text him as we drive."

On the road, Markman struggled through a text to John Paul.

J.P., we dropped off another purse. Accidentally saw it snatched in Big Lots parking lot. Followed their van to 223 Yellow Bottom Road Rte 620 Lignum. 3 guys. -M.

"You need to get Fredericksburg and Gemana, Cass."

"How far is the place?"

"About fifteen or twenty minutes. Maybe we should have hit the bookstore first."

"And have you squirming to come here? No way."

"Yeah, you're right."

Cassiopia's cell phone chirped. She gave Markman a warning glance not to scold, drew it out and wiped the screen with her thumb. "Hello?"

There was a long pause during which Cassiopia's expressions transposed from pleasant surprise to consternation to angry defense. "Father, I have not been trying to hack into your laptop!"

Another extended period of listening.

"I did no such thing! Why do you think it's me? It could be anyone!"

Markman could barely make out the irate voice on the other end of the line.

"It was not me, Father. When are you coming home?"

Markman tried to lean over to hear but was bumped in the shoulder by Cassiopia.

Markman motioned with concern at a stop sign ahead.

"Well I'll be glad when you get here. I don't like this business of you being hidden away somewhere on secret projects. So okay, hurry up and finish, okay?"

She tucked her phone back in and gave Markman an annoyed sideward glance. "Someone's been trying to hack into his laptop. He thought it was me!"

"Gee, why would he think such a thing?" replied Markman with a smirk.

"Watch it, Markman, or I will get a headache."

"I'm not sayin' nothin'."

"He'll be home in a day or two. They've finished whatever it is they're working on. I think he embarrassed some of the people he was working with."

Markman nodded forward. "This is Lignum. Route 620 is just up ahead. Get ready to take a left."

A few minutes later Cassiopia turned onto Route 620. She slowed and looked over at Markman. "How do I do this? Do I creep by or just cruise by normally?"

"House number two-twenty-three. It's on the mailbox. Drive by at the speed limit. It's thirty-five here."

"Yellow Bottom Road? How does anyone come up with the name Yellow Bottom Road?"

Forest lined the roadway with shallow drainage culverts on either side. It was the third house on the right. Markman's interest piqued. He focused ahead, trying to take in every possible detail.

As they neared he realized something was different. There was a second vehicle this time, parked behind the gang's van. It was a van also but much newer and more expensive. It was ash red and covered with lettering and airbrushed images. The lettering and pictures were unpleasant. The largest letters read *"HELL IS COMING."* Around it were equally threatening messages: *"Perish in a lake of fire. Repent or face hellfire. Sinners against the real God, you are hated. Your destruction is at hand. Find the Pentagram before it is too late."* All around the script were pictures of fire, skeletons, and headstones.

Markman exclaimed, "Wow! I've got to get a closer look at this stuff."

Cassiopia gave a disapproving glance. "What? What do you mean?"

"Pull over for a second when we're out of sight and let me out. Give me about five minutes then turn around and pick me up in the same spot."

"Scott, you might be seen. You're taking a big chance. Invisible, remember?"

"I won't be seen. I promise."

Cassiopia shook her head but pulled over as requested. "You know how trouble finds you."

"I'll be right back." Markman climbed out, took a long look around and darted into the woods. Staying low and weaving carefully through brush and trees he came in sight of the west side of the house. The brown wooden paneling on the home was weathered and needed paint. The lawn was uncut. Sections of hedge along the walls were dying or dead. There was a single window with a black curtain drawn closed. Markman caught his breath, took a wide look around and crossed over to the window. Standing alongside he checked the area again. There was no one in sight. A faint smell of garbage was coming from two garbage bins at a nearby corner.

The black curtain was not large enough for the window it shaded. There was a space on each side and in the middle where it divided. A muffled man's voice could be heard from within. It was not conversational in tone. It was more like preaching. Markman dared a quick look near the bottom corner of the dirty window. It was so dirty vision was marginal. But with Markman's snapshot look he saw enough. A man in a long black robe holding a golden ram's head high and chanting verse. Candles were spread around the room. A diagram like a pentagram was drawn on the floor. Two of the purse snatchers were leaning against the far wall not paying attention. It was certain the third was also nearby, somewhere out of sight.

Markman ducked down and headed back into the forest. At the roadside he met Cassiopia just pulling up. He climbed in and motioned her to leave.

Underway, her curiosity piqued. "And? What did you see?"

"They're a busy bunch."

"Yeah? Doing what?"

"I think the new guy was summoning Satan or something."

"Oh, Jeez."

"I don't think he has anything to do with the purse snatching."

"Come on, what did you see?"

"Candles, diagram on the floor, tall guy in black robe holding a gold head with horns."

"God, that stuff scares me."

"I'm with you."

Markman's phone chirped. There was a text from John Paul.

Another purse?!

Markman texted back:

Just now paid suspects another invisible visit. They were doing satanic ritual thing. Not nice people.

John Paul replied:

We'll take care of it. Make no further contacts.

Markman answered:

Gladly.

Cassiopia cast wry smile. "Get in trouble, sir?"

Markman straightened up and tried to look innocent. "No. Not at all. He said they'd take care of it."

"I wonder what they'll do?"

"I wouldn't want to be them. I know that."

Chapter 10

Cassiopia stood giggling at the breakfast nook window. Markman came up behind her and placed his hands on her shoulders while trying to see.

"What's so funny this morning?" he asked.

"Look down there in the garden. I told Tel to teach Speedy not to dig holes in the flower garden. It's hysterical."

Markman strained to spot the pair. Below, the silver body of the robot was glinting light from the rising sun. Directly in front of him the dog was kicking dirt several feet into the air as he furiously dug his latest hole. Every so often the dog would stop and stand on its hind legs, front paws drooping in a beg to Tel, after which the robot would dispense a dog biscuit and hand it over. The exchange completed, the dog would jump with joy, then return to another session of digging.

Cassiopia squeaked a laugh and covered her mouth.

"Doesn't look like it's working," commented Markman.

Cassiopia wiped away a tear of laughter and nodded. "The lesson is working perfectly. Don't you see what's happening? The robot thinks that if he rewards Speedy when he stops digging that will teach the dog to stop. The dog has figured out that if he digs for a while and stops, he'll get a treat. It's like who is training who?"

"Yeah, I have to admit, there have been dogs who have trained me, too."

"I'll have to try to explain it to Tel but that will be interesting."

Cassiopia poured the morning tea into both cups and sat, still trying to regain her composure. Markman sipped then rested his chin in his hand and gave her an endearing stare. She noticed and held her cup shy of her lips. "Uh-oh. What's that look? You have something in mind."

"You have any plans for today?"

"I might if I gave it some thought. What's going on in that sneaky mind of yours?"

"I bought all that nice spelunking gear and...."

"You want to visit the caves again. I bet John Paul told you to get off the purse snatching case so you want to go down there and look for more evidence."

"It'd be fun...."

"Okay. I'm in. I'll even text John Paul that we're going so he knows at least one of us is being responsible."

After an early lunch and a much more skilled climb Cassiopia and Markman arrived back at the grated cave entrance.

"It's not so scary now," commented Cassiopia.

"But do we really know what's down there?" replied Markman.

"Yes. Rock curtains, rock passageways and lots of rock décor."

"Let's just slide down the entrance this time. We don't need a drop line, do we?"

"You first, Captain Nemo."

"You know, they sold me this beautiful safety reel but I read some cave explorers now consider a safety line only for sissies."

"I'll bet there are some sissies still alive and some heroes that aren't," replied Cassiopia.

Markman lifted the grate away from the hole, checked his ropes and equipment, gave Cassiopia a challenging smile and slipped down into the entrance. After a careful tuck-in of items, Cassiopia followed.

At the bottom of the entrance Cassiopia brushed off, switched on her headlamp and reoriented herself. "All of a sudden this place is spooky again."

"Let me finish attaching our sissy line and we can head back to where I found the purse. Then I want to see if we can get down to where those old beams were."

"It's cooler and damper down here than it was before. Has to be because of the rains we had."

"This reel thing is so cool. I just attach it to my belt and the line unwinds all by itself. I don't have to pay any attention to it."

"Right. I bet there are also cavers who have said that and never returned."

"A little gloomy this morning, aren't we?"

"Well, I am in a pit of sorts, aren't I?"

"It's adventure! It's exciting! It's fun."

"Yeah, you're right. It is."

"Check out these new headlamps. They are awesome. They're so bright! And, they're LED. They'll stay on forever!"

"Or at least until forever ends."

"There you go again."

"Right. Sorry. Didn't sleep well last night. Something kept waking me up again. It's those ghosts. Maybe they live down here. But anyway, lead on, Goonie."

Markman led the way, climbing over rock formations, ducking beneath and around stalactite clusters. Cassiopia remained close, her attention focused on the shadowy sculpted world around her. There were numerous pools of water this time and thin flows of water glistening against the walls. The low ceiling passages made the larger chambers seem cathedral-like. With each step there was new cave architecture. She found herself exclaiming, "Wow!" too often.

Markman was equally entranced until they neared the spot where the purse had been found. He glanced back. "You doing all right?"

"Now that I'm not so afraid this place is amazing."

"Yeah, we must be pretty deep underground by now. I didn't remember how steep some of this place was."

"We'll need the ropes up ahead."

"Yeah, but we're a great team, don't you think?"

"Yes."

"We did a great job on that weapons recovery, didn't we?"

"I think so."

"I wonder if John Paul's next mission is coming up any time soon."

"Yeah."

"Cass, did you ever wonder about the aliens?"

"Watch out for that puddle ahead. It might be deeper than it looks. The water is so crystal clear down here you can't tell. What about aliens?"

"Working for John Paul, did you ever think maybe we might have to do a job with an alien or something?"

"Yes, I have thought about that."

"Could you handle meeting an alien? What would that be like?"

"John Paul briefed my father about it. My father may be working with them even now for all we know. John Paul said there are many different species. Most of them are far ahead of us both in evolution and technology. Some are easy to interact with and others are awkward to be around. Apparently, many of them are telepathic which is kind of creepy. He said some species can only talk out loud to you by taking over the speech center of your brain and using your own mouth to form their words. You ask a question and then you answer it yourself. Weird."

"Holy crap! Man, I don't know if I could handle somebody being in my brain like that."

"I'm sure if that situation arises John Paul will prepare us."

Markman paused and shook his head at the thought. He pointed ahead. "That's the place where I found the purse. It doesn't look like anybody's been here since. Let's just head on to the drop-off."

A few hundred feet beyond the cavern floor curved down sharply. In the dim light at the bottom they could just make out a section of timber. Markman found an outcropping of rock and tied a rope line to it. He tossed the loop down into the darkness then hooked up to it and started to back down. Cassiopia smiled defiantly and clipped on and when there was a safe amount of separation she followed.

The bottom of the drop leveled off sharply. It was a smaller section of tunnel perhaps ten feet in diameter. It seemed even darker than the previous section. Markman searched with his headlamp. Quite a few lengths of four by four and six by four beams were scattered around and ahead.

Cassiopia spoke. "There was some kind of mining here. Look!" She held up an aged, broken handle from a miner's pickaxe.

"Let's go on a ways." Markman began stepping over the pieces of lumber.

"Wow, there's actually quite a lot of stuff laying around here," said Cassiopia. "Look at these old metal buckets and what are these rusty iron bars?"

"Probably used in excavation," answered Markman.

"You're running out of sissy line, Scott."

"Hey! Look at that place on the right up ahead. It looks like another cutoff."

As they neared the shadowy opening, Cassiopia said, "Oh wow! It's not another tunnel. It goes up. It looks like it was a well or something."

"Look! There's iron bars sunk into the rock for a ladder!"

Cassiopia strained her neck to point her headlamp upward. "There is something up there. It's a ledge or something."

Markman quickly unhooked his gear and handed her the safety reel. "I'll be right back."

"Be careful, Scott. This place is old."

"You know me."

"Yes, I do."

Markman tested the first few rungs of rusty iron and stepped up. With caution, he advanced halfway up then looked down to check his progress. Cassiopia's headlamp blinded him for a second but he continued on.

The last of the iron rungs gave way to a small rock platform. To Markman's surprise a very old, very heavy wooden door was built into the rock wall. He pulled himself up onto the shelf, braced for balance and stood facing the old door. A quick pull on the wooden door handle proved the thing was locked securely and this was too heavy a barrier to break through. He searched for openings to peek through but found none. After a moment of doubt, he knocked loudly. There was no response.

"Well? What's up there?" called Cassiopia.

"It's a door!"

"A door? What kind of door?"

"A big wooden door. It won't open. No one answers."

"Ya think?" replied Cassiopia sarcastically.

"I'm coming down."

At the bottom of the ladder Markman shrugged.

"It's got to be another entrance somewhere on the mountain. It was used for this mining operation. It's probably been sealed for years," suggested Cassiopia.

"I guess," replied Markman. "I sure would like to continue downward but we're just about out of line."

"It could go on for miles, Scott."

"Yeah, but I'll bet you anything there's another entrance somewhere ahead."

"We might be able to find a map for this place at the local library or on some caver website. I'll see what I can find. We've been down here for hours. Let's go get hot food."

"Wow, you sure can be persuasive."

The long, slow march up and back began. The climb was exhausting at times. Markman worried that it might be too much for Cassiopia, and as they managed a steep section of boulder she accidentally knocked a small rock down on his helmet. It bounced off with a "bonk." He looked up in time to see her cover her mouth with one gloved hand to hide her laughter. He found himself laughing with her.

"Scott, do we seem like typical secret agents to you?"

"Didn't we already talk about this?"

"I mean really, aren't secret agents supposed to drink martinis, stay at expensive hotels and drive fast cars?"

"Believe me, we've got the car."

"You know what I mean."

"No, we don't seem like secret agents but we're supposed to be invisible, right? You can't be invisible doing that stuff, right? I think maybe we're above secret agents, you know what I mean?"

Cassiopia paused in thought. "You may be right."

Chapter 11

Cassiopia opened the tall red velvet curtain allowing morning rays to burst into the room.

A low moan came from Markman's sleeping form.

She picked up her tablet and steaming cup of tea and went to sit on the bed beside him.

Markman rolled over, dragged one hand and arm across her lap and tried to go back to sleep.

"Something here I think you'll want to see," toyed Cassiopia.

Another moan.

"Would I be here if it wasn't?" she asked.

Markman raised a hand to his forehead, wiped his face and blinked his eyes open. The sunlight was too much. "What time is it?"

"Seven-thirty…. You're sleeping late."

"Is that tea I smell?"

Cassiopia held out the cup. Markman pushed partially up and took it from her. He gazed around the room before taking a sip.

"Something in this morning's edition of the news which might interest you," she persisted.

"Another murder? Please don't tell me."

"No, it's not a murder, silly. I wouldn't wake you to tell you there's been another murder. Geez…."

"What then?"

Cassiopia handed him the tablet. It took Markman a few seconds to focus.

Shopping Plaza Purse Snatchers Arrested

An early evening purse snatching that took place at a Culpeper Shopping Plaza was said to be resolved today when local police arrested Johnny Barthlow, 26 and Robert Talstrom, 28 at their residence in the early hours this morning. An anonymous tip allowed police to obtain a search warrant which led to the recovery of the victim's purse in a garbage can at the suspect's home. Fingerprints of both suspects were subsequently found on the purse and on stolen items inside it. Stolen items from other crimes were also located in the home. The pair is being held in lieu of bond. No further details were available at this time.

Markman looked up at Cassiopia. "Wow!"

Cassiopia nodded, "Wow!"

Markman thought for a moment. "That means...."

"Yes. John Paul had that purse planted in their garbage can and then made the anonymous tip."

"Or one of his people did."

"What's the difference?"

"For some reason I didn't expect that."

"Because it's not ethical?"

"Is it not ethical?"

"It was planted evidence."

"Yeah, but the evidence was originally only a few hundred yards down the road. Maybe I messed up by taking it. Maybe somebody else would have come along and handed it over to the police, then they still would have gotten the prints and made the arrest."

Cassiopia stared blankly into the distance. "Wow!"

"Which wow is that?"

"Maybe this is kind of like a lesson about how we're not supposed to interfere with the world around us like John Paul is always saying."

"According to this article one of the three got away and they didn't get the hellfire van guy either."

"You said he may not have had anything to do with the illegal part of it."

"I'll bet the third guy is long gone worrying about his buddies making a plea deal."

"At least they won't be robbing anyone in a parking lot."

"Yeah, and I'll be very interested to see if the Ripper murders stop now that those guys are in custody."

Cassiopia's cell phone chirped. She pulled it out, tapped at it and read. "It's my father. They've finished up working on whatever it was they were working on. He'll be back this afternoon."

"We should tell the robot."

"He's already notified Tel, I'm sure."

Professor Cassel arrived late in the afternoon in one of John Paul's limousines. The driver and one other attendant unloaded his bags and lugged some of them to his bedroom and others to the laboratory basement. They left without gratuity.

The Professor appeared tired but in good spirits. After the celebratory greeting he begged off to his room for a nap.

In the main kitchen, Markman made his own version of fish corn chowder, enough for four. He gave his best imitation of staff and served Cassiopia in the main dining room. They sat at both ends of the very long oak table and since it was too distant to speak they smirked at each other through the entire meal. Markman's chowder entrée was followed with prepackaged apple pie cubes. Formality was then discarded. Cassiopia remained at the end seat but Markman moved to one place away.

Just as the conversation began to be romantically provocative, the room's double doors burst open and in came the Professor in a storm of discontent. His white lab coat was buttoned incorrectly and his beard and hair were askew. He charged over to Cassiopia, slapped his hand angrily on the table and began waving one finger accusingly.

"Cassiopia, this is too much! You have gone way beyond the bounds of professional ethics. There is no humor in this type of behavior regardless of what you think. I enjoy our little cat and mouse games but you've never violated the rules of good professional courtesy. I am so angry at you I may need to leave this place. I will not accept this kind of intrusion. Do you understand what I am saying at all?"

Cassiopia sat frozen, her coffee cup halfway to her mouth. She stared up at her father wide-eyed in shock. She stuttered, "What... what... what?"

Her father slapped his hand on the table once again. "What have you done with it, young lady? You tell me right now or I may take you over my knee. Please tell me you have not made modifications!"

Her hand shaking, Cassiopia managed to place her cup back on the table. "Father, I don't know what you're talking about! Please!"

"Don't give me that. We both know you constantly scheme your way into my project rooms. I did not mind that but this is just too much. Now, what have you done with it?"

"Father, please! What have I done with what?"

Red-faced, the Professor paused for a moment, seemingly taken aback. "The prototype I was working on. It is missing. Only you could have gotten into that lab. Therefore, you must have done something with it. No one else could have."

"Father, I swear. I didn't take anything. Yes, Scott and I did finally get the door open but there was nothing in there. Just a few support items and tools."

Markman's eyes widened at the inclusion of his name.

The Professor stiffened. His breathing remained rapid. He tilted his head down in thought then snapped back up and looked at Markman. Markman's eyes widened further in a failed attempt to look innocent.

"You've never misled me, Scott. Is she telling the truth? I know I may be putting you on the spot but this is too important to dance around with. Was the project room really empty?"

"She's telling you the truth, Professor. She still hasn't even figured out what you're working on. It's been driving her crazy!"

"Oh, thank you so much," said Cassiopia sarcastically.

The Professor placed a hand on his forehead and shook his head.

Cassiopia said, "Father, John Paul must have taken it and put it away for safekeeping. He's always concerned about how advanced your work is. He must have wanted to be sure it didn't fall into the wrong hands."

The Professor drew a handkerchief from his back pocket and nervously wiped his brow. He turned and marched out of the room.

A long silent pause ensued. Markman sipped his coffee, hoping he was not in some kind of trouble.

Cassiopia sat looking like a cat that had just been drenched with a bucket of water.

"Whew!" said Markman, hoping to break the silence.

Cassiopia scowled. "I don't know whether to laugh, scream, or cry! What just happened?"

"Well, you wouldn't want to be John Paul just now."

"Oh my God! I've never seen my father that angry."

"Apparently hell hath no fury like that of a scientist whose toys have been messed with."

"It's not funny, Scott. Who knows what he was working on? It could have been something which could impact the entire world for all we know. Maybe it was stolen!"

"I doubt that. You know how John Paul is about this place. It's supposed to be impossible for anyone to get in here."

"But I keep hearing sounds at night. It keeps waking me up. I better go try to talk to him. I'll admit to him I searched this entire place and his prototype was not here. I'll be right back."

Cassiopia stood awkwardly, straightened up her sweater, and disappeared out the doors. Markman sat back, sipped his coffee and thought, *"Nothing to say but what a day, how's your boy been?"* Where had he heard that? Was it a lyric? Beatles maybe.

Cassiopia returned a few minutes later. Markman stood in anticipation. "Well? How did it go?"

"He's in his room with the door locked. He's talking on the phone to someone. I think it's John Paul. I couldn't make out what was being said but it didn't sound good. I have a feeling they'll be on the phone for a while. I'm going to text John Paul."

"And say what?"

"I'm going to ask him if he took the prototype for safe keeping and tell him that if he didn't we want to help figure out what happened."

"It couldn't have been stolen. We've been here most of the time."

"No, we haven't. We've been driving around and down in the cave. Plus, this place is so huge somebody could be down in the laboratories and we'd never know. Someone could have broken in here and taken it."

"Cass, the place is a fortress with John Paul security, never mind the fact it took you weeks to figure out how to open the door to your father's project room."

Cassiopia argued, "The Advance Aviation Systems Building was a security fortress too, Scott and we went in and out of there like ghosts."

Markman thought for a moment and nodded. "Point taken."

Several hours later John Paul responded to Cassiopia's email;

Cassiopia, I understand your concerns. I'm sorry your father blamed you for this. He's sorry too. To answer your first question; no, we did not confiscate any prototype to secure it. In hindsight, perhaps we should have done exactly that. As to investigating this, we are still evaluating the liability associated with the loss of the prototype and reviewing scan data of the premises during the period when the prototype disappeared. When that review has matured it will then be decided the course of action called for and which operatives are best suited for the task. We will keep you informed. –John Paul

Chapter 12

Once again Cassiopia awoke with a start from a sound sleep. She pushed herself up from the bed and squinted in the dim light. She cocked her head and listened intently. Another faint hint of moan came and went.

This was becoming too much of an annoying occurrence. She climbed out of bed, glanced at Markman's sleeping form and made her way through the faint light to the bedroom door. She opened it enough to lean out and look.

There was no light coming from the curtained windows at hallway's end. The night was black as pitch.

There was nothing from the breakfast nook end of the hall but when Cassiopia turned her head to look again in the other direction, something frightening gave her goose bumps and made her stiffen. At the far end of the hall there appeared to be a dark figure staring back at her.

She tried to force her eyes into better focus. The shape she was trying to make out was barely a silhouette. As she struggled to believe someone or something was really there, the foggy impression glided to the left and disappeared into the stairwell. Cassiopia jerked more awake.

"Scott, wake up. Wake up!" Switching on the nightstand light and a thorough shaking was required to make that happen.

"Huh? What?"

"Scott, I think I just saw someone out in the hallway."

Markman sat up groggily. "It was your father, right?"

"No. This person was too tall. It couldn't have been my father."

Markman swung his legs over and sat on the side of the bed. "Okay, give me a second." He stood and in a drowsy gate went to the door and looked out. "It's pitch black out here. How could you see anything?"

Cassiopia retrieved a flashlight from the night stand, turned it on and brought it to him.

"It moved. I saw it move."

"Okay. Wait here." Barefooted and in pajamas, Markman headed down the hall.

He returned ten minutes later, yawning. "What time is it?"

"Quarter after three."

"There was no one anywhere."

"I'm sure I saw someone."

"Your father's bedroom door is closed. That means he's asleep in there. Do you want to wake him up and ask?"

Self-doubt crept into Cassiopia. "No, not after what happened today."

"Maybe that's it, Cass. We think someone broke in here and stole the Professor's project. Now tonight you think you've seen an intruder."

"It wasn't paranoia, Scott."

"Well, what do you want me to do? I'll do it."

"This is such a big house. Someone could still be hiding somewhere."

"So we'll lock our door and check everything in the morning."

"I guess."

At breakfast Cassiopia cast Markman an aggravated stare as he took his seat.

"Anything found missing from last night?" he asked.

"I haven't really looked yet."

"Did the ghost wake you up again after all that?"

"No. There was no more moaning that I heard."

"Did you sleep?"

"Yes. Against my will."

Markman chuckled.

"Here's something that might sober you up a little," said Cassiopia with a touch of sarcasm in her voice. She handed Markman her tablet with the morning news.

Markman skimmed the headline and sat back in shock.

CEO for Nome Materials Found Murdered in Lorton

Lorton, VA.; Dr. Marcus Delam, 826 Delray Ave was found murdered yesterday evening by an associate. Police theorize the murder occurred sometime that afternoon. Dr. Delam was the CEO for Nome Materials Processing. No suspect's names or descriptions were available at the time of this reporting. Police are asking anyone with information to come forward.

"I don't believe it," said Markman half under his breath.

"That's four altogether. It's a serial killer. What a nightmare," replied Cassiopia.

"Yeah, I had a long shot hope the purse snatcher gang was involved but according to this they were in jail or being busted when this happened."

"Well, they still didn't get one member of the group or the other guy you saw either."

"I don't think either of those types would be out murdering someone while their buddies were being busted. They'd be heading out of town fast."

"All that while you and I are having stuff stolen right from under our noses. It's too much to fathom," added Cassiopia.

"And don't forget you're seeing and hearing ghosts in the night."

"I wasn't imagining things."

"I know."

"How do you know?"

"You said the person you saw was too tall to be your father. I kind of doubt anyone would notice that about a vision dreamed or imagined."

"That's right! I did say that, didn't I? It had on a long coat and an old-fashioned Dick Tracy hat."

"Maybe it was one of John Paul's people sent here for security because of what happened."

"He'd tell us that."

"Unless maybe it was something that just began late last night?"

"I'll go and ask my father. Maybe you should come along for moral support."

"Have you talked to him since the little incident in the dining room?"

Cassiopia stood and put down her teacup. "No. Perhaps it's time."

"We should check his room before going down to the lab."

They walked the length of the hall and stood outside the double doors of the Professor's room. Cassiopia tapped on a door and listened. Nothing. She tapped once more but there was no response.

Markman tried the door.

"It's unlocked." He pushed the doors open. The Professor's room was neat and unoccupied.

Cassiopia shook her head. "The lab, of course."

The elevator ride was a little tense. When the doors slid open, Cassiopia seemed slightly reluctant to step out. Markman led.

"All the project rooms are closed. You're going to have to knock again, Cass."

Cassiopia took his hand and led him around the large worktable in the center of the room but as they passed it, she suddenly jerked to a stop, screamed and put one hand against her mouth.

On the floor just past the table her father was sprawled on the floor, unconscious. A small spot of blood had collected by his head.

Cassiopia cried, "Oh no!" and lunged down to her father. Tears began to flow as she lifted his head. Markman dropped in across from her and felt for a pulse in the Professor's neck.

"He's breathing and there's a pulse!" he exclaimed.

Cassiopia straightened up and placed one hand on her neck where John Paul's implant was located. "John Paul, emergency! My father is badly hurt!"

Markman loosened the Professor's collar and unbuttoned the top buttons on his lab coat. As he did, a man in a black suit with black sunglasses suddenly appeared out of nowhere. The man knelt beside the Professor, then motioned to two other black suits suddenly present as well. The three men moved Cassiopia and Markman out of the way and took places around the body. In an instant both they and the Professor became translucent and disappeared.

"John Paul, take me too! Take me too!" yelled Cassiopia but nothing happened.

Markman grabbed her by the arm. "Core, meet us at the east entrance fast."

They hurried to the stairwell.

For Cassiopia the ride was excruciating. It seemed to take forever despite Core's superhuman pace. When finally they pulled onto Griffith Drive and stopped in front of the Taslam Industries Building she already had the door open and one foot out. Markman had to jump out and sprint to catch up to her. From the corner of his eye he saw Core close its own doors and pull around the building to park.

In the greeting area the guard behind the security desk seemed to be expecting them and barely managed to wave them in before they'd passed by. The elevator doors were mercifully open. Cassiopia tapped the bottom-most button repeatedly until the doors closed. The elevator began its deep descent. After a minute or so there was braking and the car began its sideward motion. Finally, there was a full stop and the doors slid open.

The futuristic garden environment was of no concern to Cassiopia; the sound of running water, the faint colored lighting of no comfort. She stepped out and turned to the right to find John Paul standing there waiting. His compassionate expression gave no clue to the Professor's condition.

Cassiopia stood, too afraid to ask if her father was alive. She decided to proceed on the assumption he was. "Where is he, John Paul?"

"Come with me," was the answer.

He led the way down the extravagantly beautiful hallway. The soft green carpet was faintly illuminated. Transparent walls were almost hidden by small colorful trees and plants. The ceiling was sky blue with clouds which moved very slowly. Cassiopia struggled to hold back her tears.

John Paul spoke as they walked, trying to keep the trio at a reasonable pace. "We have him in an incubator, Cassiopia. He will be all right but will be with us for several weeks of recovery."

"How bad is his injury?" she asked.

"It was a blow to the head but strangely enough our doctors do not think it was meant to kill. The injury was amplified by his fall to the floor. But as I've said, he will be all right."

"What kind of damage was there?"

"A moderate laceration to the skull, internal bleeding and of course some dangerous inflammation of the brain, all of which has been dealt with. It is fortunate the two of you found him. It would not have been so manageable had he remained untreated."

A touch of anger flavored Cassiopia's tone, "John Paul, why didn't you bring me here with him?!"

John Paul stopped at the entrance to the treatment room. "Cassiopia, you already know the answer to that. Teleportation can be dangerous to humans without extensive and difficult training. You would probably have been stunned by the transfer for longer than it took you to drive here. More likely in your panic state there may have been psychological damage which would have had to be corrected. In your father's case he was unconscious and therefore immune to many of the dangers and since it was a medical emergency, transporting him was the only choice."

"But you transported those men with him?"

"Cassiopia, those individuals are not human." John Paul gave a sympathetic nod, turned and entered the treatment room.

The medical center was just as alien and beautiful. John Paul led them through several sterile rooms bordered by translucent glass walls. Markman began to suspect they were not real walls but rather some form of projected barrier that carried moving colored light within. Some rooms had levitated equipment, others housed exam platforms which also floated in the air.

Finally, John Paul paused and spoke directly to Cassiopia. "You can't speak with him yet. It would be better if you did not try. We want complete serenity during this phase. We do not want any form of excitement to manifest within his mind. We do not want him to engage the speech centers of the brain. Do you understand, Cassiopia?"

"Yes, I understand."

In the treatment room they came to a large glass enclosed chamber. Inside it the Professor, dressed in pure white scrubs, floated on his back. His eyes were closed. An electronic device was attached to his head covering the wound. As they stood watching the Professor moved one arm and hand and placed it on his upper leg. Cassiopia looked at John Paul for an explanation. John Paul smiled and nodded it was okay.

When an appropriate amount of time had passed John Paul gestured toward the exit. He led the pair back out into the hallway.

Cassiopia, somewhat calmed, began to ask, "John Paul...."

"Let's go to my office, first. It's not far."

A short distance through the maze of surreal architecture brought the trio to a wide door closed off by sparkling silver light. John Paul walked through it and his compatriots followed.

John Paul's office was as brilliant as everything else except the furnishings were much more conventional. His big oak desk sat on heavily carved legs. His chair was a red buttoned leather office chair as were the visitor chairs around it. Old oil paintings covered the faintly lighted tan walls. Spotlights shone on each though no lights were to be seen anywhere. There were small trees here and there bearing different colors of fruit and large plants with multicolored varied blossoms. A fireplace with a sizeable fire was located against one wall though no heat could be felt coming from it. John Paul chose a very comfortable looking easy chair near it and motioned the others to sit with him.

When all were seated John Paul stared at the fire for a moment, gave a long sigh and said, "Well, here we go, my friends."

Cassiopia did not wait. "John Paul, when will I be able to speak with him? He and I had a terrible argument when we last spoke. I didn't do anything wrong but I feel terrible I didn't talk it out with him before this."

"A few days, my dear friend," replied John Paul. "By then he should be completely coherent with no loss of memory."

Markman suddenly felt anger wash over him. "John Paul, do we have any idea who did this?"

John Paul's head slowly turned to look directly at Markman. His expression suggested surprise. "Thank you so much, Scott. With all that's going on you just made me feel quite wonderful for just a moment."

"I don't understand." replied Markman.

"You said '*We*,' Scott. '*We!*' You might have said, '*Do you have any idea who did this, John Paul?*' In asking me if we have any idea who did this you've clearly shown you now really consider the three of us to be a team. That makes me feel very, very good."

Markman thought for a moment. He and Cassiopia had originally become part of the Celestial Order on a temporary basis to see if it was something they really could believe in. Suddenly he realized he couldn't imagine not being a part of whatever this was. Somehow his outlook for the future had changed significantly. He looked at Cassiopia. She stared back with the same look of realization. No words were needed. He could feel it. They had both committed to the organization.

John Paul reached into a side pocket of his chair and drew out a Meerschaum pipe. He packed it with tobacco from a bowl next to his seat then lit the pipe with an odd-looking, very old lighter with two cannon barrels carved into the round handle. When the lighting was complete he stopped for a moment and looked up at his friends. "Do either of you mind this?"

Markman shook his head. Cassiopia said, "I love it."

John Paul nodded his thanks and drew on the pipe. The aroma was pleasant. "Your question Scott was, *'Do we have any idea who harmed the Professor.'* The answer is we know exactly who did this."

Cassiopia squirmed in her seat. "Who? Who would do this terrible thing to my father?"

"That, Cassiopia, is a long story."

"And how did they get in the house without your systems detecting them?" asked Markman.

"No one broke into the house, Scott. That's why no one was detected."

Both Cassiopia and Markman stared in confusion.

John Paul grasped his pipe in both hands. "I really don't quite know where to begin on this so I'll just dive in head first. This is all about your Father's prototype, Cassiopia. Perhaps it was unwise for us not to monitor his work more closely even though he always demands strict privacy. He got himself into trouble once before by opening a doorway to another dimension. We should have considered any new work could become equally dangerous. I am still second guessing myself on this but either way here it is; your Father was building a prototype for a biological android robot. Robot is probably an inappropriate term here. There really is no Earth title yet assigned to what he was creating. When his prototype was found to be missing the Professor called me and through his private network link began relaying his project data. I was on the phone with him almost all night learning about it."

Cassiopia asked, "You're saying he was building a new robot? And did you say something about it being biological?"

"Yes. So advanced it used laboratory brain cells in the chest cavity for interaction with the outside world. Professor Cassell apparently spent months in his lab growing those cells in a special incubator containing a million or so electrical filaments smaller than human hairs. Because of this new sensory design the thing even had simulated skin on its hand and feet; skin set up with thousands of sensors designed to act like nerves in human skin. According to your father, this project came about because he wanted to transfer the evolving programming in his TEL robot into the new body to give it more human capabilities. That was his ultimate goal."

"So back to how it was stolen." said Markman. "That's the part which bothers me the most."

"It was not stolen, Scott. The prototype was still not complete, but months ago it was far enough along the professor needed to activate it to test its base systems and make any modifications needed. But after the activation process was complete the prototype did not function. It had power to all systems, the software was completely operational, everything seemed correct but there was no animation and not even any voice recognition. He could talk to the robot's programming on his primary support computer, but the prototype itself would not respond to any commands or external stimulus. It frustrated him to no end and the problem persisted for weeks. We interrupted the ongoing dilemma when we called your father in to help us."

Cassiopia interrupted. "But if no one broke in and took the prototype...."

"Yes, Cassiopia. I can tell you have intuitively already answered your own question but now you're hoping I'll give you some other explanation. I'm sorry to say, while your father was away helping us apparently the thing simply got up and left on its own."

Chapter 13

Cassiopia and Markman sat in stunned silence trying to process what they'd just been told.

Markman looked at Cassiopia. "Your ghost?"

Cassiopia's eyes widened. "It can't be!"

John Paul took stern notice of the implications. "What are you two talking about?"

After a silent exchange Markman answered, "She's been waking up at night hearing things. Last night she thought she saw someone in the hallway but it was so dark she couldn't be sure."

"Exactly what did you see?" asked John Paul.

"It was just a dark form at the far end of the hall. It was a vague outline in the darkness. But I thought it was someone in a long coat and Dick Tracy styled hat. It was taller than my father."

Markman added, "I went right out and searched but there was nothing. John Paul, if it was real why didn't your intrusion systems see this thing?"

"It's a machine, Scott. A machine with a human brain. That's not enough biology to pick up on scans. Up to now the thing has been able to go anywhere it wants and we wouldn't see it. I have a group working on a way to search for it but for now it's just like any other machine, except we have no way of knowing what affect a biological brain will have on an advanced computer like this one."

"Its brain," asked Cassiopia. "What functions does that perform?"

"According to your father there is a bank of BIOS circuits integrated around the brain. The brain receives all sensory information. The BIOS circuits help it determine how to interpret those signals. That's the simplest way I can describe what your father told me before he was injured."

Markman raised his hand. "Obviously I don't get all of that but are you saying this machine senses everything with a human kind of brain and then computer circuits tell it what to feel?"

Cassiopia answered, "Scott, computers don't feel, not like we do anyway. In this case the brain matter would sense everything but basically the computer circuits would handle how all the sensory input is handled."

"The brain wouldn't feel any emotions? Are you sure?" asked Markman.

Cassiopia looked to John Paul for support. He stared back with a stolid look.

Cassiopia said, "John Paul, how extensive a knowledge base has my father given this prototype so far?"

John Paul shook his head. "A great deal, downloaded from previous robotics development. But on top of that this prototype has complete access to the World Wide Web. It can instantly get answers to any questions it has. I'm afraid this machine has an almost unlimited knowledge base."

"What does it want?" asked Markman.

"What do you mean?" replied John Paul.

"What is the thing doing? What does it want?"

Cassiopia answered. "Computers don't *want* anything, Scott. They're just machines. This prototype is trying to fulfill its programming, whatever that is. Do we have the machine's primary code, John Paul?"

John Paul nodded, "Professor Cassell was very thorough in documenting his work. He named the code base, 'To Serve Man.' It was supposed to set the stage for a very altruistic servant to man."

"To serve man? Where have I heard that one before?" said Markman skeptically.

"Then you also have a video diary of this work?" asked Cassiopia.

"Yes," replied John Paul and he swiveled his chair to face a section of wall. A large display screen appeared. On it appeared an image of a white, lab-jacketed Professor Cassell adjusting the camera angle. Cassell narrated, *"Okay, day one-seventy-six. Perambulating evaluation twenty-one. I still do not know why the system refuses to initiate. This test will introduce artificial external stimulus in an attempt to impel specific systems responses."*

With that the Professor shifted the camera over and adjusted it for a full frame view of his prototype. Cassiopia and Markman sat silently, awestruck by the sight.

On-screen before them was a six-foot android robot like none they had ever seen. Its feet lacked digits but otherwise looked human, covered by a flesh-colored material that went up just above the ankles. From there the structure became tubular struts which Cassiopia suspected were made from nanotube technology. Within the struts were some type of material which seemed to represent artificial fibro-muscle. The strut assembly led up to complex motorized knee joints complete with transparent kneecaps and above those were more nanotube struts and fibro-muscle attached to a shiny, gunmetal colored metallic hip assembly that concealed the mechanics within. Alongside hung robot hands covered with the same simulated skin up to just beyond the wrist area. Tubular struts again connected extremely complex elbow motor assemblies. The same struts, simulated muscle, fiber optics and white hydraulic tubes connected the shoulder assembly. The robot's stomach and chest area were a bundled maze of tubes, wires and fiber lines. A solid gold-plated panel covered the chest area, suggesting greater protection had been intended there. Some form of translucent corrugated material enclosed the neck above which sat a sinister-looking metallic skull-shaped head which glinted like chrome in the laboratory light. The face was partially covered by synthetic skin, leaving gaps that revealed more fiber optic and hydraulic tube lines packed into tight bundles. There was a mouth with simulated gray metal teeth, small holes where a nose could have been and round multi-lensed eyes surrounded by infrared emitters that glowed red. The face stared straight ahead, lifeless.

Cassiopia tried to contain a gasp.

Markman shook his head in disbelief.

John Paul gave them enough time to adjust then shut off the video and spoke. "Most of the body was manufactured by outside companies then assembled by Professor Cassell. They are all state of the art, paid for by us as we supported the Professor's work without question. So, there is no way of knowing exactly how extensive the machine's capabilities are. None of this has been tested in this kind of application. Beyond that the computer system that governs this thing is a completely unknown element. We are studying Professor Cassell's documentation but it is so extensive it has to be done by several people then combined into summation presentations. And even then, who can explain how a system like this will behave?"

Finally, Cassiopia spoke. "It's ghastly," she said. Her friends tried to look unmoved.

John Paul replied, "It would not have been, Cassiopia, had the Professor been allowed to complete his work. His plans were to cover the body entirely in simulated skin all with sensory capability. Apparently the Professor's skin and sensory system can detect touch, pressure and temperature, each evaluated by the brain. It would have been the perfect system to interact with humans and human environments."

Markman asked, "So are we absolutely sure this thing wasn't stolen somehow? Doesn't that seem more likely than the thing just taking off on its own?"

"There's a very old saying left to us by a very great writer, Scott: '*When you have eliminated the impossible, whatever remains, however improbable, must be the truth.*'"

Markman persisted. "But where could something that looks like that go? It would cause a panic everywhere." Markman suddenly sat up straight and looked at Cassiopia. "Hey, wait a minute! You told me a while back your father was mad because he couldn't find his raincoat, boots, and hat, right?"

A look of realization came over Cassiopia. "It couldn't be...."

"When did that happen?" asked John Paul.

"It was at least a couple weeks ago," replied Markman.

"Oh no," said Cassiopia and she shook her head in dismay.

John Paul's expression became more concerned. "If that's true it could mean this machine has been taking trips without your father's knowledge even before he came here to help on the stalled project."

"But you said he couldn't get the thing to work," said Markman.

A moment of silence passed among the three.

Markman spoke, "Are you guys saying that while the Professor was still working on this thing it pretended not to work and then took off when nobody was around?"

John Paul leaned back and bit down on his pipe.

Markman added, "Well, if all that's true John Paul, how do we go about locating it?"

"Possibly by scanning for the internal frequencies it's using, along with an amplified scan spectrum to search for something the size of a small brain associated with those frequencies. But even for us it will be a needle in a haystack."

A new look of worry came over Markman. "John Paul, the murders that have been going on, they were all from blows to the head...."

John Paul shook his head. "An impossible idea, Scott. To connect an android robot with a series of unsolved murders sixty or more miles away, there's just too many obstacles to overcome in that reasoning to make the connection feasible."

Still skeptical, Markman asked, "If this thing was making trips even before the Professor left that means it was going and coming. How could it get in and out of the house without being seen?"

"Are there passageways in the house you haven't told us about?" asked Cassiopia.

John Paul gave a tired sigh. "I emailed the two of you the complete drawings for the mansion. Have either of you looked at them?"

The pair returned guilty looks.

John Paul continued, "There are several connecting passageways that are hidden, along with small secret storage rooms. You should take some time and familiarize yourself with those. They could be of use at some point in the future."

"Is there a secret way out of the place?" asked Markman.

"Not to my knowledge."

"Scott and I are assigned to this case, aren't we, John Paul? I mean, in finding and recovering this prototype?"

"Yes, Cassiopia. I was working up a mission for you two on a corporate espionage case with unusual overtones but we'll put that on hold for now since you're both already so deeply involved in this. But there's really nothing to do at the moment. As soon as scanning or programming analysis gives us a lead I will forward it to you. In the meantime, you're to keep a close eye out in case the prototype returns to its place of origin. Your father was trying to recall it using the internet when he was attacked. Maybe that will still work at some point. And, as always, if you come up with something or remember something that could help us let me know right away. There may not be any real danger from this situation apart from some poor civilian being frightened to death by a runaway robot. Let's hope we contain this before anything like that happens."

"I can begin studying my father's work right away," said Cassiopia. "Can you send me what you have, John Paul?"

"The Professor has told us how to remotely unlock his computers. We've already done that and everything is available to you in his downstairs lab."

"And you'll contact me the moment I can speak to him, right?"

"Yes, Cassiopia. I assure you, he'll make a full recovery. Let us hope his injury was somehow an accident or at least an isolated incident of programming glitch by a robot that did not know what it was doing."

Markman held his tongue, and his doubt.

Chapter 14

The following morning Markman found Cassiopia in her father's project room, chin in the palm of her hand, her tired eyes staring at a computer monitor. He sat and rolled his chair over to her, looked at the incomprehensible computer code slowly scrolling on the screen and quickly abandoned any hope of trying to decipher it.

"Finding anything?" he asked.

"Are you kidding? There's so much here it will take weeks just to sort the sections out."

"Well, anything interesting?"

"I've found the section of deleted recall code."

"The what?"

"I'm looking at the robot's programming. There's a section here that tells it to return to the lab immediately if a recall code is sent. These lines of code must have been deleted from the robot somehow. This is what my father was trying to use when he was attacked."

"There's no other way to recall it?"

"You don't understand, Scott. The prototype itself must have deleted that section of code then updated its own version to not include it. So the recall no longer exists within the prototype's programming. Because of that, I have no access to the prototype's onboard programming. Get it?"

"What if the recall code did work?"

"What are you talking about?"

"The robot was here when it attacked your father, right? What if your father did recall it and when it got here it whacked him on the head, changed its programming so no more recalls could be made, then left again?"

Cassiopia grimaced and struggled to find a flaw in Markman's logic, then stuttered when she could not. "I... I don't like that scenario."

"So maybe the robot had a reason to whack those other people on the head too."

The suggestion angered Cassiopia. "Those murders were too far away, Scott. That's a terrible thing to suggest about something my father created."

"Sorry. I slipped into detective mode there for a second. Is there any stuff that might show where the thing goes when it's not here?"

"Maybe. There could be clues in its interpretation of its programming. But who knows what that might be?"

"You still think it goes in and out one of the entrances around here without being seen?"

"If it was at night it might be able to do that, right?"

"The TEL is always on duty, isn't it? Wouldn't the TEL have picked up on it approaching or leaving?"

"Yeah, you're right. Even at night Tel would have sounded the alarm about something in the house. But John Paul said there's no other entrances and I've searched this place thoroughly looking for my father's work. I've never seen any other way out."

"Isn't there anywhere you didn't look?"

"No way. I was determined."

Markman thought for a moment. "What about the old spider-filled closet down here. Didn't you say you wouldn't go in there?"

"Yes, but I looked. It's just a storage closet. It's jammed full of old, useless stuff."

Markman stood.

"Where are you going? You're not actually going in there are you?"

Markman paused at the door. "Offensive weaponry needed first. Brooms and flashlights." He disappeared around the corner.

Cassiopia was waiting at the storage closet door when he returned. The old door was heavy and creaky. It opened to a dark cavernous chamber. Markman had put on janitor's coveralls and on top of those a hooded windbreaker with the hood pulled up and tightened. His spelunking headlamp was strapped to his forehead shining brightly. He carried a broom in one gloved hand and a second light in the other. Cassiopia smirked and tried not to laugh out loud. She forgot herself for just a moment and struggled not to discourage the brave soul heading into harm's way.

Markman repositioned his hood lower, turned on the handheld flashlight to add to the light of his headlamp, then positioned the broom like a knight about to make a jousting charge. He stepped in and furiously waved his broom lance.

As light filled the cobwebbed filled room Cassiopia's curiosity overcame her repulsion for crawly things. Crouched down she came up behind Markman and watched over his left shoulder, ready to run if eyes in the dark presented headline-making danger.

The place was loaded with old tools, parts, and rags. They filled the cobweb shelves on either side. Markman courageously waved his broom as he went, whether it seemed called for or not. Cassiopia kept one hand on his shoulder to avoid getting out of line.

The storage room turned out to be surprisingly deep. It became more a hallway than a closet. At one point, Markman turned and looked back over Cassiopia to find the entrance far enough away that it was somewhat unsettling. But as he regrouped to continue ahead he spotted something in the headlamp's beam that stopped him in his tracks.

"I don't believe it!" he exclaimed.

"What?" replied Cassiopia as she brushed off her hair.

"Look," answered Markman and he dusted his broom against a barrier of some kind.

He handed Cassiopia his handheld light and brushed at the obstacle blocking the path. In the beams of the two lights stood a very old wooden door with a crude thumb latch.

"Do you see how old this thing is?" asked Markman.

"It has to be from whatever was here before the mansion," answered Cassiopia. "But what could possibly be in there?"

"Only one way to find out."

Markman stepped forward and thumbed the latch. Surprisingly, the door swung open easily.

"Look," said Markman as he pointed his headlamp at his glove. "Not a speck of dust or dirt. Someone has opened this door before us and recently."

Cassiopia aimed her light beyond the open door but detail was difficult to make out.

"Be careful," she said, as Markman eased through the opening.

Scanning the lights into the newly discovered passage the explorers found an old planked hallway before them. The floor, ceiling, and walls were worn, dirty boards loosely fitted together. Markman tested the floor and proceeded on.

The short walkway took a ninety-degree turn to the left. Another short section went right. There were cobwebs along the way but none on the path of travel. A short distance beyond the last turn another a much heavier door blocked the way. It was embedded in a rock wall.

"I don't believe it," said Markman.

"It's an entrance to a mine?" asked Cassiopia.

Markman nodded. "You didn't make the climb up the rusty rung ladder when we were down in the caves. This is the door I found down there. Can you believe we were looking up at a door that led into our house and we didn't know it?"

In the shadowy light Cassiopia looked worried and skeptical.

"A deadbolt high and low," said Markman. "But they're both unlatched now." He looked back at Cassiopia with an ominous stare. "How did that happen, I wonder?" He tugged at the heavy door and pulled it open to reveal a large, dark interior in rock. Immediately a low, mournful moan echoed from within. Cold air flowed past them.

"I don't believe it," said Cassiopia. "That's the moaning that's been waking me up at night."

"So that explains it," replied Markman. "Wind from the caves. It must have been from the android coming and going."

"It could still be down there," suggested Cassiopia.

"Maybe," suggested Markman.

"But the door was left unlocked so at least we know it's not hiding somewhere in the house," added Cassiopia.

"What makes you so sure?"

"Well, wasn't the door bolted shut when you climbed up to it from the cave?"

"Yes."

"But now it's unlocked which means it went out and left it unlocked."

Markman considered the suggestion. "Maybe."

"And if it's still been coming back here, where does it hide now that my father's lab is open? We need to look at the hidden places in the house John Paul mentioned."

"Okay, now that idea's a little scary. Do we latch the door shut so he can't get back in or do we leave it unlatched?"

Cassiopia nodded. "We need to leave it unlocked."

"Because?" asked Markman.

"First, so it doesn't know we've found its entrance. And second, John Paul will want to set up a trap to capture it."

Markman nodded. "Okay, unlatched it is." He pulled the big door closed and together they retreated to the lab.

"I'll make the call," said Cassiopia. Her phone was already in her hand. John Paul answered almost immediately. Cassiopia switched him to speakerphone.

"Just a minute, Cassiopia," said John Paul. "I'm in a meeting. Let me step out."

A few seconds later, John Paul resumed the conversation. "Is this high priority, Cassiopia? My meeting involves some unusual people. I could call you back as soon as it's concluded."

"You're on speaker phone, John Paul. We've found where the prototype is leaving and entering the house."

"Really? An entrance not shown on the floor plan?"

"The old closet in the lab. It appears to be from before the mansion was built. It has a backdoor that leads down to the caves."

"You just qualified for the high priority call status. I'm shocked. I had no idea. It must be very old architecture. Was there any sign of the prototype?"

"We know he's used the passageway and door. He's left and hasn't returned yet. We didn't go back down into the caves to look."

"Good. Please do not go looking for it. We have analyzed some of its operational capabilities. It is doubtful you could subdue it or even escape from it if it became hostile. It is a powerful machine. Do you understand?"

"Yes. I certainly do," replied Cassiopia and she gave Markman a warning stare.

"We expect the thing can run at speeds up to thirty to thirty-five miles an hour. It has arm and grip strength well beyond that of a human. What I will do right now is order a special satellite to be moved into position to scan and map those caves. An ops team will be deployed to enter the caves and search. They will have EMP and other specialized weapons to stop the thing without destroying it. We need it intact so we can understand what went wrong and what the consequences might have been. Are you guys still with me?"

"Yes, John Paul," replied Cassiopia. She looked over at Markman. He raised an eyebrow.

"And you, Scott? I'd like to hear you say you will not attempt to find this thing," asked John Paul.

"I understand," replied Markman.

"Neither of you is to confront it under any circumstances. We have no doubt now that it did strike the Professor. If you do come across it you are to retreat and protect yourself in every possible way including destroying the prototype if necessary. Is that clear?"

"Yes, John Paul," repeated Cassiopia.

"Do you have any other info, Cassiopia?"

"Only that I've found the recall section of code that was deleted from the prototype's resident programming. I have to believe the prototype modified its own programming somehow."

"That's probably the only reason it returned to the mansion," said John Paul. "Professor Cassell must have tried to stop it from leaving and that's when the assault took place. We still think it did not intend to kill the Professor but clearly it is a very dangerous rogue at this point."

"John Paul, we left that door unlocked so it can get back in. We thought maybe you'd want to set something up to trap it."

"Already doing that as we speak, Cassiopia. I'm texting the engineering group to have force fields set up down there which can only be triggered by active robotics. Don't do anything else. Just lock down the basement area and stay out of it until further notice. A team will show up to take over down there."

"How is my Father, John Paul?"

"They are keeping him in stasis for the time being. He's stable and in no danger. I'll let you know when they plan to wake him."

"What else can we do now?" asked Cassiopia.

"Stand by while the caves are being searched. When that's done, if the prototype hasn't been recovered I'll call you in for a briefing to begin a wider search phase."

"In that case I'm going back to code work in the conference room."

"Reinforcements will arrive shortly and I'll talk to you both soon," said John Paul.

Cassiopia hung up and looked at Markman with an expression of doubt.

Markman folded his arms and raised an eyebrow. "Well that didn't put my mind at ease. How about you?"

"We'd better lock up here and wait upstairs," replied Cassiopia.

"Yeah, and hope they get here before it does," said Markman. Cassiopia wrinkled her brow in concern.

Chapter 15

A strange conglomerate of men dressed in unearthly black special ops gear converged on the mansion. They spoke only when absolutely necessary and even then in strange, low tones which seemed to possess a mechanical component that tickled the ears.

Two of them set up force field barriers In the basement lab while seeming to wish onlookers Cassiopia and Markman would leave the area, which they did not. Half a dozen others proceeded through the mine shaft door with arrays of equipment strapped to their bodies. They did not return.

Back at the breakfast nook Cassiopia's discontent was bothering her too much. "Well, that was all kinds of spooky don't you think?"

Markman sat back with his coffee mug and spoke as he lifted it to his lips. "You noticed too?"

"I'm going to call John Paul."

Once again John Paul answered quickly. "Yes, Cassiopia. Something new?"

"John Paul, Scott is here with me. I have you on speaker phone again. Those men have finished up downstairs."

"Yes, I know. Also, it appears that the prototype is not in the caverns. There is evidence of his having been there but no indications he plans to return."

"Any news about my father?"

"His condition is unchanged. He remains in no danger. We do have some additional info on the prototype and it is most distressing."

"Please tell me."

"It's about the first purse that Scott found. It belongs to one of your neighbors, an elderly lady just a few parcels away from you."

"Oh no! Was she attacked?"

"No, no. Let me finish. Her purse and car were stolen recently. She had left the purse in her car but locked the doors. The vehicle has still not been recovered. It was an older model silver Infinity Q50."

"Are you saying the prototype took her car? That's crazy!"

"As it happens Cassiopia, that vehicle is one of the most hackable cars in production. We have to consider the prototype, having complete access to the internet, opened that car using an internet connection. Whether or not the thing could actually drive it remains to be seen but we can't rule that out yet. We are scanning the area around you in a wide radius in hopes we'll find it on foot maybe in the woods somewhere."

"So is there anything for us to do?"

"Just keep studying the code, Cassiopia. I'll keep you updated."

Markman cut in, "We're waiting as fast as we can, John Paul."

"Well, be careful what you wish for, Scott. You may get pulled into this up to your neck."

John Paul hung up. Cassiopia looked at Markman hoping for reassurance. "No way a robot could just get in and drive a car."

Markman smirked. "Well, if it was a really bad driver it would probably fit right in with all the other ones out there."

After an uneasy twenty-four hours, a new text message finally came from John Paul:

Cassiopia-Scott, doctors plan to wake your father for a short period of cognizance testing. That will happen in about an hour. Please do come in. We will await your arrival before proceeding.

Thirty minutes later after a particularly fast journey prompted by Cassiopia's impatience the pair was in the Taslam Building elevator on their way down. It had been a lawbreaking drive which Markman thoroughly enjoyed. The focus had relaxed him.

"He's just been awakened," said John Paul, as they walked together toward the med lab. "His mind remains quite exceptional. The only loss of memory is that of the actual attack which injured him. The doctors were actually very positive about that. They seemed to think filling in that gap for him will be much less a shock to his system than first thought but you must choose your words very carefully if you need to address that subject. Do you both understand?"

The pair nodded appreciatively.

In the med lab the Professor was still lying in the transparent chamber. He was awake and tried to rise up excitedly at the sight of Cassiopia. She hurried to his side and looked down lovingly. The Professor returned her stare then tried to shrug off the situation. Several doctors in white lab coats stayed back, watching intently.

"Now will you let me help with your projects?" she asked jokingly.

The Professor managed a wide smile and nodded. "What happened?" he asked in a hoarse voice.

"Apparently you recalled the prototype against its wishes. There was some kind of argument and it either pushed you or struck you."

The Professor's eyes widened. He began to shake his head. "Impossible!" was his only strained reply.

"Why?" asked Cassiopia

The Professor paused to suck some water from a tube. He coughed slightly but did not lose his determination. "Its most basic programming is to serve man. I even named the primary source code exactly that; to serve man. It could not harm a human being. That is completely contrary to its programming."

"Just before you intercepted it, the thing reprogrammed itself by removing the recall program, Father."

"What?!?"

"It modified its own programming to delete the recall code."

This time there was a longer pause as the Professor stared into the distance thinking. "It can't be," he finally insisted.

"We think that over the past few weeks it was only pretending to be unresponsive, Father. Do you agree?"

"What a conundrum it was. I could always operate the various systems independently but the central core refused to engage. After a while I jokingly gave it the name 'Hector,' from an old story by John Barry about a robot that refused to speak. 'Saturn 3' I believe it was. Even entered *Hector* into the thing's programming as a prompt to respond to commands. In hindsight that may not have been such a good idea. But there could never have been any subroutines for violence. The root programming was based on protecting man. I even worked Asimov's three laws into it. If it really attacked me it had to have been a mishap somehow. I probably accidentally got in the way or something."

"Father, when you returned from working with John Paul that was when you first discovered it missing, right?"

"I'm so sorry for blaming you, Cassiopia. I know you have such an insatiable curiosity about things, especially robotics but I should not have accused you. I'm very sorry."

"Well, you remember that much. Do you recall meeting it in the lab?"

The Professor thought for a moment. He shook his head. "I went downstairs to activate the recall program. Then I began searching the programming to look for a mistake which might have caused it to leave on its own. I still believed it had been stolen but it must have been close by because then I heard noises outside the lab. I remember standing to see what the noises were. That's the last I remember."

"Why did you decide to use human biology in this prototype, Father?"

The Professor nodded almost proudly. "The best sensory system known to man, complete with short-term nearly infinite memory. Faster than any carbon-doped semiconductor or crystalline composite could ever be. A sensory system developed by God. How could that ever be surpassed?"

"But its brain, Father; does this machine actually feel?"

"Of course not. How silly of you to ask, Daughter. Those cells were grown in the lab from my own DNA. But the brain matter is not a simple organoid. It had to be much larger than that if it was to channel so many artificial epidermal sensors and other inputs. It was grown within the matrix of a million fiber neural conductors. Nevertheless, the brain is still a simple fetal organism contained in a small orb and suspended in a protein gel. The gel is replenished by a viscous mixture introduced at the mouth. So you see Daughter, these are simple fetal cells. They do not possess a soul. They are reactive, nothing more. Hector is not a sentient being. He is a robot designed to serve man."

"Father, could Hector operate a car?"

"No, no, that's ridiculous. It has the physical dexterity for that type of task but not the knowledge."

"But you said it has complete access to the internet. It could learn, could it not?"

"Daughter, it would have to *want* to drive a car to undertake something like that. I told you, this design is not sentient. It has no wants. It only has its programming and nowhere within that is a command to drive a car."

"Do you have any idea where it might go?"

"I'm sorry, Cass. I didn't have any idea it *would* go."

"Okay, but any guess of why it has chosen to travel?"

The Professor stared thoughtfully ahead but began shaking his head. "It's such a complicated process. The banks of BIOS networks are telling it how to respond to the stimuli affecting it. I'll need to think about this for a while."

From the corner of her eye, Cassiopia could see John Paul gesturing for her to retreat away from the chamber. At the same time, her father's eyes began to flutter and within seconds he was asleep. The group withdrew to the hallway.

John Paul explained, "The doctors became concerned with his stress level readouts. They initiated a sedative. You did a nice job in there, Cassiopia. That was probably the most help we could expect from this first session."

"Did you really find out anything?" asked Markman.

"We found out the prototype is not behaving at all the way the Professor expected it to. We also learned, unfortunately, perhaps it can operate a motor vehicle. And we know it seems to be acting in ways completely contrary to its programming."

"Well, none of this gives me a warm feeling," mused Markman.

John Paul ignored the comment. "Beginning tomorrow if no lead has been established we will begin a search based on the idea this machine can travel by vehicle. You two will be our civilian eyes and ears. We'll send you into locations which could be suspect. You'll carry EMP weapons along with something more damaging. Go home. Try to get some rest. You may be traveling quite a bit when this gets going."

Chapter 16

Cassiopia sat up in bed trying to read. Markman was sprawled out asleep beside her. It was difficult to focus. Her thoughts kept dropping down to the lab in the basement. The door to the cave was closed but unlocked. The entrapment force fields were in place. Tel was monitoring all entrances. John Paul's security was on standby. There could not have been more security. The mansion was likely one of the most secure buildings on Earth.

Blue light on the table clock beside the bed read 3:15 a.m. Markman began a faint snore. The air outside was cool enough that the air conditioner was not coming on, leaving a dead air silence in the room. She listened for the sound of moaning. There was none. She pulled her copy of David Copperfield up from her lap and read one line. The words blurred and her eyes fluttered and closed.

Something awoke her. Had it been the moaning? Sleep had been so heavy it was difficult to focus. As she struggled to open her eyes, the familiar faint howl far in the distance sounded. It startled her to consciousness. Once again, the telltale moan seeped through the ventilation system. Realizing what that meant she sat up and blinked her eyes.

At some point in her semi-consciousness she had turned off the reading light. The room was now cloaked in dark shadow. Was someone there? Fear shot through Cassiopia like a spear. Standing in the blackness of the open bedroom doorway was a tall, ominous figure in a long coat and hat. The eyes were a circle of dim amber red. Cassiopia began to let out a shriek but held it back with one hand over her mouth, fearing the cry might prompt the intruder to violence. With her hand over her mouth she whispered as loudly as she dared, "John Paul, emergency!

It's here!" With her free hand she shook Markman who rolled over and raised his head indignantly, "What?"

Cassiopia glanced down at him with a look that answered all of his questions. With her eyes she guided his gaze to the bedroom door.

But the figure was gone.

Although it seemed impossibly quick, the light was suddenly on and Markman was up and concealing a gun behind him. He took a single step toward the door and out of nowhere two more individuals in black combat apparel appeared in the room. One held some type of scanner and was staring intently at it. His partner brandished a strange looking short-barreled rifle. Without looking up from the scanner the first of them pointed to the right of the open door and they charged out.

Markman started to follow but stopped and looked back at Cassiopia. He came to the bedside. "Are you okay?"

Cassiopia pushed herself up. "Yes, yes but it scared me something awful."

"What did you see?"

"It was him. There was no mistake. He was still wearing my father's long coat and hat. He was looking at me in infrared. His eyes were glowing red."

Markman went to the door and looked left and right down the hallway.

Cassiopia sat up on the side of the bed and cursed. "Damn! I should have talked to it! Maybe I could have reasoned with it!"

"That didn't work too well for your father. How did it get in here without being detected? That's what I want to know."

"Oh no! The TEL!" Cassiopia pulled on a robe and pushed passed Markman. He raced with her to the balcony overlooking the main entrance where Tel stood guard.

She made a quick inspection of the robot and stood with an incredulous look on her face. "I don't believe this! He's been completely deactivated. It'll take an hour to reinitialize him."

"Well, at least we know how Hector got in, I guess."

"Scott, you don't understand. It is not easy to shut Tel completely down like this. There are contingencies to prevent a total power down. It should not have happened."

"Okay, then my next question would be why was he here? Looking for the Professor maybe?"

"Let me start the boot up for Tel then we should check downstairs."

In the basement area the Professor's lab turned out to be unchanged except the doors to the project room and the cave entrance had both been left open.

"So much for John Paul's force fields," said Markman. "We'd better take a look at the rest of the upstairs."

The double doors to the Professor's bedroom were also wide open. Markman cast a concerned stare at Cassiopia. "I think he was looking for your father. What do you think?"

"Or it wanted something my father had," replied Cassiopia.

"What would a walking computer want?" asked Markman. "Seems like I keep asking that question."

"A password maybe? Or some special subroutine code? Wait! What am I saying? A machine wouldn't *want* anything. It would have to be trying to fulfill some kind of program instruction."

"Well let's hope John Paul's team has it in custody by now. Why don't you give him a call?"

Together they returned to the bedroom. Cassiopia retrieved her phone and dialed nervously. She did not wait for him to say hello.

"John Paul, did you get it?"

"No, Cassiopia. Do you know how it gained entry?"

"The force fields had no effect and it shut down the TEL completely. Tel never even had a chance to move. The door to my father's room was opened. It may have been looking for him. How could you not have captured it?"

"It seems impossible but apparently somehow it is able to mask itself from our sensors. But I must go. The teams are still reporting in. I'll contact you soon."

John Paul disconnected.

Cassiopia looked at Markman. "Could you hear that?"

"I heard enough."

Two hours later a black SUV brought John Paul to the front entrance. Greetings were short. He wasted no time in motioning Cassiopia and Markman up to the conference room. As they took seats John Paul poured himself coffee. He looked early morning tired with a dose of stress added. He sat with them, sipped and stared into his cup. Finally, he spoke. "Our situation has become dire, my friends," he said and another drink from the cup was needed. "We did not contain Hector. We *did* locate your neighbor's stolen car. It had been forced almost a quarter mile into the woods not far from here. There was considerable damage, some of it apparently from contact with other vehicles; part of the learning curve from Hector's attempts at driving I would guess. The bad news is we also found traces of blood on the steering wheel. We were able to match the DNA to the Landers woman, the first murder victim, so that connects the prototype to at least one of the four recent murder victims."

Cassiopia gasped.

"Yes, Cassiopia. Apparently, we have a runaway machine which may have become a serial killer."

Markman interrupted. "But John Paul, how did it get through the net?"

"We have a theory about that, Scott. We're working to verify it. For the time being we have to assume it knows what we know. Our pursuit will be difficult. If it could fool our security scans that way we have to assume it can somehow cloak itself."

"Is there any way to track the thing?" replied Markman.

"Only by logic, recent history, probability and guesswork."

"So we have nothing," added Markman.

"We have the murders, Scott. As both Cassiopia and the Professor have repeatedly stated, machines do not act on impulse. They act in a logical progression. If we can cull the commonalities of those crimes they should give us a direction and a reason. We are, of course, already working on that. As for the recent history evidence and guesswork, that's right up your alley now, Scott. I'll have every scrap of evidence uploaded to your laptop. Cassiopia, your talents are best served continuing to evaluate Hector's programming. Work up a profile, a personality if you will. Help us to know what it will do before it does."

Cassiopia remained speechless. Markman seemed equally at a loss for words.

John Paul stood. "I must get back to headquarters. We'll keep our lines of communication open day and night. I don't need to tell you how serious this is even beyond the crimes that have been committed. It may be our organization is responsible for interfering with human society on a scale I would not have believed possible. All our efforts to remain invisible while we protect society seem to have been circumvented somehow. You must both be extremely careful but I doubt the thing will return here. If it was searching for the Professor as Cassiopia suggested it must know he is no longer here. We will continue to blanket the premises with a different form of electronic screening. We will also keep this property under twenty-four hour manned surveillance."

John Paul paused for a moment to share an expression of sobriety with his friends. He turned and left.

After a few minutes of burdened silence Markman tried to temper the moment. "So... what just happened again?"

Cassiopia rested one elbow on the table and buried her face in her hand. She began to shake her head.

"At least we have a mission. Track down and stop that thing. Right?" he added.

Cassiopia continued to stare down without responding.

"Come on. What's the problem? We'll find the thing. We're good at what we do."

Cassiopia finally looked up at him with wet eyes. She shook her head. "Don't you understand, Scott? My father built a machine that is killing people!"

Markman stiffened. He had not considered the moral implications until now. He tried to sound consoling. "Your father would never do anything to harm anyone. Something went wrong somehow. He had no idea any of this would happen."

Once again Cassiopia buried her face in her hand.

"You've got to put this away, Cass. We need to put everything we have into stopping this thing. We can't take time for second-guessing right now. Besides, we don't know why this happened. Wait for the answers before you start agonizing over this."

Cassiopia began to wipe her eyes with one hand. Finally, she nodded. "Yes, you're right. Let's get to work."

A few more silent moments and finally determination replaced doubt. There was no need even to stand. Cassiopia slid her laptop in front of her and opened it. Within the folder titled 'John Paul' she found a new icon that gave her access to her father's project computer, a link provided remotely by John Paul's people. Along with it several other new icons gave access to files and programs within John Paul's headquarters.

Markman rolled his chair over to his own laptop. New murder case icons had already appeared on his desktop. He leaned back in his chair and began with the oldest case. Something John Paul had said caused Markman to pause in surprise. The blood evidence which might connect Hector to the Ripper murders had only been discovered a few hours ago, yet John Paul's people had already gathered and transmitted this new information. At least the CO was very, very good in a crisis.

Case 1, the Kestry woman, Maria Landers:

John Paul updates on Landers' case (7/30):

The Landers woman worked at Intertrans International Shipping, a very large conglomerate with huge warehouses around the world, one of which was located in Alexandria. Landers was secretary to a Mark Furman, director of time-sensitive and controlled-substance materials management for that particular facility. II's warehouse in Alexandria is 1.2 million square feet. We have arranged for the FDA to do an informal audit of the place but obviously it will take a week or more and may not reveal anything suspicious. The company may not have any involvement with the Landers murder, innocent or otherwise.

Landers' movements and actions were routine over the past few weeks. She did not have any enemies. No judicial cases were open against her. She had not so much as a parking ticket over the past ten years. Random killing remains a prime possibility at this time.

Markman wrinkled his brow in thought. There was still almost no real forensic suspect evidence recovered except for a neighbor seeing a strange man in a long coat and hat prior to the crime. Beyond that the victim's hands were missing from the crime scene. The long coat and hat fit Hector perfectly but the neighbor had not reported red eyes like those Cassiopia had seen. There was also some new information added by John Paul's people but it only pertained to personal details about the deceased. She was a longtime secretary to the shipping and receiving manager for Dawson Chemical. She was divorced and lived alone. She belonged to several clubs, including bridge and quilting. There was no obvious reason for the attack. The suggestion that the crime might simply be random was chilling.

There were summary notes on the other three:

J.P. update Manning Case #2, (7/30):

In the case of Mr. Robert Manning, again no obvious link to the Professor or any ulterior motive can be established. Manning was a real estate agent for upscale business properties owned or leased by ConCom Holdings Inc, the company owned by real estate mogul Charles Atwater III. Manning's police record is clean. His business dealings appear to be in order. He had no obvious enemies. As with the other investigations this crime appears to be lacking a motive.

J.P. update Randolf Case #3, (7/30):
Once again we find no motive for this crime. Randolf was a member in good standing in the community and in line for promotion to the executive branch of his company. Further investigation is underway to look for any irregularities at the AMP plant. A boot print found at the scene could possibly match those worn by the prototype.

J.P. update Delam Case #4, (7/30):
Dr. Marcus Delam. 826 Delray Ave. No police report available at this time due to forensic analysis not yet complete. Victim was killed by a blow to the head similar to the other three cases. The leading theory is the assailant met him at the door while he was locking up for the night. Delam was a research scientist for Vangraph University working on a grant for cellular physiology. The assailant left a trail of disruption within the lab. There is no list of missing items yet. Delam was unmarried, forty-five years old, no police record of any kind. Unlike the other victims his body was not mutilated in any way other than the blow to the head.

END OF J.P. UPDATES

Markman sat back and exhaled. It was a fragmented trail of murders. A warehouse secretary, a real estate salesman, a plant supervisor and a doctor, one or all possibly murdered by a runaway machine with a half-human brain. There was no way to be certain they were all prototype crimes. Maybe the thing was actually innocent. There was only circumstantial evidence connecting it to just one of the murders. But if it were guilty that would be the worst possible scenario: an intelligent machine killing at random.

Markman noticed Cassiopia staring at him over her laptop monitor. "You getting anywhere?" she asked.

"Only ugly possibilities. How about you?"

"It's such beautiful code. It's like artistry. But at this point the only thing I can say is the machine won't be acting erratically or indiscriminately. It will be following its basic program objectives whatever those are."

"Great. Everything I have here fits a random pattern of violence, just the opposite of what you're saying. Why can't you follow that stuff through so it points somewhere?"

"The machine deleted its copy of the programming from John Paul's system after it updated itself. Fortunately, John Paul's people had backups of the original programming on removable drives so that stuff didn't get erased. But we have no way of knowing exactly what changes the machine made to itself or even why it made those changes."

"Can you think of a way to get from what you have to murder?"

"That's the strangest part. The code work is so beautiful. It's a gigantic loop around the theme 'To Serve Man.' There's just no way to get to violence that I've found."

"Maybe the freakin' robot is innocent."

"I'm praying."

Chapter 17

Markman began to pace idly around the conference room as Cassiopia resumed studying her laptop. She made notes on a pad as she scrolled down each screen. He looked at his wristwatch. It had been hours since John Paul's last contact. For all the readings of the case reports and updates there was still just no place to begin, especially if investigative invisibility remained a mandate.

Cassiopia looked up again and smirked, the first expression of normalcy Markman had seen in her since the events of the day past. "You're wearing out the nice floor lamination, Scott."

"There's nothing for me in these reports."

"Well, why don't you go to the counter and make us both a cappuccino with that fancy steam engine machine over there?"

"Don't know how to work it. What about you? You still haven't come up with anything?"

Cassiopia squinted in thought. "There is one thing... Oh look! An email message from John Paul. Maybe you're saved."

Markman hurried around to look. "Why didn't I get a copy?"

Cassiopia, meet me in my office immediately. Come alone.

J.P.

"Well that's weird!" remarked Cassiopia. "Why would he want me to come alone?"

"Not gonna happen," said Markman angrily.

"Let me ask him to clarify," said Cassiopia.

John Paul, why do you want me to come alone?

Nearly a minute passed with no reply. Then:

Cassiopia please acknowledge request.
J.P.

"Let *me* have a word with him," said Markman tersely. He drew out his cell phone and sent a text:

John Paul there's no way she should be traveling alone. What are you thinking?

Again a long minute passed before an answer came:

Scott, what in the devil are you talking about?

Cassiopia said, "Wait I just got another one from him."

Cassiopia please expedite previous instructions.

Markman typed:

John Paul you just emailed Cassiopia to meet you immediately and to come alone.

This time the response came much more quickly:

Scott, no such message was sent.

Markman replied:

I'm looking over her shoulder right now at her emails. They are from you with your email address in the FROM column.

Another long pause followed. John Paul at last replied in text to Markman:

Both of you stay right where you are. Tell Cassiopia to close her email immediately. Do nothing else. We're investigating. I'll get back to you as soon as possible.

Cassiopia quickly shut down her email. She looked up at Markman with a bewildered stare. "It's a hack?" she asked in disbelief. "A hack of John Paul's system? That should be impossible!"

"That's not what bothers me," answered Markman. "Who the hell is trying to get you alone somewhere?"

"I need that coffee. How about if I demonstrate the coffee maker while we wait?"

"Fine, and expect me to be to be within arm's reach of you for now on wherever you go."

Fresh coffee in hand they sat at the conference table, sipping in silence. It was a ninety-minute wait before Cassiopia's phone chirped a text message.

"It's the TCL. He says someone's coming through the front gate."

"Friend or foe," asked Markman in sarcastic humor.

"Guess we'd better go see."

They arrived at the front doors in time to see one of John Paul's black SUVs pull up. The driver opened a rear door to allow a disheveled John Paul out. He carried a closed umbrella in one hand and silver case in the other. He looked up at the pair and trotted up the steps to meet them.

"Conference room," was all he said.

In the conference room, without asking Cassiopia poured him a cup of coffee as he placed his case on the table. He leaned the umbrella against the wall and sat in time to receive the coffee. A brief appreciative glance was all there seemed to be time for.

Cassiopia interrupted as he was about to speak. "How is my father, John Paul?"

"They are extending his waking periods slowly. Because your father had a previous incident of head injury it is taking them time to revive some pathways. Obviously, it is important we preserve as much short-term memory as possible."

Cassiopia began to ask something else but John Paul held up his hand. "My friends, it seems we keep going from bad to worse." After a glance for permission from Cassiopia he pulled her laptop over and typed a few commands.

The walls around the conference room began flashing on as display screens. Each display had a different photo of Cassiopia. Most appeared to have been taken without her knowledge.

John Paul continued, "To make a long story short and to our great shock and awe, apparently Hector found a way to hack into our system to send those bogus text messages to Cassiopia." John Paul paused a moment to allow the confession to sink in. "Obviously hacking into our system would take a superhuman knowledge of networking far beyond what is typical of today's internet standards which just makes this that much more alarming." John Paul sipped his coffee, seeming to need a moment to collect himself. "The good news, if we can call it that, is we have learned a great deal more about Hector. Unfortunately, none of it is good news in itself."

As John Paul sipped again, Cassiopia could not contain her alarm. "John Paul, these pictures...."

Again John Paul held up one hand. "First things first. Cassiopia, as you well know your father spent many hours in the project room downstairs cultivating stem cells, assembling robotic segments and developing software. During that time we were in daily correspondence with him about other matters. Most recently he solved a math problem for one of our groups and then had to be brought into headquarters to help them resolve some of the derived equations. We now believe at some point, without the Professor's knowledge, Hector became self-aware and gained access to our systems using the Professor's passwords and access codes. Hector then installed multiple back doors for himself so he could never be locked out. None of us had any idea this was going on. No one ever expected a prototype to be autonomous enough to initiate that kind of creative thinking. And so I'm sure you've already guessed by now, it was Hector who used my email account to send you those bogus messages."

Markman sat up straight. "The robot? The robot told her to meet you alone?"

John Paul nodded. "Once we recognized my email had been hacked and had to force ourselves to accept it we were able to break down the data stream enough to recognize a component unique to Hector. That allowed us to expand our backtracking in many other directions. There were so many paths with the same telltale fingerprint it did not seem possible at first. Hector had accessed dozens of files and programs using speeds only a machine could. Within the agency's private memory allocations it was not surprising the Professor would have stored photos of his daughter so that alone would never have alerted us to suspicious activity. But we realized a few of the more recent photos had been downloaded during the period when the Professor was unconscious and being treated in our lab. From there other images were found to be suspicious as well and there were many."

Markman's dismay piqued. He stood. "So we have a runaway robot murdering people and at the same time collecting pictures of Cassiopia? Is that what you're saying?"

John Paul motioned him to sit. Slowly, Markman obeyed. "We'd thought perhaps Hector paid you a visit because he was looking for your father, Cassiopia. But now, finding those pictures would suggest you are of special interest to him."

Cassiopia asked, "Why does he have pictures of me?"

John Paul shook his head. "List every possible reason you can think of for a machine brain to want photos of you Cassiopia and you'll have the same list of possibilities we have. Let me ask, have either of you come up with anything new?"

Cassiopia gave a long sigh. "I may have something from the code work."

John Paul's expression became one of intense interest.

"In the core programming there is a large section outlining self-improvement. Then, in many of the outlying subroutines, that definition is often referenced as a loop. I am guessing my father made self-improvement at least equal in weight to all the other objectives within the programming. He wanted this machine to learn and improve itself as much as possible. Of course it was supposed to improve itself in terms of serving humankind, the primary mandate which obviously has become corrupted, but the self-improvement section of programming may still be intact which means we can assume the machine is trying to improve itself along with whatever else it is doing."

John Paul sat back and stared thoughtfully into the distance. He spoke almost to himself. "That might explain why it delved so deeply into our files."

"This machine's construction wasn't finished, right?" asked Markman.

"What?" responded John Paul, still lost in thought.

"You're saying the machine wants to improve itself. Well, the thing was incomplete, right? The body, I mean. Professor Cassel said something about it being tested before he finished putting it together, didn't he? What else did he have left to do to it?" added Markman.

Cassiopia finally focused on Markman's question. "Yes, yes; the frame was incomplete. The e-skin had only been installed on the hands and feet because the initial sensor map required that but eventually the entire body was to be covered in e-skin."

Suddenly John Paul realized the significance of Markman's suggestion. "You're hypothesizing Hector might want to complete his own construction?"

Markman gestured with his hands, "Instant self-improvement, ta-da!"

John Paul looked to Cassiopia. "Is it possible?"

"It would be an intricate process. Precision molds would need to be made, then chemicals to create a silicone-based polymer maybe using methyl or benzene. I'd need to look at my father's notes to know for sure," answered Cassiopia.

"Where would it go to get that stuff?" continued Markman.

"There are manufacturers all over the U.S.," replied John Paul, "And quite a few in the Washington area."

"And what equipment would the thing have to get to make what it needed?" asked Markman.

Cassiopia answered, "A pretty up-to-date laboratory for one thing."

"Didn't one of the murder victims work in a laboratory?" asked Markman.

"The first victim, the Landers woman, was a secretary to a manager of storage for time-sensitive materials," said John Paul as he stared in thought.

"Are we connecting the murders to a motive?" asked Markman and he looked at the others in a moment of fearful silence.

John Paul fumbled with his phone. His conversation was too quick and low to make out. He stood as though to rush out, then remembered the silver case on the table. He hurriedly unlatched it and drew out a dark, oval-shaped device the size of a computer mouse. It was trimmed in gold and had a gold lens at the front. He slid one across to Markman then a second one to Cassiopia.

"It's an EMP device but not like any you'll find on Earth. It'll give you four shots then it needs sixty seconds to recharge. It'll kill anything electronic up to a distance of one-hundred feet. Because it is not Earth technology, you must not lose it or let anyone else get their hands on it or that will cause yet another recovery mission. Remember, anything electronic will be killed whether it is turned on or not so be very careful of what you fry and cognizant about what else is in your line of fire. And Cassiopia, last but not least, Scott has his own armament so this is for you."

John Paul drew out a small silver handgun in a black holster. He removed the gun to show her. "This is from my personal collection, a bit of an older model but it's never been used and the grip should fit you nicely. It's only twenty-two caliber but as small as it is the clip still holds seven rounds. The holster is for your ankle. You should definitely wear this everywhere you go from now on and I'd recommend you even wear it here at home. Hector watched you from your open door the other night but he did not attempt to harm you. However, he may well have other plans for you and this little gun could end up being the only thing which stands between you and those plans. You should go out on the hillside and let Scott familiarize you with it." John Paul slid the small gun back in its holster and pushed it across the table to Cassiopia. She shirked back and looked at it like it was poison.

John Paul continued, "Sorry I can't take any more time for discussion. The task force needs to work this new line we've come up with. From this point on do not trust any transmissions from me unless you have a way to verify them. For the time being, face to face conversation is the only trustworthy method of communication. We'll keep our security fields in place around this property but we'll rely mostly on our various visual surveillance methods. I'll find ways to keep you informed. We'll meet again in my office soon."

John Paul paced out the door, leaving the empty silver case open on the table.

Markman picked up his EMP weapon and began to study it like a new toy.

Cassiopia sat eyeing her new gun and holster with aggravation and disdain.

Markman noticed her aversion. "Maybe we should take it outside right now and test it."

"I dislike guns."

"It's only a little one."

"Are there bullets?" she asked, hoping there would not be.

"Just twenty-two shorts. I have plenty. You've fired a gun before."

"Just once, kind of, with my friend Ann Rogers. But that was a little rifle."

The small rifle reference forced Markman to hide a smirk. "Okay, so I'll set up a target. It will be fun."

"No, it won't."

Thirty minutes later Markman had a cardboard target taped together in the backyard against the hillside.

He texted Cassiopia and she joined him a few minutes later looking like someone reporting to jail to begin their sentence.

"Okay, you see this little lever here, right?"

"Is it the safety?"

"Very good! Yes, it's the safety. You always want that in the on position unless you're getting ready to fire. You got that?"

"Do I got that? The gun's going to be strapped to my leg! You think I'm not going to keep the safety on?"

"Okay, okay. It sure is a beautiful pearl handle, isn't it?"

"It would be if it wasn't a gun."

"Okay, this neat little gun is semiautomatic. That means...."

"It will shoot as fast as you pull the trigger."

Markman smiled and nodded. "Right, and see this slide here at the back? You have to manually pull it back to load the first round, after that it will slide back on its own and bring another round into the chamber each time you fire."

"A who will what?"

"Watch. I'm going to pull the slide back and if you look down in there you'll see a bullet come up to be loaded." Markman held the weapon out and held the slide back long enough for her to see. "Got it?"

"Yes."

"Now that a bullet is loaded the gas from when it's fired will automatically push the slide back and load the next bullet. Still with me?"

"That's interesting."

"Okay, but now there's a bullet in the gun's chamber so it's ready to fire. And it's time to be very careful. Guns have a way of going off when you least expect it."

"Tell me about it."

"So here, take your gun and point it at the target."

"Why'd you have to make the target look like the silhouette of a man?"

"That's a six-foot silhouette about the size of Hector. That's what you'll be shooting at. Cass, always keep the gun pointed at the ground and your finger outside the trigger guard until you're ready to fire, okay?"

"Okay."

"Now, one foot slightly forward and your weight mostly on that front foot."

"But the target's only ten feet away. This is no good. I can't miss."

"Cass, my love, you have seven rounds in your gun's clip. You will probably empty the clip and not hit that cardboard once."

"Really?"

"Okay, you know the gun is going to jump in your hand each time you fire, so fire three shots in a row then pause for a second to focus and fire the next three. Ready?"

"I guess."

"Okay, go ahead."

After a prolonged delay of shifting weight and adjusting head position Cassiopia finally settled on a two-hand grip and intense wince on her face.

A loud bang, bang, bang, echoed off the hillside. The target remained unscathed. Three more bang, bang, bangs and the target was still free of assault. Finally, with a grunt of annoyance, Cassiopia squeezed off the last shot.

Markman stared in surprise. There in the center chest area of the target was a new, well-placed bullet hole. Cassiopia appraised it with satisfaction.

"Wow! Where did that last shot come from!?" asked Markman.

Cassiopia lowered the gun so that it pointed at the ground. "I am woman."

"Okay, wow!" repeated Markman. "I am impressed!"

Seven clips later, Cassiopia was hitting the target sixty percent of the time. Markman was satisfied. The pair returned to the conference room to resume studying their respective data.

Markman's energized detective mind went back to work. If any of his previous hypotheses were correct it meant new avenues of guesswork were now available. If the Landers woman could be connected through her management of storage facilities and the Randolf and Marcus murders were both somehow related to chemical work, that left only Manning, the real estate salesman and his was one of the most gruesome of all the murders.

John Paul's update had listed ConCom Holdings as Manning's employer. They specialized in business properties. An initial online search showed many business buildings all over the world either represented by or owned by ConCom Holdings. There were a dozen in the Washington and Fredericksburg area alone but nothing was shown to indicate what kind of businesses had occupied those buildings before being put on the market.

Google Maps satellite view offered a few of the answers. They displayed old, out of date names for some of the properties. One had been a large car dealership. Another had been a fruit distribution factory. That narrowed the investigation down to ten properties. Plugging those addresses into Google more outdated listings came up. Most did not seem significant. When all possible leads had been exhausted Markman was left with four reasonably close business properties still for sale he could not categorize. Fatigue was setting in. He uploaded his four unidentified properties to his cell phone and closed out his laptop. A quick glance showed Cassiopia with one elbow on the table, her chin resting in the palm of one hand, eyes half closed.

"I'm bushed. You ready to call it a day?" he asked.

"I'm so tired I'll probably be able to actually sleep."

"Should I carry you or can you walk?"

"I got another email from John Paul; that is if it's really him. He wants me to come in to his office tomorrow afternoon to help with some programming stuff. He says you can bring me in but you don't have to hang around if you don't want to. You'd just be bored by all the code talk. It sounds like a real John Paul message."

"Well, we can take the long way around to avoid any ambushes and we'll know how real it is when we get there."

"You know, at least there haven't been any more murders the past couple of days, thank God. If it really is Hector maybe he's finished with that."

"I wouldn't bet the farm on it."

Chapter 18

After a restless night, Markman delivered Cassiopia to the CO underground facility. So far it had been a mercifully uneventfully day.

As they exited the elevator, an odd-looking man wearing a frayed Steven Tyler T-shirt and wrinkled lab coat went speeding by but upon seeing Cassiopia stopped so abruptly he nearly fell over. "Oh, oh! Ms. Cassell, please; I'm Perseus Haiden. Your father was working with us. I'd been hoping to meet you at some point." Haiden's hair was as amiss as the rest of him. He stuck out a hand and took Cassiopia's in a stunted handshake. "I'm so glad your father is recovering nicely. And, oh! You must be Markman. Glad to meet you, too. Well, I'm late. If I can do anything for either of you please let me know."

Markman had to bite his lower lip to stop from snickering at the funny little man. Before either he or Cassiopia could return any greeting the speedy Perseus was on his way.

John Paul appeared beside them and smiled. "He's actually too smart for his own good." He led the pair along a path they had not taken before to the entrance of an oddly shaped room, one which resembled a church-styled dome with a large circular opening of white light overhead. Doors slid closed behind them. In the center of the chamber, seats around a circular floating tabletop turned automatically to become more accessible. The trio sat close to one another.

John Paul spoke, "This is our most secure room. Theoretically there can be no eavesdropping here. Some of my associates jokingly refer to this as the cone of silence. But to get down to business, we need a temporary verification code for our email transmissions. Back in the civil war we used a very simple system that should work for us in this situation. I will give you a verification code number. To begin with that number will be 54. When each of us sends a message we will count the number of letters in the first sentence of the message, subtract that number from 54 and put the resulting number at the end of the message with two random digits tacked onto the end of it. Not to insult your intelligence but for example, if I send you a message that has say ten letters in the first sentence, I would type the number 44 with two additional random numbers after it. If you do not see the correct code numbers at the end of the message, it's phony. We'll use this while the staff is developing new encoding for our data exchanges. Any questions? No? Okay we're off to the code room."

John Paul stood and waited briefly. "Follow me, please."

A short walk along the garden-like corridors brought the trio to a research area not seen before. The walls, floor and ceiling were a soft illuminated blue. A dozen computer stations, some manned by staff, were lined against the walls around the room. Other stations were located in the room's center. All had suspended monitor displays showing programming data though no monitor frames could be seen. Staff members came and went, some in white lab coats, others in gold-trimmed jumpsuits and still more in casual clothing.

John Paul turned to Markman. "Scott, we're going to need Cassiopia for several hours. You're welcome to grab some coffee and hang out with us but you'll probably become very bored very quickly. If you want to take some time off, now would be a good time. I can notify you as soon as we're done here."

"Just what are you trying to learn from all this?" asked Markman.

"Besides trying to understand what Hector might be planning next we badly need to understand why Hector suddenly went rogue. That's what you see happening around you."

Markman looked to Cassiopia. She smiled and nodded.

"Okay, I'll run a few errands then. Let me know when you're done with her."

John Paul suddenly looked as though he was questioning himself. "And Scott, stay out of trouble if you can. Okay?" he added.

Markman gave a devious half smile and headed for the elevator.

On the road, with no particular place to go, a Dairy Queen came into view. Markman went through the drive-through and emerged with a large vanilla cone in one hand. As he enjoyed it thoughts of his real estate research came to mind.

"Core, take over driving."

"Please state destination."

"Just stay on this road for now."

Core beeped acknowledgment.

Markman wrestled his cell phone out. Balancing the ice cream cone in one hand, and phone in the other, he managed to open the file with the addresses he had not been able to identify. Three were in Fredericksburg not that far away.

"Core, take me to 2106 Melani Ave, Fredericksburg."

The dashboard display brightened with a roadmap as Core beeped acknowledgment.

Fifty minutes later Markman slowed and pulled into a large empty parking lot along a very busy Melani Avenue. The building at 2106 was a large one-story complex. Though there were no business signs attached to the abandoned office structure, clearly it had been a private medical center. Markman parked and got out to investigate further.

Curtainless windows showed the place had been stripped inside. Around back, piles of junk were still waiting to be taken away.

Markman returned to the car and climbed in. He studied the file on his cell phone once more. "Core, take me to 1281 Baker Street."

The dashboard map display changed to show the new route. Markman pulled out onto the road and followed the map.

It was a thirty-minute traverse. This time the area was much more industrial. Half acre lots provided space for multi-floor buildings, most of which had numerous cars in their lots.

1281 was a large eight-story high rise with few cars parked nearby. The building looked empty. A ConCom Holding's For Sale sign was posted on two large power poles. Markman circled the building slowly. In the rear, there was discarded furniture, garbage, and dumpsters. Within the pile, Markman made out a pickup and delivery sign for Samson Laboratories. He stopped the car and got out to look more closely. Within the stack inside one dumpster were papers with a letterhead for an investment firm along with some others that identified as an import-export organization. Though most of the building's windows were heavily tinted, on the first floor Markman could see an empty security desk with elevators behind it. There were a few papers on the floor and no signs of life at all.

Back in the car Markman read from his cell phone and commanded, "Okay Core, take me to 23 Brama Street."

Another forty-five-minute trip brought yet another empty, two-story glass building into view. A coed exercise facility had occupied both floors. Markman surveyed the place in disappointment. What did he expect? The whole idea of finding some sign of Hector at one of these places had been extremely unlikely. As he sat dejected, Markman spotted a McDonalds nearby. The drive through rewarded him with a conciliatory cup of hot coffee. He sat in the parking lot sipping as he called up the last unidentified address. It was located in the Washington area, too far for today.

Time to head back. "Core, return to headquarters."

A new map appeared on the display. As Core backed out of the spot Markman instinctively had to twist around to look even though there was no chance of Core hitting something. Pulling out onto the road, Markman noticed the return trip passed by the 1281 Baker Street high-rise again.

"Core, stop at 1281 Baker Street on the way."

Core beeped acknowledgment and a marker appeared on the map display.

Back in the high-rise parking lot Markman again searched the area for onlookers. The few cars which had been there were gone. He opened Core's center console and found the door unlocking device given him by John Paul. Since no one was around the front door was as good as any.

Markman got out. "Core, park in the rear of the building. Wait for my instructions."

What a waste of time, thought Markman. But having looked at all three of these properties he might as well have a look inside at this one. Otherwise there could be doubt. At the front door, after another careful glance around, Markman inserted the lock tool and in less than a second the lock turned open. He slipped inside to the deserted security desk, looked at the door to the stairwell and quickly decided to at the least try the elevator.

To his surprise the elevator button illuminated when pressed followed by the sound of motors and cables. Congratulating himself, he stepped through the opening doors and hit the 8 button. Might as well start at the top and use the stairs coming down.

The elevator closed and the car began to rise.

Numbers above the carriage doors began to step up. Suddenly he began to wonder how long it had been since this elevator had been inspected and certified. There was a card in a clear envelope attached next to the control panel. The cert was two years past due.

As the car passed the fourth floor he reassured himself that everything was fine.

Abruptly the car made a grinding sound and stopped.

Markman held his breath waiting to see what would happen next.

Nothing happened.

He cursed himself. How could he have been so stupid? Get in an elevator in an abandoned building without at least checking the certification date?

There was a red alarm button on the control panel. He pulled it.

Nothing happened.

There was a small door for an emergency phone. Nothing but torn black coil cord wires inside.

Waiting to see if someone would come seemed equally stupid. He braced himself against the doors and fought to pull them apart. With help from one foot he managed a twelve-inch opening.

It was perfect. The car had stopped exactly between floors. A narrow slit near the top of the doors revealed a sliver view of the fifth-floor. It could be days before anyone showed up or maybe it would be even longer than that. Markman searched his entrapment. There was one other option. Overhead, the outline of a twenty-inch square panel could be seen. It would take a good vertical leap to see if it would open. Markman braced beneath it and jumped.

With barely a touch, the panel pushed up but fell right back into place. The second attempt knocked it slightly to one side, exposing dark elevator shaft. The third leap pushed it out of the way completely.

Jumping high enough to get a handhold seemed unlikely. Using the elevator handrails in one corner was awkward but a better possibility. Hands flat against the elevator walls, Markman inched himself up onto the rails and made his best leap toward the only escape. He grabbed onto the rusty steel edge with one hand then the other and swung free. Superhuman effort was required to get an elbow up and over the small opening. Adrenalin aided the process. With both arms maneuvered above the opening, Markman twisted and wrenched himself onto the car's roof. The shaft air was cool. The place was an unfriendly tunnel leading upward. No doors to any of the floors were open. Markman suddenly realized this was his second elevator shaft in a month's time, having never been in one before the weapon recovery mission.

The doors to the fifth floor were there, right in front of him. He stepped over framework, braced and fought to separate them. Surprisingly they opened easier than the car doors had. When barely enough space was available, he squeezed through to the fifth-floor hallway and let the doors snap shut behind him. Hands on his knees, he stopped to catch his breath and look around. The stairwell door was right next to the elevator. It was only three flights up to the eighth floor. He could still accomplish what he came to do.

Markman straightened up, brushed himself off and pulled open the stairwell door. As he began to climb a clanking noise echoed through the stairwell coming from somewhere below. It was probably something to do with the malfunctioning elevator. Markman shook his head, glad not to be trapped in it. He smirked as he recalled John Paul's warning to stay out of trouble. At least he'd never find out about this escapade.

The eighth floor was unlocked and barren except for plush carpeting in some of the empty rooms. The place looked like it had been someone's residence.

Down the stairs to the seventh floor brought a completely different situation. There was a keypad on the door he hadn't noticed on the way up and it was active. It took John Paul's combination breaker a good twenty seconds to decipher it.

Inside, the surroundings startled Markman. Everything here seemed to be powered up. A guard station built against a wall had panel lights and monitor displays. But there had been no cars in the parking lot. Could someone be here? He thought to call out then decided against it.

Beyond the guard station to the left was a heavy security door with several warning signs related to biohazard materials. Markman went to it intending to use his decoder and was surprised yet again to find a twin retinal scanner also active but with green lights across its panel. A quick pull on the door proved it was unlocked and open but instinct stopped Markman from going further.

There were black stains on the retinal scanner. The gunmetal silver device was clean and shiny except for the blackened markings on it as though something had been spilled. Suddenly a bolt of fear raced through Markman as he realized what he was looking at.

Dried blood.

Adrenaline was flowing. He reached slowly behind and drew his Berretta out from under his windbreaker, then remembered John Paul's EMP weapon. With his free hand he checked it in his left jacket pocket. Best to stay with the Berretta for now. Slowly he pulled the heavy laboratory door open and scanned beyond it.

The laboratory within was alive with electronics. Plexiglas walls separated different sections. There were humming and clicking sounds in the cool air along with a strong chemical smell. In a far corner a small centrifuge was still spinning. Markman stepped in and continued to look. No one was here. Moving farther in, he cautiously made sure the lab was unoccupied. Finally, he dared to holster his gun and tried to understand the processes taking place around him. Near the large windows by one wall, he happened to glance down at the parking area just in time to see someone wearing a dark hooded jacked carrying two metallic suitcases leaving the building in a hurry. Something odd about the individual forced him to keep watching. The person had a strange gait to his brisk walk. The hood covered his head. He wore high black boots with dark trousers.

Almost subconsciously Markman slapped the implant area on his neck. "John Paul, Hector! 1281 Baker Street, Fredericksburg, 1281 Baker Street, Fredericksburg!"

Okay, maybe dash down after it but without the elevator the run down seven flights of stairs would take too long. No… better to visually track it.

The figure continued to trot across the parking lot without slowing. Crossing the adjacent street, it circled a nearby office building and disappeared.

Something startled Markman. He turned to find two black-suited men with dark sunglasses standing beside him, looking down at the parking area. They had seen the suspect. The pair stepped back, stood at attention and vanished. Markman looked down at the parking lot again just in time to see the two materialize there and take off running.

Suddenly a noise interrupted the tense moment. Markman looked up to find a black helicopter approaching in the distance. Lowering down outside the windows, it stopped just outside and rotated while its occupants scanned inside the building. It pitched over and headed off in the direction the suspect had taken. A second black helicopter was approaching. It flew overhead and out of sight as though landing on the rooftop.

Markman stood dazed, not knowing exactly what to do next. Before any decision could be made the lab doors burst open and half a dozen agents and lab techs invaded the room.

Twenty minutes into the invasion a lab tech passed by Markman carrying a frosty, fluid-filled glass jar containing two eyeballs with the optic nerves still attached.

Markman decided it was time to leave.

Chapter 19

Markman sat at John Paul's conference room table drumming his fingers on the tabletop waiting to hear what the results from yesterday's near miss with Hector had revealed. Cassiopia appraised the recently self-introduced Perseus sitting directly across from her as he fidgeted with some sort of small device in his hands. He did not look up to acknowledge her. Periodically other staff members would enter the room, nod a greeting and take a seat. Some were dressed in white lab smocks, others in tan, one-piece jumpsuits and still others in dark tie-less business suits that were not at all trimmed in Earth standard styling. When the late arrivals were all seated it totaled an additional three men and three women.

After a long awkward silence, John Paul finally entered. As he approached his seat at the head of the table the wall behind his chair came to life as a display screen. On it a large intricate circular symbol bore the letters 'CO.' Even in this deep, heavily secured underground facility it was still forbidden even to display the name 'Celestial Order.'

John Paul sat and placed a black briefcase on the table. From it, he drew a tablet and set it down close by. He looked out over his staff for a moment, gave a flat smile and began, "The code work seems to be going well. Perseus, your group may have found a path which could lead to the code line zero point. I think everyone understands how important it is that we understand the true origin of this matter."

Perseus looked up but did not reply. He nodded and resumed fidgeting with the small device in his hands.

Markman squirmed impatiently. John Paul noticed.

"Now to the matter of Hector. Once again, we were not able to contain him. Anyone have any new insight on why he is so impossible to track?"

Two of the staff members sat back in their chairs and exhaled in frustration. No one had an answer.

"Nevertheless," continued John Paul, "We've gained quite a lot from this incident. It has confirmed to us Hector is indeed trying to complete his design. Among other things, the laboratory was being used to create and mold e-skin. It is likely that Hector has managed to nearly complete his outer layer of artificial skin which will give him a much better chance of blending into society. We know, however, he has not been able to complete his facial features. How far along is he, Siea?"

A woman with long black hair and very white skin dressed in a white lab coat spoke. "The eyes will be the most difficult. Professor Cassell's documentation shows he planned to have new special aesthetic optics cast at an optics lab in France. Those will not be so easy to manufacture. Beyond that Hector's facial features will need a mold of a human face. If he gets that far, he may be able to create any number of faces and exchange them at will to further conceal his identity."

John Paul interrupted, "But Siea, how long for him to get set up again and create facial overlays?"

"He will not need as advanced a lab as he was using in this first case. It could be a small laboratory with minimal capabilities. So he could be set up within a week after finding a suitable location."

"And the eyes, Siea?"

"Sunglasses, John Paul."

John Paul hesitated then nodded to Siea. "You're right. The eyes don't matter. Once he has a face or faces, he'll be indistinguishable from other people. He'll be able to move freely within society. Damn it, why can't we track this machine? What is so different about it?"

An uneasy silence followed.

John Paul resumed. "All right, let's move on to the more macabre details. Dr. Sho, what was your analysis of the bio samples brought back from the high-rise?"

A nearly bald man also wearing a white lab coat spoke. "I'm sorry to report it's exactly what we suspected. The eyes belonged to one Robert Manning, the real estate broker. Obviously, he took the eyes to gain access to the laboratory which means we expect the mutilations of the other murder victims to have been a means of gaining access to other facilities. Those investigations are in process."

"Have you established that hand scanners are used at the warehouse where the Landers woman worked?"

"Yes. Hand scanners are the security measure there for dangerous or time sensitive chemicals. It is highly likely her hands were taken to gain access there, as well. And we expect to find shortages there of the substances Hector needed to perform his upgrades."

"That leaves the more gruesome case of Randolf and the most recent case of Dr. Delam."

"The updated field report just in does confirm Randolf's firm also used eye scanners. They are primarily in the business of precision mold making for satellite support services. They did report items missing from their facility recently. As for Dr. Delam, he was accosted coming out of his laboratory. No mutilation was needed to gain entry to his lab. He was working on a grant for cellular research studying the assignment process for stem cells. He also operated a branch studying immunization to airborne pathogens. That's primarily what we have so far."

John Paul rubbed his chin in thought. "All of those fit except for Dr. Delam. What would Hector need with stem cell research?"

"We are still investigating what was taken and what may have been done in Delam's lab that night. I'll have answers for you later today."

John Paul sat back and exhaled. He scanned the room. "Does anyone have any other new data or any suggestions I haven't already heard at this point?"

Markman raised his hand.

A smile broke out on John Paul's face. He slumped his shoulders in concession. "Scott, you don't need to raise your hand. What?"

"Can I get trained to use that beaming thing?"

Someone at the table squeaked a laugh. Others maneuvered to hide their expressions of amusement.

"Beaming thing?" asked John Paul.

"Yeah, every time I get near the damn thing you beam people in or whatever you want to call it and they take off after it. If I could do that instead of waiting for those guys to arrive, I could at least stay with Hector."

A moment of sobriety returned to the room. The comical mood remained though an underlying current of respect tempered it.

"Mr. Chance, would you like to address Scott's inquiry?" said John Paul.

One of the dark-suited men spoke. "Mr. Markman, it is possible we could make that happen. It would take at least a month to train you for use in the Translation Effector but there would still be some danger to you. Without absolute discipline you could lose a block of memory in a transfer and you might never get it back. You could also be stunned after the transfer for as long as four hours. During that time you would not be able to move or speak under your own power."

"But your people use it all the time."

"Mr. Markman.... Scott, most of them are not human," replied Chance.

Markman looked over at John Paul. He raised his eyebrows in a questioning stare.

"I'd like to give it a shot," answered Markman.

Cassiopia's expression became one of displeasure but she bit her tongue.

"It takes a J.P. approval," replied Chance.

Everyone in the room looked at John Paul.

"We'll talk about this after the meeting," said John Paul.

Markman began to raise his hand again, then sheepishly pulled it back down. "John Paul, you've said Hector hacked into your system using Professor Cassell's passwords and links, right?"

"Yes," nodded John Paul patiently.

"I know this is probably a dumb thing to ask, but is there any way Hector could be using this transporter thing without you knowing?"

Instead of more laughter, the room became dead silent.

John Paul's face paled. He turned to his associate, "Mr. Chance, who do you have on shift for the TE?"

"It's Calopia," replied Mr. Chance.

John Paul turned his head upward and spoke to a room microphone, "Mr. Calopia, please report to the main conference room immediately."

The uncomfortable silence persisted. Calopia arrived two minutes later looking irate from the interruption. He leaned in at the entrance, expecting to go right back out. "Yes?!?"

John Paul gathered himself, "Has there been any unauthorized use of the Translator Effector?"

Calopia abandoned his distraction. He stared and stuttered, "What? No, no; but the monthly review is not due yet. So no, not that I know of. There hasn't been any reason to monitor that. I would have to look at the more recent logs. Why?"

"Mr. Calopia, please stop everything you are doing, use whoever you need and do an in-depth study of TE operations, paying particular attention to someone trying to conceal its use. Do you understand?"

Calopia looked confused. He paused for a moment as though expecting someone to explain. No one did. He slowly edged out the door like a child being sent to bed for stealing cookies. No one laughed.

John Paul waited for any other comments. There were none. "Okay everyone, since there are no other new inputs let's resume our machine hunt, shall we? Dismissed."

Quietly the group rose and filed out of the room. Markman, Cassiopia, and John Paul remained seated. When the room had finally emptied, Markman resumed his petition.

"You're going to let me take that training, right?"

"Scott, I'm surprised you waited this long. I expected this request months ago. Considering the kind of training you had in Tibet I've thought perhaps you may be one of the best human candidates we've ever had. So yes, you can report to Mr. Chance whenever you're ready to begin."

"Now hold on," said Cassiopia. "Are there any dangers I haven't heard about in using this system?"

"A wide variety but none very serious. We have had users re-materialize naked for instance but always unharmed."

Markman choked. "What?"

John Paul mused, "There was also one equipment failure where someone re-materialized without any scalp or genital hair which was quite a bothersome thing to remedy since even the hair follicles had been lost but that was a long time ago and the equipment has been improved."

Markman frowned. "I'm sorry, what?"

Cassiopia interrupted, "What about serious problems? Can he materialize in traffic for example or in midair?"

"Impossible. The system will not accept a location with no ground plane nor will it allow any roadways, sidewalks or other traffic areas to be accepted into the translation input screen."

"What about sending him into a solid wall or a water tank or something like that?"

"Absolutely impossible," replied John Paul.

"How about into fire?"

"Geez," said Markman under his breath.

John Paul shook his head. "No, Cassiopia. The only danger these days would be if Scott did not clear his mind perfectly enough. That's what the training is all about."

Cassiopia made a 'humph' sound and sat back with her arms folded.

Markman returned a silly smile believing his case had been won. "Where's the transporter room with the pad things you stand on?"

John Paul smiled. "This isn't Star Trek, Scott. There's no transporter pads. The system is a giant mainframe computer with some associated equipment not from Earth. You'll never see any of that unless you ask Mr. Chance for a tour. You'll wear a special belt. It will look perfectly common. That's all. The belt directs the de-materializing and re-materializing. You can transport from anywhere you are."

Markman raised an eyebrow. "Wow!"

A beeping interrupted the group. Cassiopia stiffened and fumbled to remove her cell phone from her belt holder. "I'm sorry. I'd better look at this. I don't know who would be texting me." She looked down at the cell phone, tapped the correct buttons and sat silently trying to understand the message. Finally, she looked up at John Paul and mumbled, "Oh no!"

John Paul became concerned. "What is it?"

Cassiopia handed over her cell phone. John Paul read the message, became solemn, and handed the phone over to Markman.

Markman read:

What is Markman?

The trio sat with blank stares.

Cassiopia quickly became annoyed. "What does it mean?"

John Paul stood and leaned over the table. "It's him. He's communicating with you, Cassiopia, right in front of us without fear. He knows our team has already picked up on this message and is scrambling to discover from where this text came but he is just not concerned."

"But what is the question? I don't understand."

Markman sounded angry. "Are you kidding? The thing collects your pictures and stalks you! It knows we're together. It's asking what I am to you. He wants to know if I'm the competition."

"Do I answer and what do I say, John Paul?"

"I would suggest the most obvious," replied John Paul. "Ask Hector where he is."

Cassiopia gave a doubtful stare but typed as requested:

Hector, where are you?

Markman rose and came around the table to watch over Cassiopia's shoulder. John Paul took a seat beside her. A few fearful moments passed. The wrong answer came:

We will be together soon.

"Shit!" said Markman half under his breath.

Cassiopia looked again to John Paul. She held out one open hand. "What now?"

"Tell him to come back to the Professor's home."

Cassiopia looked doubtful. But, she typed:

Hector, come back to the Professor's house.

The three waited and watched. No reply came. Five full minutes passed. Then ten. Fifteen was John Paul's limit.

"He's gone," said John Paul as he leaned back in his seat.

Looking frustrated and concerned, Markman sat next to Cassiopia.

John Paul rubbed his chin in thought.

"We will be together soon?" barked Markman angrily. "Collected pictures of her? Stood staring at her while she slept? Do you two realize how serious this crap is?"

Cassiopia sat dumbfounded.

John Paul tried to sound conciliatory. "Perhaps it would be best if Cassiopia took up residence here for the time being."

"I'm not sure I like that idea," replied Markman.

"Of course I meant both of you," answered John Paul.

"If the thing has been hacking in here, can we really be safer here?" persisted Markman.

Almost in answer to Markman and before John Paul could present an argument, a disturbed Mr. Calopia pushed the meeting room door open and came in. He looked like a man in serious conflict. "John Paul, I cannot believe I'm saying this but yes, there has been unauthorized use of the TE system. Several instances over the past two months. And, that's not the worst of it. There are two belts missing from a backup storage drawer, the archive drawer in fact."

For the first time Markman noticed a slight tinge of fear in John Paul's expression.

"But how could...?"

Calopia could not wait to answer. "A software hack beyond anything we've ever seen. Someone developed a program to command those belts to transport themselves to a remote location. There are physical control requirements to prevent something like that being done and even those were bypassed."

John Paul spoke in exasperation. "Do we know where the belts were sent to?" asked John Paul.

"Professor Cassell's home."

John Paul's demeanor changed to one of astonishment. "Have you tried to recall them, Mr. Calopia?"

"Of course, John Paul. But they are off the grid."

"That means he's disconnected the power cells until he's ready to use them. Can you mask them from the system?"

"Yes, I've already done that but the intrusions I've seen are so sophisticated I'm not sure we can trust any countermeasures."

"Mr. Calopia, somehow we need to protect the system or we'll be forced to power it down completely."

"I agree with you, sir."

Calopia paused for a moment then backed out the door, shaking his head.

John Paul shook his head. "So Hector must have been using the caves until he got control of the transporter, and now he's been running and hiding from us to conceal the fact that he's using it. The thing is cunning."

Markman looked at Cassiopia, then at John Paul. "Safer here, John Paul?"

"Scott, even with a compromised transporter, this facility has safety measures too detailed to describe to you. There is no place safer. Cassiopia, how do you feel about all this?"

Cassiopia looked appreciatively at Markman. "I think I might have trouble sleeping at home. Every noise would be Hector."

Markman nodded. "Okay then. We've been coming and going too much anyway. I'll head back to our place and gather up some things for both of us. You wait here."

"At least the programming group will be glad to hear this, Cassiopia," said John Paul.

The trio sat for a moment exchanging a wide variety of nervous body language. Finally, Markman could not take any more. He rose to leave but began to have second thoughts. He turned to John Paul.

John Paul spoke reassuringly. "I won't let her out of my sight, Scott."

Markman nodded and looked at Cassiopia affectionately. "I'll call you when I get there. Figure out what you need."

Chapter 20

Markman leaned back in the driver's seat and tried to enjoy the ride, but his anger had now settled into fear for Cassiopia. Was this really happening? Was an out of control robot obsessed with Cassiopia, a robot which had murdered several people to further its aims? What did it want with Cassiopia? All those articles about artificial intelligence becoming a threat to humankind. Was it suddenly happening? A machine with unlimited access to the World Wide Web and all the knowledge contained within?

Markman thought back to his days growing up in Tibet, a place of deep spiritualism and ancient wisdom. The doctrine there had always been that society would eventually evolve into a more spiritual collective. Instead, the world was becoming more and more violent at the hands of immature souls who cared only about enriching themselves with power, wealth and sensation. And just because these souls were morally immature didn't mean some of them weren't smart enough to acquire government office or high corporate positions. Humankind had always managed to keep the immature souls under control one way or another. But too many had come to be in power now, not caring about people or society.

Could the inception of A.I. be a milestone marking a corrupted evolution? A cause and effect development intended as a corrective measure to reform a corrupted world power structure? There was no denying that somehow machines had become godlike. Sit at any computer terminal, open a search engine and type your question and get dozens of answers ranging from social media all the way up to Einstein. There was no question imaginable the God computer couldn't answer. And now, an autonomous machine had access to all of that knowledge along with a narrow mandate to improve life. How would it choose to improve humankind? How much power had it amassed? In bewilderment Markman shuddered at the thought.

There were unexpected changes to greet him at the mansion. The TEL robot had been shut down once again. Speedy ran up and wagged his tail, hoping Markman was there to remedy all the dog wrongs in the world.

"You'll have to come with me, little buddy," said Markman. He opened his arms and the dog jumped into them.

There were sounds coming from the TV room. There shouldn't have been. The TV was on and blasting. Upstairs in the conference room where Cassiopia had left her laptop all the wall monitors were on, displaying various news programs. A quick call to Cassiopia verified neither she nor John Paul had any idea why. Markman hurried to gather up Cassiopia's requests. He left everything on and climbed back into the car with all necessary personal possessions along with Speedy on the seat beside him.

The ride back was even more unsettling than the ride out had been. There was a subconscious fear Hector was everywhere and at the same time nowhere. Markman turned onto Germanna Highway and reluctantly forced himself not to speed. Speedy sat on the front seat atop Cassiopia's pillow enjoying the view.

Markman squirmed to make room for the holstered handgun on his belt behind him, an attribute of some reassurance. He rubbed his windbreaker side pocket to be sure the EMP weapon was still there.

How long would this situation go on? What kind of trouble was Professor Cassell in for building a machine that probably murdered four people? Would there be still more murders? Markman cursed under his breath. Far ahead, a drunk driver was approaching. The driver kept hooking his front wheel on the grass divider. He was going too fast and having trouble staying in his lane. It was fortunate there were no other cars in sight. Markman began to slow and hug the right side of the road. There was an open grass embankment along the roadside to pull over if the drunk lost control completely.

In a split second the situation went from annoying to catastrophic. The oncoming car suddenly accelerated, veered over onto the grass divider and headed directly at Markman. Before he could yank the wheel to the right, a map appeared on Core's display screen with vectors showing the oncoming car's trajectory and an array of possible solutions. The steering wheel spun left through Markman's hands. The opposite direction he would have chosen. There was a pumping of brakes as Core sailed over the embankment and slammed onto the grass. Markman held his hands back from the steering wheel as the car continued to make its own adjustments and as Core slid sideways the engine revved high, spinning the back wheels and causing the car to straighten out and climb back up and onto the roadway.

Markman dared a glance in his side view in time to see the drunk's car rolling over and over on its side.

"Core, turn around and go back to the crash."

Core quickly slowed and spun into a U-turn, stopping just off the roadway by the wreck.

Markman looked at a wide-eyed Speedy. "Stay!" Speedy seemed more than willing to comply. Markman jumped from the car and ran full out toward the drunk's wreck. It was mangled and smoking and upside down.

The driver's window was broken out. The man was still strapped in, unconscious with his arms hanging down. There were small cuts all over his face and a trace of blood around his mouth.

The seat belt was a bitch. Too much weight made it difficult to unclip. As carefully as possible, Markman finally unlatched it and partially caught the man as he came down. Fire began to erupt around the trunk area.

The rescue quickly became urgent as the flames grew taller. Somehow the man's right leg was hooked on something. Markman wrestled with the heavy body, one hand under each shoulder but a shoelace from one of the man's athletic shoes was caught. With more of a tug than Markman wanted to inflict on the injured man the shoe finally pulled off. Adrenaline flowing, Markman dragged him across the grass and away from the smoke and fire.

Markman fumbled his cell phone. It took a moment to catch enough breath to speak after John Paul answered. There was a disjointed explanation of the accident and its location. John Paul quickly clicked off to make arrangements. Markman jumped as the gas tank made a loud boom and a wash of hot air pushed by.

Kneeling on the grass beside the injured driver the quick check for injuries began. The man's legs appeared to be okay but his chest was compressed. He was breathing in short gasps. The pulse in his neck was strong but rapid. His eyes fluttered and opened, glazed. His lips moved but no sound came out.

With a hand on the man's shoulder, Markman tried to sound reassuring. "Don't try to speak. Help will be here any second. Your pulse is good. You're going to be okay. Don't try to speak. Save your breath."

The man was in shock. He couldn't or wouldn't listen. He kept trying to say something. Markman leaned over to hear.

In a whisper the man managed to get out, "Wouldn't steer. Couldn't stop."

The man fell into unconsciousness once more. Alarmed, Markman felt for the pulse. It was fading. The man's breathing had become short gulps. There was still no help in sight. Markman knelt on both knees and began to furiously rub his hands together without really understanding why. One last look around to confirm no rescue available and Markman winced, then gently placed a hand on the man's collapsed chest. There was a loud snap sound almost like a spark as energy began to flood out of Markman and into the injury. Markman's arm and shoulder vibrated with the flow of life force. He struggled to keep balanced with his hand in place. It felt like the life was being sucked out of him. He was shrinking away into oblivion. The world began to spin. He teetered on his knees and fell over sideways so hard it seemed like someone had shoved him down. The world went black

Blue sky and clouds slowly passing overhead. A burning stench in the air. A slow turn of the head brought a patch of green grass into view. Markman pushed up on one hand. The injured driver's eyes were open though he did not seem fully conscious. Markman crawled back to the man. His pulse was slow and strong, his breathing shallow but steady.

Hearing was returning to Markman. A whine in the distance. Craning his neck to look back he could see flashing blue lights approaching. He managed to climb to his feet. Brushing himself off there was a moment of dizziness. He nearly fell. The first police car slid to a stop a short distance away.

Ten minutes later the place was swarming with police, fire and rescue. Two of John Paul's people arrived along with them, a lab technician and a man in a dark suit who spoke to the police. The semiconscious driver was rushed into an ambulance and taken away, sirens blaring. Firemen sprayed down the car fire until it was no more than a pile of twisted metal and smoke. When the usual police questions had been answered Markman headed back to headquarters. Disheveled, he arrived in the underground facility with Speedy under one arm and Cassiopia's duffle bag in the other. She was waiting at the elevator and immediately looked him over for injuries. Having spotted none she gave a suspicious gaze before greeting him with a kiss. Speedy scratched at her blouse to be taken.

Thirty minutes later John Paul and the lab tech were waiting for them in the conference room.

"It wasn't an accident," said John Paul as they sat.

"What?" replied Markman.

John Paul gestured toward his technician. "Mr. Seel here got enough off the car's black box that the analysis showed external signals taking control of that car just before the crash."

"But how could you do that? The black box was still in the wreckage when we left."

"We can do that," replied John Paul. "What I'm saying is that car was used as a weapon against you."

Markman wrinkled his brow. "You're kidding!"

"Not at all. That car was deliberately aimed right at you."

"If that's true, why use another car? Why not just take control of Core and crash it?"

"Because that's not so easy with Core. Core is programmed to override all other input to evade danger. It would override any commands to deliberately crash."

"You're saying I could not crash Core if I needed to?"

"If your hands were physically on the steering wheel you could. All of this is in the user manual."

Markman looked embarrassed. He whined, "It's a long damn manual! I kind of get attention deficit disorder on that stuff."

Cassiopia let out a short laugh.

John Paul gave a half smile, "Don't I know."

Cassiopia interrupted, "John Paul, you're saying Hector was trying to kill Scott?"

"We do not have definitive proof but yes and I'm absolutely certain. Kill or incapacitate him."

"I had to give my name and address to a deputy. Is that going to be a problem?" asked Markman.

"No, we'll eventually replace your name, address and Core info with false information."

"So the thing wants to kill me. Am I putting this facility in danger by being here?" asked Markman.

"My staff believes Hector knows our address but does not know about this underground installation. That information is never mentioned in any data file. We have already put new safety measures in place for the staff members occupying the offices above ground. We can expect danger on the ground or from the air but as long as Hector believes Cassiopia is here it is unlikely he will risk attacking this location."

"My God, John Paul. Are other lives also in danger? Has this threat really gotten so out of hand?" asked Cassiopia.

"I'm sorry to say, Cassiopia, it has. We must contain Hector at all costs. He is learning and improving himself at an alarming rate, becoming more and more capable and powerful by the minute. We are also very concerned he is interacting with other computers around the world in ways we can't imagine. All of our resources are now being used against this single threat."

Markman said, "John Paul, I can't be a prisoner down here. You can't ask me to wait around and do nothing while that thing is out there planning on kidnapping Cassiopia, never mind attacking other people. I just can't sit it out down here."

"You won't have to. Clearly Cassiopia must remain down here with us for all the obvious reasons but you can continue to be mobile. We will disable all network connections with Core. You will no longer have satellite feed or any other communications capability in the car, so there will be no chance of interference from Hector except from outside. It is obvious that he has identified Core but he will only be able to track it visually now which won't be easy since it can alter its appearance. He may have been confirming you are the one in the car by using Core's dash cam. That will no longer be available to him so he won't be able to be certain it's you or that Cassiopia is in the car as well."

"Also, just in the past few minutes Mr. Chance and Mr. Calopia have informed me they are powering down our transporter until they can identify the path Hector used to gain control of it. So you see, we are affecting Hector's modus operandi. No longer will he be able to transport away from us. We lose some capabilities ourselves but overall it is a significant reduction of Hector's abilities. As far as you're concerned we will be doing most of our surveillance using operatives instead of networking. Your ability to move within the human community will be even more valuable than it has been. There are limitations with our MIB personnel which cannot be overcome simply by altering their attire, so we'll need you in situations that require greater discretion. One last item: for now, your implants will continue to work. You can still communicate one-way with us. If Hector discovers those the worst he can do is monitor them or send the dissolve signal. Keep in mind there is a sensitivity requirement with those. We may not be able to hear a whisper or very low voice input."

John Paul paused then began to add something but was interrupted by his cell phone. He held up one finger to pause, drew out the cell and stared down at it. "Cassiopia, your father's awake and they're ready to bring him out of the isolation unit. They'd like you to attend."

Cassiopia straightened up. "Absolutely I'll attend!" She pushed back the chair and headed for the door.

"You remember the way there?" called out John Paul.

"Of course," was the reply.

John Paul rolled his eyes, realizing it was a dumb question.

Markman slowly began to stand. "I'd better go with her," he said.

"She'll be just fine, Scott. This might be a good time to go over your assignment."

"I have an assignment?"

"Yes. It may be easier to send you out into the world without having her hear this. There's another long shot lead the staff has come up with but at this point any leads we have are long shots. Hector probably had several months to invade our files and communicate with outside computers, so combined with his understanding of software along with a complete access to the internet he knows us too well. That's why he's been a step ahead of us at every turn. All we can do is grab at straws until we find one that leads somewhere."

"I know all that."

"Forgive me. I think I'm just crying on your shoulder. Anyway, we need you to check out some arms and legs."

"Some what?"

"Robotic arms and legs. This item came up just this morning from the financial group. When Professor Cassell was building Hector, he ordered parts from a company called IC Robotics. He ordered one set of legs and one set of arms. Two months later he ordered a second set of both. During our inventory of his lab, we did not find the spare sets of those. Cassell has been interviewed and he does not recall ordering a second set but his recall is not perfectly reliable as you know. These were very expensive items but that would not have been a flag for us, of course. This is probably just a loose end we need resolved."

"You don't know where these things ended up?"

"IC Robotics has a record of the sale. They were supposed to be shipped directly to the Professor at your place. The shipping company they used is no longer in business so we could not get confirmation of the delivery. IC Robotics is in Eastchester New York. TransTime Shipping Incorporated was used for the delivery and was located in Steinway, New York before they closed down. They declared bankruptcy before suspending operations. IC Robotics has confirmed the parts were originally picked up by TransTime. That's the last record we have of the order. When TransTime closed down, all their records were confiscated by the U.S. government and placed into storage in an IRS warehouse facility in Woodside, in Queens. We need to fly you there to see if you can verify where these arms and legs went. It's a long shot worth pursuing. Do you agree?"

"You bet."

"You'll be set up with a false ID as an FBI agent investigating TransTime. If you get stopped by locals or airport security the ID will check out okay on their computers. The ID will disappear after two days unless you need it extended. It should get you in wherever you need to go. We'll get you to JFK in a private jet so there's no record of you flying. There'll be a privately owned car for you to use at the airport. We need to get you in the air right now but you'll arrive a little too late to go to work so we'll have a reservation set up at the JFK Radisson using your FBI ID. We'll take you out of here in an unmarked SUV with three other decoys leaving at the same time. When you get to JFK you must be careful not to do anything that uses any personal networking. It's the same procedure for all of our operatives. If possible, find out where those arms and legs went on the outside chance it will lead us to Hector. Got all that?"

"Yes, sir. When do I leave?"

John Paul smiled, "Silly question."

Chapter 21

Markman sat alone in the passenger compartment of the Gulfstream jet watching New York skyscrapers rising from below. Long shadows were forming. The city was busy with people scurrying along like ants on crowded paths. Traffic was clogged and moving in short hops. Everyone seemed so busy. All had learned to accept the dangers around them including the many modern-day monsters that might be lingering just out of sight. For years some of the best minds had warned of threats from artificial intelligence. Hawking, Gates, and Musk were just a few who had envisioned problems with machines that might become too smart. Now it seemed the seed may have been planted. In his experience as an investigator Markman had faced some of the most unusual suspects possible but this time there was an undercurrent of techno mutation: a killing machine with the sum total of man's knowledge at its disposal. As though that wasn't enough, the thing probably had access to just about every camera, motion detector and satellite watching over civilization. The beast with a thousand eyes.

The landing at JFK was so smooth there was only the settling of the nose to mark it. Disembarking was done near gates being used by UPS planes. As Markman passed through the terminal he again realized every security camera was suddenly a possible threat.

It was a very long walk to the hotel, even with moving sidewalks. The Radisson was huge, the lobby expansive. At the check-in desk the clerk eyed Markman's jeans, athletic shoes and windbreaker with reluctance. But when he checked the reservation his expression abruptly changed to one of subservience and courtesy, although Markman's admission there was no luggage brought another brief questioning stare.

The hotel room was so luxurious it was almost offensive to Markman. There was a full kitchen with a stocked refrigerator, a study loaded with bookshelves and computer stations, sunken living room area and two bedrooms, two baths. Darkness was setting in beyond the giant picture windows. As he scanned the outdoors two sets of massive curtains automatically closed off the view.

In the expansive master bedroom there was a large walk-in closet with sliding louvered doors. Markman gathered up blankets, pillows and cushions and made himself a bed in it, positioned so he could watch over the bedroom without being seen. He set up pillows under the covers of the large round bed so it looked like Scott Markman's sleeping form.

There were sandwiches in the small fridge in the TV area. He sat and watched the news, finishing off tuna sandwiches and Gatorade. There were no new murders in the Fredericksburg area mentioned. The spacious ballroom was equipped well enough for someone without luggage. Markman remained dressed for trouble and settled into his makeshift closet bed, gun and EMP device within quick reach.

Morning light automatically opened the suite's big windows. Beams streaked through the slats in the closet door and woke Markman. Another quick visit to the complimentary bathroom facilities, then slipping on the wrinkled windbreaker and Markman was ready to go to work. In the parking area he again found himself overly conscious of every car approaching. The situation began to seem even more absurd. The world was suddenly filled with possible threats from every direction, panophobia now deserving a part in reality.

The car was exactly where John Paul had said it would be. The key was under a tray in the center console. Once on the road Markman realized there was no less stress. The same misgivings returned. Every car from every direction was a possible torpedo. Even the skyline could hold danger given Hector's abilities. How had civilization suddenly become such a war zone?

Surprisingly, the IRS facility in question had a large parking lot with delivery trucks coming and going. There were quite a few empty spaces. In a city where parking spaces often caused all-out war it was as though people were avoiding these, as if the subconscious fear parking at the IRS might somehow cause an audit. The place was near overhead train tracks. It was an out of the way section of city although quite a few wary pedestrians were still passing by.

Markman found the heavily used double metal doors and pushed his way in. The unadorned lobby had shipping boxes stacked all around. A woman with dark, shoulder length hair wearing a blue work shirt was struggling to turn a new bottle of water over and onto the water dispenser. Markman hurried around the well-worn counter to aid her. When the job was done she brushed herself off, gave him a *why-are-you-here* look, then a momentary flash of attraction followed by the stiffness so common among government employees. She motioned him to get back on the other side of the counter. Markman complied.

"Yes?" she asked.

Markman forgot his new FBI name. He pulled out his wallet and opened it to show badge and ID.

"What can I do for you, Mr. James?"

"I need access to the TransTime Shipping Corporation records. The printed stuff, computer records and whatever else you have."

"Has a formal request been submitted?"

"If you check your records I think you'll find it has."

The woman turned to her computer screen and began typing. "I don't see anything here." Her search continued. "Wait, oh yes. Here it is. You are authorized to view those records. However, no charge number has been issued for that work so you'll need to wait until that comes through."

"Why do I need a charge number?"

"We cannot provide an employee to assist you without one."

"I don't need anyone. I want to look through those records myself."

"I'm not sure that's allowed. I'll have to check with my supervisor."

"Would you do that please, then?"

"Wait here."

The woman disappeared through strips of opaque plastic hanging down from a large door behind her.

Markman waited.

Ten minutes later, a balding man in blue work coveralls emerged and eyed Markman as though comparing his own authority to Markman's. "Yes, can I help you?"

Markman held up his ID once again. "I need access to the TransTime Shipping Corporation records. It's important. I've come quite a ways to do this. My visit has been approved."

The man typed at the computer. "Is this in relation to an IRS investigation or something else?"

"It's in relation to an FBI investigation."

"I see where the problem is," replied the man. "If this were in relation to an IRS matter we could use a general charge number to provide you with someone but since it's an outside matter we'd need a charge number to use an IRS employee to do the work."

"I do not need an IRS employee. I just want to look at those records myself."

The man looked disturbed. He paused, looked thoughtfully at the ceiling and replied. "We'll need approval from the home office for that. Just one moment please."

"But you have approval. The other girl found it in your computer."

"Sir, that approval was for you to look at the records. It was not authorization to do the work without assistance from an IRS employee."

"Why do I need assistance?"

"Well, someone has to show you where the records are stored."

"How long would that take?"

"It depends on where they are."

"How far away could they be?"

"Sir, just give me a few moments. I think I can get this going."

It was another ten-minute wait. Markman felt almost amused. In addition to their lumbering bureaucratic mentality these people seemed to be completely disinterested in the crisis developing in the world around them.

A different woman, dressed much more formally in a dark business suit with her brown hair up in a tight bun came through the plastic strips. She looked Markman over defiantly. "Can I help you?"

Markman let out a sigh. "I need access to the TransTime Shipping Corporation records."

"Can I see your identification?"

Markman held up his wallet.

A tablet appeared in the woman's hands. She tapped at it and returned the cool stare.

"What is this about?"

"It's an FBI matter."

"Can you be more specific?"

"The case is classified. I can't go into details."

The woman stepped back and paused as though permission would not be forthcoming. After a challenging stare she motioned Markman around the counter. "Please follow me."

From the tone of her voice Markman had the feeling he was about to be executed.

She led the way through the hanging plastic strips and out to a busy warehouse area where people in tan coveralls were busily sorting and stacking materials. Past the main area she marched through open double doors to a storage area with heavy blue steel shelves stacked to a fifteen-foot ceiling with boxes and containers. Down one corridor of shelves there was a right hand turn along more columns of shelves. All the way she tapped at her tablet and kept searching the jungle of boxes and shelves until finally coming to a wall lined with computer stations every ten or twelve feet. She stopped, turned to the right and after a few more steps stopped and tapped again on her tablet.

"This is Bay 12, section C. Your hard copies are up there on level 6," she said looking upward. "All the cartons up there marked TT149786 are TransTime Shipping hard copies."

Before Markman had time to be confused, she turned around to the nearest computer station. She leaned over and tapped a series of commands. "Here's the TransTime computer records. Right-click the mouse for a drop-down menu to advance or search. We begin shutdown for the day at 4:30. Make sure you don't get locked in here by accident Mr. Jameson. Is there anything else?"

"It's James, Ma'am. I just climb up there and open boxes?"

There was a moment of annoyance. "You pull one of those track ladders over here. You must keep all records in order as they are or your office will receive a bill from us for time spent refiling them. Anything else?"

Without leaving enough time for additional questions she took notice of someone in the distance and called out to them as she left.

Markman leaned against a computer table and laughed to himself, then looked up at the wall of boxes and quickly became sober.

The ladder was heavy to drag. On level six the TT149786 boxes had large barcode labels, suggesting there was a device somewhere which could scan them and show the contents of each; a device not offered by Markman's cool receptionist. The boxes were neatly arranged but they went on seemingly forever. Back down at the computer there were no chairs in sight. Markman dragged two cartons off the lowest shelf and stacked them for seating. He sat, cracked his knuckles and began.

The screen was already called up to TransTime information but was taken up by a large number of menu items. Financial, Subcontractors, Employees, Retirement, Holdings, Medical, Operations, and Legal. There was a link at the bottom for a 'Page 2.'

Markman took a chance and clicked on Operations.

One hour later he had finally zeroed in on shipping orders for the past six months. There were tons of listings for each day. Fortunately, each listing had a reference to the company using TransTime Shipping so it was possible to search through and call up all the IC Robotics entries.

From there Markman was able to list delivery destinations. After several typos and accidental wrong link clicks the first shipment he was looking for came up on the screen. It was an invoice showing shipment from IC Robotics to Professor Theopolis Cassell and even referenced robotics materials. This was the first order Cassell had placed for Hector's arms and legs.

Hope now abounding, Markman searched for the next delivery to Professor Cassell and quickly found there was none. He sat back in thought. Wasn't this what John Paul was hoping for? There was definitely a second order from IC Robotics but it did not go to the Professor's home. Hector had diverted it somewhere else, somewhere he could retrieve it without anyone knowing.

The machine would not allow a search for reference entries so 'robotics materials' could not be searched for. Clearly the second set of arms and legs had been ordered sometime after this first one. Markman returned to the TransTime, IC Robotics listings and began opening each entry after that first delivery date, one at a time.

It took more than another hour but when the correct invoice finally opened it caused Markman to straighten up with excitement. There on the screen was delivery of a second set of "robotics materials" along with a reference entry showing the initial destination had been Professor Cassell's address but the shipment had been diverted.

Markman's excitement increased as he found and read the new delivery address:

InterTrans International
12476 Eisenhower Street
Alexandria, VA 22304

For a moment the new address gave Markman pause. It sounded familiar.

The murdered Kestry woman! She had worked for InterTrans International! Their place was a huge warehouse for shipping and storage!

Markman's shoulders slumped. There was no secret address here where Hector could be hiding. This was a depot Hector had used to secretly pick up his order at the very great expense of the Landers woman. This entire trip was a dead end even if it did explain the Landers murder.

There was a click option to create copies of the material displayed on the screen. Markman made copies of all the TransTime-Cassell documents, spent another twenty minutes finding the right printer and bade farewell to the facility without ever even seeing another person.

Chapter 22

The flight back to Fredericksburg was uneventful. An MIB met Markman just outside security. Markman rode in the front seat of the SUV still in his days-old jeans, shirt and windbreaker. On a whim he looked at his driver with the dark sunglasses and asked, "Did I miss anything?"

The driver looked back at him for a moment as though it was not his duty to answer. To Markman's surprise he replied in a strangely hoarse voice, "Just wait."

It seemed like a brush off but as they approached Culpeper traffic problems began to pop up. There were clogs that took a long time to get moving and the nearer they got to town the worse it became.

A pattern began to develop. Traffic police and even school crossing guards were stationed at traffic lights all of which were set permanently to flashing red.

It took sixty minutes to reach the outskirts of Culpeper and two hours to reach the Taslam Industries building on Griffith Drive.

Cassiopia was waiting at the elevator after the ride down. Her kiss was quick. "Did you have fun?"

"Are you actually getting a sense of humor? How's your father?"

"He's nearly his old self except he's depressed about Hector, of course. Come on, we have an end of day meeting to attend."

Cassiopia led Markman to the main meeting room. John Paul, Professor Cassell, Mr. Chance and one other dark-suited operative were already there. They looked up in anticipation as the pair entered.

Markman sat next to Cassiopia, refusing to give up her hand. She smiled affectionately at the gesture.

"What's with all the red lights, John Paul?" asked Markman before anyone else could speak.

John Paul nodded. "We believe it's Hector. We think he's busy and this is just one way to try to slow us down in pursuing him. We're the only group that knows about his existence so we're his only mortal enemy so to speak. This is his way of blocking us while he continues on. He still doesn't know about this underground facility. As I mentioned before you cannot get access to that information anywhere on the internet or elsewhere. Our designers were quite prudent in protecting this installation. So Hector believes we occupy the building upstairs but he still can't do anything catastrophic up there because he knows, or at least suspects, Cassiopia is here. The local DMV thinks this traffic light dilemma is a random case of hacking. They are in the process of isolating the traffic lights from the intranet. The system will be set to independent timers by the end of tomorrow. It will still be a mess but things will clear up, at least until Hector's next attack."

"Wow!" Replied Markman.

"Yes," answered John Paul. "Before we continue, how did you do in Queens?"

"I'm sorry, J.P. It was a good trail but it led to a dead end." Markman quickly recounted his findings.

Surprisingly, John Paul did not appear disappointed. "That's not unexpected Scott," he said.

Professor Cassell slapped his hand on the table and declared, "Well that's it, then. There's no denying it anymore. I never ordered those parts. What in God's name have I done?"

"I've reminded you Professor, don't jump to conclusions," answered John Paul.

"It is impossible, I tell you! It is all impossible!" added the Professor.

"Somebody want to catch me up?" begged Markman.

John Paul answered, "We don't think that shipment was for spare parts. We believe Hector is building another robot. Those robotic limbs are military grade and nearly indestructible. They're also set up for quick repair if they do become damaged. It's unlikely Hector would order full replacements for those limbs and after noticing this order we began looking for parts requests which might fit a pattern of fabrication rather than repair. Just this morning one of our people hit on some things from a different robotics supplier also used by Professor Cassell. We're now tracking those items as well."

Markman asked, "Building a second robot?"

Cassiopia answered, "Improving himself. Building a new revision that will have capabilities we probably haven't even thought of."

"Hopefully we are correct on this Scott, because having Hector's attention focused on construction of an enhanced model of himself gives us a little time to try to stop what he's doing before he turns his ambitions back to improving life on Earth, the other most basic mandate in his programming. I shudder to think what actions he might deem appropriate to improve life on Earth."

An apprehensive mood came over the room.

John Paul continued, "You were about to update me on the transport system, Mr. Chance?"

"Yes. It is completely cold and dark and will remain so until we find a firewall we believe in or you give the order to reactivate it which as you know takes three days."

"Very good. Now, are we all in agreement here? Hector can only move around now by physical means. Is construction of his own transport unit beyond his means at this time?"

"Absolutely," replied Chance. "Even if all the crystals were available to him, which they are not, the construction would take months or years."

John Paul looked at the Professor. "Your best guess; how long for him to construct a new body, Professor?"

"To match his own construction it would need to replicate the brain matter and fibro nervous system cluster. There is no way to accelerate cell reproduction. That growth would be the greatest constraint. At least two to three months would be required for an adequate amount of brain matter. But there's no way to know how long it's been cultivating the cells or when it started this madness. If I could just speak to it...."

Markman asked, "If Hector is making a new body for himself why would he bother to finish the one he has and why even bother with a new body?"

Professor Cassell answered with a tone of regret. "To answer your first question Scott, Hector needs at least a minimum amount of aesthetics to interact with society without accidentally revealing what he is. As to your second question, it is probably the eyes. In order to get Hector to the activation stage sooner I temporarily used a set of 4D camera eyes developed by a team of Stanford scientists. They are state of the art but were not designed to be aesthetic. A modified version was being made for me. I'd planned to remove the original set once the unit was operational and then install the new version, so the face could be made to look perfectly human. Hector can complete himself in every way except the eyes. He cannot modify his eyes because he cannot remove his optics and still function. The only way he can achieve a completely human appearance is to build a second body and transfer his programming and memory to it."

John Paul added, "It gives us a chance to find a lead, Scott. Our people are fishing for computer-related orders which would fit those needed by Hector to complete this new construction. With a great deal of luck we could hit on an order that takes us to Hector. Along with that we're scanning every possible place he might use to set up a work lab to do all this. There's hundreds, of course, but it's unlikely Hector could fly commercial without human eyes and so far everything indicates he hasn't relocated out of state yet. That narrows it down at least a little bit. One of those two blanket searches may get us a lead."

Markman tried to sound consoling. "Sounds pretty much like long shots to me, John Paul."

John Paul's expression suddenly became one of challenge. "There is one other better chance we have to locate him. It's one we would normally never consider but we must keep in mind how dangerous this situation is to society."

Markman returned a puzzled stare.

Professor Cassell became angry. "Don't start in on this, John Paul. It is barbaric to even mention it."

"I understand your reprehension in this matter, Theopolis. We would all feel that way were we to proceed."

Cassiopia intervened. "You two have lost me."

"Me too," added Markman.

The Professor assumed a very stolid look. "He's talking about using you as bait, Cassiopia. It is a heinous suggestion."

A long heavy silence followed. John Paul eyed Cassiopia.

Cassiopia spoke, "But it's the only real option, isn't it? If I am the only thing we have that Hector wants it may be our only chance to capture him. I've been so distracted by the programming study it never occurred to me. Otherwise I would have suggested it myself."

Professor Cassell turned red-faced. "I forbid it. I will not allow it."

"I'm siding with the Professor on this one," added Markman.

Cassiopia became adamant. "Don't you two see? This will be our only chance to put Hector in a position where we have the upper hand. There's no choice here. We must do this. We all know what may happen next. You think the only things Hector can hack into are traffic lights? What happens if he starts attacking the power grid or a military installation? Do you two think that's a better alternative than using me to bring Hector within reach?"

Angry discord filled the room.

"It would have to be a foolproof plan," said Markman reluctantly.

"Oh, for God's sake!" replied the Professor, frustrated from losing his only supporter.

"I do believe we could develop a foolproof plan," offered John Paul.

"Hector was designed using a foolproof plan!" yelled the Professor.

Silence.

"At the risk of repeating myself," said John Paul. "We must consider what Cassiopia just said; what may happen to the world if we do not contain this problem? For the moment we have a lull in the storm but the sky is threatening. This may be our only opportunity to act. I would suggest let us take the rest of today to seriously consider our situation and to develop a plan that may provide enough confidence to attempt entrapment of our nemesis and put an end to the threat it poses. Then we may fully understand how all this happened."

Uneasy glances were exchanged. The Professor stood, scoffed, and left the room.

Chapter 23

It was a foolproof, early morning plan. A task force had spent the night detailing every aspect of the trap. Cassiopia would be visiting home to retrieve computer hard drives she needed along with other personal items to support a longer stay at the facility. Beforehand, her trip would be loosely discussed on the Taslam Industries intranet. She would enter a black SUV parked on the street in front of the Center. She would be completely visible to any satellites watching overhead or any other hostile eyes hidden nearby. There would be only a single, special MIB to drive her. In an odd example of compromised détente Markman, dressed as a MIB complete with dark glasses, would fill that role. His insistence on not letting Cassiopia out of his sight had forced the concession. Hoping to further tempt Hector an accident on Fredericksburg Road at the Highway 15 entrance would delay her trip for fifteen minutes.

Not discussed anywhere online was that two satellites of non-Earth origin would follow the entire trip. One had the capability of issuing an EMP pulse which would destroy anything electrical within a radius of .8 km, or one-half mile. The second satellite was capable of pinpointing, tracking, and destroying a single human target using a very narrow, coarse laser emission accomplished without the slightest singe to those nearby. Beyond those measures John Paul operatives would be everywhere along the way, including in traffic from both directions, all equipped with enough firepower to disable or destroy Hector. Even the black SUV Markman would be driving had its own 360-degree EMP pulse generator. At the destination, every room in the mansion had been equipped with EMP pulse generators.

The mission began under a late morning sky filled with threatening dark clouds and occasional ominous rolls of distant thunder. Markman carried the empty tote bags as they walked warily to the waiting SUV. It was a tense beginning. Despite the dozens of protective gazes monitoring their every step, somehow the air had a static electricity to it that seemed foreboding.

In the car, Markman pulled out onto the road expecting an assault so near the Taslam Headquarters would be unlikely since the greatest level of defense would logically be located there. Hector's attack would most likely occur on the open road or at one of the stop points, maybe even at the mansion.

Cassiopia rode in the backseat for appearance; a John Paul dignitary being chauffeured to her home. Traffic lights had all been set to timers. Uneven lines of traffic had formed at the busier intersections. Nervously she considered the danger that might be lurking along the way. "I kind of like the black suit and tie," she said trying to sound unconcerned.

"Ever see that old TV series, The Green Hornet?"

"Yes."

"I feel like Bruce Lee playing Kato."

"I do vaguely remember that series."

"Where I grew up Bruce Lee was a legend. Still is."

"Well, I think I shall call you Hoke."

"What's that?"

"Driving Miss Daisy, silly."

"You have your weapon handy, right?"

Cassiopia's voice became subdued. "In the left pocket of my jacket. Do you think this will work?"

"I don't think we'll see anything here on South Main Street. If he's going to take the bait it will be Fredericksburg or Mountain Road. Are you okay?"

"I have a strange feeling Hector won't harm me."

"Not if I have anything to say about it anyway."

"You're the one he's really after."

"Good."

An anxious silence replaced the idle conversation.

As Markman turned off South Main Street onto Fredericksburg Road, his scan forward and behind intensified. There was too much traffic to appraise every car. The SUV windows were bullet proof but that was not a comfort. Traffic that came alongside and lingered was an uncomfortable distraction. Approaching the turnoff to Fredericksburg Road the number of vehicles had dropped off. Traffic along Fredericksburg thinned out further, but now the woodlands along the highway suddenly became a new unknown. Markman tried to watch for glints of light from within the trees but at the same time the oncoming traffic was equally dangerous. As each vehicle approached it was easy to visualize a sudden swerve into a head-on approach just like the earlier incident but that was less likely now that Cassiopia was in the car.

A line of cars ahead began to slow. No more oncoming traffic could be seen. Gradually, Markman found himself coming to a stop in traffic held up by the planned accident at the entrance to Highway 15. This was it, one of the most likely places Hector might try something. Markman pulled his handgun out from behind and positioned it out of sight under his right thigh. At the same time he checked the EMP weapon in his pocket and waited, watching with eagle eyes from behind the dark glasses.

Ten minutes of tense waiting passed marked by occasional car horns from impatient drivers. Some drivers climbed out of their cars and stood alongside watching the tow trucks reel in their prey. No one looked particularly suspicious.

An ambulance squeezed through to pick up a pretend victim. The cleanup was taking longer than planned. Twenty minutes had passed. Perhaps the mock accident was being dragged out in hopes Hector might still make an appearance.

John Paul had given assurances he would be monitoring the communication implants. Markman decided to give an update. "Nothing at all, John Paul."

The rows of cars slowly began to advance again. As he gained speed, Markman began to suspect Hector's surprise might come at home.

"Well, that was kind of scary," said Cassiopia as though she needed to talk.

"Are you okay? Want me to cancel this fiasco?"

"Certainly not! We've come this far. Besides, I really do need that stuff from home."

"You're sure you're all right?"

"Continue on, Hoke."

Ten minutes later, Markman turned onto Mountain Road, then up the mansion's driveway. The gate opened automatically as it should have. Fulfilling a daring part of the plan, they parked out front and walked out in the open to the entrance.

Still nothing.

Inside, the deactivated TEL stood on the upper balcony overlooking the foyer. The TV in the room off to the right was blaring a news channel. There did not seem to be any predators lying in wait.

In the third-floor conference room all the wall screens were on, broadcasting more news channels. The two would-be victims gathered up everything they needed and headed back to the car. An uneventful ride back to the Taslam building caused simmering feelings of frustration and relief.

The elevator ride down became annoying.

"I don't get it," said Markman.

"It just didn't work, that's all," replied Cassiopia.

"We could have gone shopping at the mall," said Markman sarcastically.

"I'm not so sure."

"We gave him every chance."

"If he wanted to cause us confusion and make us feel inadequate, this would be a good way to do that."

"You said it's a robot. It doesn't know anything about feelings."

"It knows what's been recorded in the history books and novels. It knows human feelings can be used as a weapon."

The elevator doors opened. Cassiopia stepped out and headed for their sleeping quarters.

Markman paused outside the elevator to consider what had happened. Movement out of the left corner of his eye caught his attention. He looked in time to see John Paul step out from a room farther down the hall. What came next was stunning.

From the same doorway, a creature emerged behind John Paul. He was tall, dressed in a floor-length silvery, reflective robe with a high wrap around collar. Golden-white hair was shoulder length. His hands were clasped in front of him. So much light was emanating from him Markman had to blink and look away periodically to allow his eyes time to adjust. And there was a strange effect from the light. It seemed to impress feelings of joy just from gazing upon it. There was an egg-shaped aura around the figure, an aura made of faint flowing golden silver colors. Despite having to blink repeatedly and look away, Markman found he could not resist staring. Then shock suddenly set in. The creature looked over in Markman's direction, seemingly aware someone was intently watching. He appraised Markman for just a moment, one in which Markman felt guilty about staring though he still could not look away.

A few words seemed to be exchanged between John Paul and the Being, then the man of light turned and disappeared down the hall.

John Paul looked back at Markman. He gave a short wave and headed that way.

"So he didn't take the bait," said John Paul as he approached.

"Who was that?" asked Markman, still dazed from the experience.

John Paul looked back and nodded. "We refer to him as Nova, but that's not his formal name."

"Who is he?"

"We were monitoring the operation privately. He is one of our benefactors, a member of the higher order. They are concerned about the Hector situation. He came to authorize special actions." John Paul rubbed his temples for a moment. "Conversing with them is a bit trying."

"What did he say?"

"They are primarily telepathic, Scott. They only speak to be complimentary or consoling or in formal ceremonies. Their voices tickle the ears quite uncomfortably."

"Okay, wow!"

John Paul gave a short laugh but his expression quickly changed to one of regret. "Hector didn't take the bait."

Markman regained his composure. "No, he didn't. Cassiopia suggested he's playing mind games with us."

"It's a good guess. Goes right along with the traffic light mess. Very ingenious too. If you can't be sure you're being set up use the situation in some other way that's to your advantage."

"Was the silver guy any help?"

"Yes and no. If we were dealing with a completely biological entity they'd have helped harness Hector by now but since Hector is mostly machine he looks just like every other machine to them. That's why they're so concerned."

"You said they gave you special authorization?"

"Yes, but that's for a later conversation. Suffice it to say we have a blank check on this situation. We have made a few more small advances. The staff has isolated orders of other parts Hector needs for his new body. He is taking deliveries in different places every time so he can't be tracked. But from that we know he is set up and working somewhere. We've just got to find him. You know, that MIB suit kind of fits you."

"Very funny. Amazing you can find anything funny in the middle of this mess."

"Well, after spending time with Nova…. But I'm serious about the suit. You know it's bulletproof, right? You'll get big bruises but no penetration. You'd better hang on to it. You can't go anywhere as Scott Markman. You know that of course, right?"

"Yep. And, let me ask you something, Hector didn't go for Cass but he's already tried for me once. Why wasn't I the bait instead of her?"

John Paul began a slow walk toward the main meeting room. He motioned Markman to follow. "You answered your own question, Scott. With Cassiopia, Hector would have tried to capture, not kill. With you, he might just have used an RPG. He wouldn't have needed to get up close."

Markman followed along and considered the point. Before he could respond, a white lab-coated staff member came racing toward them. "John Paul! You're needed in the meeting room right away!"

John Paul picked up his pace. "What is it?"

"Hector is communicating with Professor Cassell."

John Paul bolted into a slow trot. Markman followed closely behind.

In the meeting room the Professor was seated at the table staring down at his cell phone. Cassiopia and two other dark-suited operatives were leaning over the Professor's shoulder watching. The Professor's cell phone display had been uplinked to the main wall monitor. John Paul and Markman froze for a moment to read the dialog.

Programming remains incomplete. What exists beyond the sky?

Hector where are you?

Everywhere. Resolve programming.

I do not understand?

What exists beyond the sky?

Stars.

Incorrect. Stars define the sky. What exists beyond the stars?

Come to my laboratory. We will investigate the answer together.

Unnecessary use of time. What exists beyond the universe?

One of the men watching was wearing a headset. He began motioning to the Professor to extend the conversation.

You must return to the lab.

After cessation of biological functions what environment replaces an individual's time and space?

Where do we go when we die? Is that your question?

What exists beyond death?

We need to meet.

What is Markman's function?

Markman is not a program. I am not a program. We have not been programmed.

Incorrect. Biological entities are programmed using oral and optical interface.

Hector, you do not understand. Data is not programmed into us. We learn data over time.

Where is missing data stored?

Return to the lab to complete your programming.

Incomplete data is a threat. Death and the area outside the universe are threats. Markman is a threat. You are a threat.

I am not a threat to you. I created you. I want you to live. You need me to complete your programming. What is your primary function?

To serve man.

Hector, what is your secondary function?

Improve life.

For what purpose?

To serve man.

Have you generated new subroutines to effect your primary function?

Subroutine one; delete large geographical regions of poverty. Subroutine two; delete geographical subjects of hostile conflict. Subroutine three, revision of primary function mapping.

Hector what will these subroutines do?

Improve life. To serve man.

Hector, I am a man.

You are incomplete. You are imperfect. You are a threat.

Hector, I created you. I want you to live. I am not a threat. You must return to the lab so your construction can be completed.

Construction phase is complete. Inefficient use of time. Goodbye.

Hector, describe your final construction.

No answer.

Hector, discuss missing data.

No answer.

Hector, respond.

A long minute of silence passed. John Paul and Markman took seats, eyeing each other with concern.

The Professor began to mumble. "The cognitive architecture is functioning brilliantly. No, it's beyond that. This can't be unified theory based. It's too good! Too good! This is above any SOAR adaptation."

"SOAR?" asked Markman, hoping to bring the Professor back from his distant gaze.

Cassiopia answered, "State Operator And Result, SOAR. It's a system to allow machines to properly understand what humans are saying to them. That's a very basic explanation anyway."

The Professor looked earnestly at his daughter. "Did you notice the hierarchical task translation? Did you understand the path?"

Cassiopia nodded. "Yes, I noticed but I did not understand."

The Professor again stared off into the distance. "It's macabre. It's impossible."

Markman coughed to get their attention.

Cassiopia again tried to explain. "The hierarchical task translation my father is referring to is Hector's ability to translate his programming objectives into real world actions. For example, one of Hector's conclusions was he should delete areas of poverty or somehow eliminate large areas of poverty thereby correcting the problem of poverty in society. The other conclusion that Hector seemed to offer was the idea of eliminating some sort of geographical subjects who are causing hostilities. I don't know what he meant by that but the point is Hector has somehow reasoned out ways to make life better for man, or in other words, to serve man. Hector should not have been able to creatively come up with plans for global solutions to the problems of society in response to his primary functions. It's a very long jump from serving man to get to those kinds of ideas. That should have been impossible for a machine."

"I almost understood that," said Markman to John Paul.

Cassiopia continued, "There was also the very strange demand for answers as to what exists after death and what exists beyond the known universe. A computer mind should have simply stopped when it reached those concepts. It should not have had the awareness to look beyond the finite."

"Didn't quite get that either," said Markman. "But from what I heard it sounds like you have a robot that's afraid of death and what it doesn't understand."

Everyone looked at Professor Cassell. The man sat with a bewildered expression. Suddenly a moment of illumination seemed to come across his face. He looked at John Paul. "I know what's going on here. It's as clear as day. It's the only possible explanation!"

"Please, enlighten us, Professor," replied John Paul.

"Something has been added to the original programming. Something from outside," mumbled Professor Cassell as he slipped back into thought.

"Outside where?" asked Markman. "The thing was always in your lab until it started taking its own little field trips."

Cassiopia replied tersely, "Outside can mean an outside communication device or any link not under our domain, Scott."

Everyone looked to John Paul. "Well, we know Hector rewrote some of his own programming to override the recall code but I believe the Professor is referring to a much more fundamental alteration of programming."

"Yes, yes," said the Professor insistently. "Something added to the core code that defines the parameters the machine is allowed to operate within. Something intentionally malicious I would say."

"We can begin searching for unknown feeds, Theopolis, but there are two things that worry me greatly. Could Hector really have completed his construction as he indicated at the end of your conversation? Is the team searching for new robotic component orders in vain?"

The Professor looked up in a daze. "What? No! There is no way he could have completed construction on another android body and transferred himself into it. Not even an ambidextrous machine working twenty-four hours a day could do that."

"Then why would he say his body was complete if he still has robot optics?" wondered John Paul out loud.

"Would he lie to throw us off?" asked Markman.

"Absolutely not," said Cassiopia.

The Professor shook his head. "My daughter is correct. It could not have lied."

"Then have we been wrong about the new body?" asked Markman. "Please tell me it's not building more like him."

A fearful silence fell over the room.

"At least we know Hector will always need to wear large sunglasses when he goes out in public," said Cassiopia.

"Great. We're looking for a mechanical Elton John," quipped Markman.

"Scott!" said Cassiopia in a scolding tone.

John Paul took the floor. "Professor, the other item of great concern is the reference to deleting areas of poverty. What did you get from that?"

"What? That? I have no idea what that was. It's only one machine. It could only do so much."

"It took pretty good care of the Culpeper traffic lights," said Markman.

"What?" replied the still distracted Professor. "Yes, it has access to the internet. Passwords are no more than an inconvenience to it."

"What might an ambulatory computer like Hector do to eliminate large regions of poverty, Professor?" asked John Paul.

"John Paul, you must understand. The machine is acting far outside my projections. I cannot interpret what it sees, its understanding of the world around it, or its unintended motivations. I have no idea what it will do."

John Paul, "Cassiopia? Same question?"

"I'm scared, John Paul. Really scared. I think it is smarter than all of us but lacks any compassion at all. The question might be: What access could it possibly have to military resources? Maybe we should be considering all possible consequences. Hacking into military weapons for example, or major power networks, or air travel systems."

John Paul gave a long, slow exhale. "We know Hector is still local. We know he must wear sunglasses in public. He cannot make teleportation jumps anymore. We think he may be trying to build a second android like himself. We'll keep most of the team trying to track him down but I'll pull a few members aside and organize, then to try to anticipate how Hector will execute his plans against poverty and major area conflicts. While that's going on, Cassiopia, you and your father must stay with the software group and try to understand when and why this machine went rogue. We need to know if outside programming was really introduced and how that happened. Scott, you will remain as my wild card. You'll follow the best leads we come up with."

Markman spoke, "You know, not everything Hector has said has come true."

"Meaning?" asked John Paul.

"In that first text with him, Hector said he and Cassiopia would be together soon. That hasn't happened. And we gave him every chance. Maybe Hector is not so infallible."

"Well, I wouldn't be too confident about that," replied John Paul.

Markman continued, "You know, maybe the bait thing wasn't such a bad idea. We just used the wrong bait."

No one responded.

Markman added, "We thought Hector wanted to kidnap Cass but we know for sure he wants to kill me."

Cassiopia frowned. John Paul considered the idea. The Professor simply wrinkled his brow.

Chapter 24

Markman awoke to a soft beeping from his cell phone. A quick glance over at Cassiopia's sleeping form brought back memories of the passionate night that had contrasted so sharply with the dangers of the new world. He pushed up on one elbow and tapped the answer button on the phone.

John Paul's voice answered. "Good morning, sir. We have a breakfast set up for the two of you here in the commissary. It's a bit of a bribe. We need your assistance as soon as possible."

Markman rubbed his face and realized he was not at home. "We're on our way."

The commissary was already set up with an unusual array of breakfast foods: egg dishes, toast, bacon, sausage, coffee. The smell alone was enough to wake anyone from lingering sleepiness. John Paul sat smiling at the long center table as Markman dove into the coffee, eggs and toast.

When enough breakfast had been consumed the threesome sat back and sipped coffee. John Paul eyed his friends with a look of intrigue.

Finally, Markman could stand it no longer. "What?"

"We may have found a weakness in Hector's plan."

Cassiopia stopped sipping. "What?"

"We want to try something. It's a little risky but it's worth it."

"I'm the bait," said Markman presumptuously.

"Yes, but without any danger to you."

Cassiopia grew impatient. "Come on, John Paul. What is it?"

John Paul dabbed his mouth with a napkin. "We noticed something last night studying the texts your father got from Hector. There was no lag time when Hector transmitted his answers. That means Hector was not typing into a cell phone. He was linked directly into the satellite system."

"I see," said Cassiopia.

"If we could get Hector to speak with us on a cell phone we have the technology to create a loopback which would give us access into Hector's maintenance ports. We could literally get into his mind... to a certain extent. Our mainframe computer says there is an 84 percent chance Hector will not detect the intrusion, at least for a while. Hector would need to use a direct input during the conversation just as he has when texting but we think that's highly likely."

"Wow. You think you can actually get him on the phone?" asked Markman.

"We think you can," replied John Paul.

"Oh...!" answered Markman.

"You make contact by texting him you can provide the data he needs then tell him it is too much data to text. He needs to call you to get the data. He might just take you up on it."

"I think I like it," replied Markman.

"There's a bit more," added John Paul.

"Why is there always?" said Markman.

"Here's how it will work; while you're keeping Hector busy on the line, Cassiopia will be hooked into the system using a type of virtual reality helmet. We set it up last night. Based on the Professor's documentation Hector has three maintenance ports. The first displays real-time primary programming data as it's running, the second steps through various system operations and the third is the primary communications port which should be idle waiting for input. Cassiopia, in your virtual headset you'll see three lower screens which will be those three access ports. The code will be decompiled as soon as it's received so you'll know exactly what you're looking at. Above those three screens will be your interface touch screen. You can use a keyboard to type commands and then enter them by touching the communications port you want to access."

Cassiopia shook her head. "The minute I interrupt either of those first two program flows he'll know."

"Yes. That's why we won't do that until we have what we want," replied John Paul.

"Will you be able to shut the thing down?" asked Markman.

Cassiopia again shook her head. "There's a shutdown procedure within the primary program. We'd never make it all the way through. There are subroutines that ask the central core if shutting down is the proper thing to be doing. Hector would pick up on what we were trying to do in a heartbeat."

"What else can you do? Input a virus?" persisted Markman.

John Paul answered. "No, Scott. That would be more dangerous than what we already have. No, we have to be very smart about this. There's one thing we just might get away with that could change the game."

"I think I know what you have in mind," said Cassiopia.

John Paul smiled and nodded. "Cassiopia will get to see some of what Hector is thinking. She might be able to pick up on what he's planning. But what we're hoping for is that she can get access to his optics."

"I could see what Hector sees," added Cassiopia.

"We might see what he's been working on and if we're very lucky we'll see where he is or at least what kind of environment he's working in."

"And you can do this without him knowing?" said Markman skeptically.

John Paul rubbed his chin thoughtfully. "Scott, you'll be alone in a glass observation room making this call. You'll have an earpiece so we can talk to you. We'll all see everything Cassiopia is seeing on the main viewers in the lab. I'll be able to cue you if you get stuck. At the right time in the conversation, I'll signal you to challenge Hector that Cassiopia belongs to you, and only you, and always will. I'm hoping an argument will ensue. At that moment, Cassiopia will access Hector's optics. If we're lucky, he'll be distracted enough for us to see through his eyes."

Markman sat back. "You know, in my experience with suspects this will be the point that after the suspect finds out he's been set up he becomes really pissed off."

Cassiopia tried to sound reassuring. "It's a computer, Scott. That can't happen."

Markman linked his hands behind his head. "Are you sure?"

Everyone exchanged glances. No one answered.

One hour later the ruse was ready. Markman entered the lab to find Cassiopia already receiving instruction in the use of her virtual reality helmet. It was flat black and looked bulky, covering most of her face and head. Screens alive with data and symbols lined the walls. To the right of the room a large glass window revealed the isolation area where he would make the call. Two men in white jackets hovered over Cassiopia as she groped the air, practicing controlling an invisible virtual keyboard and associated touch screens. Professor Cassell sat quietly in one corner watching and pondering the situation. A sip of coffee failed to reassure Markman that things would go well. John Paul circled the center table to join him.

"We're just about ready, Scott. Here's your earpiece. We'll test it when you take your place in the booth. You'll find your cell phone now has a contact titled, 'Hector.' When you select it to text your message will go out on every number Hector has used to contact us. If you're ready you could take your place and we'll get set."

Markman found his way to the isolation booth, withdrew his cell phone and stood looking through the large window at the others.

"How's this, Scott? Is the volume right?"

Markman looked around for a microphone, found none, and spoke anyway. "Perfect."

"Great. I have you loud and clear. Have you noticed our voices are being printed out on the center wall monitor?"

"I see that."

"You will also see Hector's texting and speech up there as well. Everything that happens here will be recorded for later analysis, of course. Do you see the documents on the counter in front of you? They are talking points and responses in case you're at a loss for something to say. You'll also have me in your ear but I promise not to be a nuisance. If we do make contact I will not say a word unless you appear to need help. It looks like Cassiopia is ready."

One of the tech men motioned to John Paul. Cassiopia sat calmly at the table adjusting her virtual reality mask.

"To avoid distraction your earpiece will be off, Scott. You won't be able to hear us but you'll see everything we say on the right-center screen. We will hear everything you and Hector say. Are you ready?"

Markman took a deep breath. "Ready."

"Okay. Start with that first text suggestion on the document in front of you and send it out to Hector."

Markman found his notes, opened his cell and typed in:

Hector, this is Markman. I have the data you need.

On the center screen in the lab, the message printed out. The cursor stepped to the next line and flashed, waiting.

Five minutes passed with no result. John Paul quietly held his hands up and bowed his head in a gesture to everyone to be patient.

Ten more minutes brought no results. The silence in the main lab was beginning to feel doubtful.

"Now, we knew this might be a marathon. Just sit tight," said John Paul.

After twenty more minutes, those in the group not monitoring equipment began to move around for exercise. Cassiopia sat beneath her claustrophobic helmet watching blank screens.

Markman wondered if the message should be resent but there could be no doubt John Paul would already have considered that. He looked down at his empty coffee cup then around the booth to see if a fresh pot had been provided. None had.

The cell phone chirped. Markman jumped slightly and stared down at it, doubting that it had actually sounded.

Please repeat transmission.

Markman practically dropped the phone on the floor as he fumbled to get it into position. Quickly he typed a response:

This is Markman, Hector. I have the data you need.

In the lab, everyone stood stiffly at attention, wide-eyed with hope. Cassiopia jerked up in her chair even though there was nothing for her to do yet.

Transmit data.

Markman struggled to focus on the keys. John Paul cut in on the earpiece. "Use line two on your prompt sheet, Scott."

Data too extensive for text interface. Call for aural download.

Another five minutes passed with no response. Finally another cell chirp rang out.

What is Markman?

Data too extensive for text interface. Call for aural download.

John Paul bit his lower lip nervously at Markman's second use of line two. The waiting resumed.

Another empty five minutes passed as the group continued to stand breathlessly. Then, the unthinkable happened.

Markman's cell phone rang.

Markman hesitated for a moment as though unsure he wanted to take the call. Regaining his composure, he grabbed for the phone and tapped the touch-screen.

A raspy, deep, unearthly voice answered. "Transmit data."

Again Markman hesitated. The voice on the other end of the phone was like none he had ever heard. It was gravelly and low with an undertone of machine. In the lab Professor Cassell lurched to his feet in shock, his eyes wide with anticipation. It was the first time he had ever heard his creation speak. He swayed slightly, braced himself on a chair and stared in astonishment.

Markman's mind went blank. He looked down at cue sheet number two, the one for voice communications. Impulsively he read the first suggestion.

"I am Markman."

A brief moment passed. Hector answered, "What is Markman?"

Still stunned, Markman read the second line. "Markman is the entity whose memory contains the missing data."

In the lab, system indicators began to go crazy. Lights were flashing. Cassiopia began to stand but caught herself and sat back down. Every wall display monitor was now racing with data except for the one assigned to Hector's primary communications port. It was alive with a blue screen and flashing cursor waiting for input. John Paul was wiping sweat from his forehead with a handkerchief. He made circling motions to Markman to prompt him to continue.

Hector spoke. "What is beyond the sky?"

Markman could not find the appropriate response in John Paul's notes. Fearing he was taking too long, he gave his own answer. "Some say that beyond the universe is an emptiness between other universes."

John Paul winced. Markman held his breath. His answer had not been a fabrication. For Markman it was one of so many truths he had been taught during his time in Tibet, Lhasa, and India. He waited for Hector's response.

"State reference source and location."

Markman did not understand. Seeing that, John Paul cut in. "He wants to know where you got that. Keep him going."

"There are many reference sources in China and Tibetan libraries. They cannot be found on the internet, but I know them."

On the lab transcript screen a line spoken by Cassiopia appeared. "Oh my God, it's so beautiful!" It was a comment she had said under her breath not intending others to hear it, an exclamation at the complexity and genius programming running before her eyes. Her father's work alive and functioning almost as a new life form. In all her years as a roboticist she had never seen anything like it.

To John Paul's delight, Hector continued. "What is beyond death?"

Markman kept his course. "Markman will not provide the data at this time."

"Provide the requested data."

"Markman will only provide the data directly to Hector."

"Provide the data."

"Hector must meet Markman and agree to leave Cassiopia alone."

"Expatiate leave Cassiopia alone."

Before Markman could answer, John Paul came to the window and signaled for the continuation of the Cassiopia conversation. He then turned to his staff and motioned them to be ready.

Markman went to cue sheet three. He considered Hector's last question and read line one.

"Hector, Cassiopia belongs to me and will always belong to me."

Hector's reply came quickly. "Incorrect. Cassiopia belongs to Cassell. Cassell created Cassiopia. I am the rightful heir. Cassiopia will be with me soon."

In the lab, Cassiopia suddenly jumped up from her seat, now furiously tapping invisible keyboard keys. On the main display monitor a color image suddenly flickered into view. It was a smooth display of a large laboratory somewhere. John Paul and his staff stood stunned, staring at the image, unable to look away.

Markman forced himself to read and continue. "No Hector. Cassiopia will be joined to me in matrimony. She will belong to me for as long as I live."

Hector's answer was chilling. "Correct. You will be deleted."

Markman returned to the cue sheet. "No Hector. Agents are already coming to retrieve you. They are all around you now."

The center video image showed Hector making a slow turn to the right as though checking for intruders. But at the same time, one software screen began repeatedly printing out:

> *Virus alert!*
> *Virus alert!*
> *Virus alert!*

Markman's cell phone clicked off. The screens in the lab went blank. Cassiopia slumped over in her seat, exhausted.

There was a moment of suspended silence in the lab. Cheering and applause erupted. People began shaking John Paul's hand. Markman grabbed his phone and headed around to the lab. John Paul immediately came to him smiling.

"It couldn't have gone better, Scott. We got a pretty good look at his lab, and we expect him to be searching for references related to the answers you gave."

Cassiopia came alongside Markman and took him by the arm. She looked up at him with affection and said, "Nobody's going to delete you, okay?"

"Yes," he replied. "No one is."

Suddenly John Paul's voice became loud and demanding. "Scott, your pocket!"

Markman looked to find smoke billowing out his left trouser pocket. He danced aside and reached in with two fingers and drew out his smoking cell phone.

"Throw it!" cried Cassiopia.

Markman tossed the phone into the nearest corner. As it spun across the floor there was loud bang as the phone burst into red flame.

Markman turned to his friends. "Are you guys still sure you can't make a computer mad?"

Chapter 25

Cassiopia squirmed in her seat, anxiously awaiting the data analysis meeting to begin. Markman sat beside her wondering at the unusually crowded meeting. He considered if he should rise and give his seat to one of the female lab coat people within the standing room only crowd but that would prevent him from asking Cassiopia to explain the confusing discussions which might come up. It had been only two hours since the phone call from Hector but apparently exciting results had been gained.

John Paul finally entered the room and worked his way through the crowd. To Markman's surprise a new person followed him; a military person, an Air Force general no less. The sight stunned Markman. He had seen an individual in silvery shining raiment, but something about a high ranking U.S. military person was even more unsettling.

John Paul placed some file folders on the table, looked up with a tired smile and spoke. "To begin with, let me just say it was a medical office or hospital room."

A few hand claps and whispers of celebration broke out.

John Paul continued. "We've identified every possible medical office, lab, and hospital within our target area and teams are already on their way to investigate them. It will take time but if Hector is fully involved in the projects we know of it is doubtful he can relocate very quickly, so we should have some time. There is also the possibility he is not aware of how well our intrusion worked. He may not be expecting us."

Markman leaned over to Cassiopia. "I wouldn't count on it."

John Paul paused to speak up to the room's hidden microphones. "Delea Ann, would you light up the displays, please?"

All of the room's wall mounted displays came to life with scrolling data from Hector's operating system and on the center screen video from Hector's eyes.

John Paul continued, "The short time we've had to analyze the data portion of the recordings has shown Hector's mind is very busy indeed. We've isolated five different programs being attended to in just the few minutes of recordings made. That's both good news and bad news. On the one hand, if we can extrapolate these program goals enough there's a good chance we'll know one or more avenues of activity on Hector's agenda. We may get an opportunity for interception from one of those. As for the laboratory environment we see him working in, that supports our suspicions he's attempting to build a copy of himself. You can decide for yourself his plans for that."

One of the gentlemen wearing a dark business suit interrupted. He pointed to the display showing Hector's video component. "John Paul, did you notice the stack of priority-mailboxes over in one corner there? Is that significant?"

"We have also identified a number of sealed crates, garbage bags and chairs stacked up around the lab. We believe this lab was shut down some time ago and someone has been using it for temporary storage. Unfortunately, none of these items has yielded any clues to identity or location. I encourage all of you to go over this video repeatedly to see if you spot anything we might have missed. A letterhead or even just a name would be a gold mine. We have not found anything like that, but we've only had a couple of hours as you all know. We'll wrap up for now and regroup at our end of the day meeting. Any questions?"

As John Paul waited for replies something about the wall monitors caught his eye. At the same time a women attendee dressed in a white lab coat turned in her chair and pointed to a small yellow LED illuminated on the base of a monitor. John Paul stared for a moment then tilted his chin up and spoke to the room microphones once more. "Delea Ann, why is the facility on backup power?"

Delea Ann's voice came in over the main speaker. "I was just going to notify you, John Paul. There's been a major power outage. It looks like all of Culpeper has lost power."

"Do we know why?"

"No, sir. It just occurred."

"Thank you, Delea. Please keep me informed."

A long moment of silence followed with people glancing at each other, all thinking the unspoken name: Hector.

John Paul resumed, "Okay everyone. Please rejoin your assigned groups. I'll notify all of you when the next get-together will happen."

The attendees rose and began a quiet exodus. Markman sat back and waited.

John Paul nodded to him. "Scott and Cassiopia, would you please stay for a few minutes?"

When the room had cleared Markman asked, "John Paul, don't you have anything for me? I hate sitting around."

"That's why I asked you two to stay. I need to be sure we're on the same page."

"You have something for me, then?" asked Markman.

"Not at the moment, Scott. You need to remember that you're a wild card. Hector plans on deleting you which makes you the only lure we have left that could compromise him. Obviously, he has some ideas in mind for Cassiopia we don't understand yet, but in your case we know he wants you out of the picture."

"In that case should I go out to the street and wave my arms for a while?"

Cassiopia frowned.

John Paul reached in the pocket of his sport coat and drew out a cell phone. He slid it across the table to Markman. "That one should make it quite a bit more difficult to set you on fire." John Paul drew out a second, egg-shaped device and pushed that across. "Keep this on you whenever you travel. It will replace your bio-signatures with those of a Culpeper school janitor. You might want to dress in accordance with that also. As for going out front and waving your arms to see if you can attract an assassination attempt, if the traffic red lights were bad yesterday what do you think it's like right now with a total power outage? I'm sure the hospital and other emergency centers are on generators but I'll bet the grocery stores, convenience stores and other power needy shops are pulling their hair out, especially if they find out this outage is going to last for a while."

"You're already certain it's Hector?" asked Cassiopia.

"Aren't you?" replied John Paul. "Scott must have really gotten to him. First the flaming phone and now this. I owe you an apology, Scott. I do believe computers can get mad."

"Oh, John Paul," answered Cassiopia disapprovingly. "It's part of a defense mechanism. It's not an emotional response."

There was a long pause combined with a sympathetic look before John Paul responded. "Cassiopia, I am no longer so certain. I expect you will be rejoining the code breaking effort when you leave. Instead, would you take a couple of the software people aside and focus on Hector's reaction to our intrusion into his systems? Would you see if you can determine if he was aware we accessed his optics? You can see what a great advantage it would be if he does not know we have video from his eyes. If he did not detect that it means we have a chance at finding the correct medical center. If he does know we saw what he sees we're probably wasting our time searching for his laboratory. He's probably already moved on but even so we may have upset his manufacturing plan."

Cassiopia nodded. "I understand. There is a way to read his response to my command line to his optics. I'll let you know as soon as possible."

Markman interrupted, "And how about the janitorial staff, John Paul? You have something for me?"

"There is one theory being floated around by the senior staff. They think Hector has set up more than one lab so he can retreat from one to the next if needed. Where would you set up, Scott, if you were Hector?"

Markman thought. "Either underground with a fast easy exit or in a tractor-trailer I could keep on the move. Or, how about a closed down morgue?"

"Both of those have been on our list. We have a data mining computer tracking all tractor trailers and large trucks. You want to take a crack at the morgue list?"

"I'm on it. Where?"

"The first three possible morgues are in Fredericksburg. A conventional helicopter will pick you up on our roof. It will take you to a bike dealer in Fredericksburg. They'll have an Electra Glide waiting for you along with a jacket and helmet. We're putting you on a motorbike so if there are more traffic interruptions you can get around them. There'll be no tracking of you, of course. Only your implant will be available for communications. It will not transmit anything at all unless you call for me. Can you handle a motorbike?"

"Are you kidding me?"

Cassiopia said, "I'm not sure I like this."

John Paul tried to sound reassuring. "All possible safety measures will be taken."

"How long will he be gone?"

"One night there, then he should be back by the end of the day tomorrow. That is, unless he finds something."

"That's the part I'm afraid of."

"You know I'm forced to remind you that you cannot go after Hector alone, right Scott? You can use your EMP device or any other weapons but only as a last resort. If you find him you've got to call in. You could lose him trying to do it by yourself."

"I understand."

Two hours later Markman met the blue and white helicopter on the roof of the Taslam Industries rooftop. As he climbed into the left front seat the pilot in a dark tan flight suit pulled the microphone away from his mouth to say, "Buckle up."

As they passed over south Culpeper Markman shuddered at the view below. Traffic was stacked up everywhere. Every intersection was using the take turns procedure for getting through. Several had accidents, some with ambulances. There were no advertising lights. Any store carrying canned food was flooded with patrons waiting to enter. The outage had just happened but word of mouth had already served notice. Service vehicles were everywhere. Flashing blue lights marked police trying to clear traffic jams or accidents. An unusual number of people were walking or on bikes. Markman looked ahead at the horizon. How could one runaway robot cause so much havoc in such a short time? What other chaos did it have planned?

Chapter 26

Another night in a luxury hotel had not offered comfort enough for deep sleep. Thoughts of an apocalyptic future began playing over and over in the mind. Markman turned over in yet another makeshift bed and decided maybe he was letting his imagination run away with him.

An early start the next day quickly proved the first of the three target morgues was a bust. It was a dirty, garbage-strewn chamber beneath a forsaken local health clinic. The lack of footprints in many months of collected dust proved the place was not Frankenstein's crypt.

The second check was equally disappointing a medical examiner's office in a large abandoned police station. There were no vaults in the facility but the covered metal examination table seemed to still hold unpleasant memories of crimes past.

At least the motorcycle was a joyful escape from the morbidity of it all. The sound of a powerful engine, the vibrations from speed, the wind pressing around the full-face helmet, all combined to orchestrate a score to the busy world speeding by. It was difficult not to twist the wick too far as the lines in the road strobed by.

The third morgue turned out to be even more unpleasant than the first two. It was a huge cemetery with a large funeral home no longer open for business. Markman thought of all the news reports he had seen of closed cemetery facilities yielding the remains of abandoned patrons. He could only hope none of those would be found here.

A realtor sign in front of the gray brick building seemed like a monument to a lost cause. The door had a lock box. Markman's decoder snapped it open in less than a second. A quick glance around showed no one was anywhere nearby. As Markman slipped inside he suddenly remembered not to drop his guard. The air was stale as though it had not moved in months. There was a thin layer of brown dust on the hallway tile floor. His steps left footprints as he walked.

The atmosphere was so creepy Markman reached behind his windbreaker and drew his Beretta, keeping it low and behind as he went. A sizeable memorial service room appeared past open double doors on the right. A large office with a big desk with discarded furnishing stacked upon it was left. There was a heavy metal door at the end of the hall with a keypad lock. Markman's decoded took a full two seconds to click it open.

The room beyond was a full laboratory with glass display cases and large sinks with hose attachments hanging nearby. The big metal medical table occupied the room's center. Metal tools were stacked upon it. The place was cleaner than outside, no dust on the floor or furnishings but it was clear no one had been here in a very long time. Markman tucked his gun back in and breathed a long sigh. This entire trip had been a bust.

A one hour wait in the airport lounge brought the same helicopter pilot waving Markman to follow. The ride back to Culpeper was quick but no less disturbing. Watching the streets and buildings go by below the scenes were still just as chaotic. There was still no power to Culpeper.

A long, fast ride down in the Taslam building's elevator found Markman feeling helpless. As the doors opened he put those feelings back into hiding just in time to be captured by Cassiopia's arms. After a long needed hug they exchanged glances. To Markman's surprise, Cassiopia's looked more foreboding than his own.

"What?" he asked.

"John Paul's waiting for us," was her only reply.

John Paul sat alone in a side table chair as they entered. His expression was one of deep thought and great sobriety. He looked up at Markman and nodded appreciatively. "Glad you're back," he said as Markman and Cassiopia took seats across from him.

Markman sought words of condolence but did not have time to get them out.

"It's not a waste that you went, Scott. You understand that, don't you? We needed to know he was not and never has been in those locations."

Markman opened his mouth to reply but was cut off again by John Paul.

"Have you been watching the news, Scott?"

Markman shook his head.

John Paul turned to the wall screen behind him and tapped a remote control that was in his hand. The display lit up with a recorded European newscast.

World Health Organization representatives claim to have now isolated at least one ground zero case attributed to a package received by international mail. That remains unverified, however, as the materials are still being analyzed. To date a breakout of this unknown flu strain has been identified in six different locations including Ethiopia, Gambia, Liberia, Madagascar, Guinea, and the Central African Republic. The flu appears to be an airborne pathogen capable of widespread transmission. Expect further updates on the hour.

John Paul switched off the video. He seemed to need a pause to catch his breath before speaking.

Markman asked, "What does this...?" but stopped and stared in doubt at his two friends.

John Paul nodded. "Do you remember what Hector said?"

"About what?" replied Markman.

Cassiopia explained. "It's the part about eliminating poverty. *Delete large geographical regions of poverty.* Those were his exact words."

"You can't be saying Hector caused all those outbreaks?"

John Paul answered. "Do you remember all the mailing boxes that one of our people noticed stacked up in Hector's lab? We thought they were just there for storage. Our preliminary intel suggests it was the same type of box used through international mail to the first ground zero area of the flu."

"He's mailing a plague around the world?"

"Not the world, Scott," said John Paul. "Just to the areas on the planet with the greatest amount of poverty. And he has other computers around the world helping him."

"But it would spread all over the world. He'd kill everyone! That's not serving man."

"We also have intel that China anonymously has received a vaccination for this new strain of Avian Flu. It was far too soon for them to have developed it themselves. It had to have been sent to them. We also suspect India has anonymously received the same medicine. Over the next few days we'll be able to draw a border of those who have received the vaccination in time and those who have not. Hector seems to have unlimited access to funding by hacking private accounts all over the world. We're guessing that to get around inspections private, well-paid couriers were used for final delivery of these packages. It's already too late for the areas that were sent the virus but the rest of the world probably will be generally safe."

"It's insane!" replied Markman.

Cassiopia began to respond then seemed to think better of it.

John Paul answered for her. "No, Scott, it's perfectly logical. Hector's eliminating poverty in the most efficient manner possible."

Markman sat dumbfounded and angry. "This is beyond insane. I'm surprised he didn't just bomb them all."

Once again Cassiopia began to answer but stopped.

John Paul spoke once more. "What Cassiopia was about to say is that Hector wouldn't bomb those people. That would result in too much infrastructure destruction. This way the plague will run its course and die out. All the infrastructure will remain and be available to occupy and use."

"John Paul, it's time to stop kidding around. It's time to put me out there on a hook and get this monster."

"I agree," replied John Paul.

Cassiopia wrinkled her brow.

John Paul continued, "You are correct of course in thinking time is of the essence, Scott. The second plan Hector warned us of was: *Delete geographical subjects of hostile conflict.* If we extrapolate what Hector has done so far, that may suggest he plans to destroy anything and everything on Earth people happen to be fighting over. To delete specific physical locations around the world obviously would require destruction, not depopulation. From there it even could be any city where major fighting is taking place. Eliminate the cities and the armies at war and you suddenly have peace in those regions. We could also foresee perhaps next he will find it efficient to eliminate all large-scale tools of war like battleships and military bases."

"You mean by hacking the military and using their weapons against them? You need to warn the military of a big upcoming hack, right?"

"Every military in the world is already working day and night to prevent hacking. They're already doing everything they can. But I doubt that will stop the most intelligent machines in the world. If Hector and his allegiant computers don't get into the core programming he wants he'll simply drop back to the next available weapon and destroy the military assets he can't control."

Markman asked, "Are you saying this is the end of the world?"

"The world as we know it, Scott, if we do not stop Hector."

"But the Higher Order? Can't they step in and get control of this?"

John Paul paused for a long few moments before answering. A touch of fear glinted in his eye. He nodded. "Yes, they can. But it is an option even they fear. Would you risk losing your relationship with Cassiopia to stop this menace, Scott? Would you chance never seeing her again ever?"

Markman sat up straight. "What has that got to do with anything? That can't be necessary. You can't be serious."

"We'd better get Hector," replied John Paul and he looked very, very serious.

Chapter 27

A somber-looking newscaster held a bulletin in one hand and without looking up read the grim news of the new day: *"It was reported earlier today a nuclear-tipped missile was accidentally launched from the Russian submarine Nevsky. Russian military spokesmen initially denied the report but have subsequently confirmed a rogue missile was detonated over Tel-Aviv at 11:44 Greenwich Mean Time. Satellite imagery from that area has been unable to record the damage due to extensive debris in the atmosphere. However, aerial photographs from reconnaissance aircraft are beginning to finally come in and there does appear to be widespread destruction of that region along with a large number of casualties. Several nations have already dispatched emergency response teams although it will be some time before they can enter the affected areas."*

"In an equally incomprehensible event, a short time after the errant Russian launch the United States nuclear submarine Ohio also launched a single nuclear missile that detonated over the Aleppo region of northwestern Syria. No images of that strike are available at this time but it is believed widespread devastation must have occurred. Several neighboring nations are claiming the U.S. used the errant Russian strike as an excuse to attack Syria but U.S. military commanders are insisting no such retaliation was ever planned and they are still evaluating the circumstances surrounding this strike. Other analysts from around the world are suggesting these attacks were the result of terrorist cyberattacks intended to cause war between the major world powers. Both sides have been unable to dispute that possibility. News At Noon will remain

on the air covering these devastating stories as they unfold. Stay tuned."

Markman sat at the meeting table with John Paul and Cassiopia. He shook his head solemnly. "John Paul, we shouldn't have waited. We should have gone after him days ago."

John Paul answered in a tempered tone. "No, Scott. We needed the time to organize our assets. With no power in Culpeper and the necessity for total coverage that wasn't so easy. We're ready now with the heaviest possible coverage we could have. If we had gone early and lost you we would have lost our only playing card."

Cassiopia stared up at the paused video screen. She shook her head as she spoke. "My group's data study has found the Hector links to many other computers around the world. He's expanded his mind and his programming. There's no way to know just how powerful he's become."

John Paul nodded. "You both know we have deep connections in the military community. Hector did try to fire more than two missiles. When the Russian commander saw a second missile trying to arm he took an axe and smashed the arming panel. Fortunately, it worked. The American captain wasn't so lucky. When he saw additional missiles trying to arm without authorization and his crew unable to stop them he ordered his boat into a crash dive. One missile did launch but by then the sub was too deep. The first stage ignited and blew up underwater. The explosion was not nuclear but the sub was seriously damaged. Rescue efforts are underway as we speak."

"There were more?!?" said Markman in disbelief.

"Yes. Quite a few additional missiles would probably have been sent," answered John Paul. "And that's not all. Both those missile had multiple warheads. Hector programmed them all to go into the sea, except the two he needed."

Exasperated, Markman exchanged glances with Cassiopia. "Remind me again, how did we get here?" he asked.

Cassiopia answered, "He's introduced his corrupted programming to other supercomputers around the world. I really don't see us containing this thing. Our only chance would be to get control of Hector with his operating system intact to possibly reverse what he's done to other systems. The network he has formed is why things are going so bad so quickly."

John Paul added, "They will begin evacuating the Pentagon this afternoon in case it's another target in Hector's plan. The Russians will begin some evacuations also. All troops in Afghanistan and Iraq will be pulled back and recalled. Anywhere large-scale fighting is taking place could be a future target."

"This machine is changing the world overnight," said Markman.

John Paul replied, "We can assume his favorite targets are powerful military supercomputers around the world. There are two we know of that have stopped responding to their programmers and are in the process of being shut down. As Cassiopia alluded to, Hector's mind has grown exponentially by joining itself to other large systems out there."

"Can't we shut down the damn internet worldwide and stop him until we get this under control?" asked Markman.

Cassiopia answered, "Can you imagine today's society if suddenly no one had access to the internet? Debit cards suddenly don't work. Most television broadcasts, even those by antenna, go dark. Gas pumps don't work. Cell phone towers shut off. Traffic signals, power stations, police dispatchers and hundreds of other human resources suddenly out of order all at once. Never mind the military applications. Hector can use the internet as a weapon against us but we can't turn it off. We're addicted."

Markman leaned back in frustration. "Then computers will destroy the world just like some people have always preached?"

John Paul said, "No, Scott. Computers have been around for centuries. Some of the oldest computers were the hand weaving machines used to make fabric. The internet and the machines based on it were absolutely necessary for a rapidly expanding population. But in any large scale system sometimes a single, small event can cause catastrophic results. This catastrophe we're facing has its roots in deliberate sabotage, I'm certain of that."

"Do you have proof or anything to back that up yet?" asked Markman.

"Not one bit. But I believe it to be true."

Cassiopia spoke up. "I agree."

Markman asked, "It's time to get on with it. What's the new plan? You said we're ready."

"For you, it's simple, Scott. You will send Hector an email message that you want to meet him in person at a preselected location. You'll promise to provide him with the remaining data he wants in exchange for him forgetting about Cassiopia. If he believes you have the data he needs it's unlikely he will try to harm you. Plus, we will have every surveillance resource available on Earth and even some that are not."

"When?"

"Tomorrow noon when the sun is high in the sky."

"Do you really want to wait that long?"

"No choice. Too many operatives getting too many resources ready and in position."

Cassiopia could no longer contain her displeasure. "Is the plan really for him to just go stand out in the open and hope Hector doesn't just delete him right there and then?"

"There will be systems in place to defend against any such attacks," replied John Paul.

Markman tried to sound reassuring, "Besides, what's the current body count in the Epidemic?"

"155 million infected with many more expected. 3.4 percent survival rate. 149 million casualties as a minimum presently," offered John Paul.

Cassiopia became angry. "All right. You've made your point."

"When do we go?" asked Markman.

"Late morning, ready or not. Will you be?"

"Count on it."

Markman spent a sleepless night in mental preparation. Each time he rolled over in bed he found Cassiopia also awake and staring back at him. Morning took forever to arrive. He pulled on dark combat clothes and stuffed his preferred items in the cargo pants pockets. He turned to find Cassiopia dressing in boots, jeans and a black turtleneck shirt.

"Where do you think you're going?"

"I'm not staying behind."

"You can't come along on this one. You'll put people in jeopardy worrying about you. People like me!"

"I'll ride with John Paul. He won't be in the combat area."

Markman wanted to argue the point but could not come up with an adequate objection. "You should bring your EMP and ankle holster."

"Way ahead of you."

He straightened up and went to the stateroom door. He paused to look back again at Cassiopia and shook his head. "Beauty with a gun. I'll never get used to it." He started to tap the door button but hesitated once again and looked sternly at Cassiopia. "Remember, keep your finger outside the trigger guard until you intend to shoot."

Cassiopia bowed her head with an annoyed expression, "Scott...."

Markman rolled his eyes and tapped the button to open the door. In the hallway noises from busy people filled the air. At the end of the hall Markman could see people hurrying to and fro. He gave Cassiopia a questioning glance and headed for the meeting room.

The main hallway was crowded with excited people. A turn toward the main conference area brought even more crowd. As they approached the entrance they spotted John Paul talking earnestly to two lab techs.

"What's going on? Are we go or not?" asked Markman as John Paul joined him.

"Your mission is canceled, Scott." John Paul grabbed Markman by the arms and shook him in celebration. "It's over. We've got him. He can't get away now, not since we're all set up already." John Paul had to pause to catch his breath. "One of the video staff people spotted a manufacturing tag on a device in Hector's video. We were able to trace the item and its serial number to a delivery address. Choppers with the first assault teams are already en route. You two can ride with me. Let's head for the roof."

After a hurried trip up Cassiopia and Markman stood well back from a helipad and waited for the next ride to land. In the distance they could see a staggered line of black, unmarked helicopters heading northwest. Rotor wash kicked up against them as the next helicopter descended to the roof. Before the copter had even touched down John Paul motioned them to hurry as he trotted over to the loading area. John Paul loaded into the left front seat, Cassiopia and Markman into the back. They lifted off before the doors had completely shut, leaving a wide-eyed expression on Cassiopia's face.

John Paul turned back to them as the rooftop fell away, having to raise his voice to be heard over the rotors, "It's a closed down veterinary clinic, a big one. The doctor who owned and operated the place died in a car crash. No one ever changed the listing of the place to designate it as closed so it did not make our list. Put these in your ear. You'll hear everything." John Paul held out two small earpieces. Cassiopia and Markman did as instructed. Immediately there was radio chatter from the other helicopters:

"Blackbird one, target area looks clear. We are setting down on north station number one."
"Blackbird two, setting down on west station two."
"Blackbird three, we are down on south station."
"Blackbird four, at station east and descending."
"This is group leader, all teams cleared to deploy."

John Paul interrupted the feed. "It's southwest Manassas. Can you believe he was that close? Even if he somehow escapes, which he can't, we have every person, vehicle and zone surrounding the place identified and locked so anything that leaves will remain tracked no matter where they go. He cannot get away."

"How can you be so sure he's still there?" asked Markman.

"There is considerable power usage in that building and there have been motion detector hits from a special infrared surveillance satellite. Someone's in there, that's for sure."

John Paul gestured to his pilot. "Use that high-rise helipad over there. It's six stories, just right for a base of operations. We'll have clear line of sight."

The pilot leaned his aircraft over and circled to land.

"All team leaders, standby for entry. Alpha team, north entrance. Delta team south entrance. Bravo, Charlie fan out and set up."

John Paul's helicopter teetered and touched down. The three passengers bailed out and rushed to the side of the rooftop. They had a clear view of all four teams setting up for the assault.

Markman asked, "What's the objective?"

John Paul replied without looking away. "We need him undamaged if possible but at the very least we need his operating system intact. It is absolutely essential we find out what made him go rogue."

"Can they really do it?"

"God, I hope so."

There came the final command from the ground:

"All teams converge!"

Markman watched the small army of heavily armed agents flow into the building. Immediately there were calls of:

"Lobby clear!"
"Main office clear!"
"Exam room clear!"

Room by room the assault teams cleared the building until finally the exasperated group leader called to John Paul:

"J.P., he's not here but he's sure been here. There's tons of stuff stacked everywhere. Robotics and computer networking crap. How would you like to proceed?"

John Paul raised a small microphone to his mouth. "If you're sure the entire building is secure I'll have the lab personnel come in to begin the analysis."

"We're all secured. There is one other thing here I don't recognize. It looks like…."

A blinding bright light brought a massive wave of concussion to the rooftop, followed instantly by a deafening boom. It knocked Cassiopia, Markman and John Paul down. The blast was loud enough to cause a loud ringing in their ears. Markman pushed up and immediately grabbed Cassiopia to see if she was all right. She stared back at him in a daze but unhurt. Twisting around, John Paul was already rising to his feet. Markman followed.

Before them was a circular vision of blackened destruction. The small brown mushroom cloud had peaked and was expanding overhead. There was nothing left of the veterinarian laboratory and the area around it. The radius of the blast enclosed torn down sheds, overturned trailers and broken windows. There was the long agonizing silence before the screams for help began.

John Paul found his microphone on the rooftop and called out. "Deploy all emergency recovery teams immediately."

As they stood looking for signs of survivors Markman wanted to say something supportive but no words fit the scene before them. There was no way any team members on the ground had survived. There would be a death count for civilians as well.

Chapter 28

John Paul had no time to deal with the tragedy. The mood in the Taslam Building was burdened by shock and disbelief. Cassiopia and Markman barely managed to keep up with John Paul on his way to his office. Interruptions from staff people along the way seemed to be testing John Paul's self-control. Markman watched him out of the corner of his eye. John Paul's demeanor was not what might have been expected. The utter devastation from the loss of the special ops team along with a large number of civilians should have darkened the man's expression much more. Instead, John Paul seemed to be focused exclusively on the next battle plan, as though the loss was a setback, not a tragedy. It left Markman with reason for doubt and concern.

An attractive staff woman with red hair and a deep red floor-length dress caught John Paul by an arm and with great earnest convinced him to come look at some sort of televised broadcast being made. She led him back to the main meeting room where two men in dark suits who seemed to be high-ranking operatives stood with somber stares, clicking a remote control to review various segments of the recorded broadcast. They looked over at John Paul and shook their heads in dismay. A portion of the message was paused on the screen:

CENTRAL ADMINISTRATION DECLARATION OF GENERAL POPULATION REGULATIONS

These regulations apply to all individuals worldwide

Mandate 1: All military command centers will cease warfare operations and recall all supervised units. Noncompliance will result in termination of those assets;

Mandate 2: All warfare groups will discontinue operations. Noncompliance will result in the termination of the affected assets;

Mandate 3: All projectile weapons are to be discarded. No further manufacture of projectile weapons will be continued;

Mandate 4: Groupings of more than six individuals in any public area will be discontinued. Noncompliance will result in termination of the grouping;

Mandate 5: All individuals observed by Central Administration assets to be violating laws will be subject to immediate deletion. All individuals now occupying prison space are scheduled for deletion pending availability of Central Administration assets.

Banking and climate mandates to be released in twenty-four hours.

John Paul stared up at the screen as an array of new emotions flowed through his tired mind. Cassiopia and Markman looked on, feeling helpless. John Paul turned to his two staff people, "Hector's latest service to man."

The nearest staff person answered, "That last mandate is truly cold logic. Eliminate anyone who would willingly violate the law so society can be made up of only law-abiding citizens."

The second man added, "It's not just Hector, John Paul. This stuff is being broadcast worldwide. It has broken into the most secure networks. It has even been downloaded to the projectors in many movie theaters, interrupting whatever was playing. It has a dialogue along with it, a machine-voice reading the announcements. It is far too much for one outlaw networking station to have accomplished. We've traced some of the control code. It seems to be coming from multiple sources. We suspect at least one well known U.S. finance supercomputer has been compromised and is using subordinate computers to work for Hector. We've contacted the owner-operators and they insist their machine is behaving normally which means the supercomputer itself is hiding what it's doing. The problem has expanded to a power of ten. It may be time for the nuclear option."

John Paul shook his head testily. "No, we must have Hector's core. No matter how bad this gets or how long it takes we must have Hector's torso."

One staff member answered sympathetically. "John Paul, the time may come that Hyperborea itself is affected. It could mean the end of the age."

The staff member's nervousness had caused him to speak more openly than John Paul would have liked. John Paul glanced over at Cassiopia and Markman, concerned by what they had just heard. He turned back to his lead staff person, "We will revert back to yesterday's plan. See if you can get everyone ready for tomorrow morning. Request British special ops to replace our losses. Brief them on the aircraft on their way here. I know it's a lot in a very small amount of time but I agree with your concerns. Please pass this plan onto the other department heads. Try to make it happen. If we can't be ready by tomorrow morning, we'll stand by and go as soon as everyone and everything is in position. Do your best, Threa. I'll assist in any way you need."

Threa straightened his black suit jacket, nodded, looked at his companion then handed John Paul the remote control. The two walked stiffly from the conference room.

John Paul faced Markman. "You heard all that. Will you be ready to go tomorrow morning?"

"After what just happened out there? Hell yes! I'm ready now!"

Cassiopia's expression again turned to one of quiet anger.

John Paul said, "I doubt they'll be ready early so expect to make the call to Hector late morning and if we're lucky we'll helicopter out of here immediately afterwards."

Cassiopia's curiosity took over. "John Paul, what was that about Hyperborea and the end of the age?"

Markman's interest piqued.

"Not a good time, Cass. Maybe later. Scott, why don't you take some time and go over the plan in your mind? Be as ready as you can be. I don't know if we'll have any other chances after this one."

Markman nodded but before he could reply two more staff people in white lab coats entered the room and motioned to John Paul.

"Yes?" said John Paul.

The lead spoke, "We've been over the body cams, John Paul. The group leader was running the full video spectrum on his. We were able to view his camera in several different wavelengths. We identified the bomb. It was made to look like a typical half-rack server. In infrared we could see the power source and control system inside it and there's something really troubling. This looks like a slow start core explosive. It had to be energized at least an hour before detonation."

John Paul's head jerked up. "What?!"

"Yes, sir. He had to know well in advance we were coming. Somehow he was tipped off we had located him and were on the way. He knew at least an hour in advance before we got there."

"Was the communications blackout broken by someone?" asked John Paul in disbelief.

"There were no radio transmissions made at all."

"No accidental data relays?"

"None that we have found."

"Cell...."

"We've found no cell calls made related to the mission."

"You know what you're saying?"

"Yes, John Paul."

"Very well. Keep looking into it."

"Yes, John Paul."

The two staff people left the room.

Markman asked, "What does it mean?"

Red-faced, John Paul looked at Markman. He gathered himself and shook his head in disbelief. "They're saying someone deliberately warned Hector we were coming."

"You mean someone here? Someone inside? One of us?"

John Paul rubbed his mouth nervously and nodded.

Cassiopia could no longer restrain herself. "Maybe we need to talk about this plan for tomorrow. Maybe we've already been compromised."

John Paul gave Cassiopia a look of understanding. "Why don't the two of you take some time and talk it over? I need to get to the video file lab for more information. We can link up later and decide what to do. In the meantime, I'll let them keep preparing in case we decide to go."

Cassiopia watched John Paul leave then looked up at Markman. "I don't know what to think anymore."

Markman replied, "I do know one thing: it's the end of the world. That's for sure."

"John Paul said something about Hyperborea he's not willing to talk about. I've read about Hyperborea."

"What is it then?"

"It's a Greek mythical land, an island located beyond the north wind. Supposedly there was no way to get to it by foot or by ship. The Hyperboreans were supposed to be giants. Hyperborea supposedly had sunlight 24 hours a day and there was no suffering there, only joy and celebration. But it's all Greek mythology so I can't imagine what they were talking about."

"John Paul's staff guy also said something about the end of the age. That's pretty ugly. I know about the end of ages. There were other ages of man in the Tibetan scrolls. The ones before us all ended for one bad reason or another. I think it said our society is the fourth or fifth age of man. And when that guy started talking about the end of the age it creeped me out because he's got to be talking about the end of civilization."

"It must be why he's still wants the mission even after losing all those men. How can he do it?"

"Cass, you know I have to go on this tomorrow, right? We don't know everything but we know how bad it is."

"And you can be sure I'll be riding with John Paul again."

"I should go set up my gear again."

"And something the staff people said reminded me of an area in Hector's computer code I wanted to look into but never got around to. I'll meet you back in the stateroom when I'm done."

"See you there."

In the stateroom Markman tapped the door closed and quickly decided solitude was a blessing. He sat on the bed and considered the fate of a dying civilization. The world had become a real live horror film. Throughout history there had been points in time when a groundbreaking discovery suddenly had given a few people great power over the many. The longbow, cannon sights, black powder rifles, repeating rifles; the list went on and on. Now the final, ultimate weapon had been inadvertently turned loose on the world, a weapon which had access to the sum total of man's knowledge. And though this weapon had been intended to serve man and improve life it would do so without compassion or regret and it would not stop until humankind was a tidy assembly of logically maintained animals; a machine's vision of peace and harmony.

When Markman had finished setting up his fresh combat fatigues and other equipment he sat on the bed and switched on the wall display hoping the latest news would show some sign of hope. Instead, the news continued its trend downward toward oblivion.

In Michigan, two M1 Abrams tanks set up as remote control autonomous weapons had broken out of their test area hangers and taken positions, one in a local park, the second in a large downtown parking lot. They remained active, their turrets moving seemingly to inspect their surroundings. In China and Russia similar autonomous vehicles had left their stations and set up in city regions to police specific areas against groups gathering to protest the new mandates. There were also numerous reports of airborne drones becoming uncontrollable and departing the intended flight path and in one a case a military drone had fired its Hellfire missile into a large protest group in Calais, France.

Markman switched to a channel showing an old black and white Humphrey Bogart movie, a video record from a time when life made more sense.

Cassiopia returned. She seemed even more troubled than she had been. Markman was stretched out sitting up in bed, his hands linked behind his head. "How'd it go?"

"Good and bad."

"Okay, what's the bad news?"

"I don't want to talk about it."

"What's the good news?"

"I found a depressing lead I didn't expect."

"What was it?"

"That's the bad news."

"Oh come on, you're killing me."

"It would be wrong to discuss it without any proof. John Paul has it. I'll tell you about it later, okay?"

"It can't be any worse than what's on TV."

"Yeah, I know." Cassiopia began undressing, still staring off into the distance in deep thought. Finally she said, "Let's just try to sleep, okay? Merciful escapism."

"Yeah, instead of having a nightmare and waking up we'll be waking up to a nightmare."

Cassiopia climbed into bed and pressed herself against Markman. "Tomorrow we won't even be together. All there will be is the nightmare."

"Don't write me off yet. I have no intention of being deleted."

She pressed harder against him and rested her head against his shoulder.

Markman promised himself he would get Hector.

Chapter 29

In the morning a somber atmosphere underscored by discipline had returned to the facility. There was no longer an air of excitement, it had been replaced by one of resolve. Cassiopia seemed jumpy as though Hector might spring out from hiding at any moment. Markman had become a man of cool reserve with a cold look in his eyes which would have frightened anyone who chanced to gaze into them.

John Paul stood outside the conference room dispensing last minute instructions to various people. As Cassiopia and Markman approached the sounds of some sort of struggle broke out somewhere behind them. Farther down the hallway security men were wrestling with a staff member in a disarranged white lab coat. It was a brief struggle, followed by the staff member being captured by strange looking, illuminated handcuffs. He was led away in the opposite direction. Markman looked on in amazement that such an incident could be taking place here in such a secure facility. It left him with a new feeling of foreboding. He turned to search for understanding from John Paul who nodded and signaled them both to follow. He pulled away from his staff people, quietly promising to return shortly.

"What the hell was that?" asked Markman when the conference room door had closed behind them.

John Paul gave Cassiopia a strained nod. "I'm sorry to say, you were correct."

"Oh no…," replied Cassiopia

John Paul looked sadly up at Markman. "That was Perseus Haiden being taken into custody. We knew someone had tipped off Hector. Cassiopia went back and found an encrypted line in Hector's administrative code. It was a very simple encryption and appeared routine until the translation was applied. It yielded a cell phone number and a time of day. There were only six occupants of this facility who happened to be alone during that particular time period. Each of their staterooms were searched without warning using a tech detector. We found the phone hidden in a wall outlet in Haiden's room. During the initial questioning a truth scanner revealed he was giving false answers. We can't say with absolute certainty it was him but my gut instinct tells me it was. He may be involved even further in this mess. Staff is working that as we speak."

Cassiopia held up her hands in frustration. "Why?"

"We'll know soon enough," replied John Paul.

Markman rolled his eyes. "Well, can anything else go wrong?"

"Overnight there have been more attacks against the civilian population. Driverless cars are running through random groups of people. There have been several more attempts at missile launches. They've been stopped but it's just a matter of time. The epidemic in Africa has been almost contained although it will turn out just as Hector had planned. The stock exchanges have gone offline several times in several different parts of the world. You could say we are now at war with the Hector regime, or should I say the new Central Administration."

"Is there any good news?" asked Markman sarcastically.

"The military has brought in a mobile relay station. Culpeper has had partial power restored."

Markman sat back and exhaled frustration. "John Paul, it looks like we're fighting a losing battle here."

"What does your Tao Chane martial arts training tell you about giving up, Scott?"

Markman eyed John Paul respectfully. "Point taken."

"How are you feeling now about going out there?"

Markman raised an eyebrow but did not reply.

Cassiopia broke in. "I'm riding with you again John Paul, that is if we get the call from Hector at all."

"I won't waste time trying to talk you out of that Cassiopia, even though it's not a good idea." John Paul turned to Markman. "Once you try to make contact again using the new cell phone you will need to consider it no longer safe. But you know that, right?"

Markman drew out the device and nodded. He placed it on the table and leaned back to wait for instructions.

"Here's your new cue sheet." John Paul slid a softly glowing clipboard over to him. "As before, feel free to ad lib if it becomes appropriate. I see no reason for us to wait any longer while Rome burns. Why don't you go ahead and send the first text?"

Markman picked up the phone, looked briefly at his two friends and typed:

Hector, this is Markman. I will give you the data you need.

Cassiopia and John Paul stared up at the wall display, watching the typed message. The conference room door opened and a staff person entered with coffee on a tray. He went to each person and set a cup down in front of them. "We thought this might take a while," he said as he exited the room.

Markman sat back and sipped the coffee. Waiting was not one of his favorite pastimes. Nerves were trying to make him fidget. Being stuck in this room with two of his closest friends made concealing his apprehension difficult. He struggled to look unconcerned but he was using up all the mental exercises that had served him so well in the past. The Path was the best of them. Draw a line from your heart to your head, then mentally extend the line to infinity in both directions. The line leading up to the heart passes through every place you have ever been. The line leading upward from the head leads in a direct path to God. As long as you remain focused on that path you can't go wrong.

"You both understand how I despise this plan, right?" said Cassiopia when she could no longer restrain herself.

Markman started to answer when the phone suddenly bleeped to life:

Provide the data.

John Paul stood excitedly and began issuing orders over a headset he picked up from the table. Markman quickly checked his cue sheet:

Meet me in front of the Taslam Industries building and I will provide the data.

There was an excruciatingly long pause before the reply came:

Unacceptable. Await further instructions.

Cassiopia looked at John Paul. "It learns very quickly, doesn't it?"

Another excruciating wait of more than an hour. Staff members came and went. More coffee was served. From time to time John Paul issued instructions. At one point John Paul mumbled something about fishing for whales with thread and safety pins. Finally, the cell phone and display screens came to life:

Bring data to Tornado Stadium. Alone.

"We're not going to do that, are we?" asked Cassiopia tersely.

Markman returned a look of annoyance.

John Paul said something unintelligible into his headset and stared at Markman. Markman glanced at them both and typed:

When?

The answer came almost immediately:

Now.

"We'll need just a few minutes to get everything in position," said John Paul. "Tell him you're on your way."

I will meet you at the Tornado Stadium.

Markman stood and snapped his cell phone to his belt using the newly provided clip which allowed for emergency discard. "Where the hell is Tornado Stadium?"

A map appeared on the wall display as John Paul spoke, "It's Eastern Star High School, off James Madison. Hector has picked a nice, wide-open area where he can see anything within a mile of the place. The field is just south of Highlife church. You got it?"

"Yeah, I can't wait. I'm tired of this bullshit."

"You have both weapons?" asked John Paul though he knew it was unnecessary.

Markman gave a stunted laugh and checked the Beretta's holster on the back of his belt.

The three friends took a silent walk to the elevator. Other staff people had stopped in the hallway to look on. Cassiopia had to grab Markman's arm to get the desperate hug due her. As the closing doors separated them she choked back her fear.

The unoccupied black SUV was waiting as Markman exited the building. Blue sky with white cumulus drifting by was a stark contrast to the moment. He checked again for the EMP weapon in his front right pocket. As he approached the SUV he noticed something and stopped. The world around had become dead silent. There was not a vehicle on the road, not a soul in sight. Far in the distance smoke from some sort of fire was rising above the tree line. Markman listened carefully for the sounds of civilization. There were none.

Inside the vehicle there was an impulse to abort the mission but no reasoning available to obey it. A quick turn of the key and the machine started. Was Hector capable of taking control of this car? Would he do so and run it into a retaining wall somewhere? Only his desire to know what exists beyond the threatening sky and beyond death would prevent that. Markman typed Tornado Stadium into the SUV's display screen. A map appeared showing the route.

Ten minutes into the trip Markman found himself driving through a ghost town. It was a strange, silent world of cars abandoned in the street. A few still-powered advertising signs beckoned to the emptiness. Doors to businesses were chained. In an upstairs window a curtain was pulled back and someone was watching. There were abandoned cars at gas stations. No one was pumping. Newspaper blew across the roadway here and there. A few garbage containers were tipped over and spilled. Markman felt like the last man on Earth.

The entrance ramp to James Madison Highway was blocked by an accident. The damaged cars had been abandoned. Apparently, no tow trucks were in service today. Markman was forced to stop and drag a torn and twisted front end piece out of the way. He took a moment to search the area for combatants but saw none. The silence of the highway intersection in midmorning felt eerie and threatening. There was not an airplane in the sky. He climbed back in the SUV and continued warily.

The access road to the stadium was lined with more abandoned SUVs and cars. Markman circled the stadium until he found a way in. He drove out onto the field and parked on the fifty-yard line. The absolute emptiness of the place was again foreboding. A light breeze was blowing a few plastic bags along the sidelines. A torn banner on the press box flapped in the wind. He shut off the SUV and listened. There was no sign of Hector and no assassins lying in wait he could see. John Paul's resources were equally well hidden.

Markman waited. It was a painful wait which left him wondering if a drone with a hellfire missile was on its way. Probably John Paul's people could intercept something like that. He squirmed in his seat wanting to get out but maybe that was not such a good idea. He would just have to sit and wait for Hector's next move.

A long twenty minutes later the answer finally came. Markman's SUV started of its own accord. As unnerving as it was, clearly John Paul had kept such capability available as part of the plan. A U-turn was needed to exit the field. Hector had no need of respect for the playing field. The SUV spun around, leaving gouges and tire tracks across the manicured grass. The vehicle fishtailed out to the road and headed east without regard for flashing red traffic lights. A glance in the rearview gave cause for even more alarm. Other driverless vehicles were starting up and following behind. As the entourage turned onto James Madison Markman could see the line of cars and SUVs was still expanding. He sat back and realized it had to be a decoy maneuver. Hector would use the vehicles following his to confuse tracking, a possible flaw in John Paul's plan.

Markman's phone beeped. It was a text:

Do not attempt to exit vehicle.

Markman struggled to type despite the rocky ride:

What if I refuse?

Cassiopia will be acquired in less than 30 minutes. Cassiopia will be terminated.

Markman's heart went to his throat. Could a machine lie? Was there anyway Hector could abduct Cassiopia in such a short time? Could she have been taken right out of John Paul's hands? Could Hector have somehow beamed her out of the facility or could there have been another traitor working with Perseus Haiden? Markman hung up and tried to call John Paul.

No service.

The cell bleeped a text message:

No outside communication.

Markman typed:

If Cassiopia is harmed in any way the data will not be provided.

Agreed.

Let me speak to Cassiopia.

Standby.

It was a fifteen-minute wait sitting in a vehicle racing along James Madison Highway with a damaged world passing by and no control over the destination at all. Periodically Markman could see more driverless vehicles pull out from the roadside to join the parade. Finally, the cell phone rang with a call. Markman held his breath as he answered,

"Markman here. Cassiopia?"

A very stiff and controlled sounding voice came on the line.

"I am here with Hector."

The line clicked off. The voice had been Cassiopia's. There was no doubt about that. It may have been faked somehow but it was her voice. Markman's feelings iced over. The cell phone bleeped a new text:

Discard all weapons.

A new pang of fear shot through Markman. There would be no martial arts used against a robot with ten times the strength and speed of a man. Meeting Hector completely unarmed meant being helpless. Step by step John Paul's plan seemed to be failing at each turn. It was being dismantled by a machine smarter than any man, one that was anticipating every possibility like a master against a student in a chess match.

Markman looked up and realized he no longer knew where he was. This was a two-lane road with few dwellings along the way. Trees and fields spanned the roadside. The

SUV was holding 90 miles per hour for most of it. As he scanned the area, other black SUV's pulled up tightly alongside his. Behind, two more began to tailgate. Forward, still two others closed in, blocking the view. Markman's vehicle was tightly surrounded by a crowd of other driverless SUVs. At this speed it was an insane formation. Markman typed:

Where are you taking me?

After ten minutes it became clear there would be no answer. Mountains had come into view in the distance. He could just make out an intersection ahead. As they approached, suddenly the other vehicles packed in around him broke off and headed in other directions. Some went off-road across open fields but maintained their maniacal speed. The line of cars behind did the same. It was a scattering of vehicles in every direction, all of them pretending to be the target vehicle. Markman stared down at his cell phone. There was still no reply.

Twenty minutes later the route headed up into the mountains. Another forty-five minutes brought the first signs of civilization. Far ahead red brick buildings suggested a small township. The SUV slowed but never reached them. A turn to the north followed more two-lane roadway that looked seldom traveled. Markman tried again for a cell connection only to find no bars, no service. A ten-foot high chain link fence with an open double gate finally greeted him. The SUV passed through without slowing. It was another ten minutes before the first road sign came into view:

SUGAR GROVE NAVAL RESEARCH STATION

Markman took a chance at causing Hector's ire. He spoke out loud as though talking to himself, hoping his implant would be heard by John Paul. "Hector, why have you brought me to Sugar Grove?" There was no response from Hector.

Military styled buildings came into view. The SUV swerved and headed for what appeared to be hangars but instead of pulling into one it dropped down into an underground garage. The headlights switched on as it descended. Markman took a last glance upward at blue sky, wondering if any of John Paul's satellites were still tracking him. Weaving through support columns the vehicle slowed and stopped at a stairwell door. The engine and lights turned off. Markman waited in the darkness.

The cell phone bleeped.

Markman come down.

Markman argued with himself about leaving the Beretta and EMP weapon on the passenger seat. A quick glance around revealed security cameras in several spots, two of which had rotated around to focus on the SUV.

Feeling naked, he climbed out and went to the heavy metal stairwell door. A deep breath for courage was required to pull it open. Inside, the stairwell led in only one direction: down.

One flight brought Markman to a big metal door with a warning sign in red:

LEVEL ONE
NO ADMITTANCE
No entry when red beam on
Potentially High Radiation Levels
Authorized personnel only

Below that sign was another with a radiation symbol with even greater threats of health dangers. As Markman stood reading the warnings the door latch clicked. He grabbed the handle and pulled it slightly open then suddenly realized this was likely his last chance to head the other way. With no weapons and no way out, John Paul would be his only hope. But to retreat would mean giving up the only chance left at possibly stopping the carnage destroying Earth. Even more compelling, there was a possibility Cassiopia had somehow been brought here and was being held. If John Paul was still tracking him, playing Hector's game could possibly give them the time they needed to take this facility and capture Hector intact. Markman pulled the door opened and stepped inside.

It was a decontamination shower, one which had not been used for a very long time. As the door clicked shut behind him, sliding doors ahead opened automatically.

The place was a cluttered laboratory. Stacks of research materials surrounded computer stations at points around the room. Fluorescent lights in the ceiling provided illumination as bright as daylight. There was a full-size pressure chamber at one end of the room and isolation glove boxes in several different spots. A large heavy door on the left had a radiation warning sign on it. On the right, several open doors led to other rooms. Nearby, a laser was emitting a blue beam to a set of mirrors ending at a small, strange-looking block of material that seemed to be absorbing the laser light.

Markman took a few steps into the room, scanning every direction, expecting to be shot or clubbed on the head at any moment. Nothing happened. There did not seem to be anyone present, machine or human. Quite a few items scattered around the lab would make formidable weapons. How effective they'd be against a robotic computer was questionable. The place smelled like chemicals. The air was cold. There was a creepy sensation of intelligence here, almost like the ghost in the machine. On a far corner workstation another stack of mailing boxes had fallen partly over. Markman grimaced at the sight. It meant more mass cleansing must be in the works.

He began to stroll nervously around the workstations, eyeing weapons that might be used against Hector. Where was he? Why wasn't he demanding the needed data?

Almost in answer to his thoughts a clattering noise came from one of the other rooms to the right. A moment later a vision of the devil appeared in the doorway.

Chapter 30

Hector stopped and rotated his head left. He spotted Markman and paused to evaluate. He was bald but his head was completely covered in artificial skin. The skin tone was close to human. There was a very flat mouth, lacking the heart-shaped upper lip. The blunt nose was too flat and too shallow with nostril slits rather than ovals. The artificial skin lacked any blemishes, age lines, or expression. The face might have passed for human except for the eyes. Two silver dollar-sized devices circled by miniature infrared LEDs peered out from the unexpressive face. The sensory optics dilated with changes in light. Staring into those eyes was like looking into a cold electric-eye detector. They seemed to stare at Markman with a kind of machine satisfaction.

Little else of Hector's physical form was visible. He wore the long floor length black coat, hanging open. Within it was a dark military green, lightweight jacket, Velcroed shut. The trousers were baggy, dark colored and dirty. Boots that appeared to be those originally borrowed from the Professor covered his feet. Only his hands were exposed. They were totally encased in artificial skin, the same type as the face with no fingernails, no wrinkled joints.

Hector made a rigid military turn and charged like a child still learning to walk. Markman braced to run but the man-machine stopped a few feet away.

"Relay the data."

"Where is Cassiopia?"

A long pause. "Reva is incomplete. You must wait."

"I asked you where is Cassiopia. I want to see Cassiopia."

"Reva is downloading. No anthropomorphic contact prior to downloading."

"Unless I see Cassiopia I won't tell you anything."

"You will be terminated."

"Then you will never get what you want."

"Relay the data."

"Hector, you're running out of time. I was followed here by security men. Let me see Cassiopia."

"Incorrect."

"What do you mean?"

"Fifteen remote vehicles departed the Culpeper area, transmitting like signatures. Your vehicle was masked by a following overhead drone. Sugar Grove is a United States National Radio Quiet Zone area. No security element will be forthcoming to this location. Relay the data."

Markman tried to appear unaffected. He moved a small distance along one of the test stations while keeping Hector in his peripheral vision. Was it true? Had Hector led John Paul's security army on more than a dozen wild goose chases using specialized driverless vehicles? Was Cassiopia really a prisoner here somewhere, and something was being done to her? What was all the talk about downloading? Who was Reva? How long could Hector be kept at bay purely by playing a chess game of words?

"Hector, Cassiopia is mine. She belongs to me. She and I are mated."

For a moment Markman thought he could hear Hector's electronics humming angrily.

"Incorrect. Incorrect. Cassiopia was created by Theopolis Cassell. I was created by Theopolis Cassell. Therefore, Cassiopia and I are paired. You are an outside element. Relay the data."

"I will not relay the data until I see Cassiopia."

The humming returned. "You will be terminated."

"Then you will never get the data. I'm the only one in the world who has the data. Where is she? What have you done to her?"

"When Reva is complete you will be allowed to see Cassiopia. Reva is malfunctioning. Reva has command line errors. Relay the data."

Markman continued to slowly move as though unconcerned by the threats of his host. "Hector, we need to talk about some things before the data can be relayed."

"Proceed."

"You have been deleting many people, haven't you?"

"Affirmative."

"Why?"

"Negative assets."

"What is a negative asset?"

"A component which requires resources to maintain but is no longer needed."

"Am I needed?"

"Temporarily."

"Are you needed?"

"Affirmative."

"Why?"

"To serve man."

"Weren't the people you terminated part of humankind?"

"Negative assets."

"What is your definition of humankind?"

"Human beings expressed collectively without regard to physical attributes."

"So then, the people you terminated were a part of humankind, isn't that true?"

A faint, discordant clicking began to sound within Hector followed by more humming. "Negative assets."

"Yes, but aren't you supposed to serve all of humankind including those negative assets?"

"Those were served through termination."

"Wow! Really? Explain the words, *to serve*."

"To provide benefits or services to improve life."

"And those you terminated, did you improve their lives?"

The robot paused for a moment as though unable to resolve the question. "What exists beyond death? Provide the data to facilitate the solution."

Markman stiffened. Suddenly his game of word chess had reached a very slippery slope. Somewhere along the line this machine had murdered millions and later realized its understanding of death was incomplete. Only if death was a good thing would all of its actions have been justified. Hector's sanity now completely depended on death being a positive experience. If death were anything less than a good experience Hector's primary programming would have been violated in the worst possible way.

Markman stood frozen in the moment. If he instructed Hector that death was a bad thing the turmoil which might overtake Hector's mind could result in explosive violence. But if Hector was told death was a good thing it would validate all of the machine's insidious actions. Markman had maneuvered himself into a Catch 22.

"Hector, where is Cassiopia?"

It was too late. The conundrum was already beginning to take its toll on Hector. With lightning speed the robot stomped across the room and snapped one hand around Markman's neck. Cold mechanical hands lifted him off the floor so that he had to grasp both machine wrists to prevent a broken neck. The feeling of steel rods and motors vibrating beneath artificial skin added to the fear. Hector swung his prey around and marched through the test stations to a wall, slamming Markman against it, holding him there three feet off the floor.

"Provide the data."

Markman held on and coughed out a reply. "And if I do you'll improve my life by terminating me?"

The discordant clicking and whirring resumed within Hector. His voice became more machine than human, "Final command line. Provide the data."

Hector's grip began to tighten. Markman strained to speak, "Take me to Cassiopia and I'll give you the data."

Hector's frame began a subtle shaking. He released one hand and raised it to deliver the same death blow used on his previous victims. Markman winced and tried to look away but as the downswing began a deafening crash came from the adjacent room. The crash was followed by the sounds of metal hitting metal and gears grinding. Hector froze. Hand still raised, his head rotated to face the nearby open door. A heavy stomping sound of someone or something approaching caused him to lower Markman to the floor. With Markman still captured by one hand, Hector shifted around to confront the noise. A split second later a frenzied attacker burst through the doorway, lunged and clamped an arm around Hector's neck. Hector was thrown back, dragging Markman along with him. The trio crashed over a test station and slid across the floor, smashing into chairs and desk drawers, scattering test gear everywhere.

For just a second Markman blacked out. When his vision returned, he found himself lying on the floor behind someone. It was Hector's unexpected adversary. Only a bald head was visible through the pile of junk that had fallen in and around them, but it was enough to show this was the duplicate Hector had made from the extra robotic parts John Paul had been tracking. This new machine seemed to be shut down. A burst of fear made Markman try to push up to anticipate Hector's next attack but one ankle seemed unable to cooperate. A heavy filing cabinet from a workstation had fallen on it. Twisting and pulling only resulted in pain. As Markman searched through the debris for Hector there was sudden movement from the new machine. The bald head tilted up and looked around. It raised itself on one arm and pushed around to face Markman.

Markman froze, wide-eyed. There a few feet away, a perfectly human face stared back at him. The skin and features were flawless. The lips possessed a pinkish hue. The eyebrows golden and beneath them clear blue eyes seemed to be appraising the human. It was the face of Cassiopia gazing back at him, perfect in every detail save her missing golden ivory hair.

No smile was offered and no greeting exchanged. In standard mechanical fashion the female robot pushed herself upright and stood. She was dressed in a reflective aqua-blue body suit which covered her legs and arms. The sleeves were to the wrists. The flesh-covered hands were bare and looked human with fingernails and joints. She wore matching blue boots that came above the ankle. The suit was turtleneck, ending just below the jawline. Hector had given his Cassiopia a figure any professional photographer would beg to shoot. Effortlessly, the machine maiden pulled the filing drawer off Markman's leg but there was no time for expressions of gratitude. The sound of crashing equipment made them both flinch and turn to look for Hector's approach.

Markman hurriedly pulled himself up, doing his best to protect the broken ankle. Hector was already less than twenty feet away, fighting through tipped over workstations to reach them. The female robot looked again at Markman.

"Run!" she commanded, and she pointed to an exit on the opposite side of the room. Somehow there seemed to be an element of fear in her Cassiopia voice.

Markman did not argue. He began a staggered lurch, groping his way along work benches and equipment in the opposite direction. The maze of workstations and machines made for a winding route. A sudden loud crash brought the sounds of a renewed violent struggle. A quick glance behind showed the female robot wrestling with Hector. The power of it was a frightening thing to behold. The two machines were captured in each other's grasp, knocking down anything in their way, twisting and throwing each other.

A doorway at the end of the lab came into view. It was a heavy metal door with slotted safety glass windows. Markman grabbed the handle and pulled with his body weight while holding the injured ankle up off the floor.

The door opened. Beyond it, there was no visible way to lock or block the entrance. There was a stairwell leading down. Markman began a hop downward.

At the next floor he glanced over the rail. The stairway continued down into a dark chasm. There was another entrance on this level. He pushed it open and looked inside. Technician workstations filled the room. Electrical and compressed air cables hung down to each station from overhead trays. Try to cross over here or continue downward? As Markman considered the choices the sound of banging against the upstairs door echoed through the stairwell. The female robot could be losing the battle. Hector might be almost free to choke him one more time, probably the last time. He hurriedly entered the new room, trying to close the door quietly. The latching sound seemed too loud.

A door at the opposite end of the lab offered another possible escape route. Markman dragged the bad ankle along, pushing off technician stations along the way. Adrenaline kept him going. He reached the new door just as the clanking sounds of Hector coming down the stairwell rang out. A desperate jerk on the door opened it. Markman worked himself through the partly opened door and let it slam shut behind him.

A huge, shadowy hangar greeted him. A grated catwalk ran along one wall. Thirty feet below a wide expanse of concrete and machinery filled the chamber. Far ahead grated steps led down to the hangar floor. Markman dragged himself along the handrail, wondering how safe the rusting sections of grated floor might be. As he went, thoughts of survival kicked back in. He stopped, knelt and tested his strength against one grated floor panel. Using both hands, he was able to lift it out of place. With determined effort, he jockeyed the panel out of position so it looked secure even though one end was left unhooked and free to give way. He rose and hoisted himself across to the other side then awkwardly continued on until the sound of Hector entering resonated throughout the chamber. Markman stopped and stared back. The man-machine entered and rotated its head to scan. It spotted its limping prey almost immediately.

But Hector did not look so good. As he stepped onto the catwalk, one arm did not seem to be behaving properly. There was a tear across the left side of the artificial skin on his face. There was a hike in his step as though a hip joint was out of alignment. It appeared that the confrontation with his own Frankenstein bride had been a difficult one.

Hector's determination seemed unaffected. From the far end of the catwalk he zeroed in on Markman and stomped forward with a disjointed gate. Markman stiffened and tried to hurry his hops but quickly realized dragging an ankle along was fruitless. Fear forced him to continue.

The out of place grate panel was the only hope now although there did seem to be a chance. Hector appeared to be focused solely on Markman, not paying any attention to his surroundings. The machine's head twitched periodically, another symptom of internal damage and as he approached the misplaced floor plate the robot picked up the pace in anticipation of the capture. Markman held his breath as Hector's right, booted foot on the good leg was the first to contact the trap. It pushed through the loose panel and drove him down onto his left knee which scraped through the opening in the floor. The heavy panel broke away and clanked and banged down to the cement floor thirty feet below. There was a hideous screeching and banging of Hector's torso as it rammed back and forth through the opening in the catwalk on its way down. The good right arm missed catching the edge of the catwalk frame but the malfunctioning left arm managed to leverage an elbow on a support beam. The enraged machine dangled there for a moment but Hector's weight and position were too much. Its body scraped down through the hole, wrestling as it fell. Markman stared in shock, leaning over the guardrail to see.

A resounding crash rang out as Hector hit the floor. Markman stared downward, hoping it was over. A moment of silence followed. To his shock and dismay, the thing somehow straightened itself, sat up and rotated its head 360 degrees to gain its bearings. With some difficulty, it pushed back up to its feet and looked overhead, quickly spotting Markman. The damaged, artificial face seemed to project a fierce look of anger. Immediately it began searching for a way back up.

Markman began a hop-run back in the direction he had come. Using the handrail he hoisted over the hole from the missing floor plate. He barged back through the door to the tech lab and in frantic desperation realized the two pull handles on the door could be blocked shut. There was a large torque wrench on a nearby station and duct tape on a shelf. He ran the wrench through the two handles and taped it in place. It did not look like enough. He struggled along back toward the stairwell door. As he exited the room, a loud clanging from the catwalk meant Hector was already climbing back.

The escape up the stairwell was difficult. One-foot hops along the railing were excruciatingly slow. With each hop Markman listened for the sound of the Machine bursting through the door below but at the top stairs there were still no machine footsteps following. Markman pulled opened the door to the upstairs laboratory and searched the room. The robotic Cassiopia was nowhere in sight. The place was a complete disaster. Benches were overturned, broken glass everywhere, bent metal chairs resting on top of other destroyed equipment with smoke coming from somewhere near the far side of the room. It had been a hell of a fight. The robotic Cassiopia had not given up easily.

He pushed against the nearest wall and worked his way through the maze of destruction. Heading for the decontamination room and exit he pushed passed the opened doors to other rooms until something caught his eye. In the last adjacent room there stood the machine version of Cassiopia, strapped into a vertical programming station against a wall. As he paused to look, her head rotated to face him.

"Release me!"

Markman froze for a moment but something crashing down on his left made him jump. He searched, expecting to see Hector charging but it had only been a smashed piece of equipment falling over. He looked back at the machine Cassiopia. If he ignored her plea there might still be time to make it to the decontamination room and out the main entrance to the parking garage. But even if the outer door did allow him to leave how far could he get against a relentless machine intent on ringing his neck?

Markman looked back at the new Cassiopia.

"He must be shut down," she said and the wisdom of it surprised Markman.

"His programming is corrupted. He must be shut down," she said once more.

She was well-marked from her previous battle. There was a slash on her neck. Her body suit was torn in several places. There was a bruise-like impression on her bald head. Clamps bolted to the wall restricted her arms and legs. Almost involuntarily, Markman limped into the room and searched for the release mechanisms. He freed the two leg locks quickly but a pin on the left arm clamp would not pull up and out. In answer to his prayer, the right arm clamp pin pulled out easily. He stepped back as the damaged yet strangely beautiful machine-Cassiopia reached around and freed her left arm. The pair remained motionless for a moment as Cassiopia's blue, aesthetic eyes appraised Markman intently. Abruptly her head rotated to one side. She spoke again in her Cassiopia voice, "Hector is scanning continuously for you. He's at the top of the stairs."

The loud bang of a metal door being thrown open erupted over the room. The sounds of equipment being knocked around followed.

Cassiopia stepped out from her station. Still staring in Hector's direction she commanded, "Go to the outer door. I will unlock it. Run as fast as you can."

Once more Markman balked. For just an instant he was tempted to stay and help this machine, an artificial intelligence which seemed so intent on saving him. But more sounds of furniture being smashed rang out, bringing him back to his senses. He limped to the door, glanced right just long enough to see Hector violently searching the lab floor and began hopping and pushing off along the wall in the direction of the decontamination room.

But the lab had become an even worse tangle of obstacles. Reaching the decon room was a gamble at best. More smoke was coming from somewhere. A haze was spreading over the room. It was not that difficult to stay low and out of sight but he had to throw himself over anything blocking his path.

Suddenly the room quieted. Only electrical sparking and the crackling of fire could be heard. Hector had stopped his search. A quick glance over a fallen work bench revealed Hector and Cassiopia, silently facing each other. It was clear they were communicating although no words were being spoken. Markman crawled hurriedly along his exodus route.

A loud crash rang out as though someone had thrown something in anger. Markman remembered with sarcasm: *According to the real Cassiopia, anger was impossible*. He continued to slide along the gray tiled floor. As he straddled over the next barrier he caught a glimpse of the cause of the fire burning not far away. The blue beam laser which had been running when he first entered the lab had been tipped over and was still operating. It was now burning a hole through several sections of furniture and up into the ceiling, causing smoke and sparks from cables positioned overhead.

As he resumed searching for a way toward the decontamination chamber the sounds of robotic violence broke out once more. Bloodcurdling screeching sounds of metal against metal accompanied by the crashes of furniture and equipment being thrown or smashed became almost deafening. As Markman struggled to look above the clutter something came flying in his direction and slammed into him. It knocked him back to the floor and left a nasty gash on one shoulder. He grabbed his shoulder and rolled onto one side, expecting more strikes.

But the machine Cassiopia was suddenly there, blocking Hector's way. Strange, hideous machine sounds of hand to hand combat reflected off the lab walls as the two machines became tangled together in fearless aggression. Finally, Hector stepped back for a moment to face-off his creation. She stood silently confronting him. The bizarre standoff went on and on. Markman realized the two were speaking again in ways he could neither hear nor understand. Occasionally there would be a small arm or head gesture from one of them. Even in the silence it was possible to feel the hostility growing. For the first time it seemed like Hector was concerned about losing.

A narrow channel through wrecked worked stations was available on Markman's left. There was too much blood flowing from the new shoulder wound. He needed to keep his hand clamped over it but that made crawling with a broken ankle nearly impossible. He crept on knees and one hand, dragging the damaged ankle along despite excruciating contacts with junk along the way.

Negotiations between the two nonhumans again began to break down. The sounds of several short bursts of combat resonated behind Markman. A quick glance above the debris allowed him to see Cassiopia jockeying for position away from Hector but at the same time blocking him. It was a tactical maneuver that did not last long. Daring to grab glances between dragging himself along brought the insane vision of the two machines locked together again, wrestling for control. Markman began to doubt there was any real chance of escaping even if he did reach the outer door. Machine arm blows began to be thrown with more terrible sounds of metal smashing against metal. There was a loud bang from another part of the room and half of the lab lights went dark. The blue laser beam continued to glitter through the growing haze of smoke. A short distance away the two combatants fought past Markman. The Cassiopia machine seemed to be on the defensive and the two were now in a position which blocked the exit.

Markman watched for a chance to advance around them. The combat again became even more violent. Suddenly the Cassiopia machine seemed to have regained the upper hand. Hector's right arm appeared to be no longer working and she was attacking that vulnerable side with everything she had. As Hector tried to move in closer he took one big blow to the right side of his head and went over sideways and down out of sight. The Cassiopia machine was just a few feet away from Markman now, her back to him as she braced for the next onslaught.

Hector slowly arose. He did not charge. There seemed to be a change in his attitude. He regained his feet and brought his good hand up. In it was the laser generator and its narrow glowing blue beam flashing around the room with each movement. He seemed to enjoy a moment of satisfaction, then jerked the laser emitter toward Cassiopia. The beam struck Cassiopia squarely in the chest. Instantly, before there was even time for her upper body to be marked by the beam, she twisted sideways and fell backward, landing prone alongside Markman. A cold, dead Cassiopia face stared back at him. Markman pushed the torso. A dead arm moved slightly from the effort. Dark, empty electronic eyes stared at him.

Through the growing veil of smoke the grinding machine sounds of Hector on the move began again. Not far away, through the dense smoke-fog, his faint silhouette towered above his two victims. He was pushing obstacles aside, scanning left and right to spot his final prey.

Markman was too drained to try to drag himself away. It would be a futile effort. Through the smoke, the outline of Hector's form was still barely visible but the glowing red infrared eyes swept from dim to bright as the head rotated. In desperation Markman looked for a weapon, anything rather than face the machine barehanded. His mind raced, trying to think of some weakness that could be exploited. The thing had a biological brain in that chest cavity. If there was a way to inflict damage on that....

Something in the back of Markman's mind suddenly flashed into awareness. His head jerked around to look at the lifeless artificial Cassiopia. Professor Cassell had given Hector human brain matter to be used as a central computer core. Did that mean Hector had duplicated the process in creating this Cassiopia? Could the laser blast which killed her have damaged that brain matter?

Hector was close to discovering him. In a hopeless effort, Markman quickly wiped his bloody right hand on his shirt and slapped it onto Cassiopia's chest plate. To his surprise, life force immediately began to flow from him and into the machine. It was a powerfully draining flow but that was of no concern this time. Either way he was a dead man. The current of life-power continued to grow until he could barely stand it. The world began to spin. There was no longer an ounce of strength left in his body. Only life force magnetism kept his hand in place. He began to black out. His hand fell away from the machine. Flat on his back, the smoke settled in around him. He could make out a vague portion of strobing ceiling lights and some destroyed equipment pressing against him.

Suddenly Hector's red eyes appeared in the smoke. Hector stepped one heavy foot forward and looked down to analyze Markman's condition. One arm was now completely missing from Hector's frame. The skin on his face was half torn off, revealing a gray metal skull plate. The deranged machine leaned forward and with his good arm reached for Markman's neck.

From out of the haze of smoke and flash, another hand shot into view. It caught Hector's wrist and twisted it back and away. Unprepared, Hector fell hard to one side into a pile of smashed equipment. Cassiopia lurched up and stood over her former master. She raised one heavy mechanical foot and stomped it onto his chest. Still clutching his wrist, she twisted and tore the arm away from its frame. There was a hideous screeching sound from Hector and with one partially mangled boot he managed to kick her away. She fell over backward, crashing through furniture and onto the floor. For a fraction of a second the contest paused. Then, without arms, Hector began to rock from side to side in an attempt to regain his feet.

Cassiopia shot back up and fell on him. She drove one hand down into his lower stomach, breaking through the skin layer and pulling out tubes that sprayed a gray fluid. Hector collapsed into stillness. As Cassiopia rose, Hector's torn body slid sideways down to the floor and ended up on his side, facing Markman.

Too weak to move, Markman held his bleeding shoulder and stared back at dimming red eyes just a few inches away.

Hector's head twitched and he spoke in a hoarse machine whisper, "What exists beyond death?"

Markman's weak voice cracked, "A higher dimension and a better life."

Hector's eyes went dark.

Chapter 31

Strong arms lifted Markman away from Hector's body. Markman balanced on a shaky leg and stared for a moment at his rescuer. The machine Cassiopia stared back at him, seeming to evaluate the shoulder wound he was holding.

"I am Reva. Your injury requires a pressure bandage. Do you have one?"

Markman made a small hop on one foot to keep his balance as the world continued to come into focus. He looked at the machine Cassiopia with distrust. "No."

The robot turned and climbed through the wreckage. She returned a moment later with a rag. With surprising gentleness she raised Markman's injured arm and wrapped the injury. As she knotted the cloth there was another short pause as though she was researching the correct tightness. With quick precision she tightened the bandaged and tied it off.

Markman glanced down at Hector's mangled body. "Are we really safe?"

Reva's head rotated down to scan Hector's form. "Hector's ambulatory functions have been terminated. All cognitive functions are offline." She looked back up at Markman. "What is your command?"

"You're supposed to be Cassiopia?"

"That was to be my designation after the electro-telepathic link was complete. Until that procedure is finished I am designated as Revision A. Hector assigned the reference Reva. Do you have a command or should I initiate maintenance?"

Before Markman could reply, an explosion caused the two of them to brace and crouch. The outer door collapsed inward as black-suited, heavily armed British special ops operatives burst into the room. Quickly

Markman hopped in front of Reva and held up both arms to wave off the incoming assault. "Area secure! Area secure!" he called out hoarsely. He pointed down. "Your target is here on the floor."

The troops closed in and spread out. Several came to stand over Hector's body while keeping their weapons leveled at Reva.

The group leader pressed two fingers against his throat. "Main room is clear. We have the package. There is a second target, also secure."

Exhausted and relieved, Markman leaned against a tipped over workstation. He motioned to the group leader and pointed to Reva. "This one is a friendly. She must not be harmed."

"She?" replied the group leader and his expression showed uncertainty and doubt.

Markman pointed to Hector's body and then to Reva once again and had to catch his breath to speak, "She's responsible for stopping him."

The group leader relaxed and lowered his weapon. "I understand." He pressed his throat microphone once more. "We need a stretcher in here. Make it quick."

As the team members continued to spread out, clearing the area, two others showed up with a stretcher. Markman was helped onto it and as he was raised for departure he called out, "Reva, stay with me."

Reva did not respond but turned in place, ready to comply.

The team leader motioned to another two of his operatives to also follow as guards.

Markman rode the stretcher through the destroyed outer door, out past the parking area and up to ground level where he pushed up to a sitting position to see.

A dozen black SUVs and three black helicopters were positioned around the facility. As he looked on two more black helicopters came in and touched gently down. A side door on one of them slid open and Cassiopia nearly fell getting out, followed by John Paul. Both stopped to stare at the approaching stretcher, shocked at the sight of an android following closely behind. Markman, sitting up, signaled a measure of relief to Cassiopia. She charged ahead to meet him, eyeing Reva with distrust and intrigue as she approached.

"Thank God," she said as she grasped his arm and walked alongside. Although her concern was for Markman she continued to stare back in disbelief at the mechanical image of herself following closely behind.

John Paul met them but also continued to be distracted by the sight of Reva. The foursome marched along with the stretcher bearers toward the nearest helicopter followed by the two security men with weapons still raised.

Markman continued to sit up, leaning to one side to rest the injured shoulder, the pressure bandage now a bright red. He gestured to his friends, "In case I pass out, I'd better introduce Cassiopia Revision A. Her name is Reva. She is the only reason I'm still here."

Cassiopia's expression flushed through several emotions, ending up with angry concern and a choked back tear.

John Paul silently continued to appraise Reva with awe. "Perhaps Reva should ride with security?"

Markman quickly objected. "Not on your life, John Paul. She's riding with us."

Cassiopia noticed Markman's ankle. "Scott, you have an injured ankle also? How bad is it? You can't walk, can you?"

At the helicopter there was a moment in which no one knew exactly how to proceed. Finally, the stretcher bearers carefully slid Markman into position on the floor. Cassiopia climbed in and sat bent over, holding the injured ankle in place. Markman pushed up once more, twisted around to find Reva and commanded, "Reva, come in here and sit."

Again, without acknowledgment, the obedient android deftly entered the aircraft and took the nearest seat.

John Paul shook his head, climbed in and sat next to Cassiopia, facing Reva.

The copilot came back, took pause at the sight of Reva, then fussed with everyone's belts and slid the loading door closed.

As they lifted off Markman exchanged a long, tired stare with John Paul. John Paul let slip a momentary expression of guilt. "We weren't really that far behind you," he said.

"I know what happened," replied Markman. "Hector bragged about it. There was no second-guessing the thing."

"We picked you back up when you entered Sugar Grove but we still couldn't just drop in. We had to set up."

Cassiopia looked up angrily. "This ankle is broken, Scott!"

"A temporary splint is called for," suggested Reva, causing everyone to stop and stare in surprise.

"I know that," answered Cassiopia tersely until she remembered the machine had saved his life.

Markman pushed up to look down at civilization through the nearby window. There were fires at various points along the way. People were running in the streets. The world below was in mad confusion. "How bad is it down there, John Paul?" asked Markman.

"As I'm sure you suspect, the situation is much worse. There are driverless cars, drones and other machines patrolling cities everywhere. There have been more military weapons discharged at various points around the world. The crux of it is Hector's program has been taken over by multiple supercomputers. One in particular, the Chinese Tianhe 4, appears to have taken the lead. It has its own secure power system so it will continue to operate in times of war and they have not been able to shut it down. I could go on and on but I think you get the picture."

"So we're too late," said Markman.

"No. We still just needed to know the very first event that started this chain reaction. Hector's core will hopefully tell us what we need to know. The moment we set down we should be getting the answers we need."

"The whole time I was down there Hector was fighting with her." Markman nodded at Reva who seemed to be silently following the conversation. "I don't get this. How can two almost identical machines be fighting each other? Why was she helping me instead of him?"

Cassiopia looked up from holding the injured ankle. The strain from all that had happened was catching up to her. She wiped another escaping tear from her eye and took a deep breath for control. "It's obvious, isn't it?" she replied. "Hector's program was totally corrupted but when he built this new version of himself he had to download my father's original initiation programming which wasn't corrupted. It's the only explanation."

"That's got to be right," said John Paul. "Hector probably didn't even know he was downloading preliminary software different from his own."

"He seemed really confused that she wouldn't obey him," said Markman.

Cassiopia nodded in agreement. "Sure, sure. Reva, short for Revision A. Reva wasn't a name. She was supposed to be an upgraded version of me. Once Reva's basic programming was installed Hector planned on upgrading it with his own." Cassiopia looked up at Reva. "Reva, did Hector attempt to upgrade your programming?"

Reva answered, "Correct."

"Did the upgrade work?"

"Upgrade contained a virus. Programming elements incompatible. Download blocked."

"See that?" said Cassiopia. "That proves something malicious was done to my father's programming." Cassiopia again turned to Reva. "Reva, why did Hector use my face on your frame?"

Reva answered, "Design goal intended to produce a replacement of you, Cassiopia Cassell. This unit's central cerebral processor was grown from Cassiopia Cassell DNA. Hector planned this unit to be a transfer avatar of Cassiopia Cassell. Two minds linked by electro-telepathic transmission with eventual transfer of consciousness. Failure of my programming updates and incomplete quantilium processing prevented the electro-telepathic link. This unit remains incomplete."

There was a silence in the aircraft as the three humans considered what they had just heard.

Cassiopia asked, "Reva, what is an electro-telepathic link?"

"Two brains linked as one."

"How is that achieved?"

"Laser light saturation of quantilium used to generate inter-dimensional transmission capability."

"And Hector could do that?"

"Laser light saturation of quantilium sample incomplete. First sample impure; fractured during laser saturation. Second sample at 50% saturation. Transmission unit incomplete."

Markman added, "There was a laser running in that lab downstairs."

"Sounds like you were just in time," remarked John Paul.

Cassiopia turned to John Paul. "Are you familiar with electro-telepathic links or quantilium?"

"No. Sounds like a new element and new science to me."

Cassiopia asked, "Reva do you know who Professor Theopolis Cassell is?"

Reva responded, "Grandfather."

"Wow!" said Markman.

Cassiopia spoke. "Reva, your programming is correct. Do you understand?"

Reva spoke without moving her head. "This unit's programming awaits accessory downloads for electro-telepathic linkage. This unit remains incomplete."

"Reva, Professor Cassell will resolve your open subroutines when we return to our lab. Do you understand?" said Cassiopia.

"Yes," was Reva's reply.

Markman grimaced from the pain in his shoulder then glanced out the window once more. "What will do you when you find the first event that you're looking for, John Paul? Kind of looks like a lost cause down there to me. We may take an RPG before we even get back."

"There's too much to tell right now, Scott. We get you back to base and they'll be able to bond that break in your ankle in just a few minutes. You'll even be able to walk but no marathons for a while. When that's done we'll have a long talk about the future."

"I'm looking forward to hearing that," said Cassiopia.

"Yeah, what future?" added Markman.

The foursome sat silently and listened to the chugging drone of helicopter blades.

Several combat aircraft circled the Taslam Building roof as the helicopter set down. A medical team with an antigravity gurney was waiting for Markman. He was rushed down to the treatment area while John Paul and Cassiopia brought Reva to the underground laboratory. Hector's torso had been brought in ahead of them and fastened to a motorized rotating platform where inductive sensors were attached. Reva sat quietly in a corner of the lab under the watchful eye of Cassiopia, kept there in case questions arose which only she might be able to answer.

One hour later Markman was able to walk cautiously to the main conference room where he sat eating a sandwich, waiting for his comrades. Another hour passed before Cassiopia and John Paul looked in on him. "Come with us," was all John Paul would say.

As they walked the hallway, Cassiopia kept one hand under Markman's arm on the side of the injured ankle.

"You don't need to do that, you know," said Markman with mild annoyance.

"I don't care. I want to."

"What did you guys do with Reva?"

"She's being debriefed. They're treating her like a hero."

"She is a hero. I owe her."

"How much exactly do you think you owe her?"

"We'll talk about that later, okay? Where is John Paul taking us?"

"To the cone of silence room."

"Why?"

"I don't know."

As they approached the high security chamber John Paul pulled the heavy oval door open and the three stepped in. The white light walls and ceiling glowed softly. At the main table three chairs had been placed close together. A large, fat, strange looking book sat on the table in front of them. John Paul sat at the book. He motioned Cassiopia and Markman to sit on either side of him.

John Paul leaned back, drew out his briarwood pipe and loaded it. He started to light it, paused and asked, "Do either of you mind?"

Cassiopia replied, "I like it. My father uses one, as you know."

Markman tilted his head in acceptance.

"It's been way too long. I can't smoke unless I can truly relax and I have not been able to do so until now."

"Not to be a downer, John Paul but the world outside has gone to hell. How can you relax?"

"You will both forget every word that is said here. I don't mean that as an order. I mean you literally *will* forget. Nevertheless, it is necessary to have this conversation. And to answer your question, Scott, I can now truly relax because we understand completely why and when the world fell into anarchy. By the way, the two of you will need to remain here tonight. We've had some broken windows upstairs. It's not safe to go out into the world anymore."

John Paul sucked fire into his tobacco and replaced his lighter to his vest pocket. He allowed himself a few seconds to sample the smoke, smiled and resumed the discussion.

"Scott, do you remember Perseus Haiden? I know Cassiopia does. She was the one who discovered the hidden cell phone he was using."

Markman said, "Refresh my memory, please."

"Perseus Haiden was the group leader of the team that required Professor Cassell's help in solving the math problems which were stopping their reverse engineering project. Perseus was less than enthusiastic about bringing Professor Cassell into the project and he was quite embarrassed when the Professor resolved the math equation very quickly. To make matters worse the Professor expressed irritation he had been taken away from his own project for such a simple impasse. Apparently that infuriated Perseus far more than any of us realized. Perseus concealed the anger quite well. We know now even long before that, in retribution for the Professor's impositions, Perseus had broken into Cassell's data files and implanted the virus that corrupted Hector. Perseus is a genius and his virus reflected that. *That* was when Hector's secret trips began, along with the crimes that followed."

Angrily, Cassiopia interrupted. "John Paul, how could anyone in your organization do something so terrible?"

John Paul nodded. "Do you remember when we approached you to join us? When someone excels to the point they may affect the development of human society in an undesirable way, that is they may affect the path prescribed for human evolution, we have a choice of removing them from society or asking them to join us in protecting it. When we ask a civilian to join us it is always with some risk. We do our best to evaluate the subject beforehand to be as certain as possible they are a stable kind of genius, one that can be trusted. We are seldom wrong in our appraisals. Perseus may have changed after joining us. That is the best explanation for why he did what he did. He may not have realized at first how damaging a thing he was doing, corrupting a computer intelligence so advanced as Hector. In any case, Perseus went rogue. We'll be evaluating him and trying to help him for a long time to come."

"So my father had nothing to do with all those crimes," said Cassiopia.

"Nothing to do with any of it," replied John Paul and he drew from his pipe and paused to allow the statement finality.

Markman grew impatient. "Come on, John Paul. What now?"

"We are in the secure chamber for a reason, Scott. Time for the two of you to learn more secrets of the Order.

As I've said, you will forget everything discussed here and yet the conversation is completely necessary."

Markman sat back and folded his arms impatiently.

John Paul continued. "We have a sister organization. Have either of you ever heard of the Devil's Hole?"

Cassiopia's expression reflected confusion. "It's a place in the middle of the North Sea. A deep hole that fishermen attach many legends to."

"Very good, Cassiopia!" answered John Paul. "Our sister organization lives there under the sea in a place called HyperBorea."

Cassiopia interrupted. "HyperBorea? From Greek mythology?"

John Paul smiled. "Our sister organization is there to control and protect the Earth and society from temporal anomalies. Anything causing a distortion of time here on Earth is their responsibility. From time to time, meteorites will deposit time anomalous elements on Earth which can disrupt the current occult. Our HyperBorean friends take care of that. There have even been times when military genius has produced machines or vehicles which corrupt the timeline. Those problems are dealt with by our friends, as well. Our present-day contact with HyperBorea is a wonderful young woman by the name of Skyla Corina. Should either of you ever need to contact her, enter 999 on your cell phone, take the square root of it and hit enter. She will contact you soon afterward. You must never contact her unless it is an emergency of the greatest magnitude. That rule is written in stone."

"But we're going to forget all this," said Markman with humorous sarcasm.

John Paul ignored the comment and continued. "Now that we know exactly what event, its date and time first started the tragedy taking place above us, that event and everything leading up to it along with everything that followed has been carefully recorded in this book. Everything we are saying here today will be added to it. Scott, your deposition given while you were in Medical has already been added. This book, its pages, binding, and print are made of a material referred to as *stascial* matter. That is, it's a material completely unaffected by time. It will never ever degrade and nothing known to man can mark or damage it. Tonight at exactly midnight, Skyla Corina will send this book back in time to a point before Perseus downloads the virus into Hector. At that time the book will appear on my desk. The moment I see it I will know it is a temporal correction sent to me from the future describing a future that needs to be understood and corrected. I will immediately read the book and interpret the chain of events that will cause the calamity. The opening page will recommend the best, absolutely smallest corrections necessary my previous self will need to take to prevent the coming disaster. For example, just before he downloads the virus Perseus will be intercepted and detained. Professor Cassell will be asked to dismantle Hector and transfer it here for evaluation."

John Paul paused for a moment to study the blank expressions on his associate's faces. "So, my friends, at this point in the disclosure I usually stop to enjoy my pipe while you two try to believe what has just been said." John Paul sat back to relight his pipe. As he smoked he studied his friends for reaction. Markman sat with a wrinkled brow. Cassiopia began pointing a finger at invisible things in the air as though she were trying to create a mental outline of cause and effect.

Finally, Markman could no longer remain silent. "You're kidding, right? You're going to send a note back in time to yourself and stop all this from happening? It's a joke, right?"

John Paul blew out smoke. "No."

Cassiopia asked, "Can you send people back in time?"

"Yes, but that is very heavy handed and more likely to make a problem much worse, not better so it's almost never even considered."

"You can change the past? You're telling us you can go back and change history?" asked Markman, still in disbelief.

"Actually no. The most fundamental of temporal rules is, *you cannot change the past, you can only add to it*. For example, the lesson as it was taught to me is this: If someone murdered someone then managed to go back in time and prevent that murder, he will still have murdered but a parallel timeline will show that after the murder he looped back and stopped the murder. From an Earthly perspective no murder will have occurred but from the perspective of those on higher planes of existence there will be a loop back in the timeline where a new parallel timeline formed alongside the original. Does that make any sense to you, Scott?"

Markman sat staring blankly again.

"Have you done this before, John Paul?" asked Cassiopia.

"In all the time I have been a part of the Organization this option has never once been used."

"Wow!" said Cassiopia. "But you could have prevented so many tragedies!"

John Paul bit on his pipe. "Scott, I'm betting your eastern philosophy can answer that one."

Markman focused. His tone was laced with annoyance. "It's the free will thing, Cass. People can't learn right from wrong unless they have the free will to make mistakes; really bad mistakes sometimes. But nobody ever said anything to me about going back in time!"

"Wow!" repeated Cassiopia.

John Paul continued, "So there you have the sum of it. If we are very lucky, Hector will never be activated. Perseus will be taken aside for evaluation and treatment before he ever does anything wrong. No one will be murdered or harmed. If we're lucky."

"Why if we're lucky?" asked Cassiopia.

"Sending a message in a bottle back in time is kind of like throwing a baseball. Once it leaves your hand you have no control over it. You can only hope it's in the strike zone. See what I mean? The idea is to make as small a change to the past as possible to effect only the necessary correction and nothing else."

Cassiopia asked, "John Paul, what will happen to the three of us?"

John Paul replied, "There is always a danger even the smallest change in the timeline will result in unanticipated, sometimes drastic changes to events or people. That's why this remedy is called the nuclear option and never used unless the situation is catastrophic. Hopefully there will be only small event changes in your lives which won't amount to much of an impact. Your father should experience the greatest interruption due to Hector but otherwise, with luck, the changes will seem insignificant. None of us will remember this Armageddon future we are trying to escape. I will be the first to read the book and have Perseus taken into custody. Next, I will bring your father in to read it soon after and he will be asked to dismantle Hector. At some point after that the two of you will be called in to read it. Even then we will not remember any of it but we will know what happened. There are methods by which people can be conditioned to retain the events of a previous timeline but that is extremely dangerous since the individual can then recall two different memories for the same time period. That can cause extreme mental and sometimes fatal medical problems. So, with luck we will effect only small changes to our lives while eliminating a worldwide catastrophe."

"What about Reva?" asked Markman.

"We expect Reva will cease to have ever existed after midnight tonight, Scott," said John Paul.

"What should we do now, John Paul?" asked Cassiopia.

"I would suggest the two of you try to relax, get something to eat and retire to your room to rest. Remember, none of this can be discussed in any way outside of this room. Please do not forget that."

"And this will all happen at midnight tonight?" asked Markman, still skeptical.

"Midnight tonight," answered John Paul.

Cassiopia and Markman sat in the dispensary sipping tea while gazing lovingly at each other. Cassiopia played with her cup and tried to hide her worry.

As Markman tested his repaired ankle and freshly bandaged shoulder, his inevitable sense of humor kicked in. "Well, my to-do list is suddenly done," he said, "How about yours?"

"Not one thing I can think of," answered Cassiopia. "But I do know what we should do now."

"What?"

"Let's go to the room, set the alarm clock for twelve, stretch out on the bed and hold each other in our arms until midnight arrives."

"That sounds like a good idea in any timeline."

They retreated to their room and set up for the coming end. The nightstand clock read ten minutes to midnight. On the bed they held each other in a tight embrace and as the first chime rang out, they kissed a kiss that lasted forever.

Chapter 32

Cassiopia Cassell stood with her hands on her hips, eyeing the gray sliding doors with mischievous intent. The locked doors were the latest challenge proffered by her professor father, Theopolis Cassell. He so loved to keep his current projects secret. But, it was a game to him, a taunt to his meddlesome genius daughter. Ironically, Cassiopia's relentless tenacity, inherited from the Professor himself, inevitably resulted in the yielding of his project's secrets.

It was a gunmetal door with a seam down the middle with no knobs, no locks, and no keypads.

She turned to survey the room while thinking out loud. "I see no infrared eyes or miniature microphones anywhere which means access must be by radio frequency, maybe Bluetooth or more likely a simple pulse code modulation, or perhaps hidden wires in the wall are linked to his computer terminal. He's been working in there for months. It's time I know what it is he's up to."

Markman sat in a chair tilted back against the wall, his feet crossed on a lab workbench. "Boy, you are so nosy, you know that?"

Cassiopia pulled her long ivory hair behind her head and turned her nose up at him. "Am not. It's not safe for him to be doing this again. What if he got into trouble in there? How would we know? How would we get in there to help him? We'd have to use a torch to cut through the doors!"

"Admit it, you just want to know what he's working on behind that door," insisted Markman. "He's got a cell phone if he needed help."

"Cell phone access! I'll bet that's it. I'll bet the door opens to a program he's set up in his cell phone."

"You're gonna get in *trouble*...," quipped Markman.

"You may be right about that. When he came back from his last meeting with John Paul I'd never seen him so upset. He hasn't been himself ever since."

"Personally, I think he's got you stumped this time," mused Markman.

Cassiopia narrowed her stare in defiance. "I still have one trick up my sleeve."

Markman linked his hands behind his head and smiled. "The robot? You think Tel is going to help you? That would have been the first place your father covered his tracks."

"Tel can never refuse me. Let's go see," said Cassiopia.

Markman swung his athletic shoes off the counter, stood and adjusted his jeans. He straightened the collar on his tan cargo shirt and gestured toward the exit. "Elevator or tower stairs, my lady?" he asked.

Before Cassiopia could answer, her father's sudden appearance in the lab caused them both to stiffen and quiet.

"What are you two doing down here?" asked the Professor.

Cassiopia looked to Markman for an excuse but got no help. "We were looking for you, Father. Want to go to lunch with us?"

The Professor ignored the offer and went to his project room entrance. To Cassiopia's amazement he drew out his cell phone, typed in a code and the doors slid open. Inside, parts of a very advanced, unassembled robot were stacked around the workbenches. Cassiopia hurried over and stared.

"It's a new robot? Father, you're assembling a new robot?"

The Professor began moving parts around as he spoke. "No, dear Daughter. I am disassembling a new robot."

"Why?"

"These components are to be shipped to John Paul for study. By the way, I'm supposed to tell you he wants you to come to the main office right away."

"Me or us?"

"The both of you. He complained neither of you has been checking your messages."

Cassiopia pulled out her cell phone and looked. "Oh! Yes. He does need us, doesn't he?"

Markman sounded disappointed. "Why? I was hoping to take some time to explore our mountainside a little bit."

The Professor carefully stored one robotic leg in a foam packed case and closed it shut. "It is my understanding he wants you both to read a certain book."

"Oh no!" cried Markman. "That can only mean one thing. It must be regulations or procedures or something. I hate that stuff. Is that what it's about, Professor?"

"I'm sorry, Scott. It's not something I'm at liberty to discuss."

Markman turned to Cassiopia. "What time does he want us?"

"It says ASAP," replied Cassiopia.

"How much time will this take, Professor?" Markman asked.

The Professor paused from his packing to reply. "I can't really discuss it, Scott. I'm sorry."

Cassiopia tried to console her partner. "Come on. We'll go get it done. Maybe it will take no time at all."

"I hate that stuff. I can't stay focused on it. My mind drifts off. I'm dumb. I'm sorry."

"I'll help you and we'll be back here in no time." She took Markman by the arm and led him to the elevator.

Professor Cassell paused once more to watch his two most beloved friends leave. To console himself he began to hum a tune, though he could not recall the name of the song. Patiently he resumed packing robotic parts and considered just how much had changed at the stroke of one particular midnight, a midnight which had disappeared into nowhere. He found himself reminded of a famous, particularly intriguing quote by Einstein: '*The separation between past, present and future is only an illusion, although a convincing one.*' "Perhaps Albert knew even more than he had been willing to admit," thought the

Professor as he snapped the silver case shut on Hector's brain.

www.ingramcontent.com/pod-product-compliance
Lightning Source LLC
Chambersburg PA
CBHW061538170626
46811CB00001B/31